THE SINGULARITY WITNESS

A Novel

DAN GRANT

MindScape Press, Inc.

The Singularity Witness Copyright © 2017 by Dan Grant
All rights reserved.
First Edition, 2018

Cover art by Cakamura DSGN Studio.

Identifiers: ISBN: 978-1-7325040-0-4 (hardcover)
ISBN: 978-1-7325040-1-1 (trade paperback)
ISBN: 978-1-7325040-2-8 (e-book)
ISBN: 978-1-7325040-3-5 (audio book)

Subjects: mind mapping-fiction | mind control-fiction | illegal human research-fiction | fiction | thrillers | suspense fiction | science fiction | adventure fiction

To learn more, see author notes and read background material, go to www.DanGrantBooks.com.

Publisher: MindScape Press, Inc.
www.MindScapePress.com

PROLOGUE—FAREWELLS

ANCRI, Undisclosed Research Facility, West of Princeton, New Jersey

CAROLINE WANG KNEW THE authorities would view her atrocities as murder. No doubt they would be right.

She shook off the thought and cast her gaze down the intersecting sterile white corridors stretching before her. Deep inside her chest, her heart shuddered as pale lighting and colorless tile seemed to run forever. Trepidation smothered her like a swimmer caught in a swift undertow, her body submerged as an endless black tide towed it away from a distant, unreachable shore.

Caroline soaked in the foreboding silence before reaching back into the morgue and gripping the gurney's stainless steel handle. In the corridor, a wheel on the gurney wobbled and competed against the echo of her shoes clicking on flooring as she navigated it through a maze of similarly placid corridors.

Caroline stopped at a nondescript door marked INCINERATOR.

Placards read: DISPOSAL OF MEDICAL NUCLEAR WASTE IS PROHIBITED. AUTHORIZED PERSONNEL ONLY.

As the institute's neurogeneticist, a biological data-farmer of sorts, she was responsible for keeping their Genesis participant alive as long as possible. But that had been a grave mistake.

Caroline cleared her throat, gripped the gurney's handle tighter, and shoved it through the hinged door, which slammed closed like a blast of thunder.

She'd never visited the incinerator room. Disposal wasn't in her job description. Gray masonry walls surrounded her. The floor's dull finish soaked up most of the artificial light. A three-foot, dish-shaped door protruded from the far wall. Beside it hung a console packed with buttons and gauges.

Angst surged inside her as she searched for composure, while her vision settled on the crisp white sheet covering the body on the gurney.

"You thought I was your friend," she said. "You were wrong."

Her gaze found the surveillance camera above the door. Through the lens of the camera, she could almost see an audience of detached observers watching from comfortable offices located elsewhere in the facility.

The bastards were watching.

They should be here. Not me.

How many rats had fled the sinking ship? Nearly all of them. Most of her colleagues had resigned, citing philosophical differences. Others disappeared along with all traces of their existence. Her mistake was staying, naively thinking she could make the breakthrough. But in a year's time, the institute had gone from resembling a thriving metropolis to a desolate ghost town. Those who stayed kept silent. Opinions were discouraged. And Caroline became no different from the hired boatman who ferried the damned across the river to the shores of Hades.

She slammed her palm into an orange, mushroom-stemmed start button. A pneumatic eruption roared to life behind the thick door of the incinerator. A thermometer needle crawled upward on an analog dial.

A waft of air filled her nostrils. The room felt different as microscopic particles escaped ventilation filters as a blower fan hummed to life. She knew what that meant. Air pressurization was a safety protocol—positive air flow introduced into the room to provide back-pressure, to keep fire and fumes from expanding, in case of a malfunction. She half-hoped the furnace would explode in a life-consuming blast, saving her from completing this mission. Disposal. Her current mandate.

But Caroline was not so fortunate.

A tear streaked down her cheek, and she fought a swelling watershed behind tired eyes.

"You didn't deserve this. All you wanted to do was impress your father."

Caroline stripped back the sheet to expose the naked body past a bony collarbone. Amy Richards, pale and stiff, was barely recognizable. Only a grotesque outer shell remained of a once-vibrant woman. Her head was shaved, including her eyebrows. Alien-like deformations and sutures arced across a leathery scalp. Thin, hair-sized lines connected the dots on her scalp to larger dime-sized gray circles, the obscure tapestry forming a fragmented set of geometric patterns. Her eyelids were sunken and shut, and Amy's mask hid a recent, horror-filled past.

A year earlier, Amy had volunteered as their Genesis participant. Now she was dead.

"This is how we repaid you," Caroline said, tracing her fingers along Amy's scarred forehead. Cold skin felt taut and rough, like starched linen.

Amy's death had shown her that the institute's Genesis program was a distorted conquest.

"I won't let your sacrifice be in vain," she said behind twitching lips.

Shielding her movements from the camera over her shoulder, Caroline withdrew a core biopsy needle from her lab coat. Using choreographed movements, she uncapped it, leaned over, kissed Amy on the forehead, and thrust the needle into Amy's heart. After rising, she etched AMY RICHARDS RIP in the pale skin along the centerline of the body with the tip of the needle. She recapped it and returned it to her coat. Next she retrieved an iPhone, held it tight to her chest, and tapped the camera feature. The phone went back into her coat pocket too.

Evidence. And an insurance policy.

The world had to know what they had done.

Caroline folded back the sheet and flattened the edges over the body. Reluctantly, she turned back to the incinerator.

With a nervous hand, she opened the door and yanked the holding carriage out of the fire box. The protective ceramic coating on the carriage rails retained little heat, allowing Caroline to manipulate it with bare hands. She positioned the gurney parallel to the carriage. Her breathing stalled as she slid one arm beneath Amy's torso, her elbow cradling the head, and the other hand below the buttocks. Amy's emaciated body was lighter than expected, and Caroline had no problem laying it onto the carriage.

"Walk with God, in a place where no harm will come to you again," she said over the knot forming in her throat. "Someday, I hope you'll forgive me."

Caroline shoved the carriage into the fire box and closed the door. After flipping up a clear plastic protective cover, she pressed a red button on the console. An inferno rumbled to life behind the door. The temperature dial on the incinerator leapt toward the 1600 degree Fahrenheit mark, where the unit would cremate the body in an hour and destroy all evidence.

Almost all evidence.

She stared at the incinerator, hoping to steal some warmth and overcome the soul-crushing cold residing inside her. It was a vain effort.

This was a funeral.

And she was the only one who had come.

As instructed, her efforts to get to know Amy Richards had been pretense, subtle coercion. Now Caroline was alone, with no one to give a eulogy when her time came to depart this life. It was a time that might come soon.

She knew too much.

And those who knew too much became liabilities.

Liabilities, well, they disappeared—like Amy.

Long black hair splashed across her shoulders as she collapsed across the empty gurney and sobbed. She wondered if the audience watching on surveillance monitors had returned to regular duties, as if this moment, the death of a human being, meant nothing.

Their Genesis participant was gone.

The world had to know the truth.

Caroline pressed a shaking hand against the pocket of her lab coat.

All will know the truth, and the truth will set us free.

MONDAY, OCTOBER 5th
THREE MONTHS LATER
PRESENT DAY

The best way to predict your future is to create it.
Abraham Lincoln

1
APPOINTMENTS

Princeton University, School of Engineering and Applied Science, Princeton, New Jersey

7:00 A.M. THOMAS PARKER considered karma a stalker, and dodged his cell phone all weekend to avoid his fate. As the elevator fourth floor doors opened, the device in his pants pocket sprang to life, signaling a text message.

He knew what that meant.

The verdict was in.

While failing to publish was egregious, it wasn't supposed to kill his career.

He checked the display. 7:30. PJs. DON'T BE LATE.

The executioner's appointed time and place.

He shoved the dread from his mind as his loafers, wet from the outside rain, squeaked against the tile floors. Wooden crates, pressurized tanks, and transitional equipment straddled peripheral gray striping along the D-wing corridor. He carried a hard-sided case, long enough to fit four human skulls, in one hand and fumbled with door keys in the other.

At the A-wing juncture, he slid his keys into the lock of a gray steel door, which opened faster than expected.

His mind came alive. Someone was in the lab, and leaving in a hurry.

The heavy door crushed him against an inset concrete block wall, trapping him between rigid objects. The abrupt force felt like a battering ram. As the door eased back, pain coursed throughout his body and his vision blurred, causing him to drop his hard-sided case.

A man in a suit with red hair and a scar etched into his chin emerged from behind the door. He kicked the case away and gripped the edges of the steel door with both hands.

Parker braced himself.

The jarring sequel robbed his lungs of air. His face kissed steel again as his head whipped back. His vision blackened and dizziness washed through him, but he managed a tenuous balance by clutching the door. The man ripped it free of Parker's hands. His knees buckled, like a boxer teetering before going down for the count.

Thomas Parker felt his consciousness wane as he hit the floor, and the last thing he saw was the man snatching up the case and extracting the pearl-faced headdress within.

Princeton, New Jersey

HEADHUNTER. IT WASN'T STEWART Richards' primary profession but an essential skill, and Princeton proved his greatest recruitment challenge yet.

Since his appointment was not for a few hours, Richards entered the Nassau Inn, grabbed a table in the Yankee Doodle Tap Room, and drank black coffee. The famed Norman Rockwell mural hung above the bar, an aristocratic poseur with a feather in his hat. Rockwell had a knack for crafting visual lexicons and vivid characters. The mural displayed a master at his finest.

Something Richards appreciated—the chance to place brilliant people in extraordinary situations.

Richards never focused on the numbers, never cared about the collective body count. Numbers were unimportant, irrelevant. The crux of his occupation came down to making the right acquisition, not a quick, foolish attempt to place another square block into a round hole.

And he had proven to be a master of all types of procurement.

Resource specialists used traditional labels to classify acquisitions—commodities or intellectual property, something of value controlled by a competitor. These coveted assets included prototypes or engineered plans. Most times, the simplest procurement came down to appropriating someone else's gold nugget idea, more bluntly, industrial espionage.

However, the most challenging acquisitions were not property but people, visionaries—those few geniuses with the potential to change the world.

Finding Einsteins required a mix of luck and skill.

His Princeton trophy demanded orchestration in advance, a bit like rigging the house rules at an Atlantic City casino. He was not about to lose this acquisition.

The cards had been dealt. The game was ready to be called.

Only one thing remained.

Thomas Parker had to come to the discovery on his own accord that his career needed a bold change. Parker had to want to be recruited.

Despite its Ivy League status, the Princeton Neuroscience Institute's programs were not as prestigious as its affluent contemporaries. Parker's fledgling research was underfunded and overshadowed in the national limelight by power schools such as MIT, Yale, Harvard, Johns Hopkins, Cal Poly, UCLA, and even Boston University's Center for Adaptive Systems.

Working on shoestring budgets, Parker made breakthroughs far beyond his peers, and funding proved to be his Achilles heel. Without it, discoveries were limited.

Even for Einsteins.

In the process of identifying candidates, Richards recognized Parker was an idealist.

Money could not be the lure, yet there were other ways to put money to work.

It had all been arranged, and he had an intoxicating offer.

After finishing his coffee, he opened a dossier to revisit Parker's background.

The candidate was married to his research. Parents deceased. No siblings. No relatives. No romantic entanglements. A loner who maintained a predictable distance between himself and colleagues. Rarely socialized. Never with students. There was only one person—a research assistant, a twenty-nine-year-old graduate student—with whom Parker seemed at ease. Rebecca Ward. Becky to her friends. On the surface, at the faculty-student level, their two-year relationship seemed paternal.

But the dossier's intimate details revealed otherwise.

Becky Ward had a crush on her advanced topics neuroscience professor.

Richards paged through the folder with a thoughtful smile.

Although plans were set in motion, he knew such a nascent relationship either needed exploiting or resolving. In fact, he counted on it.

Thomas Parker was about to be recruited.

Parker awoke to find people huddled above him. A dark-haired brunette wedged herself into the group of onlookers. She was talking to him, yet her voice struggled to break through the fog that enveloped him.

An unrelenting pain permeated his head, and he traced a lump on his forehead with shaking fingers.

"Feel like sitting up?" Becky Ward asked, kneeling beside him.

Parker's mind crawled through what had happened. Slowly, his throbbing head cleared. A man. Short red hair. Scar on his chin. He had been sandwiched between the door and the wall.

Arms took hold of him and propped him upright.

"What happened?" Becky's slender fingers caressed his face as she studied him with inquisitive eyes.

"A man," he said, clearing his throat. "I was hit with the door." He tried to look past the curious onlookers. "... my case?"

She hauled it toward him and placed it in his lap. "Here it is."

He looked it over. "The lab?"

She put a hand on his shoulder. "Don't worry about that, doc. It's the same cluttered mess it always is."

A pair of paramedics parted the spectators and drilled him with questions: name, occupation, date of birth, was he in pain, did he hit his head? One took vitals while the other checked his pupils' reaction with a pen light.

The intense beam from the paramedic's light caused Parker to lose sight of Becky as she disappeared into the swelling crowd.

A pocket in his Dockers buzzed to life. He fought off the paramedics and glanced at the display on his phone: YOU'RE LATE.

THIRTY MINUTES LATER, AFTER a healthy dose of dos and don'ts from the paramedics—which included orders to go home and rest—Thomas Parker jaywalked across Nassau Street, using his hands to shield his head from the downpour.

Inside PJ's Pancake House, he slogged past the usual sea of bodies crammed around the hostess station.

Across from the campus, PJ's was not just a local hangout, but a historical pillar, almost as much part of the local lore as the university itself. Pulitzer and Nobel Prize winners, world-renowned scientists, politicians, athletes, and pre-fame celebrities had frequented PJ's at some time or another. PJ's was etched into Princeton's history, and it felt sacrilegious to think a person could attend or teach at the university without dining at PJ's.

"Back here, Tom." A distinctly British voice rose above the clamor of conversations, Phillip Derman's accent a remnant of his English upbringing. Dressed in a smoke-gray suit, Derman had a narrow face with thinning silver hair and a slender build. His baleful look was like a finely dressed fox surveying menu choices and deciding what victim to have for breakfast.

Parker acknowledged his acquaintance with a half-wave, while dodging crowded tables until he reached the booth at the back of the restaurant. He hung his rain-soaked jacket on the hook beside the table and slid into a vacant seat.

A cup of coffee waited for him. Parker warmed his hands over it. Water beaded his mop of hair and he leaned out of the booth to shake off the remnants of the rain.

"You look like hell. Rough morning, Tom?" the fox asked.

Parker gingerly felt the lump on his forehead. "Someone was in my lab and clubbed me with the door."

Derman arched an eyebrow. "Well, at least you're not seriously hurt."

Parker grimaced, and without making eye contact asked, "Did I win my appeal?"

"Your case didn't have merit." Derman waited for Parker to look up before continuing. "The advisory committee's ruling is final."

A waitress arrived, and they both ordered the house special: a half order of buttermilk pancakes.

"Untenured," Derman said, "non-published faculty don't get breaks. Even for brilliant professors such as yourself. The harsh reality is that when the NSF" — the National Science Foundation — "cut funding, you lost your stake in the game. The spare change from my conductive polymers grant afforded you a grad student for one semester. Now you have her working *pro bono*."

They sipped their coffee in an awkward silence.

"I need more time," Parker said, his hands quivering.

Derman shook his head. "This is academia—publish or perish. For God's sake, this is Princeton. Stop pretending to be so disingenuous. You knew the rules. Everybody does. In three years, you put nothing of substance in print. Bloody hell, we indoctrinate undergrads to produce research papers from the moment they set foot on campus. Yet that's an inconvenience for you."

"I've got... data—"

"Data?" Derman gave an exasperated sigh. "Publishing is the life blood of securing tenure. It doesn't matter what kind of teacher you are or how much entitled, pompous brats swoon over your lectures. The painful truth is research dollars float academic boats. And research leads to publishing—that is how *our* game is played."

Parker chewed on his lip and searched for a counter argument. There was none. He was guilty as charged.

"Tom, you committed the greatest sin in academia. You refused to publish. When you exhausted your funding, those sins could no longer be forgiven."

Parker raised his head in protest. "My findings are premature."

The waitress returned with plates of buttermilk pancakes. "Do you need anything else?"

Derman shooed her away with a wave of his hand.

"You're kidding, right?" Derman asked, disappointment painting his face. "You know I pay attention. You've got the results. And I have no idea how you've done it." He lathered his short stack with syrup and stuffed a fork full of pancake in his mouth. "That's an achievement in itself."

Parker shot the Brit a defiant gaze.

Derman rapped the side of his head with his fingers. "You've got Pandora's box inside your skull, the details of your research locked deep inside that vacuum of space you call a brain. Because you're the smartest genius in the room, you document nothing. Trust no one. At best, you sketch a few concepts. Hell, your girlfriend doesn't get enough divine dispensation to work alone in the lab. And you two are inseparable."

Parker raised an index finger. "She's not—"

"Sorry… your graduate student. Didn't mean to imply any-thing." Derman sliced his pancakes into squares and waited for Parker to relax. "Tom, we've known each other since you arrived at Princeton. The harsh reality is, Friday you are out."

Parker picked at his pancakes and offered a vacant nod.

Derman smiled. "I have contacts."

"You've offered before."

"Listen. Take industry for a test drive."

Parker slid his pancakes aside. "I won't prostitute my work or sell out."

Derman exhaled. "See the grand picture here. Industry will provide an army of technicians to record procedures and test data—hard results you can publish. Industry will secure patents and safeguard research." He wiped his face with a napkin. "You'll get another shot at academia. You're too bloody smart not to."

Parker considered his options. "Maybe you're right."

"I'm always right." Derman finished his coffee. "Can I schedule a meeting?"

Parker dropped his napkin on his picked-over pancakes and tapped the side of his head. "Pandora's box was actually a jar that contained a vicious evil. It was never supposed to be opened."

"You're correcting my analogy?"

"If my research ends up in government hands, it'll never see the light of day. Try publishing under that scenario. Medicine won't reap benefits from it living in a dark box or jar or wooden crate."

"Is that the reason you don't publish?" Derman nodded. "I see your point. However, Zeus presented Pandora with a full jar. Oh, yes, it contained a vile evil. After she opened the bloody jar and evil started infecting the earth, Pandora realized her mistake and closed it, thus trapping the remaining contents inside—the Spirit of Hope. Tom, your work gives mankind Hope. It will give the world a new era in medicine."

Parker wrung his hands together.

Derman placed his hands on the table. "Ten, this morning?"

Parker sighed as his door-crushing headache returned. "Yeah, that works."

The fox grinned. "So how will you showcase the presentation?"

"High school kids are visiting campus. I'll work it into their science day show-and-tell."

"Brilliant way to frame your work." Derman snatched the bill out of the waitress's hand as she strolled to the table. "I'll take that."

They stood and gathered their things.

Derman set a reassuring hand on Parker's shoulder. "This is the right move for you."

2
ASSIGNMENTS

Falls Church, Virginia

KATHERINE MORGAN SPENT MOST of the night remembering the good times—how special agent Jack Wright could woo her with a smile, the handsome ruggedness of his day-old stubble in the morning, the scent of his Jivago aftershave, the crispness of his tailored suits.

Then she remembered the last night they shared a bed.

So much had changed since then.

She had changed.

As soon as Kate stepped out of her health club, she spotted his Lincoln sedan at the curb. Wright sat behind the steering wheel, talking on a cell phone. In so many ways, she wanted to restart her workout routine and pretend this morning was not about to happen.

But she had a new assignment.

Catching sight of her, he flashed a charismatic smile and ended his call.

Kate's heart skipped a beat. Not a good sign.

Toughen up, she chided herself as she patted down her business suit: harvest brown, an outfit selected specifically for this reunion. She wore no makeup. No perfume. Did not want to stimulate his senses. This was work. Nothing more. She had pulled back her shoulder-length, coffee-colored hair and fastened it with a silver barrette. On her hip, concealed by her suit jacket, was a plastic-gripped, Glock semi-automatic.

FBI special agent Jack Wright leaned across the front seat, swung open the passenger's door, and gawked at her as if she were a swimsuit model. "Kate, you look radiant."

He leaned toward her, his arms open for an embrace.

"Drive, Jack," she said, thrusting a firm hand against his chest to maintain their separation.

He stared into her eyes, challenging her conviction. Testing her waters. Hoping to catch a glimmer of past feelings. She had extinguished that flame and vowed never to relight the candle. Not with special agent Jack Wright, anyway.

He slumped into the driver's seat. "We haven't seen each other in two years and all I get is a 'Drive, Jack'?"

She knew him well. "You'll get over it."

Wright's gaze soaked her up for a long moment.

When she caught herself holding her breath, she said, "You drop clear off the radar and then magically reappear to worm your way into my life and back to calling the shots. Why pick me for your detail?"

"Well I wanted the Legat post in France," he said of the bureau's legal attaché program. "But the director declined my request and instead reassigned me. This is big. He picked me. And I picked you."

Kate rolled her eyes. "You should have chosen someone else."

"I need your expertise."

"Oh, that's a stale line."

Wright replied with a chuckle and turned his Lincoln away from the curb. They caught I-66 and the Capital Beltway north to Baltimore, where I-495 became I-95.

Kate watched a NO HAZMAT sign blur past the windows as they chatted about the weather and bureau politics. They avoided anything personal. Signs for Baltimore passed with more frequency.

He cleared his throat. "Kate, I never meant to hurt you. I'm not good at being humble. It's just, I miss being your friend."

She had prepared herself. The wounds ran deep. However much she wanted to ignore it, deny their past meant anything, she still felt something for Jack. She watched him shift his vision from the road to her.

"Friends? Is that what we are?" She mustered a guarded smile. "How about we talk about the investigation?"

He pointed to her feet.

From beneath her brown flats, she snatched up a folder bearing the black-and-white seal imprint for the DEPARTMENT OF JUS-TICE FEDERAL BUREAU OF INVESTIGATION. The folder's lower third read CLASSIFIED INVESTIGATION in red letters. The cover bore a ten-digit alphanumeric Washington Field Office case number, starting with 079.

Kate scanned the report's executive summary. "So, we believe he's missing or dead?"

Wright shrugged. "I guess we'll find out together."

Severna Park, Maryland

KATE MORGAN STUDIED THE middle-aged woman parked on a walnut trimmed settee.

Debra Ford's face was flushed from an interrupted workout. The woman was fit, with clear muscle tone encased in black Lululemon. A half-bottle of chardonnay sat on a matching coffee table between them.

Jack Wright set a digital-recorder next to the wine.

"He's dead, isn't he?" Debra Ford glared at the recorder. She uncorked the bottle, filled a thin-stemmed glass to the brim, and took a long sip.

"We don't know that," Kate said, jotting the words "morning drinking workout freak" in small letters on a notepad, and crossed her legs to position the paper so it couldn't be read from across the table. "But he's been missing for almost a week."

"That's why you're here. Isn't it?" Debra Ford took another drink and fidgeted, then returned her hands to the stem of the wine glass.

Wright shot her a look. "The bureau and Capitol Police take it seriously when a United States Senator goes missing. Your husband's disappearance is troublesome."

"Ex," Debra Ford corrected. "Sam's an ex."

"Mrs. Ford," Wright continued, "when was the last time you saw Sam?"

"I've answered these questions for the Capitol Police."

"We know," Kate said.

Debra Ford's gaze reached beyond the agents to the vast spread of water stretching outside her window. Situated on a bluff, her micro-mansion held a panoramic view of the Rock Cove, the Severn River, and a boathouse below. Outside, it was blustery. Thick, dark clouds churned in an off-gray sky.

The woman rubbed her temples. "A week ago, Sunday. Sam dropped in to watch football with our son, Josh. The three of us dined together."

Wright asked, "Did you notice anything odd about his behavior? Did the senator talk about anything unusual?"

Debra Ford laughed. "He was mad because the Redskins lost to the Cowboys."

"That's not what I meant," Wright said.

She sneered. "I know what you meant, agent." Her tone cooled. "Sam never talks shop with me and his public duties rarely followed him home. And I no longer pry. I think if anything troubled him, watching the game with Josh took his mind off it."

"How'd you first meet your ex-husband?" Kate asked.

Debra Ford smiled at last. "I was at the State Department. At the time, my father worked for the White House and landed me a position as a legal intern in the Office of Intelligence. Sam had just entered politics, full of unwavering confidence. We met at an embassy dinner for Yuri Dubinin, the Soviet's Ambassador to the United States. The Berlin wall had just fallen. Gorbachev's push for glasnost changed the world before our eyes. It was an amazing time at State. Sam came on with a pickup line: 'Miss, if you don't give me a name, I'll have to call you Princess.' I made him call me Princess for a whole month. The rest is history."

"Speaking of history," Wright asked, "is it true that the senator was unfaithful during your marriage?"

Debra Ford waved her index finger, and took her time refilling her glass with more chardonnay. "I was waiting for you to get to the dirt. The gossip. No matter. It's no secret. My shrink tells me it's okay to talk about it. Who better to share your dirty laundry with than the F-B-I?" She took a thoughtful breath. "Sam cheated on me during our whole marriage. I caught him sharing *my* bed with other women. Twice, he convinced me he had changed. I was naïve. Okay—flat out stupid. The third time, well, bimbo number three..."

"I would think once is enough," Kate added.

Wright turned and peered out the windows at the dark green river beyond.

"I have no idea how many mistresses he collected. I just know of three. There were more, of course, but three were enough to destroy any remaining trust."

"I believe you demonstrated a lot of tolerance," Kate said.

"Well, a shrink helps," she said with an alcohol-fed giggle. "What I know now, in light of Sam's behavior, our marriage was doomed. I couldn't stop it. Sam made his choices. It was only a matter of time."

Kate glanced at Wright, who was staring out the expansive windows.

"Sam and I talk more now than during our twenty years of marriage. We have an understanding. He keeps his nose out of my affairs. I don't meddle in his."

"To your knowledge," Kate asked, "is he involved with anyone now? Perhaps someone on his staff?"

Debra didn't hesitate. "Sam's an unfaithful prick, but he's no fool. He learned long ago, the office is a bad place to play house. I never worried about him sleeping around at the office. Edwards, Weiner, Sanford, and Clinton—he didn't make their mistakes. He didn't even do the Spitzer call girl circle either. At work, Sam keeps his staff out of his drawers, if you get my meaning. His personal life is need-to-know. His staff have no clue who he dates, if you call what he does dating."

Silence hung in the air for a moment.

"The senator uses a laptop," Wright finally said. "Did he have it with him Sunday?"

"I believe so. Oh, just like Tiger Woods and Packwood, Sam learned one more thing: don't let anyone get hold of your electronics." She rapped her glass with her fingernails. "You've seen it? A fancy slim computer. Its skin glows in the dark. A couple of months ago, he bragged about it being 'bullet proof,' whatever that means."

Kate scribbled notes. The case file mentioned that the three-term Oklahoma Republican senator sat on the Senate Committee on Commerce, Science, and Transportation, and he was the Chair of the Senate Subcommittee on Science, Technology, and Space. Encryption was one of the legislative areas his committee oversaw. Samuel Ford's laptop probably was "bullet proof."

"I want to get back to the senator's infidelity for a moment," Kate said.

From across the table, Debra Ford radiated contempt. "I'm sorry, miss agent who-ever-you-are again, Sam wouldn't be interested in you." She gulped down another half-glass of wine. "At this point in his life, he favors blondes, mainly because they're not hold-on brunettes like me."

Kate started a new page of notes, one without the word *lush* written on it. "Mrs. Ford, you've implied your ex-husband is discreet with his personal life. Who are his types? Please, indulge me."

"G-men must not be too bright nowadays," Debra Ford snapped. "The bureau seems to be fishing in a pretty low talent pool."

Kate crossed her arms. "Mrs. Ford—"

"Oh, you people have no sense of humor."

"Not on Mondays," Kate said flatly.

"You are both so dry."

"Just doing our jobs, ma'am," Kate replied.

Debra Ford rolled her eyes. "Oh, very well. Sam oversees a charitable trust. A Delaware corporation. It distributes academic scholarships. That's his angle. When he finds a worthy coed, his trust reimburses her for necessities: housing, food, tuition, books, and a small educational stipend."

Kate's eyebrows arched. "In exchange for a discreet relationship?"

"Figure that out all by yourself?" Debra Ford drained the last of the bottle of chardonnay into her glass. She licked her lips, frowned, and got up.

"Please, Mrs. Ford," Wright said, intercepting her, "we won't take much more of your time."

Kate asked, "Do you wish him ill for his infidelity?"

Debra Ford spun around. "You mean, do I hate his guts? Do I wish Sam was dead for the hurt he caused me? I won't answer that without consulting with my lawyer. I sure as hell will say I despise politics."

Kate nodded.

"Sam gave me three great children," she continued, her head starting to sway. "For that I am grateful. I spent my marriage raising them without a father. Politics separated Sam from his family, but through his connections, he provided for us. That was never in doubt. Our children attend private colleges. You'll find it ironic to know that two of them hate both their parents." She chuckled as if it was an inside joke. "Josh, our middle child, is the only one who comes around. I count my blessings knowing none of our children will pursue political science or law as careers. You can quote me on that. Even double underline it if you'd like."

Wright guided Debra Ford back to the settee.

"Just a few more questions," he said, studying her carefully. "What's the amount of your husband's life insurance policy, in the event of his death?"

"I need a refill," Debra Ford proclaimed. Her mouth tightened and attention faded as the empty wine glass in front of her began to hypnotize her. "This is a lot to process. And I don't manage the affairs of his estate."

"This is a federal investigation with consequences for those who mislead us." Wright leaned closer. "Mrs. Ford, from the looks of things you appear well off. A house with a killer view, posh tastes from some upscale interior designer. Lady, this shack is no dive. You got a maid who greets people at the door. Nice touch. And I saw a Mercedes ragtop in a five-bay garage. Nice treasures for a high-society woman who doesn't have a job and routinely sees a top-dollar psychologist. So without beating around the bush, what do his heirs inherit in the event of his death?"

Debra Ford's hands shook. Her eyelids closed.

Stretching out his arms, Wright leaned back and nodded to Kate.

Taking her good-cop/bad-cop cue, Kate closed her notepad and touched Debra Ford's trembling hands. "You don't have to answer that question."

Debra Ford blurted, "There's no life insurance policy, except through his Senate position. His assets reside in trusts. Around forty million."

"To your knowledge," Wright asked, "has he fathered children with anyone else?"

She stared at the agents before turning to the digital recorder on the table. Something clicked behind her eyes. Her voice turned cold. "I've answered enough questions."

Wright collected his recorder.

Kate packed her notepad. "Thank you for your time."

Ignoring them, Debra Ford staggered to the kitchen and returned with a fresh bottle of chardonnay. The cork was popped and the glass filled before they reached the foyer.

The maid stood beside a colonial-style walnut front door, holding their coats.

"When I said the FBI's talent pool was low," Debra Ford said, "I didn't realize it was pitifully shallow."

She guzzled her refilled glass. The fresh splash of vino invigorated her senses. The color in her face returned to post-workout flushness. She poured another and toasted the agents at her door.

Kate's eyes narrowed. Debra Ford knew something. Something they'd forgotten to ask.

She thought about their questions. It wasn't the mega-trust, nor his family, nor his staff, nor his laptop. It was the women. *Quid pro quo.* Coeds and discreet relationships.

"Ms. Ford, what'd we miss about his non-profit dating game trust?"

Debra Ford chuckled. "Housing allowances. You didn't ask about Sam's… love shack. That's what I call it… love shack. Wasn't that… a song?"

Kate smiled wryly. "By the B-52s."

The woman finished off yet another glass. "… heard of 'em."

"Who is Sam's current girlfriend?" Kate prompted.

"Don't know," she said, her speech beginning to slur. "Josh made his father show him a pict'r. Blonde. At'ractive. Not old enough for… nip and tuck." She burped and paused, as if she might burst into tears. After sluggish blinks, she continued, "Law stu… dent."

Debra Ford swayed and latched onto the wall for support. "Can't wait 'til Sam breaks her heart. Dumps 'em all… after 'while."

Kate nodded. "Where's Sam's love shack?"

She gave a dismissive wave with her empty glass.

"Debra, you've been most helpful."

Debra Ford staggered closer to Kate, the wine glass clutched in her hand like a torch. Their eyes locked, while she scrutinized Kate's appearance. The intake of chardonnay was beyond fragrant, and in such close proximity, Kate caught herself holding her breath to avoid taking in secondhand fumes.

"Tell ya a secret?" Debra Ford's head bobbed.

"What is that, ma'am?" Kate asked.

Debra Ford sniffled awkwardly. "I miss Sam."

Kate sensed a slight hesitancy in the woman's tone and offered a cordial smile. "We'll forward along what information we can."

-‡-

Seconds after the agents left, Debra Ford deposited her empty wine glass on the kitchen counter and snatched up a cell phone. She strolled to her living room's sweeping windows and studied the ominous gray sky over the Severn River.

On her phone, she typed in a familiar cell number and sent a text: JUST LEFT. She hit send and brought up a stored number for a beat reporter at the ABC-affiliated TV station in Washington, D.C. Another text followed the first: GEORGETOWN.

3
FRAGILE FREEDOMS

**Princeton University, School of Engineering and
Applied Science, Princeton, New Jersey**

IN HIS FOURTH FLOOR engineering lab, Thomas Parker shifted
his weight onto his knees and slid a baking sheet-sized, data acquisition blade server into the bottom rack of a coffin-sized enclosure.
The corrugated edges of the slatted platform on which he knelt dug
into his knees, and a nagging throb permeated his brain, the after-
math of violently kissing a door.

He grimaced, a sign of frustration more than recognition of
pain or discomfort.

He had become the poster child of *100 Ways to Kill Your Ivy
League Career*. His single-minded endeavors never included a fall-
back plan. In five days, he was in danger of becoming what he feared
most—another streeted academic, forced to peddle his talents to
keep his research alive.

Rising, he surveyed his neural-net lab through industrial-style
windows. A waning dream now. The two-story research space was
crammed floor to ceiling with equipment, computer servers and
monitors, nitrogen cooling tubing, and its central focus, an assessment chair.

Why would someone break in the lab and not take anything?

It didn't add up.

Apprehensiveness put him on edge, like a tightrope walker on a frail thin rope spanning a dark chasm. One fatal slip and that would be the end.

With his academic corpse not yet at room temperature, he wondered how long it would take former colleagues, stalking the proverbial fence like buzzards, to pick off his lab. Even given the Andlinger Center for Energy and the Environment expansion, research areas on campus were in limited supply. Everyone knew that Vladimir Valentine, DuPont Plunkett Award honoree and tenured professor, was maneuvering to secure a lab for his seven-figure, space-age nanopolymer research using buckyball molecular tube configurations. He would not be the only scavenger.

Valentine! Parker vowed to leave him nothing, not even a paperclip.

A phone rang beneath a mound of computer schematics and endless lines of program code. Three rings passed. He tried to tune out the interruption.

A voice barked from somewhere below. "Answer it!"

He shoved papers aside and snatched up the phone. "I'm in the middle—"

"I'm sure you are, Dr. Parker!" a woman's voice interrupted.

He spun toward the windows. Below, his second-year graduate assistant, Becky Ward, looked like a multitasking waitress juggling trays of dishes, cradling a laptop in one arm, typing on a console with her free hand, and speaking to him via a Bluetooth headset synced to a phone clipped to her waist.

"Oh, so sorry, doc," Becky said, with a mock gag. "I'm being rude. How's the head?"

He turned his head from side to side. "Still attached."

"Well, while you've been recovering from head trauma, I compiled initiation sequences. Did your work too: clarified interface exchanges, filtered oscillatory noise in cellular clusters, and sequenced neuro-grid routines—all done. *Fini*," she said in a bad French accent.

Parker massaged his brow. "Are you sure nothing is missing?"

"I'm hurt you don't believe me. Yes, yes. I did a thorough once-over. The lab is fine."

He sucked in a frustrated breath. "My apologies, Ms. Ward."

"What are you not telling me?" she called up to him, not using the phone. She returned to the phone. "We lost the appeal?"

"We? That's an admirable deduction," he said. An awkward moment passed. "It was decreed that I depart at midterms."

"Midterms? That's Friday!"

"An ABD," he said — an all-but-dissertation Ph.D. student — "will cover my remaining lectures."

"That's so bogus!" She was yelling again, this time into the phone.

He hung up and slumped into the chair behind the desk.

The metal floor to the mezzanine platform rumbled with thunderous vibrations, and he could hear her ranting as she bounded up the stairs and bolted into the office loft.

"This reeks of bureaucratic incompetence." Her breathing grew labored as she approached. "Other universities would never drop you—not in a million years."

"Those programs might have cut me sooner." Parker watched her march across the room and back again. He'd come to know his confidante as a rabid, vocal, marathon pacer. Becky had a habit of walking off miles in white Nike cross-trainers.

An intense energy radiated from her face and sobered her youthful features. Silently, she churned over potential solutions to a current problem—his problem—their "we" problem. A keen intellect was hard at work.

Over the past two years, he had grown to appreciate her vibrant mind. He held up his hand. "Rebecca, I'm grateful for your incredible dedication."

She inched closer. "Doesn't this outrage you?"

He rose to meet her halfway around the desk, before she could trap him behind it. If not kept in check, Becky had a habit of encroaching on personal boundaries.

"What now?"

"Not sure. I'm in uncharted territory." He turned away to avoid eye contact. "We have a guest joining us."

Her eyes narrowed. "You swore you'd never sell out."

Parker pondered her statement. "Perhaps there's a higher order at work? Karma telling me that reality trumps ideology?"

Her expression softened, like an ice sculpture melting under a splash of spring Jersey sun. She glanced away as if to show him that she grasped the complex realities of acquiring tenure at an Ivy League institution. She slid a red elastic band off her wrist and tied back her brown hair into a ponytail. As she did, he caught sight of her bare wrist and a tattoo.

Last summer, after an earth-shaking day in the lab, Parker broke his rule of fraternizing with students and bought Becky a pint of Sam Adams at the Ivy Inn. Over another round and wings, Becky admitted to having two tattoos, but declined to say where the second one was located. He speculated, but never asked. None of his business. The visible one encircled her wrist. A three-colored Pisces-bracelet of red, blue, and green dolphins cresting an endless stream of ocean waves—swimming through an open sea of freedom.

Their days of unrestrained freedom had just ended.

"What happened?" she asked, breaking the silence. Her white Nikes took wide strides as she started to pace again.

He could see she was hurt. "I grew addicted to the rarefied air of academia, and I thought our research would keep the bureaucratic hazards at bay."

"Dr. Parker, this may not be the right time. If someone takes on your research, I want to join you."

"No. Complete your studies. Publish. That publish part is what I took for granted. Don't repeat my mistakes."

"I believe in our work, so I'll work for free."

"That you already do, Ms. Ward. Although, I will admit, I wish I could live up to your lofty standards."

"I won't take no for an answer."

"That's presumptuous."

Her eyes sparkled. "Absolutely."

He pointed to the stairs. With a nod, she disappeared without another word.

As the rumble of footsteps trailed off, doubt germinated inside his already aching head.

Parker leaned against the windows and took in his neuro-net lab below.

For more than four years, Princeton had been the closest thing he had known as home. And because he refused to heed the call to publish, he had squandered everything.

CAROLINE WANG EXITED AN SUV in Princeton's North Garage and checked the pocket of her peplum jacket for the biopsy vial and her iPhone. She issued simple directives to her massive WrestleMania-like security escort behind the wheel and snapped open an umbrella to shelter her from the dreary weather.

She glanced behind to make sure her escort didn't follow. He was not to be trusted.

Even in the rain, Olden Street was alive with student pedestrians and bicyclists, not unlike most of the streets through the nearly three-hundred-year-old Princeton campus. A short walk led her to the Engineering quadrangle. A yellow Princeton Public Schools bus took up a no parking zone across the street.

She glanced at her watch to confirm the time. Under her umbrella, she leaned against a stone landscaping wall and waited for a man for whom she'd held the utmost disdain.

Minutes later, a Lexus sedan parked behind the school bus, and Stewart Richards stepped out of the car and into the rain.

Caroline greeted him at the base of the steps.

"You are not supposed to be here, Dr. Wang," Richards said.

She caught her breath. "The board wants an unbiased observer present."

"Your participation adds no value."

"That may be true, but I have my orders," she said, fighting shakiness in her voice. The last three months had been spent working under the cold-blooded murderer, the same calculating bastard who sanctioned the death of his own daughter, Amy. And Princeton was her opportunity to deliver payback.

Snatching her wrist, the one holding up her umbrella, he reeled her in until they were intimately close. He adjusted his gorilla-like grip until her umbrella sheltered both of them. A waved of students parted around them, paying them no attention.

Richards whispered, "If you undermine this recruitment, your body will be found floating lifeless in Carnegie Lake. I am clear?"

Caroline nodded. Message received, loud and clear.

RICHARDS MOVED CAROLINE ASIDE to study the modern-looking structure. Constructed in institutional red brick, the engineering quad was devoid of the same architectural characteristics that Princeton was renowned for—the distinctive historical landscape featured in Ivy League recruiting brochures. A reddish-brown crumpled metal J-hook, something called modern art, sat offset to the School of Engineering and Applied Science's main entrance.

From the refuge of a vestibule, a gray-haired man opened the doors to the building's lobby, careful to avoid the rain.

"Traffic enforcement will ticket you if you park there," Phillip Derman said, gesturing to signs posted at the curb. "No parking."

Richards passed through the entry, flicking rain off his overcoat. "I'll take my chances."

Derman's gaze darted back and forth between them. "I only expected you."

He ignored their greeter and took in the two-story lobby. It was an open, inviting area with plenty of exterior windows and stairs leading to the second floor. The engineering library was just to the left. Intersecting corridors ran north and west.

Classes appeared to be in session.

"Which way?" he asked, impatiently.

Derman pointed. "The elevator is this way."

Richards strode forward, leaving Derman to play catch up and Caroline lagging by several paces.

"He received authorization to conduct human research?" Richards asked.

Derman flashed a pat-yourself-on-the-back grin. "It's cataloged as equipment calibration."

"That's an understatement."

From the start, Richards had been unyielding in laying the groundwork for this procurement. He left nothing to chance, with all manners of contingencies implemented. Whether by philosophical ideals or an aversion to bureaucracy, Thomas Parker had proven unwilling to collaborate with government scientists or accept direct avenues of funding. Interested parties had managed to keep an eye on his fledgling research all the same—and that was where the services of Philip Derman proved valuable. Six million dollars to date, in exchange for monitoring Parker's research and funneled another million through various non-profit avenues to supply Parker with backdoor equipment. The majority of the black budget investment originated from three entities: the Defense Advanced Research Projects Agency (DARPA), the Defense Intelligence Agency (DIA), and the office of Intelligence Advanced Research Projects Activity (IARPA).

This was a big game acquisition.

And the headhunter was about to acquire another trophy.

They stepped into the freight elevator and Derman tapped the button for the fourth floor. The elevator jolted as it ascended.

Derman offered his hand to Caroline, and she apprehensively took it.

The Associate Dean of Development for the School of Engineering and Applied Science launched into rapid fire of facts and propaganda about research programs undertaken by the engineering college, along with their joint doctorate program with the Neuroscience Institute.

Richards disregarded the spiel, lost in his own thoughts.

He considered it ironic that while other prestigious institutions also cultivated the bright young minds of tomorrow, his quest for a future genius had brought him to Princeton, best known as the place where Albert Einstein had spent the last years of his life.

Stewart Richards had come to Princeton to recruit the world's next great genius.

And it was shaping up to be such a great day.

4
CONTEXT

**Princeton University, Engineering Quad,
Princeton, New Jersey**

In the neural-net lab, decked out in a white lab coat, Becky made final preparations. A swarm of enthusiastic biology seniors from Princeton High School mashed their faces against the large paneled windows that separated the cramped observation area from the lab. Students watched in awe as one of their peers climbed bravely inside a Transformer-like cockpit, called "the chair."

The contraption was more machine than teenager.

Wearing an aviation-style flight-suit, Amanda Conley settled into a cockpit of gadgetry and slid a crude-looking helmet over her head. A spherical array of fiber optic cables flowed out of the helmet and its spray connected to clusters of terminals that surrounded her. Spaghetti-thin bio-readout circuits pierced her suit and connected to yet to more terminals.

Becky secured Velcro straps over Amanda's wrists and ankles. It was for her own safety, to keep their volunteer from interfering with the vast amount of delicate electronics. Next, Becky sealed stimulation goggles across her face, leaving only a smile revealed.

Amanda stuck out her tongue, which raised a chorus of chatter in the observation area.

A hands-free microphone below Becky's chin projected her voice over the lab's speaker system.

"Images sent to Amanda's eyes," Becky said, "stimulate her retinal inputs, which then generate neurological responses inside her brain."

"They're gonna fry her, man," gloated a male classmate. "She's a goner."

Another boy chimed in. "Burnt toast, baby!" He high-fived other boys around him. "I'm starting to smell smoke."

"Oh, shut it, loser," a girl snapped.

"Someone dial 9-1-1."

"Okay. That's enough," their biology teacher said as she squeezed herself between the growing factions of boys versus girls. "Behave. All of you."

"Amanda, you rock!" a girl called, which started a whole new wave of banter.

Becky paced with measured strides in front of the chair. Her fingers adjusted knobs and slides on a hand-held wand she carried. A thick, snake-like umbilical cord dangled from the wand and slithered across the floor as she walked.

"Amanda," Becky asked, "how are you feeling?"

"Fine," the teenager in the electric chair replied. "This is cool."

Becky checked the teenager's vitals: blood pressure one-ten over seventy, pulse sixty-four. Everything looked fine.

Becky glanced to her young volunteer. "I want you to recall one of the colored shapes in our data set. One at a time. Just like we rehearsed. Close your eyes and visualize one object. See every edge of the object—the fullness of its color. Say the shape and color aloud in your mind, but do not say anything aloud. After the computer makes its selection, give us your choice."

"Got it."

Becky counted steadily down from five.

Ding. An electronic game-show-like bell sounded. An LED projection screen produced a red diamond from among the three hundred plausible shapes.

"What did you choose?"

The teenager said, "Red diamond."

Overhead speakers passed along distant cheers.

Amanda beamed. "The computer read my thoughts?"

Becky nodded. "It did indeed."

The process continued. The screen cleared the diamond. Moments later it flashed a green hexagon. Amanda gave her response. More cheers followed. The board was cleared again. The computer made another selection: a blue gecko silhouette. Amanda's response: "Blue gecko."

The students applauded again.

IN THE BACK OF the observation area, Thomas Parker hovered in a splash of darkness, where lights and console illumination did not reach, away from the intrigued mass of high schoolers. He was a reticent observer, careful not to upstage his research assistant. He watched Becky conduct the experiment like a TV game show host with a live studio audience clinging to her every movement.

His gaze shifted to the applauding students. While their genuine vigor for science was reassuring, it could not supplant his doubt.

Derman was right. Not publishing his findings had been a mistake—nascent steps demonstrating that a human could telepathically converse with a machine—the ability to technically follow a chain reaction of microelectrical pulses and chemical transfers as they propagated across the brain's internal landscape, until they arrived at a destined set of neurons and synapses, and then translate that miniscule ionic transfer back into something the outside world could comprehend.

The burden he carried had nothing to do with performance anxiety, but with the precipice on which he stood. A declaration of mind-machine interfaces and neurological mapping would fuel extravagant tabloid headlines: *Man Conquers the Mind! Make Your Dreams Come True!* The distorted exposés would thrive in the stratosphere. In more threatening ways, malicious exaggerations could claim the ability to alter conscious and unconscious behaviors: *Creating Mind Warps! Mind Control! Social and Mental Conformity! Cure Insanity!*

Parker sighed and checked the Casio on his wrist. His interviewer was late.

ILLUMINATION FROM THE CORRIDOR bled into the tiny observation area as Stewart Richards led Caroline Wang and Phillip Derman into the cramped space. Derman shut the steel door behind them, and the swale of light disappeared as quickly as it had emerged.

Richards allowed his eyes to adjust to the adumbrate conditions. Through garage door-sized windows, he spotted the neuro-net lab. It was bright, white like heaven. Overhead speakers carried a female voice. He matched her to Parker's dossier. Rebecca Ward. Graduate student. A lab coat draped past her knees. A snarl of black wires trailed behind her as she strolled about the lab. She spoke to a seated figure encompassed by a massive throng of wires and cables. With the exception of a glimpse of flesh-toned skin along the jaw-line, it was hard to tell where a human being ended and where a machine began.

Richards fell speechless.

The impressive technological achievement on display was created by two people working on a shoestring budget—damn near an impossible scenario to pull off. And Thomas Parker was doing it for infinitesimally less than his own program, which pursued the same breakthroughs. In total, the compact lab used stacked platforms to optimize space. Very academic. Exactly how he'd imagined it. Of course, he had seen photographs in his scouting dossier, which he considered gap information and part of a broader contingency plan.

Richards watched, entranced.

He had indeed found his Einstein.

—¦—

THOMAS PARKER SAW THE newcomers enter the observation area. A man with a gray eyes and a mop of frosted hair led the threesome, and he recognized the devilish rock star immediately. Stewart Richards was a man whose reputation preceded him—former Nobel prize runner up and a stalwart in the field, ranking among the top thirty experts in the field of modern neuroscience. A Chinese woman and the associate dean stood on opposite sides of him.

"Wanted to escort them up myself," Philip Derman added.

The man's gaze targeted him. "Stewart Richards. Glad to finally meet you. And this is Caroline Wang."

They shook hands. Richards held their grip longer than normal, in a masculine, measuring-kind of manner, and while maintaining eye contact. On the other hand, the woman offered a meek handshake before retreating to the observation window.

Parker forced a polite smile and motioned to the action in the lab.

"How'd she get to be the lucky one?" Richards asked, leaning in behind the teenagers.

"They drew straws for the chair."

"The chair?" Richards said with a hint of amusement. His gaze panned the lab, taking in its every detail. He pointed. "Is that a Cray?"

"Very astute," Parker said.

In the back of the lab stood two supercomputer lineups, each equivalent in length to five industrial-sized double-door refrigerators side by side. Large bundle of cables stretched across the floor from the computers to the base of the chair.

Richards eyed the cabling next. "You're using fiber optics."

"Roughly a thousand strands." On a monitor, Parker brought up a multicolored schematic, which resembled a shattered plate of stained glass more than it did an illustration of tiny wires and connections. "Fiber delivers the real-time communication rate needed for neural tracing. Our brains can perform ten-quadrillion calculations, all while running on around twenty watts. Brain waves, I call them brainstorms, are thousands of pico- to micro-ampere electro-chemical currents bouncing back and form between neurons. And a single neuron can interconnect with up to ten thousand neighboring neurons. So, by the sheer math alone, the brain hosts a lot of neurotransmissions to track. Sensitivity in our interface sensors was paramount."

"You're using superconductors?"

Parker furrowed his brow. The man was sharp. "You've done your homework."

The man shot him a confident smile then flashed an apathetic shrug directed at Caroline Wang. "For her edification, tell us about your neuro-sensors, in layman's terms."

Parker considered his response. "The quantum-based circuits detect transfers of energy dashing across synaptic junctions and translate that neuro-chemical movement back into light using multi-layer, nanowire-based transistors and optoelectric supercon-ductor wafers."

From a table, he retrieved a pyramid-shaped, clear-glass paper-weight and immersed it in the incandescent glow of a desk lamp. White light beamed through the glass pyramid and evolved into a prismatic rainbow on the other side. He rotated the glass object in his hand, causing a stream of polychromatic radiance to splash across the desk.

Parker continued. "The computer science community strives to deconstruct life, strip it down to a discrete spectrum of black and white, binary zeros and ones. Science cannot ask two hundred thousand years of evolution, the human brain and its inhabitants, to be reduced to disingenuous fractions of data—on and off values. At its max, the brain can have around a hundred-billion neurons. And the steady state charge conditions in neurons vary, with more of a sliding scale of impulse triggers for activation: different threshold voltages and action potentials. Neurons are mated to other interneurons and tuned to certain triggers—meaning they develop resonance-like as-sociations and come alive when they hear specific musical notes or see colors of light. Our sensors detect neurotransmitter migration and synaptic discharges and mirror it as wavelengths of light—not unlike the spectrum of visible light."

Richards processed the disclosure. "Where a rainbow of color becomes a symphony of neural musical cords?"

Parker chuckled. "Something like that."

"Neurons are tuned to respond to specific inputs?" Caroline said, more as a statement than a question. She tossed Richards an icy glare.

Parker added a lit LED pen-light next to the incandescent lamp source and a whole new array of rainbowed brilliance sprayed across the desk. Some of the cascade of colors became muted, others intensified, and others gelled together into a rich kaleidoscopic brilliance.

"As you know, the human brain has as many as ten thousand different types of neurons. Many perform specific, if not limited, physiological functions. Some neurons are only stimulated when they are showered with an intense barrage of electrical-chemical pulses, and others are hypersensitive and sparkle to life when any amount of energy is sprinkled upon them. The trick is to identify those patterns, decode their relationships, and create algorithms to turn those stimulations into traceable, repeatable outcomes."

Caroline looked intrigued. "How is your research different from what others are working on?"

Derman interrupted. "You can forget those large-scale money-sucking programs: *The Brain Initiative*, *The BigNeuron*, *The Blue Brain*, *The Human Connectome*. Dr. Parker's work is *the* first step in mapping the real human consciousness."

Parker grinned. "Well, we've leapfrogged hurdles that others struggle with: cellular variability, biological resistivity, synaptic targeting, and tracking of neural associations."

On a display, he brought up a graphical image of a human skull. Using his fingers on the interactive screen, he removed the skull and the meninges membranes to reveal the folds and fissures of a visceral brain.

Derman and Richards crowded around the screen. Caroline lurked behind the taller men.

Everyone's gaze homed in on the images.

Parker gestured to the modeled organ. "Most neural sensing techniques require penetrating the skull to implant electrocorticography electrodes in a subdural grid on top of the brain. That's medieval when you think about it. Our non-invasive neural targeting approach is external to the skull. No folds of gray or white matter are picked through. No electrodes are implanted. No microchips or electroencephalography electrodes are embedded under the scalp or buried in the brain. No impractical, dumpster-sized magneto-encephalography sensors mop up stray brainwaves. Our pragmatic method carries on a rudimentary two-way conversation between a human being and a machine, via a brain-computer interface."

Derman grabbed Parker's shoulder. "His work advances science dramatically. In the future, based on his research, amputees will control biomechanical limbs and paraplegics can learn to walk again. A blind person can witness the amazing brilliance of a sunrise. The deaf can hear another human voice. Advancements in treatment methods will allow doctors to improve post-event conditions and reverse disorders like dementia, Alzheimer's, and Parkinson's."

The students broke out in laughter. A purple oval was the next selection.

Parker noticed Caroline Wang leaning in for a closer inspection.

"Describe the bloody map," Derman prompted.

On the monitor, Parker sliced a horizontal plane through the digital brain to reveal its neuroanatomy. "Our teenage volunteer spent an hour in PNI's" — referring to the Princeton Neuroscience Institute — "3-Tesla MRI scanner looking over elementary objects. Tested and retested until reliable repetition was established. After her scan, our Cray digests the data, configures it, and constructs an interactive 3D neuro-map built on the test population. Once the road map is ready, our guessing game begins."

"Using a limited population."

"Accuracy on complex element neurolinguistic mapping remains elusive."

Richards' gaze narrowed. "Expand on your difference between elementary and complex objects."

"Okay. Let's say a person recalls a red hexagon. The computer gets it. Ding. No problem. But now ask a person to think about a stop sign, the relational structures in a fixed neuro-net matrix become more challenging."

"Why is that?" Caroline asked.

"It's due to an exponential jump in cognitive associations."

Richards gestured for Parker to continue.

"Neurolinguistic context. Cognitively, a stop sign is a richer, dynamic element. It's more than a red shape containing white lettering. It bridges over to our social and physical world. For a driver, the comprehension of a stop sign can mean the difference between life and death. Let's say I hold up a stop sign. How does your mind interpret it? Do you see, think, or say the word STOP? Do you see a holistic object with a deeper meaning, STOP? Or do you think of the STOP sign you ran last week when you were running late to work? No one cognitively processes a red hexagon imprinted with white letters. In neurolinguistic terms, humans memorize dynamic objects with varying degrees of substantive context."

Parker pointed. "Our volunteer targets one two-dimensional image out of three hundred distinct objects. Limited external and peripheral context. In our test population, a square is a square, a color is interpreted as that color."

Richards' expression turned serious. "Have you grown and varied your test set?"

Parker gave a wry smile, knowing where the question was leading. "Comprehension of higher-level cognitive functions? The recognition of another human face?" Other researchers, he explained, had used the faces of celebrities to pinpoint neural activities in the medial temporal lobe region. Using implanted electrodes, researchers showed the photos of celebrities like Jennifer Aniston, Clint Eastwood, Halle Berry, Tiger Woods, and Ronald Reagan to patients with epilepsy and tracked their neural activities. They then mapped similar visual stimulation to physical locations, such as the White House, the Eiffel Tower, and Leaning Tower of Pisa. In certain cases, patients could trigger common neural responses between a person like Ronald Regan and the White House. What the researchers could not map were individual neurons, merely approximate cognitive locations.

Richards nodded thoughtfully. "How is your neurological map defined?"

"Thought you would never ask." Parker tossed the digital brain into a symbolic trash bin and grew a new translucent, three-dimensional model of a human brain. The walnut-like topography of the organ bristled with a sparkling luminescence of tiny hot spots and revealed deeper fibrous regions within it. Descriptive tags highlighted high-level brain structures, such as cerebral hemispheres, parietal lobe, occipital lobe, temporal lobe, hippocampus, thalamus and hypothalamus, corpus collosum, and the cerebellum. Minuscule red dots pulsed and flickered within the rough landscape, like tiny cars trekking along microscopic highways. "Most medical researchers, non-AI holdovers, acknowledge that our brain does not process data like a computer. It's easiest to say our brains are fluid and reshape and reconfigure themselves over time. It takes a couple million neurons firing simultaneously inside our skulls to create the most trivial memory—a simple thought of a juicy apple—the faces of John, Paul, Ringo, and George—the remembrance of song lyrics to *A Hard Day's Night*. Thousands of physical or sensory or psychological or emotional stimulations can alter a given set of neural firings and make them different from the next."

Richards pursed his lips together. "How do you track brain activities that don't repeat, much less build a map for that kind of variation?"

"Imagine a red apple." Parker's eyes shone with excitement. "The object is perceived through our eyes. Its image rockets along the optic tract and processed by our visual cortex, which divides the apple into distinctive physiognomies: color, geometric composition, warmth, weight, etcetera. Inside our mind, the image contains fundamental parts for translation. Our visual cortex is where the avalanche of neural explosions start, sending a cascade of parallel neural firings racing wildly throughout the entire brain. This barrage of micro-signals talk to other neurons, until there is enough neural activity that higher levels of consciousness begin to reassemble the impulses. The process is tuned, similar to a feedback loop. Past associations and memories are drawn upon to create a visceral interpretation of the *apple*. We recognize its ruby red color, identify the object as a fruit, see it as edible—an object that cures hunger pains."

Parker joined his hands in front of the computer monitor, stretching his fingers over varied regions of the modeled brain. "We built neuro-association-based models that limit inter-neural references."

"You filter neural activity through pattern-based algorithms?" Richards asked.

Caroline nudged Derman aside to take a closer look.

Parker pointed to Amanda's virtual brain, alive with tiny eclectic red dots flickering and pulsing within and across its various bumps and folds. "Our map is a cheat. It mates to specific regions in her brain she uses when seeing the objects the first time. It takes a thousand algorithms to build a limited-context neuro-map. We want a green gecko silhouette to be a green gecko silhouette every time, minus the GEICO critter. The computer uses this template to predict individual synaptic firings. It limits the neurological neighborhoods it has to search to identify the chosen item—our green lizard. By the time Amanda actually sits in the chair, the computer parcels her virtual brain into fifty thousand 3D neighborhoods, each neighborhood about a quarter of the size and thickness of a postage stamp. It knows which neurons to search and which ones to ignore."

Parker pointed to the monitor again as it displayed a new image. "Her current selection."

Caroline's gaze locked onto the monitor. "An orange crescent moon."

The students laughed in the background.

"Our volunteer cannot think of anything she wants. It's not an open-ended population."

Richards' eyebrows shot up. "What happens with an open-ended test population?"

"Cognitive similarities infiltrate the template. A silhouette of a green clover begins to look like a green tree. Green eyes versus blue eyes."

Richards studied Parker for a long moment. "My program is an endeavor much in line with your own efforts. We're focused on surpassing what you might define as open-ended control items—to use your label, neurolinguistic context."

Parker knew what was coming.

"Visit my lab. We've got all the toys. You'll be impressed."

"Sounds government-like," he said with a look of indifference mixed with reservation.

"We're funded from a variety of sources, but we're very autonomous."

"Happy face," Amanda announced over the loud speakers.

They all turned to a monitor. A yellow happy face beamed on the display.

Parker chuckled. "Happy Face bring us to our finale."

Over the speakers, Becky gave departing directions to the crowd of onlookers. The high schoolers formed a congested line to shake Parker's hand before filing out the observation area. Through the windows, Parker saw Becky start the laborious process of unplugging their teenage volunteer from the monstrous contraption engulfing her.

"Friday," Richards said, over the wall of teenagers swelling between them. "That is, if you're available."

Parker turned to Derman, then back to Richards. "Who will I be meeting?"

The man's expression turned poker-like. "Doctors, scientists, like yourself."

Still shaking the hands of departing students, Parker asked, "Not government scientists?"

Instead of responding, the man handed Parker a business card across the strong current of passing students. "Friday morning. My facility is west of Princeton."

Richards shook his hand and thanked him for his time. Caroline Wang followed and her dark, chocolate brown eyes radiated a deep determination. She mouthed "thank you" and left without another word.

Derman elbowed a teenager aside. "Congratulations, Tom," he whispered into Parker's ear, while giving him a firm slap on the shoulders. "You killed it."

"Thanks, Phil."

"Dr. Parker," Richards asked, lingering at the door, "can I pose a hypothetical question to you?"

Parker scrunched his forehead. "Fire away."

Richards drew a breath. "What would it take to read an un-mapped mind? Decipher a memory from scratch? Carry on a two-way conversation with a total stranger?"

Parker laughed. "How about a bloody miracle."

Richards looked skeptical. "Friday, then."

5
REFLECTIONS

Princeton University Engineering Quad,
Princeton, New Jersey

TEN MINUTES AFTER THE visitors had left the lab, Parker collapsed in a chair in the observation area. Illumination from a monitor washed over him, a record of their volunteer's neuro-modeling activities. Through the observation windows, he watched Becky, wearing ear buds, sing along to Katy Perry. She danced across the congested lab as she stowed away equipment. Her voice was not as good as the pop singer's, but worth listening to nonetheless.

"Do you ever feel, feel so paper thin..."

Becky gave a whole new meaning to "whistle while you work."

At his feet were the remains of a Crown Royal bottle. He savored a splash of whisky in his I ♥ NY coffee mug and flipped the business card through his fingers.

Thick, white card stock with black embossed letters.

ANCRI.

Just a company title and address. Nothing else.

Uneasy, Parker ran routine web searches and found little of significance. Professors berated students for treating Google search results as gospel. He felt foolish for falling into the same feeble trap. The obvious results mattered least. A couple of LinkedIn and

Twitter references. *Associació Nacional de Criadors d'Oví de Raça Ripollesa*—which seemed extremely irrelevant, since it linked to the National Association of Sheep Breeders in Monells, Spain. He ran similar checks against the American Medical Association database. Nothing there either.

Clearly, ANCRI wasn't raising sheep or concerned about animal husbandry.

ANCRI's lack of openness meant it was probably a government-sponsored lab. Parker had never been associated with anything secret before. At University of Colorado's School of Medicine, he had overheard colleagues talking about the Phoenix program when its director toured campus on a recruiting visit. Phoenix was funded by a federal agency called DARPA, out of its Tactical Technology Office. Their research sought to integrate neurological-based artificial intelligence into geosynchronous earth-orbiting military satellite systems, seeking ways to get the low Earth orbit (LEO) technology and robotic platforms to think more autonomously, human-like, in terms of self-generated problem solving strategies.

A flash of movement distracted him from his thoughts.

Becky, her long chestnut hair flowing across the shoulders, peered at him through the observation window. Her lips were still moving. Singing, her mouth snapped out the lyrics as if they were hers. Her eyes locked on his.

"*Maybe a reason why all the doors are closed...*"

"Not all doors are meant to be opened," he said, knowing Katy Perry had a point.

"Hell yes they are, Dr. Parker!" she shouted and pointed at him. "I've been your freakin' slave for two years. You owe me. Massively. Big time. Colossal. There has to be a word bigger than colossal, and, whatever it is, mister, you owe me that too."

Parker cracked a strangled smile. "Ms. Ward, what kind of compensation do you have in mind? One that won't get me fired?"

"The latter has already occurred."

"True enough."

Her two years of servitude was one reason their neuromapping system worked as well as it did, and he knew it.

"Ivy Inn? Burgers. Beers. Several beers, now that I think about it." She was back to singing. "...*you're a firework.*"

Parker watched her do an about-face and return to storing equipment. Her contributions had made a difference. Certainly, he owed her. Dinner and drinks seemed like a cheap out.

He turned his attention back to the business card.

It felt like a get-out-of-jail-free card. He set it down and anchored it with his empty I♥NY coffee mug, as if to secure his chance at keeping his research alive. Sell out to industry and get a damn hall pass.

Friday. His last day at Princeton. And an interview. The events were linked. Perhaps to reinforce acceptance of any offer that Richards felt obliged to present.

ANCRI was involved in brain mapping. Complex neurological events. Searching for memories. And their surreptitious little institute needed his unique expertise.

That fact troubled him. Neuroscience was specialized, and he assumed he knew the prominent institutions working in it. Never heard of ANCRI.

Friday proved a pivotal point in his career or one that would end it.

Firestone Library, Princeton University, Princeton, New Jersey

CAROLINE WANG SHOWED HER credentials at the check-in desk. Firestone Library was a historical landmark in the style of a stone cathedral. Over the years, modifications and upgrades around the core structure had expanded its footprint above and below ground. Gone were the old-fashioned card catalogs and wooden shelves, replaced by an expanse of modern counters and computer terminals. While the collective facilities held more than seven million works and 50 miles of shelving, traditional shelving had been cut back to make the library appear spacious and bright. Tracked, high-density storage systems housed its remaining books and periodicals, with the library now embracing the cloud, SearchIt database systems, and electronic media to supplement antiquated printed materials.

Fearful of being followed, Caroline took the stairs. She weaved through rows of shelving until she came to the PS3550 section on the C-floor. Only a few students were scattered about. After waiting for a student to clear an aisle, she wheeled over the rows until she reached PS3610 periodicals, the SpringerProtocols. She snatched a cardboard shoe from the top shelf and plucked several periodicals out of the container that held a collection of journals.

From inside her jacket, she retrieved her iPhone and snapped a photo of the periodicals and library catalog sequence. She opened the periodical to a random page and tore it out of the journal. On the torn-out page she scribbled:

`Singularity close. Princeton. ANCRI. Killed by father. Senator is next. Thomas Parker new hire.`

She heard heavy, determined footsteps from another aisle. She didn't think her heart could accelerate any faster, but it did, wrenching and tightening the twisted knots that already bound her stomach.

She snapped a second photo of her handwritten notes then emailed everything to the only contact in her phone's address book. She rolled the phone and the vial in her jacket into the sheet of paper and stuffed the bundle into the cardboard shoe, packed between the remaining periodicals. Then everything went back to the top shelf.

As she turned to leave, she ran into a human wall of muscle. Her WrestleMania-like ANCRI escort plowed straight into her, causing her to stumble backwards and onto the floor, like a tennis ball blasting off a practice backboard.

"You idiot!" she snapped, hoping he had not seen the journals. "Watch where you're going."

"Dr. Wang, you were to return to the vehicle." He hovered above her, offering no help up. "You're not authorized to be here."

"Really?" Climbing to her feet, Caroline stalled and gathered her thoughts.

At her feet were the journals she had removed to make room for her phone and the vial. She scooped them up and shoved them at her mammoth security escort. At the institute, she rarely engaged the man. His duties were different from hers. His current mandate was to drive her to Princeton. She tried to remember his name, something to personalize a conversation. It was simple, dark. Gross. That was it. Only one name—no initials. Just Mister big-as-Hulk Gross.

"What are these?" he asked.

"Well, Mr. Gross, they're SpringerProtocols pharmacology and toxicology issues. ANCRI needs a refinement to our PT2 sedation compounds. Lab tests show that under extended durations, participants experience side effects. Disorientation and seizures. Seizures are bad."

Gross thumbed through the journal contents. The semi-glossy pages carried lots of plain text, numbers, charts and graphs, and referenced chemical compounds.

He studied the aisle before returning the journals to her. "Back to the car, doctor."

"Absolutely." Caroline rolled her eyes and marched off.

6
GEORGETOWN

Georgetown, Washington, DC

KATE MORGAN'S IMAGINATION RAN wild as she churned through scenarios awaiting them: a "love shack," a missing senator, a coed. It sounded like the storyline for a Danielle Steele miniseries. Lost in thought, she tuned out the hum of car tires on wet pavement and the slapping of windshield wipers.

How long can the bureau keep this story under wraps?

Behind the wheel, Jack Wright crossed the Potomac and drove past the Pentagon, taking a shortcut through Virginia. The cell in his suit jacket buzzed and he passed it over.

"Am I screening your calls?" Kate mused.

Wright laughed and gave the numerical password to his phone. She keyed it in. "It's a text. Unknown number."

"Activate the TrapCall icon." A mobile app, TrapCall unmasked blocked numbers and displayed the Caller ID.

Kate frowned. "The listing is 000-000-0000."

"Huh." Wright swerved around slower traffic. "What does it say?"

She read it twice.

"Well?"

Kate frowned. "IGNORE THE GIRLS. FIND THE COM-PUTER. Jack, who else knew about our interview with Ford's ex?"

Jack looked puzzled. "Just the deputy director."

The phone jingled again. Another text popped up.

"What's it now?"

She turned the screen toward him. "DON'T TRUST ANYONE."

Her cell rang next. "Hello?"

The voice on the phone relayed the exact address in Georgetown.

Kate put the phone on speaker and asked the task force agent to repeat the message.

Wright nodded. "We'll be on scene in fifteen minutes. Execute a search warrant for the premises and mobilize a crime scene detail. Put CIRG" – the bureau's one-stop-shop Critical Incident Response Group – "on alert in case we encounter trouble."

The agent reconfirmed the directives and hung up.

Kate wondered what Wright wasn't sharing with the rest of the team.

Ignore the girls. Find the computer. Don't trust anyone. What the hell did that mean?

A dedicated task force at headquarters had a myriad of human and technical resources at its disposal to achieve anything from sifting through credit card statements to tapping DC District Court judges for the execution of search warrants. The task force process streamlined exchanges between the bureau, the Departments of Homeland Security, Justice, and Treasury, and Capitol Police. Unlike TV crime dramas that portrayed gathering the gospel truth with a single mouse click, collecting intelligence on people in the government was not that simple.

IRS statements and campaign finance disclosures from the Office of Public Records yielded a tangible lead. Samuel Ford sat on the boards of three Delaware trusts. Behind the facade of lawyers and accountants, such domestic and overseas corporate trusts were shell games for the wealthy: places to stash money, assets, and manage liability, both tax-wise and personally. The records revealed property holdings scattered across the globe, including a condo in Georgetown.

The Georgetown condo was *where it's at!*

FIFTEEN MINUTES LATER, SHE took in the mix of old and new on the narrow residential street. Wind whistled through courtyards and alleyways, carrying in moisture from the Potomac waterfront. The Whitehurst Freeway, a raised east-west DC expressway, ran parallel to the Potomac and cradled the southward edge of the college town. Below the freeway, K Street lay in near obscurity to the thousands of commuters who drove the Capital's concrete corridor each day. A block north of K Street, red-bricked condos towered above a street, aptly named Potomac.

Street parking was impossible. Wright parked in an alley and placed an FBI placard on the dashboard, in case the federal license plate wasn't enough to deter the city's ticket-writers.

The rain had thinned to a mist.

The biting cold caught the neckline of Kate's overcoat and snaked its way down her back. She buttoned the collar tightly around her neck and clipped her FBI badge to the front of her overcoat to make it visible.

She watched Wright fidget with his blue FBI windbreaker.

"We waiting?" she asked.

Kate knew what he was thinking. Once a swarm of federal agents arrived, it would be like throwing gasoline on a campfire. Paparazzi and news crews would follow. Sooner or later someone would spill the beans. Missing U.S. senators, younger-than-he-should-have girlfriends, and "love shacks" would headline talk radio and everyone-needs-to-know TV programs. Any fragment of truth would fade behind the gossip, until everyone in the modern world knew the intimate details of Samuel Ford's personal life.

The media complicated things.

He shook his head. "Let's go on up."

Kate blocked his path. *"Ignore the girls. Find the computer?"* She pivoted on her heels, taking in the streetscape: the red-bricked Papermill condos formed clustered groups, the intersection of Grace and Potomac, and the elevated freeway and K Street beneath it. She glanced in the direction of the waterfront. Beyond the freeway lay National Harbor and a park that hugged the river. "Why is an informant sending you cryptic messages?"

Wright sucked in a breath of cold air. "Can't say."

She glared at him. "Is this investigation compromised? Are you?"

Wind-splashed hues started to frost his face. "No."

"Jack, I don't believe you."

"You have to trust me."

"No I don't." She thrust her hands onto her hips. *Bang bang bang on the door baby*, she thought. What an invitation. "Okay, boss, let's go find our *girls*."

They headed up a breezeway between condominiums. The residence of interest was a red brick unit like its neighbors.

Wright tried to peer through shut curtains in the front windows. Nothing distinguishable was visible inside. Kate gestured to the door and he rang the bell.

No one answered.

Wright rang it again. And again.

Nothing.

Kate pounded on the door with an open palm as B-52's lyrics resonated in her head. *Who is it?* she mocked to herself. *Oh, I'll tell ya who it is: how about the F-B-I!*

The task desk phoned in an updated ETA. The search warrant and crime scene unit were both three minutes out.

Kate camped out on a planter and glanced around. Just another neighborhood, most regular folks could never afford to live in.

"You know, Jack," she said with a chuckle, "I think Debra Ford was hot for you. Your hard-ass persona sucked her right into your suave lady killer magnetism."

Wright rolled his eyes. "Right. That lady was groomed since birth to be privileged. Probably been an alcoholic mess forever."

"Nah. She's not as naïve as it appears." Kate made a cat-like growl. "The gig was an act. Deep inside, beneath her socialite façade, she's a man-eating cougar."

He laughed. "Good thing you were there to watch my back."

"I would have paid her to eat you alive." She took a breath and changed the subject. "You realize Debra Ford and her son may be the last people to have seen the senator."

"The thought crossed my mind."

"What does the bureau know about her time at State?"

"Her file is classified but I doubt there's much to the lush. She's an easy book to read. Came from a family of money. Married a young senator on a fast track into politics. Daddy's connections landed her a job at the State Department. From what I know, her only newsworthy assignment involved an op with the Italians and the Russians and misappropriations in the European banking system."

A distant screech of tires echoed in the breezeways between the tightly grouped red stones and caused Kate to glance south, toward the canal path and rows of condos.

"Stake out the door, cougar killer," she said, jogging off in the direction of the Georgetown waterfront. "I'll bring in the cavalry."

PARKED AGAINST A PLANTER, Kate watched Wright confirm operational directives as a technician disabled the home's alarm, insert a master key in the lock, and open the front door.

Inside, the expensive townhome was middle-class bland, without a distinctive style. Minimal knickknacks. Cheap watercolor reprints hung on the walls, nothing personal or intimate on display. No photographs of Oklahoma Senator Samuel Ford.

"Do we know who lives here?" Wright asked.

The warrant agent, the last one inside, said, "Because of confidentiality concerns, the senator's trust executor is refusing to cooperate. So we ran the address by the registrar's offices at nearby universities and came up two women from George Washington. Both law students. Tiny Marie Newberry and Melissa Von Abrams."

Kate and Wright exchanged glances. *Ignore the girls?*

She swept her vision from wall to wall, taking in the modest furnishings: suede pillows on a teal leather couch, matching brass table lamps, curtain drawn windows, white front door. Something made her back up. The door's brass safety chain. It dangled in two halves.

Kate gestured to the door.

Without touching it, Wright examined both ends of the chain. "This was cut."

"Clear," various agents called out, one at a time.

Wright frowned. "Damn, the place is empty."

Someone yelled from upstairs. "We have a locked door."

Kate hit the stairs, clearing two steps at a time, and entered a bedroom overlooking Potomac Street. An agent wearing latex gloves stood beside a closed door.

Light brown spots painted light-lavender walls and a bed mattress. The bed was stripped of its sheets. Its pillows were missing.

Kate recognized the small splotches of brown spots as blood. She studied the rest of the room. A queen-sized bed stood against one wall, flanked by nightstands and a small dresser. Basic furnishings. No photographs. A Ritz-Carlton Central Park Do Not Disturb sign hung on the knob of an adjoining door, which likely led to a bathroom. A sliding closet door faced the foot of the bed. A faint odor, barely distinguishable, seeped into the room. Years of forensics told her what it was; she knew it as death.

She examined the knob—it had a run-of-the-mill locking mechanism. A small hole in its center allowed access to the lock.

Sliding a closet door open, Kate pushed aside dresses and matching outfits hanging on the rack. Women's shoes littered the closet floor. Boxes upon boxes were stacked on the shelving. She slid a garment off its wire clothes hanger and bent the hanger's hook straight. Inserting the straightened hanger into the hole of the bathroom's doorknob, she depressed the button-style latch inside the knob. The lock disengaged with a soft click.

With the handkerchief protecting his hand, Wright twisted the knob and opened the door.

Stale pungent air filled the bedroom.

Kate entered the bathroom first.

In the bathtub, under a plastic shower curtain, lay a woman's naked body.

Ignore the girls?

7
CONFIRMATIONS

**Friend Center for Engineering Education,
Princeton University, Princeton, New Jersey**

ON THE SECOND FLOOR of the library, Parker hunkered down at a computer and coded up a Java web spider to optimize URL queries and parse HTML files. On the floor beside him was his coveted skullcap hard-sided case. Sun filtered through the building's glass walls and rained into the workstation, its warmth invigorating him, while he scanned the spider's progress on a monitor.

Unlike the stateless, thin client desktops relegated to students, the faculty computer had more spark under its chassis; the university's IT department had upgraded it with a host of software tools, including BitTorrent protocols, Tor onion-style routed communications, and anonymous search engines. In a quest to track down ANCRI, his spider condensed the vastness of the Internet, skipped the traditional web-trash, thinned the Internet herd and streamlined queries to focus on viable government and scientific-community content. After an hour, the results narrowed from more than 30,000 to under 30.

Thirty was manageable.

He flipped ANCRI's business card through his fingers and studied the top results.

Nothing looked too auspicious. The top results were a slew of intriguing articles related to the 1978 published work of a British researcher named Ancri: the diagnostic possibilities of the radio-pharmaceuticals thallium-citrate and technetium-pertechnetate in cerebral lesions. Spanish, French and German citations of those articles followed. The university motto "publish or perish" had given the British Ancri a ton of mileage from his original work. Parker was half-tempted to skim the German version, having had three years of the language as an undergraduate, but continued down the list.

ANCRI seemed invisible.

Google Earth failed to confirm a physical address west of Princeton. The satellite image of the address on the card showed an undeveloped property near a couple of farms, a wooded preserve, and Zydus and Bristol-Myers Squibb pharmaceutical facilities.

Parker rubbed his brow and clicked the next results.

It took a moment before his eyes transfixed to the monitor.

A chill fell over him and he squirmed in his wooden chair.

It was a simple web-page with sparse text. It was about him.

He read every word twice.

ANCRI TO RETAIN THE SERVICES OF FORMER PRINCETON PROFESSOR THOMAS PARKER. PARKER HOLDS A PH.D. IN NEUROBIOLOGY FROM YALE'S BIOLOGICAL AND BIOMEDICAL SCIENCES PROGRAMS. PRIOR TO JOINING PRINCETON, PARKER COMPLETED A NEUROLOGY RESIDENCY AND FELLOWSHIP PROGRAMS AT THE UNIVERSITY OF COLORADO'S SCHOOL OF MEDICINE. HE IS BOARD-CERTIFIED IN COLORADO AND NEW JERSEY.

The word **ANCRI** was highlighted in bold blue text to indicate a web link.

He clicked on it.

A new web page appeared.

ADVANCED NEUROLOGICAL AND CYBERNETIC RE-SEARCH INSTITUTE.

Alone on the screen, black text lingered on a white background. No additional references. The web address in the browser contained a numeric URL. No host IP address domain, no domain name server.

A green button appeared on screen, looking like a doorbell.

Parker looked around to make sure no one was watching him.

He clicked it and a new dialog box appeared.

DR. PARKER, LIVES ARE AT STAKE. HELP HER OR OTHERS WILL DIE. BE CAREFUL WHOM YOU TRUST.

Parker ran his mouse across the screen, hoping to find another link. Nothing. He clicked the BACK tab on the browser.

The web page vanished, as if it had never existed.

He spent another hour retracing his steps and running more queries.

No new results appeared for ANCRI.

Dejected, he glanced at the Casio on his wrist and realized several hours had passed, leaving him with little time to get home and shower before his dinner date.

The Ivy Inn, Princeton, New Jersey, 5:20 p.m.

BECKY WARD SAT ALONE in a red vinyl corner booth of the neighborhood pub. In front of her, two bottles of Sam Adams stood on coasters, getting warm. She selected a red dress for the occasion, with a low v-cut front and a black shawl for her shoulders. A touch of blush accented her cheeks, and red was the color of choice for newly painted fingernails. She hadn't gotten this prettied up in years, preferring her usual attire of jeans and lab coats.

Her indifferent eyes scanned the crowd decked out in football jerseys: Eagles, Giants, and a lone Jets fan. Most of the jersey-wearing tribe of men seemed engrossed in the Monday Night Football pregame activities leading up to the Giants-Cowboys game.

Becky felt a bit overdressed.

She watched a rowdy crowd form a line at the dartboard at the far end of the pub, and another raucous crew gather around a pool table. Grab-and-go off-license beer coolers ran a steady business.

Her fingers worked away on her cell phone.

I KNOW HE'S LATE. IT'S NOT MY FAULT. HE'LL BE HERE. AND OUR AGREEMENT SAID NOTHING ABOUT HURTING HIM!

Frustrated, Becky silenced her phone and stared at the Sam Adams closest to her.

"Thomas Parker will pay his tab," she whispered, "*cause he's my damn fireworks.*"

Firestone Library, Princeton University, Princeton, New Jersey

CAROLINE WANG'S SECURITY ESCORT, Mr. Gross, returned to the university library an hour before closing time. He waited outside the staff entrance and slipped inside after a custodian brought out the trash. He returned to the third floor, where he had found her earlier.

Something troubled him. Something about her story did not add up.

She was his responsibility. He'd lost track of her after the engineering quad.

Not a good thing for an escort.

The C-floor of the library was dead quiet.

Study tables were vacant. Gross made his way to section PS3550. The adjustable shelving had moved from earlier in the day. The exact aisle she used had been rolled closed, in order to make room for another row.

Gross racked over the row to free up the original aisle.

When he'd tracked down Caroline Wang earlier, he literally mowed her over, their encounter a surprise to both of them. He grinned, recalling her distress and seeing her land on her pompous, self-righteous ass. She'd handed him journals when she got up. SpringerProtocols. But she never actually said the documents were important.

His gaze panned the long row. The catalog numbers and bound references looked too similar to a science novice. Nothing distinguished one journal from the next. He yanked a random journal holder off a shelf and flipped through them. He tried to recall the exact titles of the periodicals he'd seen earlier. To him, everything looked the same.

It would take hours to search the aisle.

He didn't have hours. The library would close soon.

Gross looked around. He spotted one periodical holder appearing ever so slightly out of place, slightly askew. On the top shelf. Catalog set PS3610.

Gross pulled down the cardboard box. His eyes widened.

"Jackpot!"

Wedged between periodicals were a smartphone and a vial that looked like it contained blood. They were wrapped up in a page torn from a journal. He saw handwriting on the paper. A message.

Gross tossed the unneeded journals to the floor and turned to leave.

The blow to his Adam's apple was lightning fast. Vicious.

He heard the cartilage in his throat crumple before he felt the pain. His eyes teared up. Gagging and choking, Gross dropped the secret stash and brought his hands up for defense.

Blurry vision made it hard to identify his assailant. He sensed a man, shorter than he, with dark hair.

His large physique gave him an advantage.

Instincts took over. *Re-establish control of the situation, then kill your opponent.*

Gross landed a crushing kick to his attacker's midsection, then pounded his face with a jab, which provided a momentary respite. But before Gross could recover, a barrage of books hit him, hardbacks coming from his right and left, then left and right—everything spine-forward made contact. His attacker used the edges of hardbound books as weapons and seemed to have the entire library at his disposal.

Gross's throat filled with blood and he hacked out a frantic breath.

He took another strike to his trachea and gasped again.

A blow to his temple and another to his cheek followed. Spinning toward the shelves, he used them as leverage and protection. His attacker was relentless. Gross knew he had to change the conditions of engagement. His hands reached for anything he could grab and he flung journals and boxes at his attacker. Papers flew everywhere. The carpeted floor grew slippery, littered with slick-surfaced periodicals. He hunched over, taking the onslaught of strikes on the back of his head, his sides below his ribs, and his kidneys.

His head grew cloudy. Gross knew he had to act fast.

He pretended to drop to his knee, and drew his opponent closer. Drawing the deepest breath he could muster, he lunged, fists and forearms blazing. His attacker was shorter in stature and he locked onto his target, as his Delta Force training had taught him. Using his legs, Gross drove both of them into the oversized book aisle. Their bodies crashed into shelving, sending books everywhere. Gross managed several blows to the head and body before his stamina drained, the result of lack of oxygen; his lungs, unable to carry a breath, deflated like a balloon. As his airway swelled, his breathing labored. Blood trickled from his nose and mouth.

He took another blow from a book across the side of his head, a temple shot.

Gross crumpled to the floor, his vision blurred even more.

A vague, dark-haired silhouette loomed him.

His attacker rolled Gross onto his back and straddled him.

The hardbound edge of an encyclopedia-sized book pressed crosswise against his throat. Unable to breathe, Gross flailed his muscular arms at his attacker. The pressure increased, methodically crushing the remaining cartilage of his larynx.

Gross knew he was being suffocated.

Darkness overtook him.

8
IN THE WAKE OF CHAOS

Georgetown, Washington, DC

THE RESIDENCE BUZZED WITH FBI crime scene technicians. Kate stood watch at the townhome's open front door as Wright coordinated activities. A laptop lay on the coffee table, tagged with an evidence sticker.

She shook her head, thinking of the texts to Wright. *Ignore the girls. Find the computer.*

It was hard to ignore a dead coed in a bathtub.

Samuel Ford's love shack was certainly "where it's at."

A man with a goatee walked briskly toward the condo. Kate recognized him as the District of Columbia's chief medical examiner. Another man trailed him carrying plastic tackle boxes.

She greeted them and gestured upstairs.

Her radio crackled. "Reporters!"

"All right, people, you know the drill," Wright barked into his radio. He stepped outside to take stock of the situation. "Keep that news crew fifty yards back!"

Calls of "freedom of the press" echoed as the media surrendered their positions to a phalanx of jacketed FBI agents. One tenacious ABC news reporter thrust a microphone at the agents blocking her access. Behind her, a backpedaling cameraman recorded the scene—teaser clips for the evening news.

"Heaven frowns on us today," proclaimed a short, fireplug of a man wearing a navy-colored suit. FBI Deputy Director Stan Baker studied the residence. "This is a downright mess."

Wright leaned to Kate and whispered, "Better wait at the car."

"You sure?"

Wright grimaced. "Yeah. This could get ugly."

She chuckled and left Wright under the intense scrutiny of the shorter man.

WRIGHT TOOK A BREATH, knowing an ass-chewing was imminent.

"Agent," Baker growled, his pin-sized eyes fixated on Wright's, "your incompetence is turning this investigation into a public relations nightmare. What part of 'low key' did you not comprehend?"

"My apologies, sir," Wright said, as humbly as he could.

Baker sneered. "The director selected you for this investigation, without my endorsement. But I assure you, ineptitude will not be tolerated. Any idiot can spawn media mayhem. I have half a mind to reassign you to some shithole desk in Alaska."

"Noted, sir," Wright said behind a deadpanned expression.

The deputy director was known as a micromanaging bureaucrat who considered J. Edgar Hoover a role model. The man had slimed his way into the position after his well-respected predecessor was run down by a drunk driver. As a former DC prosecutor, Baker had built a career out of injecting himself into the investigative process and bullying his way around until he got *his* desired results.

Wright despised working under ladder climbing hacks like Stan Baker.

He jabbed a thumb at the condo. "The investigation took an unexpected turn when we found a dead woman. It was prudent to have the coroner collect the body."

Baker rolled his eyes. "You should have done it at oh-two-hundred, when the media is less prepared to mobilize."

"With all due respect, a ripening corpse was making it hard to work."

Baker shook his head. "Any indication Samuel Ford was behind her death?"

Wright shrugged. "No way to know. The deceased's name is Melissa Von Abrams. A George Washington law student. Possibly the Senator's girlfriend, but we have nothing solid to confirm that. Shot twice and dumped in a tub. We won't know more until the coroner weighs in. Right now, it's dangerous to speculate."

"Wright," Baker said with a scowl, "if you botch this further, not even the director can keep you on as SAC." – referring to Wright's Special Agent-in-Charge position on the investigation detail – "Am I clear?"

Wright searched for a pity reply but mustered a nod instead.

Baker cursed and stormed into the condo.

"Sir," Wright called, trying not to sound too mocking, "you have any further guidance?"

Baker turned to him, irate. "The director updates the president at oh-eight hundred tomorrow and is scheduled to meet congressional members at ten hundred."

Wright let his gaze drift to the mouthy news reporter in the distance. She patrolled the boundary of yellow "crime scene do not cross" tape like a hungry tigress.

He knew what was coming, and wanted nothing more than to squash Baker like a cockroach.

"I could care less if you sleep. You will have a list of suspects and a brief that details motives by oh-six-hundred."

Wright started to speak, then let his mouth fall open. It was going to be a long night.

FBI Headquarters, Hoover Building, Washington, DC

FOUR HOURS LATER, WRIGHT wrestled with two decisions. The first would get him fired. The second could get someone he cared about killed.

It had turned out to be one hell of a day.

On the tenth floor of the J. Edgar Hoover building, Wright stared through a conference room's smart glass windows and into an operations area of the Strategic Information and Operations Center (SIOC), where his investigative detail had assembled. The operations area blazed with monitors displaying photos, maps, credit card statements, and personal documents. Agents and technicians filled rows of computer terminals that faced a long wall of a flat screen monitors. Just like on the first day of school, paperboard titles sat above each workstation. Live news streams from CBS, FOX, CNN, and CNBC ran common lead stories: Oklahoma Senator Samuel Ford. Red digital clocks displayed time zones. East coast time read 1800 hours.

Wright had recruited half of the case agents, and Deputy Director Stan Baker populated the others. The team consisted of an Assistant Special Agent-in-Charge, field agents, tactical intelligence analysts, forensics experts, a profile specialist, a criminologist, a representative from the US Capitol Police, an agent from the Department of Homeland Security, and a logistics coordinator. And then there was Special Agent Katherine Morgan—his freelancer. Additional agents had been dispatched back to the U.S. Capitol to comb through the senator's political life. From the Oklahoma City field office, a senior resident agent chased down leads in the senator's home state.

Trust no one, he thought.

Wright rapped the windows with his knuckles and motioned to the only person he could trust.

Kate entered the briefing room, frustration painted on her face. He closed the door and energized the smart glass windows between the rooms. The polarized glass frosted over. They were alone.

"Updates?" he asked.

She clicked on a digital flat screen on a wall and drew on it with a blue dry erase marker, linking digital photos and case notes together. The case number, CLASSIFIED/079-WFO728S ran along the bottom of the screen. The collage of photos included crime scene shots of the love shack: blood-stained walls, a graphic view of a 24-year-old blonde dead in a bathtub, driver's licenses of two female coeds, phone and credit card statements. But one photo stood out from the rest: a shot of a thin notebook computer on a coffee table.

"We located her roommate in London," Kate said pointing to one of the girls' driver's licenses. "She's been there since the start of the semester on an internship with a law firm."

"That narrows the list of suspects."

Kate nodded. "We know a partial chain of events. Perpetrators disabled the home's alarm five days ago at 1930 hours and entered the residence undetected. Melissa Von Abrams sustained two GSWs," she said of the gunshot wounds. "The bullets passed through her torso and lodged in the walls. Both slugs were recovered, and ballistics is evaluating them for rifling."

Wright's face hardened.

Kate read from printouts. "Powder residue indicates Abrams was shot point blank—once in the abdomen and then in the chest. Based on the quantity of blood lost after the first shot, several minutes passed before the fatal shot was delivered."

He sighed. "So what does that tell us? The killer or killers wanted the poor girl to suffer? Torture her then kill her? It sounds too much like coercion."

Kate took the marker and drew on the frosted smart windows, linking scenarios, suspects and victims, and timelines. She drew two empty and unconnected logic boxes away from the others. "The crime scene detail says the place was clean. No prints. No fibers." She took a long breath. "This is speculation on my part. But let's say Senator Ford was at the condo having an interlude with his paid-for-girlfriend and he didn't kill her. Maybe someone broke into the residence to grab him. Maybe Ford was into something real deep.

They only needed the senator. His girlfriend was nothing more than excess baggage. A decomposing body ripens. The killers didn't care if she was found, just that she was found later rather than sooner. Ditch her in the tub, close the door, and walk out with the senator."

Wright considered the possibilities. A clean crime scene meant pros. Not street punks or gang bangers or rent-a-thugs. These were contract assassins. And that kind of skill did not come cheap. Someone had spared no expense.

If Kate's speculation was correct and Ford was a victim and not the killer, the senator had to have value. Nab him. Ditch the girlfriend. But why? What did the Chair of the Senate Subcommittee on Science, Technology, and Space possess? Was he a threat? Did he have information? Contacts? Congressional legislation impacting a sector of technology? Federal appropriations?

There were two typical approaches to solving a homicide: focus on the killers and victims, the evidence left behind, and the MO, the modus operandi, which was the bureau's typical brute force method; or focus on those who made it happen—the financiers—people who gained from the crime. Neither tactic gave him overflowing confidence.

Their priority was to find the senator: a missing person, a person at risk, or a murderer.

He was cynical about finding the perpetrators, but the task force would still plow down that road—a tall order to track down careful professionals. He knew they needed to concentrate on who hired the killers.

Find the money men then solve the crime.

And that meant putting his freelancer in harm's way.

Wright studied Kate's flowchart, then pointed to her empty boxes on the frosted glass.

"Those represent what you're not telling us," she said.

"I didn't think I was that easy to read." The color drained from his face. Using the cuff of his shirt sleeve, he erased her empty block-and-line sketches.

"Jack, you're withholding information."

She tugged at his shirt sleeve, now stained with blue marker. "Those texts you received weren't the first ones. Were they?"

He shrugged indifferently.

"Who's your informant?"

"Can't say."

"You can't or you won't. *Don't trust anyone?*"

Wright took a breath. "Maybe the investigation is compromised, I don't know."

Kate shook her head. "If that's true, how high does this go?"

"Higher than us. Maybe to the director? The White House? Just about anyone in D.C. Pick your player."

"You said the director selected you to lead the investigation. Is he involved?"

"Kate, this is Washington. You're not appointed director of the F-B-I without knowing where political bodies are buried." He paused to collect his thoughts. "Everything is plausible."

He wrote the word TECHNOLOGY on the frosted glass and boxed it out.

She twitched her nose. "Samuel Ford's congressional platform regulates technology. Something with a huge payday, making murder and kidnapping a small investment?"

From the floor, Wright retrieved a laptop case, set it on the table, and unzipped it.

The device was plastered with FBI evidence decals from the bureau's Operational Technology Division (OTD).

"Do we know what's on it?" she asked.

"I need you to take it to Princeton."

"Excuse me?" she snapped.

"Relax," Wright said. "OTD is working off a clone. Ford's laptop carries multi-layer, asymmetrical, lattice-based encryption architecture with interlaced schemes in the chipsets, the BIOS, and the operating system. Its protective fortification is bulletproof. We're good, but this is a whole other level of encryption. If the bureau wants to know what's on it, our best chance is to tap an outside resource."

She frowned. "Jack, there is no authorized chain of custody transfer here. You're asking me to take key evidence to someone outside the bureau? The moment I leave this building with the computer, it's no longer admissible in court."

He nodded in semi-agreement. "That may not matter, if we don't find the senator. Ford chairs a subcommittee with jurisdiction over numerous sectors: science, technology, space, and you can probably throw in medicine and pharmaceuticals. Worldwide, the industries under his political influence generate trillions of dollars in revenues. Ford might be a murderer. He might have been kidnapped. He might already be dead. We don't even know that this is his laptop, but based on its encryption levels, it holds information we need."

"I don't like the sound of your conjecture."

"I'm not prognosticating anything," he said. "For the sake of argument, let's say Ford is alive. He won't stay that way for long. He could have been snatched to protect billions of dollars in game changing tech. Maybe this is just the tip of the iceberg."

"You're laying a lot on me." Kate zipped up the computer case. "This morning, I asked you why you picked me for the detail."

His face hardened.

"Newsflash, Jack. My specialty is forensics. I work with dead people. You have other forensics agents on this detail. Clearly I am not needed." She waited for a response. Getting none, she continued, "Why in the hell did the great Jack Wright choose me?"

"I needed someone I could *trust*."

"*Trust no one*." She jabbed a finger into his chest. "You need a delivery boy who will break the rules—void an evidence chain of custody—and that's not me."

Wright put his hands up. "I know I'm not in a position to ask."

"Then don't."

He gave her a pained look.

"No." She de-energized the frosted windows, making them visible to the team inside the TOC. She backed away from the laptop case.

"Kate, you have every right not to trust me. No doubt, I am an unfaithful SOB. Guilty as charged. But this is bigger than the two of us. Sure, I know the texter's identity. I've known all along. He's no random informant. *Ignore the girls. Find the computer. Don't trust anyone.* Every word is true. He is one of the good guys. And I *trust* him with my life, like I *trust* you. You may not want to hear it, but I need you to take that computer to Princeton."

She shook her head.

"Boots is expecting you," Wright said with a cocky smile.

"Boots?"

"It's a pet name. He hates it." His expression turned serious. "Kate, I picked you for your versatility. Not with forensics, but with medicine. Boots has an assignment. Hypersensitive. Top secret. Even I don't know what it is. You cannot discuss this assignment with anyone. Not a soul. No one in the bureau. Not even me. Your directions are in the computer bag." Wright turned to leave. "You're expected in Princeton. Noon, tomorrow."

"Jack, what the hell are you into here?"

"Not sure." He paused. "Kate, be careful. This may become one of those cases where everyone is expendable. Everyone."

He opened the door and left the room.

Kate glanced at the laptop bag.

What the hell was in Princeton?

TUESDAY, OCTOBER 6th

*Every forward step we take we leave some
phantom of ourselves behind.*
John Lancaster Spalding

9
UNEXPECTED AFFAIRS

Over the Southern Pacific Ocean,
East of Christchurch, New Zealand

TWENTY HOURS AHEAD OF U.S. eastern standard time.

In the dreaded middle seat of a five-seat row, Cassondra Meir was exhausted, having just completed a 24-hour shift at McMurdo General Hospital before boarding the flight off the frozen rock called Antarctica. She clutched her red extreme cold weather parka in her lap and fought a swelling nausea. Sweat beaded her brow and dripped into bloodshot eyes. A bitter, metallic taste lined her mouth. Her stomach churned, feeling as if it might explode. As the metallic taste worsened, she let her eyes close.

Five hours into the uneventful flight, packed with a horde of exhausted passengers, the cramped and noisy converted cargo hold of a C-17 Globemaster III vibrated with a constant mechanical thrum. It seemed impractical that people could sleep on the military-style cargo jet, but somehow, most of the returning scientists, civilian contractors, and various Air Force personnel found a way. The flight from Pegasus Field at McMurdo to Christchurch ran just under six hours.

Only an hour of flight time remained.

Meir told herself to hold on. She could make it. With her feet on solid ground, the airsickness would be behind her.

Meir's polar research stint for the National Science Foundation had turned out to be an ordeal, not exactly what she'd anticipated when signing up for the two-year commitment. Anxious to flee the South Pole's version of Dodge City, she'd taken the first job available. Anything to escape the stale living conditions of McMurdo.

Her bout of nausea worsened. She could not last until Christchurch. Through gritted teeth, she clutched her parka for dear life. Crackles of light pierced her vision like an electrical storm rippling through her brain. A rusty smell joined the bitter metallic taste and preceded a thrust of bile from her gut. Meir tried to hold back, but it was futile.

Vomit sprayed everywhere, covering her and the men in the seats beside her.

Angry voices barked at her.

Her body succumbed to intense spasms, muscles twitching and contracting in a *grand mal* seizure. Her eyes rolled back as her body flailed and wrenched. The crackling lights in her vision faded, and everything turned black.

Princeton, New Jersey

5:00 A.M. BECKY WARD yearned to stay. She smiled and watched Thomas Parker beside her, his chest rising and falling in slumber. For two years she'd wondered what it would be like to wake beside him.

Now she knew.

But she could not allow herself the luxury of staying.

Overnight everything had changed. On so many fronts, their worlds had changed.

And she needed to leave before he awoke, and disappear. Forever.

Shifting her body to the edge of the bed, she was careful not to let the mattress recoil and announce her stirring. Her bare figure, illuminated by a streetlight beyond windows curtains, slid out from beneath the covers.

She mouthed "goodbye" to him before searching for a discarded red dress. She retrieved her previous night's garments from where they had fallen, and headed downstairs naked and barefoot to reassemble herself.

Becky left his house as quickly as high heels allowed. The air was brisk and her low-cut dress, thin shawl, and impractical heels were inadequate for a morning walk. She passed through shadows blanketing the quiet neighborhoods of Princeton. Overnight rain had left the trees damp and leaves rustled in a cool breeze.

Her apartment was ten minutes on foot, if she cut through the Princeton cemetery. The gates did not open until dawn, but she'd scaled the five-foot wrought iron before. The effort wasn't very lady-like in a dress, but she managed. Heading east-to-west, she passed memorials of dating as far back as the late 1700s, from small head-stones to flat sarcophaguses to attention-drawing obelisks. Grover Cleveland, the 22nd and 24th President of the United States, lay somewhere among them.

She'd been afraid of the dark, once. Army training regime under the Central Security Service (CSS), a tactical group integrated into the National Security Agency (NSA), had drilled that out of her. Now she had more dangerous things to worry about—such as being caught and court marshaled as a traitor. Her objective: get to her apartment, pack the bare essentials, and flee the country and cash in the monster paycheck that awaited her in an off-shore account.

Wet, spongy grass slowed her pace. She wished her Army field training had included ground navigation in challenging feminine footwear.

At the west side of the cemetery, Becky hopped the fence again and cut through backyards to pick up Witherspoon Lane, which led to Clay Street.

Ahead, an unfamiliar SUV caught her attention. Two masculine silhouettes sat inside. And the vehicle had a solid view of her apartment.

People were waiting for her.

Not good at all.

Becky slid out of her heels and stepped into the shadows, retreating around the apartment building next to hers. Once out of sight, she walked barefoot to the back of her unit, which was invisible from the street. Quietly, she slid her keys into the lock and opened the door. Once inside, she tossed her keys on the kitchen counter and secured the deadbolt behind her. She avoided turning on lights.

Cautiously, she drew back a corner of the front window curtains.

"Enjoy your evening?" a man asked, breaking the silence.

Becky spun around with a jolt and scanned the darkness of her apartment.

She'd walked into a trap.

Her mind raced through options. She could cause a distraction, get to the door, and run for it. That felt weak. And she had little within reach to use as a weapon—a candlestick off the coffee table or a table lamp. Neither was adequate.

The owner of the voice switched on the light from the adjoining bedroom and stood in its doorway. She had no trouble recognizing the intruder: Gene Thornton, the red haired man who attacked Parker outside his lab.

His emotionless eyes locked onto her and he held her CSS service weapon, a Sig Sauer P224 9mm, in a way that made her believe he knew how to use it.

"What are you doing here?" Becky glanced around.

He appeared to be the only intruder.

She kept the coffee table between them and lingered near the front door. She did the math in her head. Two seconds to the door. A half second to open it.

Not fast enough to beat a bullet.

Thornton shook his head. "Ms. Ward, where's the lab equipment?"

Her eyes narrowed. "I upheld our bargain and provided you an opportunity."

"No. You double crossed us."

A smile formed at the corner of her lips. "You should've kept the skullcap when you mugged Dr. Parker. By the way, nothing was said about harming him."

"We need the entire lab, not a single component."

"That's not my fault."

A tense silence lingered in the air for a moment.

Becky took a solemn breath. "It appears Philip Derman scooped up all the treasure. If you have a beef with missing research, take it up with him, not me."

He motioned for her to sit. She shook her head.

"So, what kind of girl carries a nine-millimeter?" He waved her pistol around the room. "It's light. Well balanced. A bit small for my hand, but fits a woman's grip."

"It's for protection," she said without hesitation. It was a rehearsed response. "My father gave it to me when I left for college."

Thornton laughed. "I'd buy that if you'd gone to college in Newark, Trenton, or Philly. Princeton isn't really a high crime district."

He was toying with her. "What do you want?"

He dropped the magazine out of her semi-automatic and pulled back the slide to ensure the gun was not chambered. He laid the pistol and its magazine on the coffee table.

"Does Thomas Parker know you sold him out?"

"No." She gestured to the window. "Those men… outside. They with you?"

His eyes twinkled.

A chill shot down her spine, and she wondered how much Thornton really knew. Derman paid her ten million over his bid. Certainly, the man dared not kill her before he got answers.

He'd torture her to get what he needed then kill her.

Becky yearned to see Thomas again, if for no other reason than to say she was sorry.

There was little time to waste, and Becky turned her attention to the threat.

On the other side of the table, the intruder hovered at an equal distance from the gun. If she was quick, real quick, she had a fifty-

fifty chance. If she killed Thornton, the two blunt instruments in the SUV outside would prove no problem at all.

Recalling her field training, Becky visualized the movements she'd need to make.

Then she sprang into action.

Dropping to one knee, she snatched the pistol and the magazine and slapped them together. As she raised the weapon, a red laser light settled on her chest, followed by a familiar pop. Two needle-sharp stainless steel barbs from a Taser buried themselves in her chest above the v-neckline of her dress.

Pain exploded in every nerve of her body.

Becky's vision blurred as her body shuddered. 50,000 volts surged through thin wires into her flesh. Her brain recognized the tick, tick, tick of the weapon. Paralysis and muscle spasms competed for equal attention. Time shattered into fragments as she crumpled to the floor.

Thornton loomed above her, his face glowing.

She struggled to focus on him.

He taunted her with the Sig Sauer before striking down with the butt of the weapon.

SUNLIGHT SPLASHED ACROSS PARKER'S face, trickling in through the bedroom curtains. He woke to a quiet house, which was the norm, except this morning he'd thought things might be different. He rolled over and saw the indentation on the adjacent pillow.

He blinked the sleep out of his eyes and frowned.

From a chair, he grabbed a faded "Princeton, It's Lonely At The Top" T-shirt and a pair of battered sweats. He slid them on and padded barefoot across hardwood floors. He skipped his morning bathroom routine and checked out the other rooms of the house as he made his way downstairs. His hundred-year-old Victorian, a five-minute walk from campus, was cluttered with things not considered home furnishings. Bedrooms were crammed with shelves of three-ring binders, computer workstations, and test benches topped with soldering irons and littered with integrated circuit parts. Wiring schematics and flowcharts filled any blank wall space. Only the master bedroom and bath, dining and kitchen, living room, and a foyer were furnished like an ordinary house. Everything else resembled a geeky hermit's cave.

The aroma of fresh coffee brewing filled the air as he approached the kitchen. He half expected to find his companion in the small dining room, but it and the kitchen were empty.

He rubbed his morning stubble and hoped the interlude was not a mistake in judgment—while rarely an enforced policy, everyone in academia knew the rules—professors did not sleep with students. He chuckled. Technically Becky was a research assistant, he was no longer faculty, and he'd entirely missed the professional conduct memo, along with the one about publish or perish or you'll lose your damn job.

The smell of coffee made him hungry.

He glanced at the coffee maker on the tiled counter. A Post-It note was stuck to the appliance's digital clock. He peeled it off, revealing the time: 9:05 a.m.

Parker had slept longer than usual. He hadn't had that kind of night in a long, long time.

He read the handwritten message.

THOMAS, THANK YOU FOR EVERYTHING. I'M SORRY ABOUT THE LAB. PLEASE, BELIEVE ME. IF YOU ONLY KNEW WHAT THE FUTURE HOLDS, AFTER A HURRICANE COMES A RAINBOW. MORE THAN A FRIEND. ALWAYS. LOVE, BECKY.

10
PREPARATIONS

Advanced Neurological and Cybernetic Research Institute (ANCRI), New Jersey

WEST OF PRINCETON, NEAR the town of Pennington, Gene Thornton drove to an indistinct checkpoint off the main road. No corporate signage was visible. Nothing identified the property. Next to a guard shack, a military-style DoS K12 crash barrier rested flush in an asphalt drive. STOP was painted on the pavement in bold white letters. If required, a panic button inside the guard shack could send the protective barrier blasting upward with enough energy to spike a 68-ton tank. On either side of the gate, V-barbed deterrent fencing with electronic sensors enclosed the property. Beyond the gate, a grassy knoll parted a forest of foliage.

A pistol-armed guard greeted his Mercury sedan.

Thornton lowered his car window, made eye contact with the security guard, and showed his credentials. The guard checked his photo ID against a record on a tablet.

"Thumbprint," the man said, holding up the device to be touched.

Thornton pressed his thumb against an illuminated biometrics square. It blinked green.

The guard scrutinized the interior of the vehicle before waving it through.

This was his fifth visit in a span of two months. Four too many for his liking. And he frowned on house calls. Client visitations added complications, personally and professionally.

ANCRI, however, was no ordinary client. And this was no ordinary visit.

As he drove up the isolated drive, the knoll gave way to a small meadow.

The billion-dollar state-of-the-art facility stood on acres of wooded hills and scattered meadows, between municipal roads on two boundaries and Stony Brook on its western edge. By design, the complex was obscured from the property's perimeter. Crescent-shaped ponds encircled a parking lot and fronted a large, main building. The clinical neurophysiology annex rose three-stories tall. The structure incorporated a series of protective measures, the least of which was a Faraday cage, an embedded copper mesh that prevented electronic eavesdropping.

A research annex and a dormitory, as nondescript as the main building, formed an enclosed courtyard. Only the central plant was a detached structure, serving as the mechanical heart of the operations, providing compressed liquids, chilled and heated water, and water and waste treatment functions through a series of underground service tunnels.

Thornton parked in the lone handicapped parking spot. The rest of the lot was empty. ANCRI did not have visitors, nor did its employees commute to the office. ANCRI was a 24/7 secured complex, locked down to protect its intellectual property.

He strolled across a wooden bridge that spanned the ponds and linked the parking lot to the clinical neurophysiology annex.

Thornton saw beyond the architectural design of the ponds, recognizing them for what they were, defense barriers—the proverbial moats to protect the castle from invasion. Intricate force protection measures. The clinical neurophysiology annex was the soul of the institute, and the guard station protected the only way into and out of the campus.

ANCRI had secrets to protect.

And these secrets offered a prosperous future for everyone involved.

Hisses and honks surrounded Thornton as he waded through a gaggle of Canada Geese refusing to clear the footbridge. He stomped his foot and the congestion of waterfowl relented, and let him pass.

A second guard met him at a sally port into the clinical neurophysiology annex, a hardened barrier separating the outside world from the secrets within.

Thornton badged in and waited for his security code to clear.

A placard above the door read: AUTHORIZED PERSONNEL ONLY. NO CELL PHONES OR CAMERAS ARE PERMITTED.

As board appointed external oversight, he was exempt from such petty mandates.

The bulletproof automated doors parted with an electronic whoosh, and Thornton stepped through in search of the man who ran the place.

STEWART RICHARDS PUFFED ON a Monte Cristo cigar and took in the grandeur of his sanctuary. The neurophysiology lab inside ANCRI's clinical neurophysiology annex was his cathedral, his apostolic palace. He, however, was no Michelangelo. Nor a chief architect, or a master craftsman, or even an artist extraordinaire.

The talented hands of others had built these hallowed grounds.

Richards was merely the administrator, which didn't bother him.

While he carried the accolades of a world-renowned neuroscientist, he could never rise to Michelangelo's extraordinary genius. He possessed different talents: resourcefulness and transformation, the ability to bring other people's visions and abstract concepts to life.

For ANCRI, imminent Phase 2 trials meant securing new virtuous and technical staff, and, of course, a new crop of research participants.

As ANCRI's director, everyone reported to him, Caroline Wang being the rare board appointed exception. Every meticulous staff interview had been conducted in person—except one, a neural physiologist named Cassondra Meir. She had been inaccessible, wrapping up a two-year stint at the McMurdo Antarctic research center. A former U.S. Army major, Meir specialized in clinical evaluation of isolated, high-stress human performance situations. Her research was so relevant that NASA adopted her preparatory evaluations to screen applicants for future manned missions to Mars. Her work focused on the psychological effects of stressful deployments for embedded staff. A Skype interview accommodated her unique circumstances. A contact at McMurdo confirmed that she boarded a flight out and was headed back to the States.

That left Thomas Parker to round out the right mix of brilliant minds.

He studied the cavernous room and a billboard-sized, high-resolution LED screen that broadcast neon lightning across a vast darkness. The spectacle's designers called it the Wall of Knowledge, borrowing the label from displays in military command centers. To the casual observer, the enormous screen was similar to those in Times Square or in Tokyo.

But it was more than that.

The lab's auditorium-like surroundings resembled ground control at Cape Canaveral. Control stations overlooked neat, conforming rows of empty pods. The pods were cocoon-shaped encasements resembling high-tech cockpits in sophisticated fighter jets, empty and awaiting pilots to fly them into battle.

Thirty pods spanned the room. Twenty-nine sat empty.

One was occupied.

Smoke from his cigar drifted upward. The fragmented light radiating out of the Wall of Knowledge sculpted ghost-like silhouettes out of the hazy air. On his way down to the main floor, Richards passed rows of unmanned control stations and ran fingertips across dormant consoles.

His gaze fell on ANCRI's only activated pod, wreathed in brightness.

Richards finished his cigar, flicked its smoldering butt to the floor, and took in the near magical-like essence of the pod.

A black fibrous, amorphous astronaut-style suit encompassed the human figure lying supine in the pod. Tiny bio-lines penetrated the fabric of the suit, creating a thick, web-like tapestry that connected the suit to conduits on each side of the pod. Spike-like contact nodes, mounted on the non-metallic helmet enveloping the participant's head, connected a nest of brilliantly lit fiber optic leads to an array of receptacles.

In the containment vessel, the man was barely recognizable.

The Wall of Knowledge towering above men and machine flickered through biometric data as massive supercomputers located elsewhere searched for recognizable and repeatable neurological patterns, unique pieces to an enigmatic jigsaw puzzle. High-resolution goggles, similar to those used in virtual reality applications but with eyeball lubricant systems, covered the participant's stitched-open eyes. Input feeds channeled audio into his ears.

"Senator Ford," Richards said, "a penny for your thoughts?"

As skilled a researcher as he was, the streams of data lay beyond his comprehension.

Richards felt like an infant discovering an alien new language, unable to unveil its true meaning. So far, no one had been able to decipher the cryptic neurological message or reduce the biometrics into simpler, more digestible terms.

ANCRI's rudimentary approach involved hyper-stimulating sensory impulses and recording those cerebral reactions through pattern recognition algorithms. But the technique failed to provide viable results. The empirical shortfall was in decoding the qualitative neurological data and assimilating it into discrete outcomes.

And that was where the skills of Thomas Parker fit into the program.

—┼—

SAMUEL FORD FELT AS if fire consumed him from within. A chronic, scorching sensation broiled inside his head and sent a torrent of heat radiating down his spine, into his extremities.

He was a lobster inside a boiling pot.

Pain resonated along every nerve in his body as his life decayed into an unending, incarnate nightmare.

Time was continuous, without beginning or end.

With no physical reference, Ford was unable to locate where he was or what was being done to him. He vaguely recalled being harnessed into a contraption of some sort. His comprehension of his current state eroded into disjointed thoughts and formed a living purgatory.

He knew only that he was held against his will, with no hope for escape.

Broken reflections passed through a battered consciousness. He tried to recall the world he knew, people he knew. He tried to hold onto coherent thoughts, but they eluded him. The constant throbbing inside his head made it difficult to concentrate. He was a helpless passenger in a burning automobile as it tumbled over the side of an endless cliff.

He tried to scream, but could not utter a sound. Not even a croak or moan.

The endless pain.

Samuel Ford wanted to die and end his insufferable hell.

11
THE MEASURE OF DECEPTION

**Princeton University Engineering Quad,
Princeton, New Jersey**

THOMAS PARKER NORMALLY WALKED to campus, which was as fast as driving and trolling for a parking spot. This morning he ran, starting in a sprint and deteriorating into a winded jog. He bolted out of the house unshaven and hair a mess, as if he'd just rolled out of the gutter. The pot of coffee left for him remained untapped, and he took just enough time to change from sweats to khakis and loafers. He still wore his worn, snarky Princeton T-shirt.

In the engineering quad, he pushed past students and bustled up the stairs. When he got to the fourth floor lab, his side ached from the exertion. Hunched over, with his hands on his knees, he caught his breath. Staring down between his legs, he spotted bands of dust-laden footsteps and black smudges on the sheen of vinyl floors. The remnants of foot traffic and dolly marks swept from his lab toward the service elevator down the hall.

"What the hell?"

Wrestling his keys into the lab's door lock, he was careful to avoid being clobbered by the same door two days in a row. Slowly, he reeled it open.

What he saw felt like a sucker-punch to the gut. Staggering into his lab, Parker slumped to his knees. Stunned, his gaze absorbed the empty space.

Only debris remained.

The observation windows had been torn down and tossed into a trash pile to facilitate hasty removal of equipment. Everything was gone: the chair, the headgear and its superstructures, supercomputers and server racks, cabling, and nitrogen tanks.

Two years of his life vanished, overnight.

His attention returned to the center of the room.

An empty Crown Royal bottle and his I♥NY coffee cup lay on the floor, mocking him. Only the day earlier, he'd daydreamed of not leaving Princeton Professor Vladimir Valentine even a damn paperclip.

Poetic justice.

Whoever stole his lab equipment wanted to make it personal.

Who?

The red-haired man with a scar on his chin? He had scoped out the lab. Obvious now. Besides university maintenance staff, only two people possessed keys.

Becky was the key master.

Anger surged. His feelings for her were one-sided. More than a research assistant, she had been his closest friend, a confidante— and, in the end, a back-stabbing lover.

She had played him like a chump.

Why?

He retrieved her note from his pocket and reread it. She must have scammed him from the day they met. Their dinner and night of passion a ruse, a way to get him out of the way long enough to allow an army of thugs to pillage his life's work.

Becky had sold him out.

Even so, she needed help. There was one other candidate—Dr. Phillip Derman.

Somehow, the two of them were linked. It seemed inconceivable.

And how was ANCRI involved?

He recalled the website message: *Dr. Parker, lives are at stake. Help her or others will die. Be careful whom you trust.*

Nothing added up.

The her is Becky? Why help her now?

Parker struggled to his feet and took one last look at his barren space.

He needed answers. First from Phillip Derman, then from Becky Ward.

PARKER STORMED INTO THE dean's office and demanded an accounting.

"You need to leave, Dr. Parker," said the gray-haired executive assistant, rising from behind her desk.

"Where's Phillip Derman?" Parker hated being stonewalled. "Did he authorize the removal of my research equipment?"

"I understand you're upset," she said. "But I will not repeat myself."

"Where is the dean?"

"Away. Away at a conference."

Matching wits with the twenty-year gatekeeper gained him nothing.

She snatched up the phone. "Dr. Parker, leave on your own accord or I call campus police. It's your choice but make it now."

FIVE MINUTES LATER, ON the E-Quad Dock, Parker located the assistant coordinator of the engineering quad's shipping and receiving.

"Hey, Jake, I need a favor."

Jake Fisher frowned as he approached. "Sorry, Dr. Parker, the answer's no, per the dean's office."

"Whoever gutted my lab used the freight elevators. Look, I need answers. That's all. Come on, they took everything. What do you say?"

Fisher shuffled awkwardly.

He led him to a darker edge of the dock. "I won't tell anyone you're a hell of a guy."

"I can't help you." Fisher swallowed hard and tried to push past.

Parker snatched his arm. "Nothing comes and goes without you guys knowing about it. You hear things. See things. I need to know who loaded up my research. It happened between six p.m. and six a.m. It's a lot of heavy equipment: supercomputers, server racks, specialized gear."

Fisher scratched his forehead. "You did not hear this from me."

"Absolutely."

"People are all jacked up. Yesterday, the dock supervisor tells us to knock off early. With pay, mind ya. Out early? Man, that's a righteous deal. Then I overheard the super talking to Dr. Derman."

"Now we're getting somewhere."

"Derman was in a foul mood, throwing his weight around and all. Said a logistics crew was authorized to demob your equipment. They required a cleared dock to facilitate loading. So, this morning I show up for work. No dock superintendent. It was a snatch and grab, man. The dean's office orders us to talk with no one, without approval from their office and the university legal counsel. So what gives?"

"Has Derman been around today?"

Parker reflected on his predicament. As a faculty member in the Princeton Neuroscience Institute (PNI), he had no prior association with the School of Engineering. PNI didn't have the available space or funding to support his work. The Associate Dean of Development for the School of Engineering and Applied Science, Phillip Derman appeared like a savior, offering a lab space and funding support.

Derman had orchestrated everything from the start. And in the end, took it all away.

"Not since last night."

Parker pointed to a CCTV camera mounted above the dock. "Is that just for show?"

Fisher flinched. "No. It's real. But it won't do you any good."

Parker took a breath. "Why?"

"Someone disabled the security head-end unit in the electrical room. Alarm loops were jumpered out. We found the sabotage this morning. Nothing got recorded."

He cursed.

Fisher licked the side of his lips. "Hey, doc, I know it's none of my business, but how much is your gear worth? Come on, ya got a ballpark figure?"

Parker frowned. "I haven't thought about a street value. The research might be worth twenty million to the right buyer. Maybe more. Damn, I got stung by a pretty bad fire cracker."

Fisher's eyebrows shot up. "Wow. Lucky bastards."

"No, lucky bitch." Parker sighed. Maybe Becky was angry about losing her graduate position and wanted cash to fund her own spin off. A fully functional interactive neural scanning system, an up-and-running enterprise solution, could command fifty to a hundred times the bare equipment value alone to the right buyer.

"Bummer you got screwed."

Parker rolled his eyes. "Where I can find your boss?"

Fisher tore a shipping and receiving form in half and scribbled down an address.

"Thanks," Parker said, patting him on the shoulder, and then heading out to track down the Engineering Quad's dock supervisor or Phillip Derman. It didn't matter which warm body he found first, as long as he got his equipment back.

12
CLEARING OF THE DECKS

Advanced Neurological and Cybernetic Research Institute (ANCRI), New Jersey

GENE THORNTON WALKED UNESCORTED through the AN-CRI's clinical neurophysiology annex, its well-lit main corridor void of staff. At the neurophysiology lab, cleanroom-style, hands-free doors isolated the corridor from an anteroom and the sterile environment beyond. Industry-recognized warnings announced its entrance.

```
AUTHORIZED PERSONNEL ONLY
    BEYOND THIS POINT
  BIOHAZARD RADIATION
```

He waved his security badge at a proximity card reader. Doors slid open with a whoosh, parting in the middle. Stepping forward, the doors closed behind him. After air pressure equalized, another set of doors opened and presented the inner sanctum.

While his original amazement had waned, he still found the technology impressive. He took in the vastness of workstations and rows of empty pods—enormous egg-shaped, space-age-like capsules with open tops.

The air held a faint odor, odd for sterile conditions, and he detected traces of cigar smoke.

A streaming spectrum rained down from the Wall of Knowledge as colored rays crackled with energy and penetrated hazy air. It was like standing in the proverbial glass bottle and witnessing lightning being captured and drawn inside.

Caroline Wang intercepted him. "You're late."

He found himself studying her and noticed that she wore a mask of exhaustion. ANCRI had two independent board appointments. He was external. She was internal. He recalled her age being somewhere around forty, although it appeared she had aged ten years in a span of three. Her youthful appearance had vanished under hours of intense research. Wrinkles creased her face around tired brown eyes and thin lips.

"Program update," he asked, his words coming out like an order.

"Ask the director," Caroline said matter-of-factly as she retreated to the periphery of the pods to await further instructions.

He headed down to the main floor. Under the brilliance of the panoramic billboard-sized screen, he saw a tall, gray-haired observer standing beside an occupied pod.

Stewart Richards.

Thornton had the fleeting impression of a medical-like-Moses standing before the Burning Bush, waiting to converse with God. To him, though, Richards' lab-coated features resembled more of an enigmatic Vincent Price than a vintage Charlton Heston. While Richards was a recognized pioneer in neuroscience, he wondered if the same man, who had grown more eccentric by the day, would see the program to the end. It would be unfortunate if ANCRI's director required premature termination.

Thornton's gaze found the occupied pod.

He had never been this close to an actual participant—they'd had two to date.

The first was a female volunteer whose results turned out to be a complete disaster and an event that required disposal.

The unexpected second—well, the man appeared not to be faring any better than his predecessor. The only visible feature was a pale lower jaw. Gadgetry engulfed the occupant. He wore a bulky spacesuit with cables and tubes streaking out of it. Bundles of multicolored fiber optic wires connected to a helmet covering his skull.

Thornton broke the silence. "Dr. Richards, the board is displeased with the program's broadening risk exposure."

Richards shrugged. "They think I am reckless?"

"The board is… concerned. Risk must be mitigated."

"The board hasn't risked anything."

"They disagree."

Richards typed at a terminal attached to the pod. A low-pitched shock reverberated throughout the lab as it faded to darkness. The enormous screen fell dark, except for a continuous stream of data values scrolling horizontally across it, moving right to left. The endless series of characters were a combination of neon green binary strings separated by a space and yellow hexadecimal values. "Risk is inherent to our endeavors. It cannot be eliminated or micromanaged out of existence. The board must embrace those truths."

Thornton threw him a stern look. "Results matter more than ideological truths."

Richards nodded. "I concede there have been diversions. However, Phase One laid groundwork that cannot be discarded. The risk is trivial." He gestured to the lab. "The prototype materials that you delivered allowed us to reverse engineer more effective data mining techniques and overcome technical boundaries. We stand at the doorstep to discovery. If it's results the board seeks, it must commit to Phase Two without reservation."

"Samuel Ford was never part of the plan. His presence adds considerable risk."

Richards laughed. "Mr. Thornton, you brought him here."

"At your insistence."

Richards threw up his hands. "What was I to do with him? Lock him in a closet until you got around to interrogating him? No. I put him to use."

"Hindsight tells me I should've ditched him in the Potomac."

"Ah, but here, he's served a grander purpose." Richards pointed to the information on the vast screen. "Two trillion bits of neurological data, give or take several hundred billion. It's a modeled sequence of cellular-level energy transfers—the elusive human consciousness—thoughts, memories, and emotions. Phase One yielded breathtaking strides in chronicling the mind's micro-energy impulses. But Phase Two delivers the real treasure."

Thornton focused on the empty pods. Years earlier, before the implementation of the White House-sponsored Brain Initiative, the BigNeuron, and the Human Connectome Projects, a national security initiative had authorized the creation of ANCRI. Its premise, labeled the Frontier, targeted mapping the intricate structures of the human brain and identifying biological intelligence processes. The initiative's goal was to replicate neurological architectures and establish an adaptable algorithmic process for interactive neurological interfaces.

ANCRI's goal was neurological singularity—interactive mind mapping.

The government's end game—at least the military's version—was mind control.

The Phoenix Consortium, the board as it were, hired him as an unbiased external representative to keep ANCRI's primary mission and mind control on track. Caroline Wang was the board's inside medical liaison.

Thornton peered up at the Wall of Knowledge.

There was no turning back. Not for ANCRI. Not for its board.

Expanded human trials were the logical step. Phase Two. An enormous risk.

Thornton motioned for institute's mad scientist to continue.

Richards typed commands on the terminal at the pod. Seconds later, the big board exploded into a myriad of colored graphs, data-filled charts, and 3D neuro-maps. The modeled human brain on display sparkled with activity.

From the corner of his eye, Thornton caught movement.

The body in the pod convulsed uncontrollably.

"Our guest is experiencing hyper-sensory stimulation. The Helter-Skelter electro-physical sensations saturate not only his visual cortex, but other sensory nerves as well. The brain has no pain receptors. The organ itself does not feel pain. Pain is merely a perception, an unpleasant activation of sensory nerve cells. Our shotgun method doesn't discriminate between which nerves are activated and which are ignored. Eventually, if he survives the Phase One gauntlet, he'll be driven mad."

"Your point is?"

"Without Phase Two, ANCRI's at an impasse."

Thornton ground his teeth. The writhing man continued to spasm. It was senseless torture, akin to electronic waterboarding and reminiscent of shock therapy, except with no value gained.

Richards appeared to be enjoying his chance to play a vengeful god, inflicting callous punishment as he desired.

"Enough," Thornton ordered.

He waited for a reply. Receiving none, Thornton retrieved a Sig Sauer semi-automatic pistol and leveled its steel black nose at Richards.

"I acquired the gun this morning, and I wondered if I'd have a chance to use it. Dr. Wang, come and stand beside Dr. Richards."

Caroline's face flushed as she took a wide arc around the pod and her hands shot up as if she faced a bank robber.

"Turn it off."

Richards mocked him with a grin. "You're not high enough up the corporate ladder to make executive decisions without the board's approval."

Thornton shrugged and called the bluff. "They'll consider it risk reduction."

From his lab coat, Richards withdrew another Monte Cristo. He snipped its end off and lit it. Puffing on the cigar, he grew a cherry that glowed like a small torch. Smoke crept across the cavernous room, curling up in the flickering light from the massive screen. He shot a hard glare at Caroline and she lowered her arms.

Thornton held the gun firm. "I won't ask again."

Richards shook his head and typed again on the console.

The broad screen reduced its magic content to reveal only physiological statistics: pulse rate and oximetry, blood pressure, respiratory rate, and body temperature.

A motor hummed to life and the pod crawled upward like a bizarre humanoid astronaut rising out of an enormous eggshell. The patient platform settled at a 60-degree vertical angle to the floor, with a host of trailing sensors and tethers adjusting accordingly.

Richards motioned for Caroline to remove the goggles from the participant's face.

Strapped in the contraption, Samuel Ford's eye sockets looked hollow. His bloodshot eyes dilated to a burnt slate color. Disoriented, he remained motionless, staring at nothing but blank space.

Despite himself, Thornton felt awe. He saw not a man but a lab experiment, a sacrificial host connected to a rat's nest of technology—a monstrous thing to do to another human being.

He felt rigid, unable to tear his gaze away from man and machine.

"Senator Ford," Richards announced, rapping his knuckles against the pod, "this is Gene Thornton. He too was a public servant, much like you, and spent years in servitude to the U.S. Navy, before becoming a consultant to our government. It's him you have to thank for your week's vacation with us."

Thornton growled. "What the hell are you doing?"

"Making introductions."

His finger tightened on the pistol's trigger. "I don't do introductions."

The man's bloodshot eyes sputtered to life. His weak gaze found Thornton.

Samuel Ford tried to speak, but couldn't utter a sound past twitching lips.

Richards puffed on his cigar. "By my own admission, the senator's visit has been an excellent extension to Phase One trials. But he's clearly not a viable candidate for Phase Two."

Thornton felt manipulated, led someplace he desired not to go.

Richard's cleared his throat. "It's time to deliver on your obligations."

Ford gasped. His feeble pulse rate ticked up on the readouts.

"Mr. Thornton, if I recall correctly, you made the rank of Lieutenant Commander. Well, sailor, it's time to clear the deck and make this station available. But please, resist the temptation to damage the accessories."

Ford's body shuddered as he found the strength to mouth the words, "Kill me."

Thornton felt nothing but disdain for Richards. But the need was clear. Reluctantly, he slid back the slide of the pistol and chambered a round.

Ford mouthed, "Thank you."

Thornton squeezed the trigger.

The shot resonated through the open room. Stepping back, Caroline let out a scream and took refuge behind an unoccupied pod. Her hands bolted up in the air again. Even though he was confident his first shot was fatal, Thornton fired a second for confirmation. Two dime-sized holes sliced into the bio-suit's fabric, inches apart over the heart. Ford barely twitched as his stitched-open eyes fell vacant.

A nearby monitor chimed to life and relayed the obvious.

Richards clicked off the equipment and the lab fell quiet.

Caroline brought her hands to her mouth.

Richards' cigar smoke lingered in the air like a smothering blanket as they stood under a halo of illumination from above.

The purgatory of a tortured man had ended.

Thornton was no novice at killing. It had been part of his craft for nearly 30 years—first in the Naval intelligence and then as a gun for hire. Each time was different. Sometimes killing required a complex sequence of actions. Sometimes it was simple, like pulling a trigger and walking away.

It gave him neither satisfaction nor remorse.

Killing was a cold man's game. Rarely did he reflect on his victims. But the sight of a tormented Samuel Ford would linger in his psyche for some time. In all his years, he had never put someone out of their misery.

"Pull this stunt again," he said, "and you'll be able to smoke your cigar directly through a bullet hole I put in your chest." He tossed Caroline his car keys. "There's a woman in the trunk. Subtract her from my quota."

Thornton turned to Richards.

"My team will deliver Phase Two participants in two days. And let me be clear. No more increases in the program's risk profile. No more selective anomalies, regardless of their scientific potential, or you, Dr. Richards, will be dispatched as quickly as Samuel Ford."

13
BEING AT CHURCH ON TIME

**University Chapel, Princeton University,
Princeton, New Jersey**

KATE MORGAN CHECKED HER watch. Just before noon.

The fall colors were well underway across the university as a broad host of oak, maple and elm trees displayed their seasonal tapestry of orange, gold and brown. Fallen leaves sprinkled cobbled sidewalks as she approached the Gothic-style, sandstone-colored structure. She entered the chapel through inset doors, set below a towering inlay of stained glass. An arched, wood-paneled ceiling of a narthex greeted her. Architecturally speaking, the chapel felt like Hogwarts' Great hall, with its tall sculpted stone arches, stained glass, wooden pews, hand-crafted pipe organ, and colorful banners.

Voices lurked ahead of her and she stopped in the nave of the sanctuary, which was open to the public. A few tourists loitered and conversed in hushed tones. The historic setting called for reverence. The last time Kate had set foot in a church had been years ago, for a mass funeral after a disaster claimed the lives of railyard workers and coal miners in West Virginia.

She spotted a man alone in a pew, his head bowed, hands in his lap as if in prayer.

No one bothered him. He appeared to be her contact.

Kate unclasped the holster on her hip for access to her service weapon, just in case. Before drawing closer, she focused on her composure. During her training at Quantico, instructors marked her down for gun-shy moments. Nerves got the best of her. Early on, one thing became evident: field work would never be her forte.

In the dim light of the chapel, she could make out the man's features as Asian. Chinese. Sixty, probably older. A full head of thick black hair thinned to patches of gray by his ears. He appeared fit, but not muscular. Business-style dark suit. Black dress shoes. He sported a bruise across a cheek.

She took a breath. "You Boots?"

The man cocked open an eye and motioned for her to sit beside him. "Take out your cell phone and remove its battery."

She recognized no distinguishable accent and he sounded like a native speaker.

Kate scanned the chapel before taking a seat in the pew.

No one paid them any attention.

Dismantling her device, she separating its parts in her lap then let her hand drift to her weapon.

"Closer," he said, "like you want to whisper in my ear."

She reflected on Wright's words to be *extremely careful.* Thinking it prudent, she withdrew her Glock and pressed it into his side. "This is close enough."

"Don't insult me. Your entrance was amateurish and predictable." He let out a disapproving sigh, but continued not to look up. "Agent Morgan, please reconsider."

She lowered her gaze and noticed that somehow he managed to be aiming a similar semi-automatic at her midsection. He hadn't possessed a weapon earlier. She'd seen his hands in his lap. The man was magician-smooth, and probably lethal.

Kate's pulse quickened. *When alone, never yield control of a situation, especially to an informant.* Great advice, after the fact. "What now, Boots?"

"Kiss me. On the cheek."

"Excuse me?"

"People won't bother us if we're affectionate. And besides, you really think you can get a shot off before I do? If that's the case, you won't be walking out of here, Special Agent Katherine Morgan."

She took a deliberate breath and pressed the barrel of her gun into his ribs. There would be no more slight-of-hand diversions, and she was not getting suckered into giving up equal leverage.

"Under no circumstances are we getting intimate."

"That's unfortunate." He faced her. "The bureau's statistics indicate 75% of shooting incidents between agents and suspects occur within nine feet of each other. I'd say our rather close quarters is essentially point blank." He shook his head. "I know a great deal about you, Kate. Even your Quantico qualification score. You shot the bare minimum with a handgun: forty-eight out of sixty. You had to take the course twice. One more failure and you might have been drummed out. Your instructor cited nerves, anxiety, as the reason for a mediocre performance. Well, even with your meager sharpshooting skills, you could put me down from here. That is, if I don't shoot first."

Neither of them budged, their eyes locked onto one another.

Her pulse thrummed inside her chest as she noticed her breathing pick up and her nostrils flare. She could smell traces of spearmint on his breath.

She studied his eyes: mahogany in color, intelligent, confident. *Eyes are the windows to the soul.* The way he spoke and held his gun told her that she faced an experienced killer. There was no advantage in manipulating the status quo.

Kate forced herself to hold her poise, and waited for her contact to make the next move.

Their impasse continued, the man content to play along, until his eyes darted away to watch an elderly pair of tourists walk from the chancel crossing, down the center aisle, and out of the church. Two tourists still loitered, inspecting the stained glass above the chancel area.

He kissed her gently on the cheek.

The abruptness of his gesture caused her to twitch, and she inhaled a stuttered breath. Instinctively she released her finger from the pistol's trigger and placed it on the trigger guard, grateful for not twitching and blowing a hole through the stranger's rib cage.

God probably reserved extra damnation for those who gunned people down in churches.

He cracked a flat smile and calmly laid his gun in his lap.

She felt his hands gently press down on her Glock, lowering it. She didn't resist, deciding to play along. As the tenseness in her shoulders eased, her breathing slowed.

"So, Boots," Kate asked, wanting to get to the point, "you text Jack Wright?"

"I hate that nickname."

"There's a story behind it, I think?"

He stroked her shoulder length hair and pulled it back behind her ears.

Kate felt a guarded uneasiness stir. She had never much been into role play, and felt uncomfortable having a dangerous stranger so close, intimately close.

The emerging warmth of his gaze seemed to take in every detail of her face. Sensing she was blushing, she forced herself to return the gesture. Age lines formed at the corners of his eyes. Faint freckles dotted the bridge of his nose. Creases etched his forehead. The bruise on the crown of his cheek seemed fresh, as if it had hurt. She wondered how he'd been punched.

She decided to regain some personal space and drive the conversation. "You know what happened to Samuel Ford?"

"Not exactly." The glow in his eyes faded. "What did Jack tell you about me?"

Her eyes narrowed. "Stay on topic, Boots. He said you needed me."

"True," he said with a shrug. "Randal Wang, Colonel, U.S. Army. I work for U.S. Strategic Command at the Pentagon. Currently I am assigned as a liaison to the Deputy Director of CYBERCOM," he said, the United States Cyber Command component to the NSA.

"You're out of uniform, Colonel," she observed.

He nodded.

"At the Defense Department, who do you report to?"

"Several directorates, but I mostly support cyber security, cryptology, and a Pentagon think tank that covers advanced initiatives."

"Advanced initiatives?" Kate arched an eyebrow. Cryptology. Well, that made sense. "What can you tell me about the disappearance of Oklahoma Senator Samuel Ford?"

"We scheduled a meeting for last Monday. He missed it."

"What do you think happened to him?"

"I believe you know what happened. You just don't know why it happened, or who is responsible for his abduction."

"Is he dead?" She watched him closely.

Wang shrugged.

"Okay, tell me who is responsible."

He handed her a page torn from a medical journal. The SpringerProtocols, with handwriting in black ink.

Singularity close. Princeton. ANCRI. Killed by father. Senator is next. Thomas Parker new hire.

"You're saying the senator is going to be killed?"

"That's the way it sounds."

He passed her a photograph of an emaciated body on a gurney. AMY RICHARDS RIP was etched into the woman's bare skin. Her macabre, gaunt features were unnatural. She was bald with no eyebrows. Graphical markings were imprinted across her scalp. A row of sutures ran along the medial line of her skull. Cheeks were drawn, almost hollow.

"What happened to her?"

"That's what you need to find out."

She scrutinized his expression. "How, exactly?"

"By infiltrating a research facility."

"That's the job you have for me?" she snapped, disdain filling in her voice. "I don't know what Jack Wright told you about me, but undercover work is not what I do for the FBI. I am a forensics agent assigned to the District of Columbia."

His face softened. "The technology that Ford got exposed to was not by accident. Two months ago, I put him in that situation. My DoD position has sensitive limitations. Restrictions. On the other hand, a ranking member of the Senate Subcommittee on Communications, Technology and the Internet comes with a platform. My intent, our intent, was to find out what kind of research this covert lab was conducting."

Kate absorbed the news. "Singularity?"

"My daughter passed on this information, at great personal risk."

"Is your daughter a mole or an informant?"

"Does it matter? If they find out she leaked intel, Caroline's dead." He released a sigh. "Ask anyone inside the Beltway, and the Advanced Neurological and Cybernetic Research Institute does not exist." He kissed her hand as the students strolled by talking about architecture styles of the 1920s. "Even with my resources, ANCRI is at best a ghost site. But that's where the FBI will find who is responsible for kidnapping Samuel Ford."

Covert operations were far from Kate's specialty. At Quantico, she'd attended a lecture by Helen Duramy, a professor of international law at Stanford, on "Effective Models for Interagency Cooperation." During the presentation, one of cadets pressed Duramy about the erosion of liberty pertaining to interagency engagements that sanctioned the use of torture and the divestiture of traceable operational assets. Before an argument side-tracked her lecture, Duramy covered the legal distinctions among dark sites, black sites, and ghost sites. Dark sites emerged from the need to have a covert or crisis management ready-to-go process in place to release interactive, web-based information at a moment's notice. Governments and multinational companies built dark sites. Their use could be innocuous, mission-sensitive, or sinister. On the other hand, a black site was the military term for a secret location, which fell under the sanctioning of the parent agency and was financed by federal appropriations or paid for under an operation's accounting code or fiscal line item in a department's budget. Safe houses were such assets. Black sites had come under fire for human rights violations and concern about legal protection for enemy combatants. Once ghost detainees were imprisoned at offshore black sites, CIA operatives used any means necessary, including physical torture and behavioral distress, to extract information.

Ghost sites, however, could either be technological or physical—an abandoned website no longer maintained, or one acting in a secretive manner as a pirate operation for the distribution or retention of data, or most notably, an illicit, covert research facility systematically disassociated from its federal entities. A ghost site was similar to a black site, with subtle variations—the most common being a third-party, self-managed facility or established operation funded by the government in the form of a grant or appropriated research. The legal separation between a ghost site and its clandestine program and the funding institution circumvented deeper fiscal scrutiny. That allowed a chain of command to disavow any alleged, questionable, inappropriate activities and invoke plausible deniability, should said activities ever become public.

ANCRI, it seemed, was a ghost site.

Going undercover there would cut her off from the bureau.

Kate understood her options. She could refuse and return to D.C. to confront Jack Wright for putting her in a compromising situation. That was probably not the brightest of ideas. Neither was agreeing to go undercover and getting involved in events she knew nothing about.

She frowned. "Colonel, I don't work for the NSA, so I'm not an asset for you to use."

Wang drew closer. "ANCRI is working on a technology called the Frontier. Ford asked questions that made people in high places very nervous. It appears powerful people removed a member of congress to protect secrets."

Kate pondered this. "If Ford was eliminated because he learned too much, and, by correlation, some sinister society of twisted geniuses want to keep their brainchild technology hidden from prying eyes, then proprietary control and money is the basis for their actions," she said. "If ANCRI is a ghost site, then a federal agency is financing this so-called Frontier. A Department of Treasury accountant or even a bureau one could search for comparable fiscal appropriations and match expenditures to suspected agencies. If that's all it takes, then there is absolutely no need for me to go undercover."

"Except for one important detail."

She crossed her arms. "What's that?"

"By the time a Washington bean counter finds the paper trail, much less pinpoints incriminating transactions to an establishment of a ghost program, Samuel Ford will be dead."

Her eyes drifted away in thought. "Who do you think funds ANCRI?"

"I'm working on that," he said, his expression flat, like that of an experienced gambler.

"Care to fill me in?"

"It's best if I don't."

His reply made her doubt his method for tracking down fiscal transfers. Leave it to the NSA to linger in the gray areas of the law.

Kate redirected the conversation back to the basics. "You knew about the senator's on-call coeds. You said *ignore the girls. Find the computer.*"

He nodded.

"What's on his computer, Colonel Wang?"

"I'll show you," he said, as if it were an invitation.

"It's encrypted."

A broad grin stretched across his face. "I'd be disappointed if it wasn't."

Kate rubbed her temples. "Those texts you sent Jack were not the first ones, were they?"

"Agent Morgan, you're within your rights to be skeptical. You told Jack that he '*should have chosen someone else.*' His response to you was '*I need your expertise.*' Those were my directions to him. *I need your expertise.*"

She strained to reflect on earlier conversations with Wright, who seemed complicit in orchestrating her involvement.

Wang took her hands in his. "Jack trusts you. That means I trust you."

"*Don't trust anyone,*" she retorted.

"Three people know you are here—you, Jack, and me. If anyone else knew, inside or outside the bureau, it'd be a matter of time before we're eliminated from the conversation."

Kate rolled her eyes. "Colonel, you work for the NSA and the Department of Defense. If anyone has the connections to bust this conspiracy wide open, it's you."

"There is a degree of separation in play regarding government-sponsored programs and federal support for ANCRI. In this instance, murder appears to be an inconsequential expense." He exhaled. "Don't believe the propaganda. First, the NSA tracks and collects secrets. We monitor and share intel with other agencies and intelligence communities, unless you happen to be a malcontent named Snowden. Second, there are structural elements inside the U.S. government that are not necessarily *for the people.* Singularity will usher in the new generation of intelligence gathering. It will transform the geopolitical landscape. Foster environments where super-intelligence capabilities rule. The NSA wants in on that action, as will all intelligence agencies, foreign and domestic. It's a simple conflict of interest. Those who control this brave new Frontier will rule the world."

"Oh, please," she said, "the Frontier will bring about a New World Order?"

"Don't be dismissive. Regimes will fall. Remember, 'History doesn't repeat itself, but it often rhymes.' History reminds us that most coups produce autocrats. There will be victims and new threats to democracy. For those in power, secrets will cease, become im-material, because the Frontier will know all secrets."

"You know, I am no poli-sci major, neuroscientist, or techno whiz. Some days my smart phone is smarter than its user." She took a breath. "So what good am I to you?"

"You are board-certified in forensics. You are trained to investigate, question, and analyze. And while you're not stellar with a handgun, you think on your feet." He handed her another photograph of a dark-haired woman. "Cassondra Meir. Neurophysiologist. M.D. Upon her return from the South Pole, Dr. Meir fell violently ill and was prohibited from clearing customs. She resides in quarantine, ninety-day isolation. The New Zealand authorities suspect Meir was weaponizing bio-agents with the intention to sell her work to international terrorists. When and if she recovers, Cassondra Meir won't be going anywhere for a long time."

"What does this Cassondra somebody have to do with me?"

He grinned. "Luckily, she's your spitting image. Similar features. Brunette. Late thirties. Even your fingerprints match."

She cringed. "I have no siblings, so how's there a coincidence?"

"While you're not twins, you'll take Meir's place at ANCRI."

"Security checks and a simple print comparison with IAFIS will rat me out," she said of the bureau's integrated automated fingerprint identification system, the largest biometric database in the world. "Every agent has their prints digitized when they join the bureau. I won't get past the front door."

Wang chuckled. "I work for the NSA. Altering a federal fingerprint database file is not that taxing."

"I bet you hardly broke a sweat doing it."

He passed her a large envelope. "Your new identity, Dr. Meir. There's a passport full of stamps. Cash. Credit cards."

"Let's say by some significant character flaw, I consider your scheme... then what?"

"We move on Thomas Parker. He was recently dismissed by the university. His termination was no accident. Our job is to win him over. Parker's our way into ANCRI."

"What if he says no?"

"Quid pro quo."

"You have leverage on him?"

"You can say that." Wang rose to his feet, her hands still in his. He kissed them as he watched a chaplain enter the sanctuary.

"You're not going to give me a choice, are you?"

"I never planned to, Kate." He gave her an inviting smile. "Let's take a walk."

They strolled outside, where the air warmed under a midday sun. A breeze bristled leaves in the tall trees surrounding the chapel. Students meandered about between classes.

Wang handed her a different cell phone.

She looked puzzled. "With all of this cloak and dagger stuff, I'm surprised you're going to permit me to make a call."

"Not a call."

"Says the mysterious texter." Kate studied the phone. "Texts don't leave voices for people to eavesdrop in on. I presume this device is disposable."

"Jack said you were smart. It's equipped with software developed by the NSA as a spinoff to its Co-Traveler program. The software pushes out deceptive caller IDs and truncates traceable transmission routes. A text, like a call, is a message that is transmitted to a local cellular tower as it's picked up and distributed by various providers until it reaches its final destination; but in our case the localization criteria for the multilateration of radio signals is manipulated. In short, we're in Princeton, but to prying eyes it'll look like the text originated from a device in Washington, D.C. The software resets the repeater signal flags after the signal travels through its last carrier's network router, only allowing the last cell tower to be traced."

Kate frowned. "Not only does the NSA have the ability track every electronic conversation in the world, it has technology to let a person communicate invisibly from any place on Earth?"

"The public has a jaded perception of what the NSA really does. Some of it is valid, of course. Much of its just media hype, normal paranoia. The NSA collects, processes, analyzes, and disseminates information. We prevent enemies of the State from gaining access to sensitive networks. But most of all, we're paid to think—develop new ways to outsmart foreign and domestic enemies, international terrorists and state-sponsored actors, global crime syndicates, and freelance hackers. Creating software that lets people go untraceable allows us to dissect those same software architectures and find ways to beat the bad guys before their breakthroughs hit the open market. Sure, the NSA snoops and collects secrets, but we protect secrets too. Our real mission is to keep this nation safe by doing what others cannot."

"George Orwell said a few things about *Big Brother is watching you*. It's now at the point a girl doesn't know who to trust." She rolled her eyes. "Since you're calling the shots you going to tell me what to say?"

"Be vague, cryptic. Make inferences. Jack will know who it's from."

She keyed in Wright's cell number and typed out a text.

AT THE STORE. GETTING HELP AT THE COUNTER, IT'S GOING TO TAKE LONGER TO FIND WHAT I NEED. DON'T WAIT UP. BE SAFE.

She revealed the message before sending it.

He nodded sheepishly. "You have National Security Agency potential."

"Oh, please." She tapped send and returned the phone.

Wang smashed it against the ground.

"Now yours."

Kate's eyes narrowed. "Mine?"

"Yes, yours."

Reluctantly, she relinquished her disassembled phone and watched him slam it against the sidewalk as hard as he could.

"I hope you enjoyed that." She retrieved the fragments of plastic and metal scattered across a landscape of fall colored leaves painting the sidewalk. With shards of phone in hand, she gestured to a nearby garbage can.

"Not here." He cocked his head.

In the distance, police cars lined the curb as a congregation of campus, local police, and sheriff's officers gathered outside the

University's Firestone Library. The collection of uniformed officers pointed to the upper floors of the building.

"What happened?" she asked, checking Wang for a reaction. The ripped out page from the SpringerProtocols, with handwriting—someone had found that page in a library. Coincidence? No. The bruise on his cheek told her it came at a cost.

Wang studied the cops. "We best keep moving."

Kate wanted to ask what kind of incident involved the local authorities, but held back, knowing the events at the library were somehow related to their case or Wang or both.

The Frontier will know all secrets.

That was damn frightening.

14
INDOCTRINATION

NSA Safe House, Princeton, New Jersey

KATE STUDIED THE NSA's safe house, a 1920s two-story Victorian a quarter-mile from the heart of Princeton. Elm trees spread a patchwork of colors above a bricked pathway that dissected a cozy backyard.

Randal Wang led her to an out-of-sight access pad near the back door, typed in a four-digit number, unlocked the door, and headed inside.

He glanced at the watch on his wrist. "I have a call to make. Go ahead and settle in. Your room is upstairs. Last one on the left. If you're hungry, help yourself to whatever's around."

She eyed him wearily. "If you're sexting Jack, tell the bastard I hate him for outsourcing me to the N-S-A."

Wang chuckled, then disappeared up a flight of stairs.

She listened to hundred-year-old floors creak as footsteps treaded across slatted wood above her, and heard a door close.

Still clutching the bureau's laptop bag, Kate wandered the house, taking in its thrift shop décor and sparsely decorated rooms. The back door led into the kitchen and dining room, allowing for easy entry without alerting the neighbors. Perfect for the NSA. She opened the kitchen cupboards and found a man's essentials: coffee,

PB&J, macaroni and cheese, and Top Ramen. She bet the freezer was full of microwave dinners and frozen pizzas.

In the dining room, she set the laptop bag on the table and scrutinized the materials Wang had given her in the church: the journal page with handwriting on it and the photograph of a dead naked woman on a gurney.

AMY RICHARDS RIP.

The photograph troubled her on many levels.

How did the woman die? What hellish plight had she suffered?

Her name had been scrawled into her chest. Odd. Was that before or after she died?

Difficult to tell from the picture.

And how was Amy Richards connected to Samuel Ford?

15
LOOSE ENDS

Federal Bureau of Investigation (FBI) Headquarters, Washington, DC

THE OFFICE OF FBI Deputy Director Stan Baker was posh in a way seldom seen any more. Like its twin, the director's office, Baker's eleventh floor office had been passed down from a long line of deputy directors. At one end of the room was a mahogany executive desk, with a matching credenza behind it; at the other, a conference table.

A career public servant, Baker prided himself on handling complicated relationships and situations, skills acquired from Dale Carnegie's classic *How to Win Friends and Influence People*. With a results-first mindset, he had the unique ability to convince, manipulate, and even coerce people into doing things his way.

But Jack Wright's meddling had undermined everything.

"Sonofabitch," he growled, reading a mirrored text off Wright's cloned cell phone.

AT THE STORE. GETTING HELP AT THE COUNTER, BUT IT'S GOING TO TAKE LONGER TO FIND WHAT I NEED. DON'T WAIT UP. BE SAFE.

"Did Agent Morgan send this?" Baker called out.

Gene Thornton stepped in from the secretary's station outside the office. "Don't see how. Her phone is cloned like Wright's. She's neither sent nor received texts in two days. Her last GPS ping registered as Mercer County, New Jersey."

Baker appraised his ginger-haired contractor. "Princeton?"

Thornton rubbed the scar in his chin. "The message's cellular transmission points to a DC-metro origination. We're tracking down caller ID now. Once we have that, we'll nail Wright's accomplice. But I don't see how it's Morgan."

Baker looked skeptical. "Did you acquire the research equipment?"

Thornton grimaced. "Unfortunately that proved a missed opportunity. But I have a lead, and men working on reacquiring what we lost."

Baker shook his head. "That Princeton professor give you any trouble?"

Thornton cracked a smile. "None."

His gaze turned serious. "Find out who Wright is communicating with. Don't be misled. Katherine Morgan being in Jersey is no coincidence. She's on an errand for him."

A year of moves and countermoves centered around one endeavor: securing a radical technology before rival agencies. Everything was on track until a senator from Oklahoma started asking the wrong questions. Baker suspected the CIA, DIA, or State Department—one of those were behind Ford's disappearance. Which entity actually had the guts to eliminate an elected official? It didn't matter. Samuel Ford had become a threat. His disappearance benefitted everyone at the table, including the Federal Bureau of Investigation.

Neurological singularity was worth acquiring, at nearly any cost.

Baker turned to his hired gun. "Where's Jack Wright?"

Thornton swiped his fingers across a tablet screen and brought up a high-definition satellite map: Washington D.C., daytime. Buildings and green lawns were visible. A red spot throbbed in the heart of the nation's capital. Tiny objects, seemingly tied together, depicted real-time traffic patterns moving in a web.

Thornton pointed to a red spot on the tablet. "Near the Capitol. He's on foot."

Baker squinted, getting his bearings on the map.

"Sir, if I may?" Thornton enlarged the image with his thumbs.

The streets of Washington emerged, revealing cars in traffic. The red spot crystalized into a red dot. Labels tagged locations. The U.S. Capitol dome was clear and visible.

Baker's brow creased in concentration. "Where's he headed?"

Thornton zoomed in on a slow-moving dot skirting the Capitol and migrating along Independence Ave as it approached the James Madison Building.

Baker recalled that a triad of buildings formed the national library. The most famous and oldest of the siblings, the Thomas Jefferson Building garnered most of the attention with its famed cathedral-like, domed ceiling arching high above a circular reading room. The John Adams Building opened years later, and the James Madison Building followed by another span of time. The facilities officially served the U.S. Congress, while functioning as well as living museums of American history and traditional libraries.

Madison was more utilitarian than the Jefferson Building and attracted few tourists. Named after the Father of the U.S. Constitution, Bill of Rights, and the Fourth President of the United States, the complex was a tribute to the man who inspired the nascent idea of a national library.

"Maybe he wants to check out a book?" Thornton said dryly.

Baker shook his head. "Intercept Wright. Take him somewhere quiet. Make his death look like an accident. Then head up to Princeton and kill Morgan in the line of duty. Make hers tragic, yet not too memorable. Leave no loose ends."

16
CHANGES IN COURSE

James Madison Memorial Building, Washington, DC

JACK WRIGHT ENTERED THE Madison Building from Independence Avenue, passing under the four-story bronze relief of "Falling Books." He flashed his FBI credentials at the officer manning the metal detector and studied the lobby. He counted four officers. No way to know how many more were in scattered throughout the complex. The metal detector pinged and a red indicator flashed, telling the officer that he carried something made of metal.

"Federal business," Wright said.

The officer examined his badge and waved him past.

Wright took the bronze core elevator up. After its doors opened, he entered the fourth floor's green quadrant and walked past the U.S. Copyright Office. Using an unmarked proximity card, he accessed the copyright hearing room and ducked into a narrow hall feeding a series of breakout rooms, eventually reaching a room marked LM 480J.

The small room looked as if it were setup for a meeting.

Wright slid his fingers beneath the conference table and located a tablet and a satellite phone, both held in place by Velcro.

He parked himself and powered up the tablet, which required a password.

MADISON1809! Easy to remember: the fourth President of the United States and the year of his election. It automatically linked to a secured Wi-Fi—not part of the public domain—that asked for another password: BELLEGROVE1751, the place and year of Madison's birth.

The thought of Madison and history stirred a memory. He recalled the director denying his legal attaché promotion. Returning to his workstation, he found a sealed envelope. A handwritten message inside read: JACK, THIS COULD GET DANGEROUS.

An inauspicious note from the bureau's top boss.

Within hours, a call from an old friend, U.S. Army Colonel Randy Wang, told him the FBI was not alone in its concern over Ford's disappearance.

Wang was old school, a veteran of the pre-9/11 "spy vs. spy", interagency rivalries, and global espionage.

Room LM 480J was a physical dead drop, where he was about to enter a virtual one.

During the Cold War, clandestine exchanges were required in a spy's tradecraft. Dead drop or mail drop places were locations where parties swapped information. The Computer Age made it more akin to a drop box on the Internet, except the worldwide web was plagued with systemic tracking algorithms and prying eyes.

On a website called ChatCrypt, Wright logged into a secure chat room named SINGULARITY! The on-line service used high-tech encryption schemes to fend off eavesdropping and cyber sniffing.

His device populated username and password fields automatically.

Three cascaded windowed screens appeared, layered like pages. The top window was the chatroom's dialog box; the middle, four framed black-and-white videos; the third, an embedded security add-on called MidnightEclipse, which protected against snooping programs and data mining schemes. If MidnightEclipse detected a communication breach, it deployed the "nuclear option" and vaporized the tablet, leaving no trace of user activities.

In the dialog window, Wright clicked on the phone image. The icon rattled to indicate that a call was being placed.

While he waited, Wright enlarged the black-and-white live-action video feeds. The frames showed four different aspects of the Madison Building: Independence Ave, the tunnels to Jefferson and Adams, and the first floor lobby. He was tapped into closed circuit surveillance.

The library's police office was on the ground floor. Someone there undoubtedly would be watching similar feeds. Since 9/11, high-definition cameras at high-value targets streamed video to a server farm run by the Department of Homeland Security. Fiscal limitations meant that some cameras were higher-quality than others, as were some video feeds. The Madison Building was not particularly a high-value target, and its surveillance coverage reflected that.

The chat window popped up, minimizing the surveillance feeds. IT'S ABOUT DAMN TIME!

Wright cracked his knuckles and typed. BEEN BUSY. GOT KATE'S NOTE.

FOR A MOMENT I THOUGHT SHE WAS GOING TO SHOOT ME.

Wright grinned. YOU DESERVED IT.

JACK, YOUR PHONE IS HACKED.

He shrugged. THANKS FOR THE CONCERN.

YOU GOT ABOUT 60 SEC. BAKER'S ASSOCIATES ARE COMING FOR YOU.

That news fueled broader suspicions.

Wright resized the chat window to examine the video. On screen, two men came in from Independence Avenue, looking as if they were on a mission. Not a hard one to figure out—take down Jack Wright.

Sixty seconds. He decided to let events unfold.

Wright spotted a few details in the video. Two stiffs wearing off-the-rack suits. Both had short haircuts. Fit, if not muscular. Feds? No. Probably just hired consultants.

The metal detectors flashed. The men briefly conversed with the security officers before splitting up to cover more ground.

Wright retrieved his cell and started the device's clock app. He set it to one minute and tapped the second hand into motion. Sixty seconds, counting down.

An image of an emaciated dead woman appeared on his tablet. Wright zoomed in on words written across her exposed chest: AMY RICHARDS RIP. She lay on a gurney in a room constructed of masonry brick. He noticed a decal on the wall. Operating instructions for an incinerator.

More photos appeared, not in any particular order: an iPhone, a vial of dark fluid, and a page from a journal with handwritten library catalog numbering and a note.

He typed. WHO'S THE DEAD GAL?

DAUGHTER OF A MAN RUNNING A RESEARCH LAB.

Wright already knew the answer to his next question, but asked anyway. WHAT'S IN THE BOTTLE?

BLOOD. FOR DNA TESTING?

Another photo revealed a handwritten note: SINGULARITY CLOSE. PRINCETON. ANCRI. KILLED BY FATHER. SENATOR IS NEXT. THOMAS PARKER NEW HIRE.

Wright glanced at his phone. Thirty seconds.

WHAT DOES THE SENATOR IS NEXT MEAN? IS HE DEAD?

NO INTEL.

Wright frowned. Princeton seemed like the place to be. Exactly where he'd sent Kate.

WHO'S YOUR SOURCE?

CAROLINE.

Wright exhaled. He had known Randy Wang since their days in Army Intelligence. Their friendship survived Wang's time at the Pentagon and the NSA. Wright had been a groomsman in his wedding and watched his little girl grow up. As a child prodigy, Caroline garnered dual degrees: an M.D. in neurology and a Ph.D. in neurogenetics.

What had Caroline gotten herself into?

And how did Ford fit with singularity?

He stole a glance at his phone. Five seconds.

CAROLINE WORKS FOR ANCRI? Wright typed.

The answer was slow. IT'S A GHOST SITE.

His phone dinged.

Clandestine operations? The government rarely permitted top secret programs to see the light of day without a fight.

DON'T TELL ME WHAT YOU TWO ARE DOING. BUT I NEED FORD'S LAPTOP RETURNED.

Wright closed the application and wanted to restow the tablet. But there was no time now. Since the library's surveillance system had recorded his presence, anyone with half a brain would circle back and find it.

He powered off the device and tucked it under his arm.

His phone's clock app read a concerning 0:00.

He was living on borrowed time.

17
TROUBLE

CARRYING HIS NEWLY ACQUIRED tablet, Wright dashed into the main fourth floor corridor and was greeted by the noise of footsteps emanating from the Green Core stairwell.

A red-haired man rocketed through the door and moved with an athlete's ease. He turned in the opposite direction and let his right hand hover at his side, ready to grab a sidearm.

Time had expired.

Wright was in the open, with nowhere to run. It was too late to retreat. Options were few, but he had one advantage: the man hadn't seen him yet.

He took a step forward and dropped to a knee. Lowering his head, he pretended to tie a shoelace. He leaned the tablet against the wall to free his hands.

The man locked onto him.

Wright's pulse pounded. He let the man approach and when he could see his adversary's shoes, he clenched his fist and swung it sideways, smashing the glass cover of the fire extinguisher nestled in the wall. He wrenched the extinguisher's door open and snatched the canister. Unsnapping the pin, he brought the hose up.

The man reached for his weapon as Wright blasted his face with fire suppression chemicals. The man stumbled, raising hands to protect himself. He advanced, swinging the butt-end of the canister upward, catching the man below the chin and knocking him back-wards, feet clearing the floor.

The man thudded against the hard tiled floor.

Wright brought up the fire extinguisher again and slammed it against the man's face, shattering nose cartilage. Blood splattered everywhere. The red-haired man went limp.

He tossed the half-drained extinguisher aside and rifled through the man's pockets, collecting a phone, a wallet, and a federal identi-fication badge attached to a lanyard.

The laminated ID badge held the name of Gene Thornton. A photo matched the man on the floor, before a close encounter with a steel container full of monoammonium phosphate.

The ID was the same as his, except for the color. Federal Bureau of Investigation. Washington Headquarters. Thornton's badge was green, classifying him as a civilian, unlike Wright's, which was blue and reserved for federal employees.

He pocketed the ID, cell phone, and wallet. A semiautomatic was extracted from an open holster—no sense leaving an adver-sary's weapon behind—and he retrieved his newly acquired tablet.

A commotion of people grabbed his attention. Time to leave. The quickest exit was the same stairwell that delivered his assailant. In a downhill half-run/half-gallop, the five flights to the basement went quickly, without further confrontation.

Wright strolled by the cafeteria and kept to the pedestrian side of the tunnel linking the Madison Building to the other libraries. Unbeknownst to the general public, the tunnels were semi-sterile security and the main thoroughfares for transferring artifacts and displays between facilities. He followed signs to the Adams Building and grabbed an elevator to the ground floor and exited onto Second Street.

Wright thumbed through the man's wallet. A driver's license matched the ID. Gene Thornton. He kept the ID and tossed the wallet and other contents in a trashcan on the corner. Spotting a DC tour bus at the curb, he seized the moment to slide his own cell phone under the front edge of the bus's back tire. It was out of commission the moment the bus pulled away.

Where now? Hell if he knew.

He watched a throng of tourists and pondered his predicament. If Thornton acted under orders, even as a federal contractor, those orders came from high up. Executive assistant level or above. That narrowed the list of suspects considerably. No more than two dozen within the bureau had that kind of authority.

Wright felt like a sacrificial pawn in a larger chess gambit.

He needed time to sort things out, so he headed up East Capitol Street and kept walking.

Whom did Samuel Ford threaten? Wright considered the possibilities. Within the bureau, that would be the Director, Deputy Director, Associate Director, Director of Intelligence, Director for National Security or his assistant, Director for Cyber and Response, Director for Science and Technology, Director for Information and Technology, the Chief of Staff, Director of Special Agents in Charge, or the Executive for Congressional Affairs. An influential twelve high-ranking men and women. Someone in that crowd risked their career for a political or philosophical cause and championing a larger conspiracy.

Instincts told him that Deputy Director Stan Baker led the shortlist of suspects.

But what proof did he have? Wang's suspicions? Hardly evidence.

His hand ached. Glancing down, Wright noticed blood trickling down his fingers and dotting the sidewalk. It was a small cut, but bled like a gusher. He yanked up his jacket sleeve to conceal the injury.

He passed the concrete posts in front of the Supreme Court and noticed Capitol Police walking the crowds and listening to the radios to their ears. News traveled fast.

Act normal and keep on trekking.

Just another business suit out for a walk after lunch. That's all he was.

At the intersection of First Street and Constitution, the uniqueness about the Senator from Oklahoma popped back into his thoughts. Ford chaired a committee with oversight authority over secret research and deadly technology: ghost sites, neurogenetics, who knew what else. Singularity. Whatever it was, someone was willing to remove Ford to keep him out of their business, and kill anyone else who interfered.

Wright needed to talk to someone he could trust.

And that someone—two of them, actually—were in Princeton.

18
DIFFERENCES IN JUDGMENT

NSA Safe House, Princeton, New Jersey

FROM THE KITCHEN, KATE watched Wang descend the stairs, his dark eyes distant in thought.

"You said make yourself at home." She licked a dab of pizza sauce from the corner of her lips and held up a slice of Tombstone oven-baked pizza. "I had doubts the NSA was springing for dinner."

He loosened his tie and tossed her a thin smile. "Save me any?"

"It'll cost you one answer." Kate took a shot in the dark. "You and Jack have a good chat?"

Wang acknowledged the question with a tilt of his head.

Bingo.

Kate grinned at the confirmation. "Should I be concerned?"

"Hard to tell. He's dealing with logistics at the moment."

"Logistics? As in moving vans or as in Jack's neck deep in crap?"

He didn't flinch. "Care to elaborate?"

"No."

She wanted an explanation. "Colonel, you brought me here. Think about playing nice, if you expect cooperation."

Wang, like Wright, seemed damn proficient at keeping secrets. Knowing no answers were forthcoming, she slid Ford's laptop out of its case and pointed to the evidence decals plastered on the device.

"I want assurances the bureau gets this back."

Wang perked up. "Of course, Dr. Meir."

"Who?"

"You need to get used to your new identity."

"Oh, yeah. Dr. Meir. The icicle pop, neuro-shrink from the South Pole." She rolled her eyes. "So, Boots, that bruise under your eye tells me you took one heck of a shot. How'd you get it?"

"None of your business."

"Whatever you say, Boots." She pointed to the computer. "Our technology teams couldn't get past its encryption."

Wang laughed as he got to work. "I didn't expect they would."

Kate turned away. Against her better judgment and the bureau's code of conduct, she had followed Wright's directives. She was out of her element, about to go undercover on a questionable assignment. The bureau taught cadets the difference between decisions and choices: decisions were a process of analyzed steps with actions executed based on gained understanding and established knowledge, while choices were mindset-based actions often made without sound judgment and from a perception of right or wrong. Kate had allowed loyalty and personal insecurities to influence her choices. Bad choices, possibly.

Wang handed her a file. "Better read it."

She took a seat on the living room couch. The file was a brief on Thomas Parker, printed on plain paper as if no one dared take credit for its existence. A chronology dissected the not yet forty-something doctor. As she read, a theme emerged. Regardless of other events, his life focused on his research. The anonymous author could only be someone close to him.

The NSA had a mole inside Parker's research lab.

Kate's antennae vibrated. She slid forward on the couch and placed her elbows on her knees, marking pages of the biography as she continued. A lot of pages got dog-eared.

"How long has the NSA been on Thomas Parker?"

"Two years," Wang said, without looking up from the laptop. His voice distant and flat.

Kate frowned. "You lied, Colonel. You said it had been a couple of months."

"No. I engaged Samuel Ford in mid-summer. That's a couple of months. We've been on Parker and his research for two years. ANCRI, much, much longer. Until three months ago, all we had on ACNRI were rumors, little viable intel. It's a hard nut to crack. It was just a matter of time before ANCRI acquired Parker. He was too valuable an asset to pass up. We just didn't know what methods they would use to secure his services until now."

Kate looked up from her file. "We?"

"You have what you need to know."

She folded his arms. "That much I've gathered."

Wang sighed. "Two years ago, I paired the professor with a first-time field agent, Rebecca Ward. CSS snatched her straight out of advanced training at Swick," the U.S. Army's John F. Kennedy Special Warfare Center at Fort Bragg. "Becky's brilliant and was fresh out a master's in biomedical engineering. Like many candidates, she was eager to change the world. I put her undercover as his grad student, where she became his *yinyang*."

Kate held up the brief. "Your undercover coed wrote this?"

"Parker was mapping neural interfaces and targeting repeatable synaptic associations. Innovative work on minimal funding. Becky provided a shopping list and through a few creative avenues, the NSA back-doored Parker several less-than-used supercomputers and network solutions. Surplus materials, we call them."

She returned the file to the table. "If the university terminated Dr. Parker, where does that leave your tag-along super-agent?"

Wang's shoulders slumped. "Last night, Parker's lab got ransacked by actors unknown. This morning, Becky was abducted from her apartment."

Kate's eyebrows shot up. "Abducted? You have confirmation of this?"

Wang nodded.

"Colonel, why would someone kidnap your agent?"

"For the same reason someone snatched Samuel Ford. To protect secrets."

The phone clipped to his belt vibrated. Wang typed in an access code and studied the screen.

Concern flashed across his face. "Thomas Parker's heading into trouble."

Hopewell, New Jersey

PARKER HELD THE STEERING wheel of his late-model Jeep Grand Cherokee with a white-knuckle grip and waited for the owner of a ranch-style house to come home.

Thirst for revenge was a powerful motivator. And this house was his last chance to get information: who stole his lab equipment? How could he get it back?

He wanted to call the Mercer County Sheriff, but doubted they'd get involved in university affairs. Officially, his research agreement stated that all equipment belonged to the university anyway.

But no one had the right to take his stuff until Friday, not even the university.

Stalking others wasn't smart and it was if his I.Q. points evaporated by the minute. Stops at the associate dean's house and Becky's apartment yielded no leads. He even questioned their neighbors. No one knew anything. He thought that while a university administrator could ride off into the sunset before fencing stolen equipment and raising capital, a shipping and receiving manager would probably need the money first.

Everything that defined him had vanished overnight: his teaching position, his research, and—as odd as the thought seemed—his best friend and lover.

Parker considered his next step as a familiar silver Audi swooshed past and screeched to a halt in a driveway.

Got ya!

Parker jolted upright in his seat and grabbed the door handle, then thought better of it. He started the car instead.

A barrel-chested man hopped out of the passenger's seat of the German-made luxury car.

He recognized the man as the shipping and receiving manager. Phillip Derman opened the driver's side door and gestured at his accomplice to hurry up. Derman scanned the neighborhood, turning his head until he looked directly at Parker.

His grip on the steering wheel tightened further.

Derman froze for a split second. Parker did not.

Adrenaline raged through his veins. He slapped the gearshift into drive and crushed the accelerator pedal. His Grand Cherokee lurched like a racehorse bolting out of a starting gate. Wheels churned against asphalt.

Derman retreated to his Audi.

Parker ripped the wheel hard. The SUV clipped a lamppost and barreled through the front yard. The impact with the Audi's read end was violent. Sheet metal buckled. Glass shattered. The Jeep's air bag exploded, obscuring his vision. He kept his foot mashed against the gas pedal. The cars recoiled and heaved. Tires squealed. The two vehicles shuddered, one resisting the path of movement, one forcing it. Smoke churned from the tires. His Jeep broke the Audi loose of the driveway and rammed it through the house's closed garage door.

Parker's ears rang. He fought against the inflated air bag, slugging and pounding it into a submission. When he was clear of it, he sprang from the car, leaving it in drive.

"You bastard!" Parked yelled, climbing through the twisted sheet metal of the garage door. "Phillip Derman, show yourself!"

Snap. Snap. Snap.

The noises came from inside the house, like sticks slapping against one another.

Parker ignored the noises and peered into the Audi.

It was empty.

He crept into the mudroom attached to the garage.

More crackling sounds sparked from somewhere deeper inside the house.

Snap. Snap. Snap.

Parker heard movement and spotted bodies shuffling through an open doorway.

What was going on? There wasn't a clear view.

The wall beside him exploded with random, dime-sized impressions.

His thirst for revenge evaporated, replaced by fear. People were shooting.

Stumbling into the mudroom, like a drunk stepping off a curb, Derman came at Parker, his arms flailing. He latched onto Parker for balance.

He readied himself to knock out a set of pearly white front teeth, but then Derman slumped, his eyes wide with terror.

Blood trickled from the corner of Derman's mouth.

Their eyes riveted onto one another.

"Tom, please—" Derman croaked, his shirt daubed in growing splotches of blood.

"Where's my—"

Parker caught sight of two men decked out in body armor, wielding firearms.

A red dot streaked across the side of Derman's face, like a laser light in an arcade, and settled on an ear hole. Parker saw a flash and heard a snap. Blood sprayed everywhere. Derman's body collapsed to the floor, like a puppet cut loose from its strings.

Parker gasped, his mouth tainted with the warm spray of blood.

He fought panic and dropped to his knees, rolling away from the dangerous neon rays.

More snaps rang out.

He dove for cover as pain tore through his side, like being stabbed by an ice pick, and scrambled on all fours toward the garage.

Snap. Snap. Snap.

Fragments of walls, door frames, and cabinets splintered all around him as gunshots followed him, coming fast and furious.

Something struck the side of his head and blurred his vision. His hands, coated in Derman's blood, gripped the orange shag carpet that covered the mudroom floor.

"Stay down!" a voice yelled. "Down!"

Dazed, Parker lumbered in a vain effort to escape. His movements were sluggish, like crawling through a maze of tree roots. Everything moved in slow motion. He squinted through smears of blood, his breathing labored as saltiness filled his mouth. The pain jabbing his side competed with an ache in his head. When he found the door, a hand mercifully reached out and jerked him to the cold, hard concrete slab of the garage.

Parker screamed in pain.

Groggy, flat on his back, he craned his head, trying to see his tormentors.

Blood covered his face, blurring his vision.

Boom! Boom! Boom! Gunfire rang more loudly, a contrast to the silenced shots inside the house.

A new figure crouched above him. A woman.

Boom! Boom! Boom! More rumbling in the distance.

"Dr. Parker," she said, her hand pressing against his wet cheek.

Her face pulsed in his vision, blurring in and out.

"Stay with me, okay?"

Stillness washed over him, its cold wake leaching his strength, leaving any will to fight anchored to bedrock. The pain in his side became a knot-filled numbness.

His eyelids felt heavy.

"Stay—" a woman yelled.

Then everything went black.

19
INTO THE FIRE

KATE'S HEART POUNDED FASTER than she could ever remember. Randy Wang was a madman behind the wheel of a car. He skidded into the driveway of a house on Taylor Terrace, blocking an idling Grand Cherokee that was half-in, half out of a shredded garage door.

He bolted from the vehicle with his semi-automatic leading the way.

Kate shouted after him. "Colonel, you're rushing into a situation you know nothing about!"

She refused to let herself get suckered into a potential conflict.

Wang disappeared into the garage. Without backup. Without a plan.

This is insane! Kate slowed to a methodical pace, her Glock held firm in two hands. She swept the interiors of the two cars. Once those were cleared, she stepped through the mangled garage door.

Snapping sounds clicked off. She recognized the noise as suppressed gunfire.

Ahead, Wang crouched at a transition between the garage and the house.

"Stay down!" he barked. "Down!"

A second later, Wang flung a man onto the floor of the garage, moving him out of harm's way. He pressed his shoulder against a doorframe, took aim, and fired in short, measured bursts.

Kate trailed closer, pistol at the ready.

A clamor echoed inside the house: not gunfire, more like people running for their lives.

She spotted Wang settled low, like a lion in the grasses on the African plains. He sprang into action behind the roar of his semi-automatic.

Kate crept to the man Wang had saved.

She recognized him from the NSA's file. Thomas Parker looked confused, almost panicked. His face was washed in blood.

"Dr. Parker," she said in a business-like tone. She placed a hand against his cheek and checked his head wound. Mild graze. He'd live, at least from that one. Shock started to take hold of him. Getting shot did that. "Stay with me, okay?"

Shock. She had seen patients fade away from it in the emergency room. An unseen gravity pulled at him, like a compass needle dialing back to magnetic north.

"Stay awake!" Kate yelled. "Come on, Thomas! Stay with me, damn it!"

His eyes closed and his body went limp.

"Thomas!"

She heard more snapping and crackling, returned fire from suppressed weapons.

Wang had yet to eliminate the threat.

She checked for a pulse. His carotid artery thrummed under the pressure of her fingers. He was steady enough. For now.

Kate leapt to her feet, knowing Wang needed backup.

Wang's weapon discharged again.

She resisted the temptation to call out.

Silence was an advantage and she prayed she wasn't walking into friendly fire.

Kate dialed in her senses. Her breathing quickened, though still not as fast as her pulse.

Moving swiftly on her toes, she kept both hands on her pistol, one around the grip and the second cupped below the first, her finger held tight to the trigger. Behind her Glock, she cleared corners and doorways just like her instructors at Quantico had taught her. Two crumpled bodies lay just beyond the entrance. She suppressed the impulse to check for vitals.

Movement stirred ahead.

The ranch-style home split in two directions, a living room to the right and a kitchen to the left. She listened for more movement.

She spotted a third fallen figure, a man in body armor who had taken a bullet below the chin, a place where his protective shielding left him vulnerable. His lower jaw was nothing more than a shredded mass of skin, bone, muscles, and blood. Beside the dead man, in a broad pool of red, lay front teeth. A silenced, laser-sighted pistol rested just beyond his fingertips.

Professional killers.

Heavy feet barreled toward her.

Kitchen!

Kate pinpointed the source of the noise.

Time slowed, her movements synced to the oncoming threat.

A deadly red neon beam streaked her way.

"F-B-I!" Kate barked. "Freeze!"

The red dot reached her eyes.

She pulled the trigger. Twice.

A man wearing a black, armored vest like his companion's tipped backwards, his face taking a strike of lead.

Kate's mouth fell agape, breath trapped in her lungs, weapon trained on the limp gunman sprawled across the kitchen floor.

Her whole body shuddered and she couldn't take her eyes off of the perpetrators—bookend twins with matching spongy crimson faces.

"Wang," she snapped, "two down. Are we clear?"

"Clear," Wang said, coming around a corner from somewhere deeper inside the house. "I saw two. Damn it, did you have to kill the SOB?"

Kate swallowed over a hard lump in her throat. She had never fired her service weapon, other than at monthly shooting range exercises. Never even had a reason to draw it in the field.

"We needed the bastard alive." He shook his head. "You sure as hell picked a day to improve your marksmanship."

"Well, excuse me. You should have winged your guy, and not left it up to me to keep his BFF alive." She pointed her gun at him. "You pull another kamikaze stunt and you'll go it alone. I'll wait outside and polish my pretty little nails, then shoot whichever one of your dumb asses comes out last."

"Kamikaze is Japanese. I'm Chinese."

"You're an asshole! Kamikaze, Chinese, clinically deranged. All labels work for you."

"Check those two," Wang said, pointing to the two bodies near the mudroom.

He patted down the two gunmen. No IDs. "Is Thomas Parker okay?"

"How the hell should I know?" she asked.

She felt the two victims for pulses. With the number of gunshot wounds each had taken, she didn't need a medical degree to declare them dead. Neither had an inkling of a pulse.

Wang rifled through the kitchen cupboards.

"What the hell are you doing?" Kate asked.

He pulled down a box of Life cereal and emptied its contents into the sink. After turning the box inside out, he dipped the fingers on the right hand of each dead gunman in their own blood and pressed them against the box's inner cardboard.

"Collecting fingerprints."

Kate shook her head. "Let the crime scene detail do that."

"If these guys served in the military, federal agencies, or law enforcement, they'll have prints in the NGI," he said, referring to next generation identification and the automated fingerprint identification database system. "Since you killed your guy before we could interrogate him, we need to track down his employer. By the looks of it, the hired muscle came here to tie up loose ends."

"Don't pin this on me. I shot my guy in self-defense. You're the lunatic. And just to set the record straight, you dragged me into this mess."

He took a breath. "Kate, we need to leave before the authorities arrive."

"Excuse me? I can't leave a crime scene. You may not care what branch of government you serve, but I work for the FBI. This must be reported. I don't get to walk away. Every agent-involved shooting gets investigated."

He snatched her arm. "We have no time to debate this. Until we secure this technology, you and I are expendable. I guarantee more thugs like these two will be coming. If we stay and report this, by-the-book, we'll both be dead by morning. Trust me, there'll be time to sort it out later. But we need to go. Now."

The scene stunned her. Four dead, killers and victims.

She thought of the Georgetown killers and their professional operation. If these killers were connected, one of these perps could be the triggerman. It gave her a small satisfaction to think she might have shot the man responsible for the dead coed in a bath tub.

At least they'd died with the same brutality they'd shown others.

"How many shots did you fire?"

The question caught her off guard. "I don't know."

"Count them out. Close your eyes and think."

Adrenaline clouded her memory. "Why—?"

"Figure it out fast. Pick up each ejected shell casing for the shots you fired. Bullet casings contain fingerprints. Right now, those prints belong to a woman named Cassondra Meir. You don't want to leave evidence behind that could send Meir to prison, do you?"

Kate took a long breath and backpedaled through the ordeal. She counted. Two shots at the same target. Retracing her steps, she found her brass scattered on the floor, no more than a foot apart.

Tampering with evidence. That alone would get her fired.

She slipped the brass in her pocket.

Wang squatted near one of the victims and turned the man over until he found a wallet.

Kate shot him an incredulous look. "Are you stealing from him?"

He slid a thick credit card out of the wallet. The name and logo read Royal Bank of Canada Cayman Islands. Wang popped open a USB attachment embedded in the card.

"Phillip Derman was the mastermind behind the theft of Parker's research. He no longer needs the proceeds and those funds will cover other endeavors now."

Wang pocketed the card.

"You're downright unbelievable." She gestured toward the garage with her head. "What about Dr. Parker? He needs a hospital."

"Let's get him into the car. We'll go from there."

20
THE CONSEQUENCES
OF RESCUE PLANS

NSA Safe House, Princeton, New Jersey

"I SAID THIS IS a bad idea," Kate barked as they lumbered through the back door of the safe house. "Listen! This man needs a hospital!"

Wang strained with Thomas Parker's dead weight, in a fireman's carry over his shoulders. Gone was his suit jacket, his button-down dress shirt streaked in Parker's blood.

Knocking files and half-drunk cups of coffee to the floor, Kate cleared off the dining room table.

He grimaced. "You said his wound wasn't life-threatening."

"You asked for a quick assessment. That doesn't mean you can deny him medical care just so you can interrogate him."

Wang rolled his eyes. "Interrogation? That's a bit strong, don't you think? Hell, if I wanted to waterboard him, we'd do that in the bathtub. Okay, if you want to feel better, there's truth serum in a box in the closet. That lets us skip any waterboarding."

She threw him an exasperated glare. "You'd better know what you're doing, Colonel."

Wang spun the unconscious Parker around.

Legs bumped the light that hung low above the thin-legged dining room table. The spindled fixture swung in a wide arc, throwing splashes of light across the room.

"I do," Wang said, rolling the unconscious man onto the cleared table, which creaked under the weight.

Kate's blood-soaked hands cradled Parker's head and she felt for a pulse on his jugular. Blood saturated the right side of Parker's shirt. She'd shredded Wang's suit jacket and used it as an impromptu field dressing.

"He's lost over a pint." She turned to Wang. "I can't do this."

"Yes, Kate, you can."

"You're insane." She pointed a wet, sticky finger at him. "I can't tell you how many procedures we've violated. The NSA may not care, but the FBI does." Like most bureaucratic agencies, the FBI had more policies and rules than an agent could remember—but it had was a code of conduct and a set of ethics every agent strove to live by. *Give rigorous obedience to the Constitution of the United States; Show respect for the dignity of all those needing protection; Show compassion and fairness to all who were served; Accept responsibility for actions and decisions and the consequences, and demonstrate uncompromising personal integrity and institutional integrity.* All of which seemed at odds with her dilemma. "Two men are dead because of us."

Parker let out a faint groan.

"We were justified in our actions," Wang said, before disappearing into a pantry. He reemerged with two black-ribbed plastic gear boxes, decorated with red crosses inside white squares. One at a time, he hefted them onto the kitchen counter. He pointed to Parker. "Our presence saved this man's life."

"What we're doing now may kill him," Kate said. The edges of the hard-sided field combat containers were scuffed from use, although the decals indicating the specific branch of service had been removed. "Where in the hell did you get those?"

He was noncommittal. "EBay. Military surplus. Fifty percent off."

"I doubt that." She unlatched and flipped back the lids to both triage containers. She surveyed the contents. "I'm going to get my ass fired."

"That won't happen."

"Easy for you to say. You don't have a license to practice medicine on the line." She rifled through the triage kits for what she needed, shoving aside suction kits and tubes, surgical tools and rib spreaders. She snatched up surgical gloves, a stethoscope, pressure dressing and gauze, and QuikClot. She donned the gloves and a surgical headlamp. Precluding damage to the intestinal track or other organ damage, everything she needed was in one of the boxes. Almost everything. A portable X-ray or MRI scanner would have been useful.

She thrust a finger in the air and pointed. "Apply pressure on his wounds."

Wang did as directed.

Kate had left general medicine after her residency, and was much happier for it. As gruesome as it sounded, forensics and dead people didn't provide the same level of stress as being responsible for another human life. The FBI had been the perfect refuge. And now it seemed she was about to screw it all up.

She stared at her shaking hands, wet and sticky with blood—someone else's blood.

Wang noticed her apprehension. "Trust me."

"*Trust no one.* Those were your words."

"Agent Morgan, we need to get into that research facility. If we take Dr. Parker to a hospital, you'll never find Ford or his girlfriend's killer."

She elbowed him aside to strip back Parker's shirt and reassess the gunshot wound, peeling back fragments of field dressing. The bullet hole was on his right, in the obliques, below the tenth rib. "He needs an x-ray. He could have unseen internal damage."

"We can't risk it."

"Listen, you may be willing to play with a man's life, but I can't do that." She clicked on the lamp strapped across her forehead and grabbed a chlorhexidine wipe, which she tore open with her teeth. She unwrapped gauze and dabbed it against the wound. "Just because I have a medical license doesn't mean I am a qualified to be a combat medic. It's a lot like trying to pretend you're a neurosurgeon in front of a bunch of gun-carrying lunatics."

"He's our way into ANCRI."

"Oh, go to hell, Colonel."

On the table, Parker let out a more conscious moan.

"Thomas, hang in there," Kate said. "We're trying to help." She tugged at his side, stretching skin taut and away from the wound to open it up for inspection. For a gunshot wound the penetration was incredibly clean, without tearing or feathering of the skin.

She reached beneath him and probed for an exit wound. Her gloved fingers found a saggy, wet dimple. The light off her headlamp glistened against a source of oozing blood. "Thomas, a few inches to the left and we'd be talking about you in the past tense. The bullet made a clean exit. That's welcome news, meaning I don't have to try to carve a bullet out of you. It appears to have nicked a rib, passing through mostly oblique fibers, missing the large intestine by a hair."

Kate directed Wang to apply gauze and pressure on the both sides of the wound. "Colonel, stop being a putz and lean into it!"

She slid on the stethoscope and probed Parker's abdomen with gloved fingers, listening to the normal gurgling of bubbles making their way through the intestinal tract.

Parker's moans deepened.

Kate leaned over Parker's face. "Settle down, Thomas, no need to thank me yet." She glared at Wang, the beam of her headlamp targeting him like a convict in a prison yard. "I regret meeting you, Colonel. And at my first opportunity, I'm going to kill Jack Wright for sacrificing me like he did."

Wang's face basked in the glow of hate-me-if-you-will illumination. "Let's get through this, shall we? Tell me what you need."

Through gritted teeth, she said, "Put on gloves. Grab lactated ringers. Hang it on a pole. When he comes to, he's going to feel really bad. So dig through those boxes and get the mother of all hangover drugs."

While Kate assessed vitals, Wang retrieved the necessary supplies, erected the stainless steel IV pole and hung the clear, prefilled bag. He stripped down the IV line, meter dial, and popped back the tip to expose the intravenous needle.

She waved him off.

He raised a confident palm. "I've done this a time or two," he said, wrapping a pressure cuff around Parker's arm and tapping his forearm to find a vein. He marked the spot with a pen for an optimal insertion point.

Remarkably, Wang seemed to know what he was doing.

Kate frowned. A damn scary thought.

"Don't tell me. You stayed at a Holiday Inn Express," she said, recalling the company's commercials. "So now you're an expert with field traumas?"

"Like riding a bike." Wang slid the needle into a vein, taped it down, and set the IV drip.

"I'm extremely terrified to know that."

"Do you ever feel you're already buried deep six feet under..." The Katy Perry song forced its way through the thoughts crowding Parker's mind. Singing. The voice was familiar. A silhouette with strands of dark hair cascading past slender shoulders emerged from an opaque tapestry. The woman reached for him. He reciprocated the gesture, their fingertips inches apart. Almost touching. But an invisible barrier trapped her beyond his reach.

Through his haze, Parker strained to put a name to the ghost.

"There's a spark for you, you just got to ignite..."

Becky?

A streaking light, like the trailing flash of a meteor racing across a night sky, whistled through their somber, slate-colored world.

Becky's singing stopped. She retreated and the aura of her face sank back into the darkness.

Another streak of light blazed between them, this time louder than a thrumming whistle, like a rumble of thunder. The darkness around them faded. He felt the pressure of hands. Pain cascaded through his body, fracturing his dream-like state. He groaned.

Becky called out to him, her voice trapped in a different world. *"Thomas, find me!"*

When he opened his eyes, Becky and her shadows had vanished.

"DON'T GO," PARKER CROAKED, startling awake and bolting upright. "What the—"

He fought to clear his blurred vision and a throbbing head.

Sounds around him coalesced from garbled noise into clarity.

"Grab him!" a woman snapped.

"Leave me..." Parker wrestled against hands that attempted to restrain him.

Blurred faces loomed over him.

The pain in his side worsened. Groaning, he collapsed onto his back and yielded to the hands. A cheaply made, five-spoke chandelier swung in oval-shaped arcs above him. Two of the lights in the spokes were burnt out and the offset of light cast surreal shadows across the room.

He saw a pinpoint of intense light, as if he were stepping out of a dark tunnel and coming face-to-face with a head on locomotive, or, worse, being caught dead-to-rights in a meteor's path.

"What are you doing to me?" he managed to say.

"We're trying to help," a woman's voice said. "Please remain calm. Thomas, listen, you've been shot."

"Shot?" Parker asked, struggling to catch up.

A halo framed the outline of a woman's featureless face. She reminded him of the woman, Becky, behind the glass, but somehow he could tell they weren't the same person.

"Where is Becky?" Parker asked, angst surging as he saw the syringe the woman held, its needle glistening in the light. He felt cold and weak. He tried to resist. "What's... that?"

"Are you allergic to any medications?" she asked, placing the palm of her hand on his chest. "It's okay. My name is Kate."

"Who?"

"Kate," she repeated as she peeled off her headlamp.

His vision cleared. The woman named Kate had coffee-colored, shoulder-length hair that curled ever so slightly as it touched her shoulders. Her eyes studied him. She wore blue surgical gloves and bore the same strained, counterfeit smile ER residents often wore when they handled patients for the first time. Blood was splattered everywhere. His blood.

"Are you allergic to any medications?" she asked again.

"I don't think so." He struggled to take in the room around him. He was inside a house. A kitchen was behind him. "I was shot?"

"Afraid so." She injected the milky white contents of the syringe into a knob of clear tubing stringing down from an IV bag that hung from a plastic pole. "Do you remember anything, Thomas? Can you tell us who shot you?"

"No." His nervous eyes continued to scan the room. "What's in the bag?"

"Lactated Ringers," she said, the hospital cocktail for fluid replacements during surgical procedures, a clear chemical mixture of sodium, potassium, calcium, chloride, and lactate. "It's to compensate for blood loss."

Seeing the IV helped explain why he felt so cool, but didn't account for everything.

"What did you give me?" he asked, apprehension lingering in his voice.

"Propofol," she said. "You should begin to feel tired."

"I know what propofol does," he snapped, beginning to feel the drug seep its way through his system.

"Of course you do, Thomas," she said. "Be a trouper. Don't fight it."

"How do you... know my name?"

The cold dampness lingered, but its effects seemed less of a concern. He made a futile attempt to resist the wave of sleep overtaking him. The swaying chandelier above them seemed spellbinding as if it were a tool of entrancement. He willed himself to concentrate on their conversation yet found himself ignored, the third person in a two person conversation.

"Restrain him," the woman named Kate directed. "I have to probe his wound before we stitch him up, to make sure he's got no strands of clothing caught inside, and no intestinal rupture. And grab a bottle of antiseptic wash for irrigation."

Kate reattached her lamp and started to probe his side with forceps. Her companion, an Asian man, removed the belt to his pants and strapped it around a wrist.

He tried to follow their conversation.

"I just want you to know," she said, "last time I did emergency medicine was during my residency. Things did not turn out well."

"How so?" the man asked, using tubing to strap down the other arm.

"A lot of people died under my care."

"Sorry to hear that," the man said.

Parker yielded to chemically induced exhaustion. His world turned dark and quiet.

"I DON'T TALK ABOUT it," Kate admitted, irrigating the wound. "It was the last year of my family med residency at Hopkins. As part of community outreach, the hospital did a staff exchange with rural clinics. Nothing ever, ever happened in my little coal mining town. The staff joked I'd be sobering up drunks and bandaging farm injuries. They were wrong. It was the worst day of my life."

After flushing both ends of the wound, inspecting it to make sure no fragments of clothing had been lodged inside and convinced the intestinal tract had sustained no damage, Kate determined that internal sutures and cauterizing were unnecessary. A QuikClot sponge helped slow the bleeding, before she closed each side of the bullet wound.

"It rained for two days straight," she said, a distance straining her voice, but in such a manner as to keep rhythmic company with her basting, inversion-style suturing. "Everything was wet, including me. The hospital's primary doc got called to a mine accident, abandoning me to the night shift when all hell broke loose. The doc was treating a blunt force trauma when a methane safety valve blew. The whole mountain exploded. We felt the shock ten miles away. Doc Mandel was burned over seventy percent of his body. He died first. Four arrived DOA," she said. "Five others died while I treated them. I was stacking and racking wounded in a two-bed ER. Not more than five minutes lapsed and a woman carrying triplets got dropped off, her cervix dilated ten centimeters. Her three boys seemed to arm wrestle the whole way out. My first solo delivery. Deliveries. To close out the night, a runaway locomotive supporting rescue efforts lost its brakes and plowed into a fuel tanker. The explosion scattered men like dominos. Another six DOAs. Six more died under my care. God cursed the mining town of Elk Pass that night. And I did little to help them."

Wang touched her hand. "Sounds like a night from hell."

Kate shrugged and started to lay down a string of nonabsorbable sutures to close the wound, her hands nimbly holding the threaded needle and forceps.

"I wrapped up my rotations at Johns Hopkins, took my boards, and switched to forensic pathology. After that, I never wanted to be responsible for another human life ever again."

She continued the basting stitches: through, loop and hook; through, loop, and hook.

"As a pathologist," he pointed out, "you still save lives."

"Nah. It's different. Morbid, yeah. Forensics makes it easier to restrain emotions. Remain detached. Stay objective. When a crime involving a fatality occurs, you program yourself to listen to the corpse tell its version of a story. Pathologists develop a warped sixth sense, like scientific tea leaf reading on dead people." She sighed deeply. "Grab the scissors, will ya? I'll tie this bad boy off and then we can flip him over to close the other side."

"You're good at this," Wang offered.

Kate shrugged. "At what? Saving a man's life?"

Wang smiled thinly. "I think you know what I mean."

She gave him a look. "Every body I work on gets stitched or stapled back together. So, yeah, bobbing and weaving, like knitting, is eventually mastered. Haven't received a complaint yet."

Kate placed a thoughtful hand on Parker's bare chest.

"I hope Thomas appreciates my patch job, because the Federal Bureau of Investigation doesn't offer malpractice insurance."

WEDNESDAY, OCTOBER 7th

The wolf will hire himself out as cheaply as the shepherd.
Russian Proverb

21
AWAKENINGS

NSA Safe House, Princeton, New Jersey, 6:00 a.m.

FOR NSA STALWARTS, HACKING security protocols and encryption schemes was hardly a monumental effort. In fact, it was rather routine. Using a technique akin to offensive forensics, Randy Wang circumvented boot and registry files and executed a twist in the operating system on Ford's computer. The device no longer resembled much of a laptop, stripped down and spread across the dining room table, its varied parts and pieces interconnected by jumper cables with a few intermediate proprietary components mixed in.

As hyped, his laptop lived up to a partial billing—a near impenetrable—a formidable obstacle for a run-of-the-mill script kiddie. And no offense to the tech wizards at the FBI, but Wang understood this kind of prize lay beyond their white hat expertise. As part of a DoD Advanced Technology CYBERCOM task force, he had constructed comparable semi-bulletproof platforms for a long list of sensitive federal entities: the White House, Pentagon, NSA, CIA. Since Samuel Ford was the chair of the Senate's Science and Technology Committee, he too fit that category, using an NSA NCIT MR-295S Alpha prototype underlayment.

The rivalry among America's intelligence agencies was real. Whose cryptologists were the brightest: the NSA, CIA, FBI, or DoD?

Ten years spent at the Pentagon and the NSA told Wang that the NSA cultivated the most talented cyber-freaks in the world. Hands down, from what he saw from the trenches. No slouch himself, with a master's in cybersecurity from George Washington University, Wang worked with NSA cipher-virtuosos on a daily basis. Their talents focused on outsmarting the myriad imminent digital traps across the globe, searching for the next cyber-terrorist threat, or developing new disruptive technologies for the government.

Ford's computer was hackable to the right person.

Encryption schemes and ciphers acted like gatekeepers, technological barriers. Doors and keys. Without the secret handshake—the digital or biometric password or passcode—there was no way to get past the front door. Traditional hacking methods took one of three approaches: the brute force method of pounding on the door until it broke down; searching for aberrations in software allowing a person to use a back door; or somehow tricking the door into opening.

For in-hand assets, the NSA had developed a fourth method. Create an alternate reality and then have the gatekeeper, the door, and its cipher adapt to a new reality.

That was Wang's approach.

Commercial encryption tools were rule-based systems. Sure, in recent years, superior encrypted systems had become adaptive, transformative systems, but their functional premise remained the same—non-hardware encryption schemes were mere overlays to a choreographed subbase. To an NSA encryption specialist, those overlays provided all the vulnerability needed—much like being able to create a chink in a suit of armor.

The ploy altered the Windows-based operating system rules, tweaking the reality until the computer's world construct transformed into whatever an outsider wanted it to become. Creating a set of new realities meant the proverbial door could be manipulated, moved, or softened enough to permit a person to open it from either side.

Wang finished the extreme modifications. The slick change worked like a charm. A surrogate passcode satisfied the encryption scheme and granted access to the machine.

He wasted no time cloning all information to a passport drive: Congressional Budget Office records; finance and line item budget allocations for DARPA, CIA, FBI, NSA, and DoD; congressional transcripts, federal emails, security clearance requests, and authorized contractor awards.

If Wang's hunch was correct, Ford's laptop held a who's who of agencies or individuals who wanted him dead.

Using a script, Wang categorized emails and documents pertaining to ANCRI and its Frontier. He quickly found the incriminating evidence: through a multi-agency grant, the DoD directed DARPA to distribute funding. Pentagon officials had authorized a firm called the Phoenix Consortium to manage the secretive research. RMG Global Solutions, an engineering and construction firm headquartered in Washington, D.C., had upgraded the ANCRI campus to include state-of-the-art analysis labs, a new generation of quantum-based mainframe supercomputers, and upgraded security systems.

RMG was the weakness in ANCRI's suit of armor.

RMG was his way into the covert lab.

From the files, a Government Accountability Office report piqued his interest.

The GAO inquiry reported a massive purchase order in the amount of $110 million. There appeared to be payment anomalies, even though ANCRI took possession of the massive 2,048 qubit array quantum supercomputer. This was odd, because the NSA had tried unsuccessfully to procure the same technology at a similar price.

An email from the National Security Advisor to the President of the United States established a direct link to the White House, showing the President knew about the covert program months before Ford learned of them. Under national security objections from both the White House and the Pentagon, the GAO inquiry had been redacted. Around the same time, a second email from the President's National Security Advisor to the Deputy Director of the FBI informed the bureau that the Pentagon viewed the associated technologies, public and private, as a grave threat to the national security of the United States of America. The National Security Advisor stated that the government should forcibly sequester all similar technologies.

A month-old email from the President's National Security Advisor to the Secretary of State warned that Oklahoma Senator Samuel Ford was initiating a witch hunt, and that his "irresponsible actions" were "a clear and present danger" to the nation's security concerns, and direct provocations to the White House.

Overnight, Ford became an obstacle worth eliminating.

After closing the laptop's hard drive, Wang purged files tied to the NSA and DoD, while leaving enough digital breadcrumbs to link DARPA, the CIA, the FBI, and the White House to ANCRI.

THOMAS PARKER WOKE AND forced his bloodshot eyes to flutter open. His view transitioned from cloudy to clear as he took in his predicament. He lay in a bed, torso elevated, bare-chested. Bandages encircled his midsection. A blanket covered his lower extremities. A bag of clear fluids dangled from an IV pole next to him.

Across the room, a woman slept in a chair. A patchwork blanket was drawn tight to her chin. Sunlight snaked through a gap in window shades and splashed across her face. On the floor near her feet were manila folders.

Parched, he smacked his dry lips in search of moisture.

The woman's eyes opened, as if she'd been waiting.

"Good morning, Dr. Parker."

Discarding her blanket, she moved to his bedside, checking his pulse and feeling his forehead with the back of her hand.

"No sign of a fever."

She dialed back the IV drip line that snaked its way to the crook of his elbow. She offered a small plastic cup with an orange liquid in it.

Bewildered, he took it. The soft tissues of his mouth absorbed the semi-salty, semi-sweet fluid before reaching the cotton ball slug in the back of his throat. He gulped the rest, swishing it first before swallowing.

"Where am I?" he asked, looking around the sparse bedroom. He was in a house, on the first floor. He could see the outline of trees through the fabric of window curtains. A crease of daylight breaking through the windows and painting an uncomfortable-looking chair across the room told him it was morning.

"Most people would probably ask, what happened?"

"I'm not in a hospital?"

She shook her head.

He frowned as he struggled to sift through jumbled images and events buried in the recesses of his consciousness.

The woman looked at him with curious eyes. "Do you remember anything? It's okay, you can trust me."

He gestured to the white bandages starting above his belly button.

"Single bullet wound, which left a slight abrasion on your right, tenth rib. Couldn't discern more without an X-ray. Thankfully, there appears to be no sign of further damage. You have a cut on your head. All said, you will make a full recovery."

"How long was I out?"

She glanced at a watch on her wrist. "About fourteen hours. The drugs helped."

Slowly and randomly, sights and sounds clicked through his haggard mind. His research had been stolen. He'd set out to find Phillip Derman. Flickering images emerged. Bright red rays of light. Faces both known and unknown. Men. Armed men. Blood. He glanced up at her, studying her features. Shoulder length dark hair with a bit of a curl touched her shoulders. "You were there."

She gave him a smile.

"You a cop?" he asked.

She shrugged.

He fluffed up his IV tubing with his hand.

"Doctor?"

"You can say that."

"Am I under arrest?"

"No, Thomas. Matter of fact, we need your help."

"Where is Phillip Derman? I saw him shot."

"I'm afraid your colleague did not survive, if that's what you're asking."

"Didn't turn out to be much of a colleague," he muttered.

"Why do you say that?"

He looked away.

"When I was tending to your injuries, you asked about a girl."

The woman in his vision—the singing woman trapped in a world of gray. Becky.

The woman doctor handed him a crumpled note.

"This was in your pocket."

With a sigh, he read it again. TOM, THANK YOU FOR EV-ERYTHING. I'M SORRY ABOUT THE LAB. PLEASE, BELIEVE ME. IF YOU ONLY KNEW WHAT THE FUTURE HOLDS, AFTER A HURRICANE COMES A RAINBOW. MORE THAN A FRIEND. ALWAYS. BECKY.

"Was she there?" he finally asked.

The woman shook her head. "Thomas, something has happened to Becky. We need your help to find her."

After a long, awkward pause, he remembered. "Your name is Kate."

"Yes. Doctor… Meir."

"Glad to see Dr. Parker is awake," a new voice said.

They turned to see a man standing in the open doorway.

"Dr. Parker," Kate said, pointing, "this is Randy Wang. Cryptologist."

Disjointed events in Parker's mind began to fall into place, like jigsaw puzzle pieces merging into a broader tapestry. Memories started to clear. He remembered crashing into Derman's Audi and confronting him. Others were there. With guns. He had been shot and woke up on a kitchen table with two people tending to his wounds.

Wang nodded. "You're in good health, thanks to Dr. Meir."

Parker looked from one to the other, waiting for a more thorough explanation.

The man named Wang gave her a non-verbal cue, as in "we need to talk."

Parker seemed to be the only person left out the conversation.

As they started to leave, Kate glanced back. "Let me know if there is anything you need."

"I could use a real drink," Parker said, licking his lips again. "Absent of that, I take coffee, black with two shakes of sugar." Awkwardly, he jiggled his hips and registered soreness in his side. He sensed a discomfort much lower in his body. Something was inserted between his legs. "And at your earliest convenience, I'd appreciate it if you could remove my catheter and disconnect me from the rest of these tubes."

Kate froze in the doorway to the hall. She gave him a thin smile. "I'll start a pot, then we can negotiate your wishes, Dr. Parker."

DOWNSTAIRS, KATE ENTERED THE dining room and caught a glimpse of Wang returning one of the field medic containers back to the pantry. The dining room table had been cleared, except for the senator's computer, a black soft-sided gym bag, and a satellite phone. In the living room, CNN ran *Breaking News* on the television. A tragic story about missing college students. Boating accident. University of Miami.

The gym bag drew her attention. It was about the size of an overnight bag, and bulged at the seams. "Going somewhere?"

He shrugged. "You could say that."

Kate waited for a better response. "Where you headed?"

Wang replied with a defiant silence.

She picked up the bag and glanced inside: medical supplies. What would Wang want with medical supplies?

He snatched the bag away from her. "Don't ask."

She glared at him. "You're up to something — illegal?" Getting no reply, she asked, "What did the laptop tell us?"

Wang arched an eyebrow. "It's an open book. Yours for the reading." He rubbed the day-old stubble on his chin. "Return it to Jack. He's driving up from D.C. But whatever you do, and, this is paramount, steer clear of direct contact. If the transfer goes south, do not come back to this safe house. Pass off the laptop covertly. Use a dead drop. Jack is radioactive. He knows it. As of yesterday, Deputy Director Baker took control of your investigation. Baker wants both of you removed from the case, in life-threatening ways. Don't risk blowing your cover and losing your chance to find out what happened to Ford."

"Why would the deputy director take over the investigation?"

"Peruse the emails between the FBI and the White House. You'll learn a lot. And don't trust Deputy Director Baker. He's implicated." Wang lowered his voice. "Kate, I'll try and make contact when you're inside ANCRI."

Kate couldn't believe what she was hearing. "What if our guest wants to leave?"

Wang rested a hand on her shoulder. "You just saved his life. Stitched him up after being shot. That ought to be worth something. He'll bond with you. Convince him. Thomas Parker needs to know his life is in danger. Naturally, he wants answers. Give him what is needed. Nothing more. He'll want his research back. The NSA can arrange that. And in a perfect world, he probably wants his stuffy old teaching position back too. That's our leverage. He helps us, we help him."

She searched his face. He was playing to Parker's needs. "Quid pro quo only gets us so far," she said.

"Stick to our plan," Wang said. "If this goes our way, all the good guys win." He drew a breath. "Thomas Parker is the mission now."

22
MOMENT OF REVELATION

NSA Safe House, Princeton, New Jersey

THE ANGST GRIPPING PARKER bleached out a sense of purpose, like a winter gust sucking warmth straight out of the body. Staring at the plastered ceiling above his bed, he searched his memories leading up to getting shot. He probed his bandaged wound with his fingers, testing his threshold of pain. Only a modest amount of pressure against muscle fibers sent a dagger to his brain.

The quandary he found himself in nagged at him.

In less than a week's time, his life, career, and research had fallen apart.

He remembered Phillip Derman's panic-stricken face, his eyes full of fear, confronting an imminent death.

"Tom, please—" Derman had pleaded, blood oozing from the corner of his mouth.

"You—" Parker's fists tightened.

The red dot had landed on Derman's head.

Parker shrugged off the gruesome memory, leaned forward in bed, and forced himself to dwell on something else—anything other than dead colleagues. An IV tether yanked at his arm. Looking around the room, he noticed details he hadn't seen earlier. He was on the first floor. A throw rug lay on a wood floor. A hot water radiator steamed away under a single hung sliding window. His eyes gravitated to his caretaker's nest. A patchwork blanket lay wadded up in a chair. Manila folders on the floor. Beside the files were his clothes folded neatly into a pile, as if someone had done his laundry.

He wondered how well the bloodstains had come out.

Thoughts cluttered his mind, like an approaching storm building up energy. Questions. Why wasn't he in a hospital? What had happened to the killers? Who were the man and woman, really? Were they connected to his stolen research? To Becky? Derman? The lab called ANCRI?

And why rescue him?

Nothing added up.

The further he leaned forward in bed, the more his IV restrained him.

Enough of that. He stripped off the bandage over the crook of his elbow and detached the IV. Next he slid his naked buttocks off the bed. Every bend and twist came at a cost. The pain of moving distracted him from the discomfort he was about to address.

Standing, he located his ball-and-chain, a translucent, plastic Foley bag quarter-full of urine that hung from the mattress edge. A thin clear tube connected his penis to the top of the bag. Self-removal of an IV line in an arm was less intimidating than the catheter riding up between his legs. The low tech solution of a male Foley catheter was a simple premise: anchor a tube in the bladder using a liquid-filled plug, and allow a split tip tube to drain urine into a bag. There was no painless way of removing the catheter without deflating the balloon, which was where a drainage syringe normally came into play.

The problem was that he had no drainage syringe.

Parker spotted a pair of scissors on the windowsill, presumably used to trim his bandages. With Foley bag in hand, he ignored the pain in his side and waddled naked around the room, making stops in a large arc along the way. First, he snatched up the woman's blanket. Upon lifting the blanket from the chair, he caught sight of a black object beneath it, wedged between the seat cushions. A handgun. He shook his head at the revelation.

With blanket in hand, he waddled to the scissors on the heater, and finally returned to his bed. He dropped the blanket to his feet, and lowered the Foley bag onto the blanket. With the scissors, he snipped the inflation tube to the balloon in his bladder. He could feel the pressure inside him subside as fluids drained onto the makeshift catch basin at his bare feet.

"Shi—!"

He cringed and slowly reeled the clear tube free.

Once detached from his anchor, he fetched his clothes and put himself back together.

He desperately needed a shower. It would have to wait. First he needed answers.

He snatched up the gun.

It was a semi-automatic. He felt its weight. He was no firearms aficionado, but knew the basics. Flip off the safety, aim, and pull the trigger. He studied the weapon and noticed it had no safety. The gun went in the waistband of his jeans.

Next, he spread the files from the floor across the bed. The first folder was a biography of a neurophysiologist named Cassondra Meir. The woman's picture did not match the so-called doctor he'd just met. The real Meir worked a world away, at the South Pole.

So who was the woman taking care of him?

The second file was a compilation of notes on ANCRI. Stewart Richards led the institute and Parker recognized the man from his interview. Another photo was tagged as Gene Thornton. The red-haired bastard had assaulted him with a door. Thornton's previous assignments included time with Naval Intelligence and the CIA.

The last file was a compilation about him and his Princeton research. Nowhere did the file mention Rebecca Ward.

KATE WASN'T BUYING THE NSA spy commander's tale, not in its entirety. The NSA and secrets. Inseparable. Wang's objective seemed tangential to her mission, which was to find Samuel Ford.

This covert institute was only superficially linked to his disappearance, as far as anyone knew.

After Wang left on his mysterious errand, she yanked down the medic boxes from the pantry and set them side-by-side on the dining room table. Wang had filled his gym bag with contents from the cases. She rifled through them, assessing what could be missing.

Wang was about to do something illegal. That much was clear.

The question was what?

The kits came with no stocking logs, leaving her to make an educated guess on what had taken. She noticed an IV bag was missing, along with the syringes pre-filled with amphetamines and benzodiazepines, BZDs, a broad range of hypnotics and sedatives.

The U.S. Drug Enforcement Administration classified both amphetamines and BZDs as controlled substances. Amphetamines treated a wide range of conditions, anything from nasal congestion to cognitive enhancement. BZDs were a class of psychoactive drugs, commonly used as tranquilizers to help reduce anxiety, insomnia, and reduce the impacts of seizures and muscle spasms. Mixed, the sinister combination could be used for more nefarious purposes, anything from date rape to narco-analysis. That was damn troubling.

Next she moved to the senator's laptop.

A handwritten yellow sticky note read: FRONTIER28. A password.

She grasped the reference to ANCRI's Frontier. But what did the 28 connect to?

Then she heard it. From the other room. Twenty-eight. Wang had deliberately left the TV running in the background, tuned to CNN's news coverage of a south Florida boating accident. Twenty-eight students from the University of Miami were presumed drowned after their catamaran mysteriously sank. Crewed by students, the sailing vessel had set out on an evening cruise. As the Coast Guard searched for survivors, families feared the worst.

Kate read the newscast caption: 28 STUDENTS LOST AT SEA, KEY BISCAYNE, FLORIDA. A wind-swept reporter stood on a tan stretch of beach, his back to the semi-murky expanse of the Atlantic Ocean. Billowing white clouds littered a steel blue sky.

"You steal my research?" an angry voice called.

Kate spun around to face the barrel of her own gun.

"Lady," Parker said, "you flinch and I'll put a bullet hole in you that no one can stitch up." He aimed the nob and notch sights of the pistol at a shocked Dr. Meir, or whatever her name was. He tossed her files to the floor and scanned the house for the other guy. "Where's your partner?"

"Easy now, Thomas." Her eyes scanned the room, and she brought her hands up for him to see. "I'm one of the good guys."

"I don't care. Answer my question. Where's the Chinese guy?"

She took a breath. "Out. On an extended errand."

He gestured with the pistol to the couch. "Keep your hands where I can see them."

She did as directed, offering no resistance, and took a seat.

Parker panned his gaze, searching for her accomplice. The front door of the house was ten feet in front of him. With her gun in hand, he could escape. He noticed the woman had been watching television. A dining room and kitchen were off to his left. He caught a glimpse of the chandelier hanging above a table, the one he'd seen when she stitched him up. On the table were a laptop computer and hard-shelled containers filled with medical supplies.

His eyes narrowed. "I'm leaving and I need my shoes." He looked again for the man. "You're not Cassondra Meir. I read all about her."

"It's my cover."

Parker frowned. "Well, Dr. Fraud, who are you really? Who do you work for?"

"I have ID." She gestured to a front pocket of her jeans. "I work for the Federal Bureau of Investigation. Special Agent Kate Morgan. And I am a doctor, board certified. Forensics." Slowly, she retrieved her bi-fold badge and tossed it at his feet. "I'm investigating the disappearance of Oklahoma Senator Samuel Ford."

Unable to bend down and retrieve it without pain, Parker flattened the badge open with his toes. A glance down revealed a matching picture, identified as Katherine Morgan. It was official looking. FBI. Blue lettering. A gold shield with an eagle perched on it adorned the right side.

He looked back at her. "Kate, eh? Well, what does a senator have to do with me?"

"Everything," she said. "We believe Samuel Ford was abducted from a Georgetown residence, an incident that left his girlfriend dead. Murdered. Indications are that someone at ANCRI may have played a role in his abduction and her murder."

Parker held the pistol on her, unwavering. "Becky was your mole. She helped the government steal my research."

Kate shook her head. "I can't speak on behalf of other agencies because I work for the FBI. But do you really think there's an overarching conspiracy to appropriate your research? Sure, Rebecca Ward was an undercover agent working for the National Security Agency." She took a long breath. "My partner, as you call him— Randal Wang—is a Colonel with the Army. At the time, he thought it prudent to have Becky engage you, as a resource, in case things turned ugly. And, well, obviously, Dr. Parker, they did."

He stiffened. "So sorry if I'm not buying into your fairy tale."

She pointed to the folders at his feet. "I learned about you yesterday, hours before you ended up on that table over there. Okay, you've read the files. We know you lost your faculty position and were recruited by a man named Stewart Richards. We know about Friday."

"Sonofabitch." The color drained from his face. "You people sold me out."

"That's not true. On the contrary, we saved your life. If we had not intervened, you'd be dead. Process that fact, Dr. Parker."

He fell silent. Who was he to believe? His own interpretation of events, or the story from a stranger?

Kate stood. "There's a video you need to see."

He steadied his aim. "Stay right there."

"Or what?" She kept her hands where he could see them. "Thomas, you're not going to shoot me."

Parker walked to the front door while keeping the gun on its target. He unlatched the deadbolt with his free hand.

"Phillip Derman sold you out," Kate said. "The NSA tracked a thirty million dollar wire transfer in his name to the Bank of Canada, its Cayman Islands branch. The funds were his birddog fee. He delivered your research and collected a fat tax-free incentive." She walked into the kitchen to retrieve his shoes and held them up. "You'll want these if you intend leave on foot."

Parker glanced to his feet and wiggled his toes. She had a point.

She managed a thoughtful smile. "Thomas, I read the lyrics Becky quoted in her note to you. Yeah, Katy Perry is on my playlist for the gym. You might be surprised to hear that I think Becky was trying to protect you."

"Protect me?" Parker frowned.

Kate raised an empty coffee mug. "How about you put down my gun, I pour both of us a cup of coffee, and we talk about how we can help one another."

23
ACQUISITIONS

Advanced Neurological and Cybernetic Research Institute (ANCRI), New Jersey

Caroline Wang crept behind a wall that jutted out from the institute's two-story dormitory wing and overlooked a courtyard surrounded by buildings. Trees filled the courtyard with brilliant fall colors, while the flagstone terrace became triage central. Crews in green and gray medical scrubs unloaded people strapped to backboards from a gutted recreational vehicle and transferred them to gurneys. Security guards formed a perimeter around the unloading zone.

"So this is Phase Two," Caroline whispered, taking in the scene.

She'd wondered how ANCRI would procure a new generation of test subjects.

Now she knew.

"Get these participants processed!" a man yelled.

Dressed in navy-colored scrubs and loafers, Noam Levine, the institute's newly promoted neurological lead, shouted more orders and directed traffic. Beside him in his traditional pressed white lab coat, Stewart Richards, his face exultant, stood amidst the organized mayhem and smoked a cigar.

Crews processed the unconscious participants through pre-defined stages. The treatment had an unsympathetic, callous assembly line feel to it. Staff in gray scrubs performed routine assessments, logged each participant, and passed them off to nurses in green scrubs. The acquisitions, unconscious to the world around them, were stripped naked and their garments discarded into a pile for incineration.

Twenty-six hours earlier, after the senator's execution, the staff had been ordered to withdraw from their workstations and confined to their living quarters. As far as the staff knew, the quarantine happened because of a toxic ammonia leak in the clinical neurophysiology annex, known as the CNA.

Caroline suddenly wished she participated in the house-arrest mandate.

If caught, they would kill her, like Samuel Ford.

Her urge to flee was held in check by her promise to Amy Richards.

The world needed to know the extremes that ANCRI undertook to secure its Frontier.

While the guards watched over the unloading, Caroline edged to the far end of the wall, hoping for a chance to slip unnoticed through the courtyard and into the CNA building. She timed her movement with shouting from Noam Levine, as he tried to micromanage the frenetic process. Bounding into the gap between the dormitory and the RV hauler, she crossed the open space as fast as she could, then straightened her posture and reminded herself to walk with a purpose, as if she belonged there.

Her gaze swept the scene. She counted twenty people on gurneys, maybe more. Enough to fill most of the pods inside. She passed a young man who looked like he'd just graduated from high school, unconscious, naked, and being prepped for depilation. A lead nurse ran grooming shears over his head. Another nurse slathered his body with a milky white chemical cream. A technician in gray scrubs recorded vitals with a laser scanner and barcoded the information onto a toe tag on the participant's foot.

She wondered where they'd all come from, slowing her gait to take in more detail as she skirted the edge of the crowd.

"That's the last one from Miami," an armed handler said, pointing to a stretcher as came off the makeshift transport.

Caroline snapped her head around to look.

"Dispose of the vehicle," another man said.

She recognized the second voice as Gene Thornton's and noticed that the man looked as if he'd come out on the losing end of a brawl, sporting a bandage across a very black and blue nose.

"Dr. Richards," Thornton said, rapping the side of the RV with his hand, "that completes our agreed upon delivery of twenty-eight participants."

"Outstanding." Richards took a few celebratory puffs on his cigar.

Thornton patted Richards on the shoulder. "Now you have a single seat left at the table."

"Yes. Quite right. I should turn my attention to that matter." Richards crushed the remainder of his cigar under his shoe.

Caroline darted to her right, far away from Thornton as possible, and headed into the CNA building.

ANCRI's neurophysiology lab was on the ground floor. Beneath it was a restricted lower level and Caroline's destination.

The CNA basement housed radioactive isotopes, such as radioactive iodine, cobalt, and cesium used for nuclear medicine. It also housed an infirmary, a state-of-the-art operating room, fMRI and PET scan suites, a pathology-autopsy suite, and an incinerator.

ANCRI incinerated all of its waste, including its participants.

The basement was where she had said goodbye to Amy. She hadn't been down there since.

Caroline badged into the exterior stairwell and headed into what the staff called "the maze" because of its winding hallways and endless series of storage rooms. The area reeked of antiseptics and cleaners. Corridor lights showed white walls and vinyl tiling.

She took a short detour to rifle through a janitor's closet for an aerosol can of one-step floor wax. With the can in hand, she moved to a door marked ANATOMICAL PATHOLOGY.

The wall beside the door displayed four universal notification placards: pathology, biohazard and radioactive hazards, and safety shower. Another sign on the wall read: WARNING: PATHOGENS MAY BE PRESENT. EATING, DRINKING, SMOKING, AP-PLYING COSMETICS, AND HANDLING CONTACT LENSES ARE PROHIBITED IN THIS AREA.

Caroline elbowed the door's wall-mounted operating pad. It slid open with a whoosh. She shook the can, popped the cap, leaned ever-so-slightly into the anteroom, and emptied a third of the can on the lens of the surveillance camera above the door. She pinched her nose closed to avoid the fumes, and stepped inside the ante-room. The door closed behind her. Air pressure equalized and she entered the pathology suite.

Beside the door stood an emergency safety shower with an eye-wash station. She deposited the can of wax in the eyewash's catch basin. Ignoring the signs reminding staff to follow standard operat-ing procedures, she headed into the lab area. It was a world of stain-less steel furnishings: exam tables, sinks, counters and test benches. A trench drain ran down the center of a tiled floor. Translucent sliding glass doors led to adjacent rooms, marked with signs for an autoclave, biospecimen cold storage, simulation lab, radiology and clinical imaging.

At a computer terminal, Caroline keyed in her access code. A wall-mounted LED display came to life, showing digitized scans of a human brain with embedded photograph links. A wireless headset used for hands-free transcription during clinical procedures, such as autopsies, rested next to the keyboard, reminding her to call up the autopsy results first.

The images amazed her. A patient record listed the physiologi-cal features of ANCRI's Beta Participant. MALE, 60 YEARS OF AGE. CAUSE OF DEATH: CHF DUE TO EXTREME BLUNT FORCE TRAUMA THE RESULT OF FOREIGN OBJECT PEN-

ETRATION INTO THE RIGHT VENTRICLE. Caroline knew CHF meant congestive heart failure. Samuel Ford had died from a bullet through the heart. CRANIOTOMY PERFORMED. BRAIN HARVESTED FOR FURTHER STUDY.

A link in correspondence implicated an obscure researcher named Riley Johnson.

She frowned thinking Richards, Levine, and Johnson were part of a larger conspiracy.

Caroline moved from the terminal to an adjacent room, the translucent sliding door to the Biospecimen Cold Storage closing behind her. They had no catalog resource, so she had to search the old-fashioned way—snoop around until she found what was looking for. She opened a bank of stainless steel and glass refrigerated drawers and cabinets.

"Come on, it has to be here somewhere."

To her left, the translucent door to the wash door room slid open.

Startled, she swung around, her pulse quickening, and came face-to-face with a tall, gray-haired man in an immaculate white lab coat.

"Dr. Richards?" she managed.

Stewart Richards stepped through, carrying a lidded glass jar. The container was clear, large enough to fit a basketball. A human brain floated in a semi-clear solution—formaldehyde, to denature proteins and harden it for preservation.

"I presume you're looking for this?" Richards exuded the confidence of a man in control of his surroundings. He placed the glass container on an examination table. "Magnificent specimen, wouldn't you say?"

She stammered. "I was just—" Her mouth fell open as words escaped her. She brought her hands up to her mouth, her eyes glued to the brain in the jar.

Samuel Ford's brain.

The container's label read BETA.

The best way to conduct post-operative forensics on a brain was immediately after cranial removal, when the brain was malleable, like the soft fibrous insides of a ripe tomato. In the newly harvested state, however, brains were susceptible to deformation. They could not be left to settle under their own weight. The reasons to embalm Ford's brain were to keep the specimen for later research, which was unlikely, or display it.

Richards was collecting trophies.

She swallowed hard. "Sir, I wanted to offer my assistance on a postmortem of Beta."

Richards cocked his head. "You had us fooled, Dr. Wang."

Her heart plummeted. "Excuse me?"

Richards smiled grimly. "Dispense with the pretense. We know that you leaked information, contacted people. It's too late to deny that. And now your actions have created a predicament. One that must be addressed."

She doubted he knew everything. How could he? No one knew. She backed toward her only way out, through the autopsy lab.

"Sir, I did everything you and the board asked of me."

"True." Richards put an open palm on the jar and stared at it as if he were reminiscing with an old friend. "But you weren't invested. You hid secrets. Neurological singularity is our destination. The Frontier will disseminate information to the world at large."

Behind her, a translucent door whisked open. Hands latched onto her.

She fought to break free. "Dr. Richards, this is a mistake!"

"Hello, Caroline," said a cocky voice.

She turned to see Noam Levine saunter past her, smug and full of himself.

He slammed a photograph down onto a stainless steel table. A crime scene photo. The security guard named Gross lay on a carpeted floor. He was dead. Perpendicular bruises crossed his Adam's apple. Books littered the floor around him.

"After Thomas Parker's interview, you disappeared. Somehow you managed to pass sensitive materials to people outside the institute. Mr. Gross retraced your steps and gave his life to protect The Frontier."

Caroline mocked him. "That's nonsense. If you are implying I am involved in his death, that's not true."

Levine's eyes narrowed. "Who did you tip off? What did you leave behind?"

She shook her head. "Nothing. Nothing at all."

"You befriended my daughter." Richards stepped toward her, his gray eyes ablaze. "Amy would have never volunteered for Genesis without your influence. Her death, although tragic, was essential. Amy served her purpose. Perhaps you'll get a chance to get reacquainted with her and atone for your sins."

Caroline screamed. "Please—!"

Levine turned to Richards. "You think she's going to tell us?"

Richards smiled. "The Frontier will know all secrets, Caroline."

From behind her, a gloved hand reached around and smothered her nose and mouth with a damp pad. She caught a whiff of a semi-sweet aroma. Her mind shrieked, *Chloroform! Don't breathe!* She clenched her jaw shut and held her breath, hoping to wait out the liquid's natural evaporation.

Richards hefted the brain in the jar up for her to see.

She tried to look away. Restraining hands made that impossible. Her lungs burned as the air trapped inside lost its oxygen content. Her body trembled. The anesthetic began to take effect. Her teeth chattered behind clinched lips. Rigid hands clasped the damp cloth tight to her defiant face.

"The researcher who is useful to me," Richards said, "is the one who boldly embraces our quest, without reservation, applying their mind to solving the impossible, paradoxes not yet discerned." He turned to her. "*Nothing is so well learned as that which is discovered.* Sacrifices, as painful as they feel to us, are required. A price for admission must be paid by the pioneers who champion our cause."

Caroline watched Levine slide in behind her.

A hard fist rammed against her right kidney, making her gasp in pain.

Caroline cringed, knowing the consequences of an inhaled breath.

A cool, unadulterated sweetness filled her nostrils. Her eyes drooped as she took another breath, no longer resisting.

FLAT ON HER BACK, Caroline woke in horror to find a swarm of people in scrubs surrounding her. The peaceful patchwork of colored leaves spanned the sky above. She was back in the courtyard. Voices clamored in different conversations. She tried to move. It was a futile effort; her wrists and ankles were strapped down. A plastic bit in her mouth kept her from crying out. As gloved hands moved across her body, she realized she was naked, her exposed skin tingling in the cool fall air.

The prep team had begun depilation.

"No!" she tried to scream, but only a guttural groan came out. "Listen to me! They're killing people! Don't do this! Please stop! This is madness!"

She retested her limbs, trying to squirm free, but the restraints held. She shot an incredulous glare at those around her. Going about their assigned tasks, none of the robot-like scrubs dared to make eye contact. They were cold-hearted, soulless demons, without compassion, without sympathy. Indifferent to her plight, they processed her like the rest of their victims, filling the quota of participants.

Caroline knew she rounded out the group of thirty test subjects.

Inside her chest her heart raged, yet the helpless violation she experienced sapped her resolve. Her lungs felt constricted, as if she were drowning from the burden of failure. The world no longer had enough oxygen to sustain her life.

Noam Levine's face emerged from the crowd and his admiring eyes took in her bare, exposed figure.

He gave her a crooked smile. "This is a new look for you, Caroline."

She cringed and looked away.

His fingers caressed her bare skin, causing chills to ripple through her.

He waved a syringe in front of her, its black plunger maxed at the 1.0 cc/ml mark.

"Sux-prime," Levine said.

The needle glistened in the daylight. A drop of clear fluid formed at its tip.

He pinched her neck to locate her carotid artery.

"You bastard!" Caroline screamed to no one but herself. Only growls and snarls escaped the bit in her mouth.

Caroline tried to wrench her head away, at least to make his job harder, but the straps held her immobile, including her head. She knew what the delivery of the chemical meant. "Sux-prime" was clinical shorthand, a slang term for a lab-modified derivative of succinylcholine, a neuromuscular blocking agent that targeted select regions of the motor-end plate without producing the adverse side effects of cardiac arrest or respiratory depression to the point of apnea.

Levine wanted her to be aware of the torture she was about to endure.

Witness what it was like to become a participant.

The needle pricked her neck.

No! Caroline closed her eyes, clenched her jaw against the bit as tight as she could, and tried to flail her neck. As the fluid merged into her bloodstream, she could feel a change deep inside. Her heart pounded. Blood coursed through her veins. Her nostrils flared as she commanded her body to fight on.

But the outcome was never in doubt. Medically-induced muscular paralysis.

Levine dropped the discharged syringe into a sharps container. He placed bare fingers over her exposed left breast and felt for a pulse. His lips twitched as he counted heartbeats.

Among all those around Caroline, Levine was the only one to make eye contact with her.

He had hazel-brown eyes, filled with a bright, evil intelligence.

His smirk faded. "Your vacancy afforded me a promotion. Imagine that. I'm second in charge, just as you once were."

His fingers caressed her face, then traced through her long black hair.

She watched him with contempt as the control of her extremities faded. Paralysis. In less than a minute, she knew, most of her voluntary muscular control would be out of reach.

His fingers glided along her naked torso and he seemed to enjoy the moment of vulnerability.

"I'll do my best to make sure your sacrifice will benefit the Frontier. Enjoy your new role, Caroline. I'll be watching you."

Levine grabbed a fistful of her long dark hair, tangling it between his fingers. He tugged at the knotted strands to pull against her scalp, revealing to her what was to come next. He gave a directive nod to a nurse before leaving.

Her tear-filled eyes darted toward the sound of electric shears, their grinding vibration catching her attention. Helplessly, she watched as a nurse in green scrubs leaned across her body to shave off her long, dark hair.

Paralyzed and unable to close her eyes, Caroline did the only thing she could and prayed. *Please, God. Save me.*

24
ALTRUISMS & TERMS OF SERVICES

NSA Safe House, Princeton, New Jersey

PARKER PUSHED HIMSELF AWAY from the dining room table, almost falling out of his chair in the process. He had just watched Becky's abduction on a laptop. The date and time stamp on the video log was thirty minutes after she had left his house. A man had been waiting for her.

The attack was brutal, difficult to watch.

Parker felt a shiver. "You think Becky's still alive?"

Kate's face softened, her eyes revealing concern. "If he wanted her dead, he would have killed her in the apartment. For some reason, he wanted her alive. Colonel Wang thinks Becky was coerced into protecting you, keeping you alive in exchange for selling you out."

He thought of their night of passion. Two years of buildup. He could still smell the scent of Becky's lotion, and feel the softness of her skin. He should have never allowed her to seduce him or their friendship get sexual. Her feelings had been an act, an illusion. She was a secret agent going through the motions in order to complete her mission.

Their relationship had been a mirage from the moment they met.

"You think she was kidnapped to help them with research or hand over my lab equipment as part of a trade?"

"Hard to know. What's so special about your equipment?"

"It's a significant leap in technological innovations," Parker said. "It's a bridge between where we stand today in cognitive understanding and neurological interfaces and where this singularity-driven Frontier exists."

Kate sipped her coffee. "Maybe it's less about your work and more about you."

Parker shook his head, not seeing the larger picture. "If that's the case, why shoot me?"

"Those hitmen were tasked with eliminating Derman and his university accomplice. They didn't expect you to be there. They may have not even known who you were."

She retrieved a photo from one of the folders and handed it to him. "This is speculation on my part, but my guess is that ANCRI is experimenting on human test subjects. Maybe Becky's their next victim."

A chill shot through him as he saw the message AMY RICHARDS RIP on the woman's emaciated chest. He noticed the dot-and-line markings imprinted into her barren scalp. Geometric patterns.

He pointed to the woman's head.

"Those are cranial terminal placements, based on ten-ten, 64-electrode EEG terminal positions. Primitive. There's not enough neurosensory definition with that scheme. Researchers use this matrix to construct rudimentary brain-computer interfaces, BCIs." He thought for a long moment. "ANCRI needs my research to construct a better interface. The electrode-studded skullcap that Becky and I developed at Princeton is not EEG-based. It has far more zip to it. We use multi-thread, fiber optic microchips—sort of like a reverse microchip laser, bonded to a substrate of superconductor sensors to get beyond the skull's impedance and target synaptic energy transfers."

"So, you'll help?" Kate asked.

He paused. "You or them?"

"Becky," she said matter-of-fact.

He chuckled. "You think me gullible? Drumming up sympathy? Appealing to a sense of masculine valor? An NSA agent played me for a fool. I wouldn't expect her employer to treat me differently."

Kate nodded. "Colonel Wang informed me that the NSA will help return your research and push for faculty reinstatement. If you want, you can go back to your life."

Parker's gaze sharpened. "You didn't answer my original question. You or them?"

"A fair question, I guess." She flashed him an agreeable smile. "This sounds selfish. I'm here to look into the disappearance of a U.S. Senator, tasked with investigating a missing person's case and a homicide. Now, we have evidence that a man working on behalf of ANCRI abducted an NSA employee. That's kidnapping and assault. If Becky is alive, and let's pray she is, it's not a stretch to assume she's in grave danger. You've been shot. Two other men have been killed. That's attempted murder and first degree homicide. Then there's the theft of your research. I don't know what federal or state statutes were broken there, but we ought to have something on the books to cover it. And what about Amy Richards, whoever she is? Tortured? Killed? Even if she gave uncoerced consent, her death alone could bust ANCRI wide open on violations in federal law for the protection of human subjects."

He rose and walked to the windows overlooking the backyard.

Kate handed him a warm mug and nudged him with her shoulder.

They stood together in silence and sipped coffees.

"ANCRI is a covert facility," she said. "It's not supposed to exist. But it does. To complicate matters, there is a chance that the FBI and White House may be involved. Both have ties to this Frontier, endorsing its activities, if only implicitly. We need answers, and I need your help to get inside that lab."

"It feels like I'm making a deal with the devil."

Kate glanced at her faint reflection in the window. "You sure know how to insult a girl."

Parker fumbled for a response. "I didn't mean you... even look like... I just meant—"

She laughed. "I understand, doc."

"Call me Tom."

"Tom it is, Dr. Parker."

For a fleeting instance, their gazes locked onto one another.

He felt a shiver return and course through him. "After my interview, Stewart Richards asked, 'What would it take to read an unmapped mind? Decipher a memory from scratch? Carry on a two-way conversation with a total stranger?'"

"Neurological singularity," she said. "That's what this is about?"

He nodded.

"What was your response?"

Parker voice hardened. "How about a bloody miracle."

Kate clinked her mug against his. "Tom, maybe you're that miracle."

25
ARRANGEMENTS

FBI Headquarters, Hoover Building, Washington, DC

IN THE BUREAU'S STRATEGIC Information and Operations Center (SIOC), Stan Baker broke the team's midday huddle and sent the tired-looking agents back to their workstations. Before him, a string of monitors displayed time stamps and maps of the capital offset against a collage of public space security camera stills of the National Mall. Prominently in the center was a photo of an agent. A caption read: FBI SA JACK WRIGHT WANTED FOR OB-STRUCTION OF JUSTICE, EVIDENCE TAMPERING, AND FELONY ASSAULT.

Baker's cell phone buzzed. He checked the number before answering. "Princess, I was thinking of you."

On the other end of the phone, Debra Ford said, "Stan, darling, don't call me Princess. You know I loathe that sobriquet."

Baker laughed. "Yes, Princess. I read the transcript of your interview. You shouldn't have mentioned it to Agents Wright and Morgan, nor your ties to the State Department. Both points are forever part of a federal investigation."

A moment of silence, then, "A mistake on my part."

He checked his watch. "Love, I brief the director and President's Chief of Staff in an hour. But after that my calendar is clear. How about we meet for a round of drinks?"

"Not tonight," Debra Ford replied. "I have a bit of June mail for you."

Now she had his full attention.

The bureau hadn't used the term "June" or "June mail" in years, probably not since the seventies. "June" meant confidential, classified, or sensitive sources; "mail" was any type of transferred information.

Baker stepped away from the agents working at their stations.

He lowered his voice. "I'm listening."

"You owe me a parcel."

Baker frowned. "I am aware of that."

"I know where you can find your agent and my parcel. I'm leaving within the hour. You need to be present." She sighed. "Stan, please, no more delegating. No more cardboard contractors. Handle this business in person."

Baker glanced at Wright's picture on display.

He mulled over her directives, feeling a sudden rush of excitement. Debra had guided a junior senator from Oklahoma to prominence on the national stage; now she was doing the same for him, offering guidance and a political boost as he rose from a run-of-the-mill DC prosecutor to second in command at the FBI. Their on-and-off affair was more for her entertainment than his, but there was no way he was dismissing her mandates.

Debra Ford had never led him astray.

"Understood, love," he said.

Kingston, New Jersey

A DOSE OF VICODIN helped Thomas Parker settle into the passenger's seat of an NSA-provided car as Kate Morgan drove to a quarry northeast of Princeton. The pain in his side lingered, while a double espresso from Small World Coffee fought off the drug's side effects.

Non-locals would hardly suspect that a rock and gravel quarry sat in Princeton's backyard. Kate pulled into the employee parking lot and parked next to Parker's Jeep Grand Cherokee.

"Compliments of Colonel Wang," she said as they got out. She left the NSA car's keys under the driver's seat. "The NSA managed to intercept your car before the Sheriff's Department towed it to their property and evidence impound. A Newark body shop worked all night on repairs. I'm told it should be as good as new. And it has new plates and registration."

Parker studied the front end of his SUV. Good as new, as if nothing had ever happened. Far from the condition he'd left it in after ramming Derman's Audi.

He peered through the driver's side window, seeing Kate on the other side of the car.

"Thomas," she said, "you don't have to help me or the NSA. This can be your out, if you want it. I won't stop you. You can walk away."

He eyed her wearily. "During an Internet search on ANCRI, I stumbled upon a disposable webpage. Just for me. I was at a library computer, as anonymous as anonymous can be on the web. I don't know if it was your NSA pal or others, but someone knew I would be querying ANCRI."

She came around the car. "What did this mystery website say?"

"*Help her or others will die. And be careful who you trust.*" She had helped rescue him from hired killers and stitched him up from a gunshot wound. Kate had saved his life. How could he not trust her? "Are you the *her* I'm supposed to help?"

Kate hesitated. "I'm out of my element here, Thomas. I would like to think so, but honestly, I have no idea who reached out to you, or what they meant by the message."

Severna Park, Maryland

DEBRA FORD DISMISSED HER maid early and walked down to the shore of the Severn River. Inside her estate's boathouse, she retrieved a day bag from a flotation cushion storage locker and set out along the bank of the river, careful to remain out of sight of the security cameras that watched her property. She knew precisely where each camera was located and its field of view. Once she'd cleared them, she cut back into the forest. A black executive Lincoln Town Car waited at the private drive leading to her riverside mansion.

The driver in a black suit opened the car door. "May I take your bag, Mrs. Ford?"

"Not today, Kenneth," she said. "I've got this."

She got in and he closed her door before climbing in behind the wheel.

From the front seat, he said, "I have us on an unregistered excursion to Princeton. Drive time will be approximately five hours. I expect to encounter rush hour traffic the closer we get to Philadelphia. I'll do my best to make up what time I can. Ma'am, you'll find the usual course of refreshments for your enjoyment: chardonnay chilled to sixty degrees and a decanter of brandy at room temperature."

"As always, Kenneth, you take care of my every whim," she said. "But I'll stick to water on this outing."

Washington, DC

THE DC POLICE DEPARTMENT'S Air Support Operations (ASO) hangar was not a destination found on tourists map. FAA aviation restrictions and no-fly zones around the White House and Capitol made the ASO helipad the closest non-threat event pickup and drop spot available.

Baker cleared DCPD security and boarded an idling McDonnell Douglas MD 530F Little Bird. The 500-series Little Bird was a larger version of the light duty tactical rotary aircraft called the Killer Egg. A pilot and copilot from the Tactical Helicopter Unit (THU) a subunit in the FBI's Critical Incident Response Group's Tactical Aviation Unit, sat behind the controls.

"Thanks for the lift!" Baker shouted over the heavy thrum of the rotating blades.

The copilot motioned that they could not hear a word he was saying and pointed to headphones lying in the passenger seat. Baker buckled in, slid the headphones over his ears, and spoke into the microphone that swung down below his chin.

"Thanks for the lift."

"No problem, sir," said the pilot, his voice coming in over the intercom. "Where to?"

"N-K," Baker said of the Newark field office. He twirled his fingers in a circle. "I'm on the clock. So let's get a move on!"

"Roger that," the pilot said, managing the controls as the helicopter lifted off and swung east, then north to straddle the Anacostia River.

Princeton, New Jersey

PARKER STEPPED THROUGH THE front door of his house. Kate trailed a few steps behind. He stopped in shock, taking in the cyclonic ransacking inside.

"You need a maid," she said.

"How can you tell?"

They waded through discarded piles of books, papers, broken chairs, desk drawers. Every room in the house was in a complete shambles.

"What do you think they were looking for?"

"Something they missed at my lab."

They passed the kitchen. The contents of drawers and cabinets cluttered the floor, pots and pans scattered about. His four-seat dining room table only held two objects: an empty I♥NY coffee mug and a drained bottle of Crown Royal, its iconic purple sleeve cast aside.

Another message from the ransack artists.

He hefted up the empty whisky bottle. Bone dry. Not a drop was left.

Parker spun away and led Kate downstairs, into an unfinished basement. The trend of trash and clutter continued, but with a cooler, musty aroma. Incandescent lamps lit what would otherwise be a dungeon. They slipped past toppled-over workbenches and headed to the corner of the basement, behind the home's boiler. He pushed against a water-stained, plywood panel. The false wall broke loose, clicked into a metal channel and slid aside with ease, revealing a small stone-lined wine cellar.

Racks sat empty except for a few bottles of Le Petit Cheval Blanc.

In the cellar's corner stood an antique bank and hotel safe, manufactured by the Cary Safe Company of Buffalo, New York. The name of the safe company was hand-painted in scripted gold leaf, with a date of 1896 and the name of the safe's original owner, Princeton Bank and Trust.

"A previous home owner was a bank manager in the 1930s. It seems his employer upgraded to a larger safe and the manager got the hand-me-down."

Parker spun the numerical dial several times then wrenched the handle. Inside, a pearl-colored face greeted them—the skull cap prototype from his Princeton lab was formed over a mannequin's head. Fiber optic cables and terminal leads swept away from the head to reveal colorful dreadlocks. He lifted it out of the safe and passed it to Kate, then retrieved schematics and two portable hard drives.

She peered at the angelic, ghost-like face in her hands.

"What's this?"

"Our meal ticket." He grabbed a hard-sided carrying case, placed the skull cap, the schematics, and the hard drive inside foam inserts, and closed the case. He gestured to the wine rack. "The bastards drank me dry on whisky. Check the merlot for dinner options. I'll be upstairs packing."

26
OBTAINING THE KEYS

Residence, McLean, Virginia

IN AN UPSCALE RESIDENCE along the southwestern edge of the Potomac, Peter Stanton sat in a trance-like state, absent of expression and strapped to a hard-backed, dining room chair. Dressed in perspiration-soaked sweats, Stanton gazed at a plate-sized happy face leaning against a gym bag on his dining room table. Tied to the back of the chair, a mop stick functioned as a makeshift IV mast. An IV bag hung from the stick's head. A tube traced from the bag to a catheter needle in the back of the man's wrist. Music played softly in the background: *Rondo Brillant in A Major, Opus 56 for Piano and Orchestra*, by Johann Nepomuk Hummel, a compilation from the New York Philharmonic Orchestra.

In an adjacent room, a home office, Randy Wang typed at a computer.

What he was doing was beyond illegal.

However, the end justified the means. He needed the keys to the kingdom.

He tracked down Stanton's credentials on LinkedIn: Principal IT Manager at RMG Global Solutions, a premier engineering and construction firm in Washington, D.C., specializing in federal projects ranging from simple border crossing stations to military installations to state-of-the-art U.S. embassies.

As Stanton returned home from an evening jog along the river, Wang had approached from behind and injected him with a sedative that produced a semi-conscious state of twilight sleep.

The gym bag on the table was Wang's "baker's box," a spy's collection of lethal implements, the kind of instruments governments dared not acknowledge. Tools for the inhumane practice known as enhanced interrogation. The CIA's 1963 KUBARK manual established procedures for counterintelligence interrogation, but the former Soviet Union had dramatically improved upon the coercive techniques with a chemical cocktail code-named SP-117YA. The CIA called this truth serum "the payday drug." Wang took a payday cocktail-filled syringe and injected it into the knob of the IV drip line.

If Wang did his work well, his interviewee, would never know he'd been interrogated. Peter Stanton would awake from his ordeal with no memory, but scared to death of what he could not remember.

"It's randomly generated each morning by the server," Stanton said in response to Wang's question about the encrypted VPN access code that connected child-based peripherals to the parent technology structures. Years earlier, Communist Party-sponsored Beijing University of Technology students had hacked Stanton's company, RMG Global Solutions, searching for government intel. A comprehensive overhaul of RMG's security measures followed the hack, but the damage had been done. The security breach cost RMG its federal contracts and two hundred million dollars in penalties. The company teetered on the brink of bankruptcy until a group called the Phoenix Consortium engaged the company about building a top-secret facility—ANCRI.

"Peter, what is the pass key to the RMG firewall?"

The man hesitated in his drug-induced stupor. "Fire 56245 exclamation exclamation"

"Is the word 'fire' all capitals, lowercase, or mixed characters?"

Stanton blinked slowly before responding. Drool formed at the corner of his mouth. "You ask so many questions... what's your name again?"

"Focus, Peter. Is the word 'fire' in all caps?"

"Capital F, the rest lowercase," the man said.

Wang typed the executive passcode into a dialog box. An Ethernet cable stretched from Peter's computer to Wang's laptop to record keystrokes and access operations. It was less risky to use an employee's corporate VPN access to enter RMG's secured network.

If a person wanted to break into a company, Wang knew, the most important contact was never its president or CEO. The information age had rewritten those rules. Corporate keys resided with many people. Presidents and CEOs led companies and provided vision; financial officers and CFOs managed finances. But the most valuable person was the one who protected its secrets. A company's greatest vulnerability was its IT manager. If you're out to rob a bank, skip armed robbery or snatching the branch manager or a teller; swing for the fences and nab the information technology guy instead. At RMG, that was Peter Stanton.

Stanton held the keys to the kingdom, for both RMG and ANCRI.

"Thank you, Peter," Wang said, seeing the passcode clear the RMG firewall and log on to its network server.

Once in, he ran a scripted algorithm. The breach would never be traceable. It was something Wang had executed numerous times before.

Confidentiality agreements meant that firms like RMG rarely used the client's real name for their most sensitive projects. A simple query of the company's legal servers revealed that RMG's code name for ANCRI was Atlantis. Wang found the Atlantis billing statements and accounting records, revealing that a company called the Phoenix Consortium owned ANCRI. A master service agreement listed the federal agencies using ANCRI's services: DARPA; the CIA; the State Department; and the Defense Medical Research Development Program, an oversight entity under the operational support of the Department of Defense via a congressional initiative called Congressionally Directed Medical Research Programs. The CIA's funding was funneled through its Office of Innovation and Integration.

Billing statements and purchase orders painted a clear picture of the agencies standing in line for a stake in neurological singularity—the Frontier.

An archived server posted ANCRI's data center and computer network passwords, the keys to ANCRI's kingdom.

The electronic fishing expedition took just over an hour. Stanton had succumbed to the sleep effects of the Russian cocktail and passed out forty minutes before Wang finished.

Before logging out, he uploaded a destructive worm called CreeperReaper—CR for short—to bring RMG's servers to a crashing halt. CR was an elegant leviathan Wang had developed in an NSA think tank, its name paying homage to one of the first self-replicating virus programs that infected early generation computer networks in the 1970s. Reaper was the program created to delete Creeper.

Wang's use of CR was cover-your-tracks sabotage.

Stalin called it a scorched earth policy. That worked in the digital world too.

After a few days of being electronically dead-to-the-world, of course, RMG Global Solutions would rebuild its company servers from cloud-based backup systems. But by then, any traces of Peter Stanton's unwitting betrayal would be undetectable.

27
SETTING THE STAGE

FBI Newark Field Office, Newark, New Jersey

ALONG THE PASSAIC RIVER, just east of Rutgers University near an abandoned river dock renamed Minish Park, the FBI helicopter delivering Stan Baker touched down. Dirt churned in the air as the aircraft's rotors slowed. Cupping his eyes, Baker gazed in the direction of the bureau's Newark Field Office.

A black SUV awaited him on the drive sweeping out of Claremont Tower, compliments of the local Special Agent in Charge. He had called ahead to make the necessary arrangements. His demands were simple: unmarked vehicle, no driver, no escort, no questions.

An agent standing beside the vehicle handed over the keys.

"The tank's full, sir," the agent said. "You need directions?"

Baker shook his head. "No."

"Sir, Newark's nuts during rush hour. You'll need to add about forty minutes plus to your drive if you're headed south, or an hour and a half if you're headed into the City."

Baker climbed behind the wheel and started the vehicle. He checked his watch.

He almost smiled. "Thanks for the tip. Tell your SAC I appreciate the ride."

Baker turned onto McCarter Highway and followed the map on his phone. He expected a detailed address, yet the app merely displayed a general location. Princeton. It was just a matter of time before his rendezvous location was forwarded.

Debra Ford always took care of him.

Peretsman Scully Hall, Princeton University, Princeton, New Jersey

KATE HAD PLANNED IT out, but that didn't mean she had to like it.

Wang's directions were rigid.

The handoff would go down in a disassociated manner.

A dead drop seemed overly old-fashioned, completely unnecessary.

She was still an FBI agent who followed the rules. Ford's laptop belonged in the hands of FBI evidence teams, and Jack Wright seemed to be the mechanism to make that happen. If other entities were involved, she couldn't risk blowing her mission by meeting Wright in person.

But that didn't make executing a dead drop easier.

Thomas Parker proved helpful, selecting a broad green space at the university, ringed by sports fields, academic research buildings, the university central plant, ice rinks, a residence hall, and a student-run radio station, WPRB.

The location was perfect.

His faculty badge got them into the Psychology Department, the sister wing to the Princeton Neuroscience Institute (PNI) and into an unoccupied fifth floor corner office.

After hours, they had to place to themselves.

The office offered a premiere vantage point, overlooking soccer fields and the southeast corner of a green space tabbed as Poe and Pardee Fields. As part of its environmentally friendly design, the

PNI-Psychology complex had a twin-skinned, glass curtain exterior that made the structure almost glow at night.

She fired off an anonymous text to Wright's sat phone with time and location.

Ford's laptop, in its soft-sided case, was stuck to the bottom of a park bench outside the PNI building's entrance. Kate had copied its files onto her own bureau-issued laptop as an insurance policy, in case the computer never reached the bureau.

Parker used a portable laser liberated from an aerospace engineering lab to burn out the lamppost next to the bench, leaving the drop point alone in darkness.

Takeout chicken marsala from Teresa's in Princeton paired with a bottle of Parker's merlot took the edge off things. They ate on the floor, like an awkward, first-date picnic.

She avoided any intimate conversations, preferring the relative safety of chitchat.

"The wine's great," Kate said, swishing it around in a paper cup.

"Glad to be of assistance, Agent Morgan."

"Thomas, I don't blame you if you feel manipulated. That was never our—my—intention."

He raised his cup of wine to her. "I understand the situation, even if I don't like it. Still, I find it rather kind of you to come to my rescue and play doctor."

"I was scared to death you were going to die on me."

"Glad that didn't happen." He paused. "I've given some thought as to the research this Advanced Neurological Cybernetic Research Institute might be into."

Kate moved closer to listen.

"Singularity is an intersection," he said, "the moment where two paths cross. A threshold where the mutual function defining two conditions takes on an infinite value. Technological singularity is the moment where artificial intelligence becomes autonomous, self-aware, exhibiting a superintelligence surpassing the finite limitations of human understanding. I presume ANCRI's spin on neurological singularity is similar—the technical achievement of fundamental synaptic mapping, not just of the brain, but the creation of an interactive map of human consciousness. ANCRI wants the ability to interface with the mind, read memories, and perhaps even alter them."

She finished off her merlot. "Sounds radically dangerous. Colonel Wang said, 'For those in power, secrets will cease, become immaterial, because the Frontier will know all secrets.'"

Parker frowned. "Your colonel friend might be right."

Kate got up and gravitated to the windows to start a nervous watch over the bench.

An hour before the handoff.

The wine failed at diminishing a swelling anxiety.

Although she was warming to Parker's presence, she yearned to talk with Jack again and regretted snapping at him before leaving Washington. His words to her were more ominous than ever: "This may be one of those cases where everyone is expendable."

She hoped that wasn't true.

Parker stood beside her and they gazed into the darkness together, the office lights off to reduce any chance of being seen from outside the building.

"You FBI agents do this kind of thing a lot? Stake out benches?"

She smiled thinly. "I've had nothing but firsts this week, including stitching up a bullet wound on a guy. How's the side, doc?"

Parker shrugged. "You think your boss will show?"

Kate nodded. "Jack will be here."

Princeton, New Jersey

IN AN EFFORT TO blend into the crowds milling about Nassau Street, Wright swapped out his tailored suit for university branded sweats pulled off a clearance rack in the school's bookstore. His assault on a federal contractor back in Washington had left him a wanted man. He stuck to black sweats, rather than the U's catch-me-if-you-can bright orange.

He ordered a burger and gin and tonic at Alchemist & Barrister's open bar. The pub seemed packed for a weeknight. A keyboard musician started his set, opening with the modified lyrics to a Billy Joel song: *It's ten o'clock on a Wednesday, the regular crowd shuffles in...*

Wright raised a toast to the piano player. "Thanks for calling me an old man."

Amid a row of strangers, Wright finished off his tonic and gin and thought of Kate. He wondered how she was holding up, whether she thought of him or even missed him. If she'd made headway on the whereabouts of Samuel Ford, or gained access to the secret lab. He felt guilty for misleading her and relegating her to an NSA clandestine mission. In thirty years, his pal had never been wrong about threats to America. ANCRI's Frontier would be a threat.

Once again, Wright had stuck his neck out a little too far.

He hoped playing along with Wang's brand of madness wouldn't end his or Kate's career, or get either of them killed.

On a bar napkin, Wright scribbled out a *in case someone finds me lying face down in a ditch* note, in case the night turned out poorly. But most of all, he wanted to tell Kate that none of it was her fault.

He still loved her, and always would.

The clock on his sat phone pinged, jolting him out of self-pity.

He tucked the bar napkin note into the pocket of his sweats.

Wright paid his tab in cash and headed out for a healthy stroll across campus.

Poe Field, Princeton University, Princeton, New Jersey

BAKER PARKED HIS LOANER SUV in a lot west of the university athletic fields and double-checked the map app on his phone. As he'd expected, Debra Ford forwarded a target beacon—a signal leading him to a specific location on the Princeton campus. Somehow, Debra knew when and where the transfer of Samuel Ford's laptop would occur. He suspected his on-and-off, part-time lover had planted a GPS tracking chip on her ex-husband's laptop while the chump watched the Cowboys-Redskins game with their son.

But knowing the device's exact location did not translate into knowing the time of the exchange. For that part of the equation, she needed an inside source.

The red dot on his phone remained motionless.

He was twenty minutes ahead of schedule.

Baker checked for a full magazine in his FBI-issued Glock, then moved to the shadows under a continuous line of trees and made his way to a spot identified as Poe Field.

28
REDUCTIONS IN FORCE

**Poe and Pardee Fields, Princeton University,
Princeton, New Jersey**

STAN BAKER BREATHED IN the coolness of the night air.

The star-laden sky above made it perfect for killing.

With Glock in hand, Baker prowled the shadows of trees around the twin fields. He kept his gaze up and targeted a knoll of grass as he slipped past structures overlooking soccer fields. Taking advantage of a towering oak, a swath of darkness cloaked his presence, no more than a hundred feet from the drop point.

Baker could not see the laptop, but sensed the prize was there. He thought of nabbing it first, but understood the situation called for patience.

Let events play out.

From the north, a jumble of noise drifted across the grass, a mix of voices and music from the dormitories. It reminded him to silence his phone.

Taking down Wright in possession of stolen evidence would cement the perception that the rogue agent was a threat to national security. Baker sensed this was *his* moment, another step leading him closer to a grander stage—all thanks to his beloved confidante, Debra Ford.

Jack Wright would be an easy kill.

All he had to do was show patience.

THE WALK GAVE WRIGHT time to sharpen his senses. He assumed Wang had cracked the laptop's protective measures to reveal a treasure trove of incriminating information. Surely the files implicated the Deputy Director Baker in a grander conspiracy or even the bureau.

He had committed the campus layout to memory. A bench on the southeast side of an open field. A logical, innocuous location for a dead drop.

Heading south, he bisected the heart of the Princeton campus and passed a ruckus of students engaged in a game of glow-in-the-dark hacky sack, the luminescent footbag passing between contestants as they circled a revolutionary war cannon buried nose-first in the ground.

Inset stone and cobbled paths led him past the dormitories of Wilson College. The cool night air carried scattered conversations and music.

He stopped short of the grassy expanse, taking in the darkness under the majestic tapestry of stars.

A park bench fronted a science building.

His sweats gave him just enough pockets to carry his semi-automatic, sat phone, badge, car keys, and the in-case-someone-finds-me-dead note. He put his hand on his pistol and placed an index finger on its trigger guard.

He saw no movement. Adrenaline quickened his pulse.

Jack stepped onto the spread of grass and closed the distance.

KATE RECHECKED HER WATCH. 10:05 p.m. Parker stood beside her in the darkness.

"There," Parker said, pointing at an outline approaching.

The figure made a beeline to the bench.

Kate squinted. "It's about damn time, Jack."

She keyed Wright's number into her sat phone. Her finger hovered over the green send button. The plan was to ring his phone should trouble appear.

It was the only way to give him any kind of heads up.

WEST OF THE POE field, in the parking lot of the university's chilled water plant, a Lincoln Town Car rolled to a stop under a splash of peach-colored sodium light. Decked out in a black pantsuit, black fanny pack cinched around her waist, and black driving gloves, Debra Ford climbed out of the vehicle. She pulled her hair back into a ponytail and secured it with an elastic band, while studying the parking lot packed with white maintenance vehicles.

She glanced to her driver. "Kenneth, dear, keep the engine running. I won't be long."

With fluid movements, like a cat stalking prey, Debra Ford darted to the edge of an open field.

WRIGHT KNELT AT THE bench and rested his weapon against his shoe. He cocked his head left, then right. The left was clear. To his right, trees cast ominous shadows but he saw no movement. Directly ahead, the intersecting sidewalk cutting between the science building and the soccer fields sloped out of view. Anyone could approach from the south and be on him instantly.

The position was more vulnerable than anticipated.

His pulse accelerated faster. *Grab the damn thing and bug out, Jack!*

A knot in his throat made him feel as if he'd swallowed a desiccant packet.

Beneath the bench, he located the object. Grabbing the case, he broke it loose from its hiding spot.

BAKER TIMED HIS MOVE when the man's attention was drawn to an object beneath the bench. The ambient starlight was not enough to discern an identity, but the figure's outline revealed athletic, masculine features. None other than FBI Special Agent Jack Wright.

Baker stuck to the soft grass to muffle the sound of his footsteps. His Glock was locked dead onto its mark.

KATE AND PARKER WATCHED a man kneel at the bench.

She let out a pent-up sigh. "Hurry up, Jack."

They watched Wright set something down beside his shoe, glance in both directions, and dislodge the laptop bag.

Parker poked her shoulder. His voice was full of alarm. "Kate—"

She spotted a ghost-like form break from a cropping of trees.

It was a man. And he was aiming a gun.

WRIGHT'S MIND ALARMED AS his hearing detected footsteps.

A figure rushed him from the shadows. Instincts told him the assailant was armed. He grabbed his gun and leapt to his feet.

Using the laptop case as a shield, Wright swung his semi-automatic in the direction of the oncoming threat.

A shot blasted with an orange muzzle flash, sparking in the blanket of darkness.

Before Wright could squeeze off a round, he felt the violent impact of a bullet strike his right shoulder, knocking him off balance and sending him down to a knee. Pain tore through his body. The Glock slipped from his grip and clattered to the sidewalk. He dropped the laptop and reached for his gun with his left hand just as a shoe kicked it out of reach.

A short, stocky man stood above him.

Deputy Director Stan Baker held a pistol on him, picked up the laptop bag, and stepped out of reach.

"You removed key evidence from an investigation, Jack," Baker said, his voice cold, calculating. "Good thing I came to stop you, before you destroyed it."

The combination of pain and adrenaline was nauseating, and the bullet to his shoulder left Wright's shooting arm limp.

"Is that your story?" Wright asked. "What dirt did Ford have on you, Baker? When his laptop disappeared from evidence, you got real nervous, didn't you?"

Baker cracked a grin, barely visible in the night. "Jack, you were allowed to walk out with it. See, what the bureau needed was for your NSA associate to get past the machine's encryption. It was a setup from the start. We needed to secure his documents first."

Wright's breathing grew more difficult. "You bastard. You sent your chump Thornton to kill me. His close encounter with a fire extinguisher foiled your plan? Now what? You here to finish what your minion couldn't?"

Baker laughed. "True enough. Thornton failed. But this Jack— oh, this—I'm afraid has worked out much better for me."

Wright feigned a stagger and inched closer to his weapon on the ground.

"Neurological research? What does this secret tech give the mighty Stan Baker?"

"Store credit," Baker admitted. "Enough to propel me to Director of the FBI."

The excruciating pain in Wright's shoulder sharpened. He blinked his eyes repeatedly to keep his vision clear. His pistol was within arm's reach. All he needed was a few more seconds.

"You plan to eliminate the director next?" Wright asked.

Baker steadied the aim of his weapon. "Something along those lines."

"No!" Kate screamed.

She watched in horror as Wright spotted his attacker too late. A muzzle flash erupted from the darkness. They heard the discharge from inside the office.

Wright dropped to a knee and lost hold of his weapon.

Kate felt trapped between action and inaction, disassociation and engagement.

Parker's jaw dropped. "That guy just shot him."

Kate hit the preset send button on her sat phone to dial Wright's matching sat phone.

"Dr. Parker," she said handing him her phone, "if someone answers, keep 'em talking. Make something up. Anything. I'm going after Jack. And, doc, under no circumstances are you to leave this building!"

Kate unholstered her Glock and sprinted into the fifth floor hallway.

Wright took a coughing breath, readying himself to leap for his pistol.

The sat phone inside his pocket rang to life, its chime disrupting the conversation with Baker.

"Hello, fellas," a woman's voice announced, from out of nowhere.

The two men turned to find Debra Ford's gloved hand holding Wright's Glock. Armed, she moved with a smooth ease and aimed the pistol chest-high at Wright.

Baker grinned. "Princess, glad you joined us."

Wright slumped. "You're involved in this? Never saw that coming."

His satellite phone continued to ring. He started to answer it.

Baker raised the level of his aim to Jack's head. "Don't."

Debra Ford smiled. "Stan, dear, let's see what this good-looking agent of yours carries in his pockets—besides balls." She smooched Wright and jabbed his own pistol into his chest. She rummaged through his pockets, emptying their contents out onto the ground. She gave him an extra squeeze down low for good measure. Retrieving the last object, his phone, she glanced at the call ID number and clicked off the device.

Wright shook his head in disbelief. "You're the dipsomaniac ex-wife?"

"Oh, figure that out all on your own, did ya?" She chuckled. "I told you when we met, Special Agent Wright, the bureau seems to be fishing in a pretty shallow talent pool."

Wright pushed aside the questions forming in his mind and focused on surviving the next several minutes.

Still aiming at Wright, Debra Ford stepped to Baker and gave him a passionate kiss. "Stan, darling, you're so ruthless when you want to be."

Baker flashed a smile. "Princess, I have you to thank for bringing it out in me."

She kissed him again and slid Wright's pistol up between them. A blast thundered.

Baker's eyes widened with shock as the bullet tore through his chest, ripping his heart apart. His shoulders slumped, and he collapsed to the ground.

Stunned, Wright pushed forward to reach for Baker's gun.

With the swiftness of a cat, Debra Ford spun around and trained the gun on him.

"I told him not to call me Princess," she said.

She snatched up Baker's pistol, his cell phone, and the laptop briefcase. She tossed Wright's weapon into the grass.

He grimaced in pain. "You orchestrated this entire thing? Had your ex-husband abducted to protect technology?"

"Sam was in over his head," she snapped. "His foolish crusade left powerful people in Washington few options but recourse and removal." Her eyes narrowed. "I didn't mind putting down his college whore. That was payback for his cheating. Actually, I enjoyed torturing them both. I would've blown Sam's balls off, if I didn't have to deliver him to a third party."

Wright felt weak. "A third party as in the State Department?"

"State, the White House, your FBI." She laughed coldly and glanced down at Baker's lifeless body. "I just served as the broker who brought the interested parties together."

To the west, a woman bolted out of a nearby building. "Freeze! FBI!"

Wright spotted Kate sprinting toward them.

Debra Ford spun him around to face her, using him as a human shield. A smile curled at the corner of her mouth as she squeezed off two rounds.

The close quarter muzzle flashes accompanied crushing impacts to his chest. The air inside his lungs evaporated and he crumpled to the ground. His head struck the sidewalk, locking his stunned gaze in a single direction. Darkness clouded over his vision, and the last thing Wright saw was Debra Ford sprinting away with the laptop.

DEBRA FORD CUT ACROSS the grass as shots sped past her, the woman sending a barrage of gunfire in her direction.

Taking refuge behind a tree, Debra steadied her aim and returned fire.

Handguns were ineffective past a certain range, often requiring sheer luck to hit anything. Her shots got damn close, though, sending the woman diving to the ground. She had no clear view of her pursuer's face, but assumed it was none other than Wright's interviewing partner, Special Agent Kate Morgan.

The thought that Morgan needed a new partner made her smile.

Between them, Wright and his boss lay dead.

Debra Ford fired another short burst before using the trees as cover and darting back to her chauffeured sedan.

—∤—

IN THE OPEN, KATE had no refuge. The young oaks in front of the PNI-Peretsman Scully Building offered little protection against gunfire. The night sky made it easy to locate the shots coming from the trees above the soccer fields.

She returned fire, hoping to get lucky.

More flashes led to bullets screaming at her, so close Kate felt as if she could touch lead as it streaked past. She dove to the ground, her gaze drawn to the two bodies. One of them, she knew, was Jack's.

Kate's mind desperately tried to catch up.

She remembered the man who shot Jack. Clearly he wanted the laptop. But in the minute it took to get out of the building, a woman thrust herself into the mix. The female assassin had gunned down Jack and his attacker, and claimed the prize.

Kate spotted distant lights in the direction the shooter had fled.

The gunfire ceased.

Kate crept toward Jack, who lay face down on the ground.

She felt his carotid artery for a pulse. Nothing.

Rolling him over made the situation clear. Even in the starlight, she could see the wet, rippled depressions in his chest. Precision shots to the heart.

Her eyes welled with tears.

"Jack," she screamed, "don't do this to me!"

Blood painted her hands as she pounded his chest in anger, fear, and grief.

Across the fields, random lights blinked on in the distant dormitories. It took her a moment to tune into the broader situation. The campus was coming to life.

Parker clambered up beside her. "Can we do anything for them?"

"Damn it, doc, I told you to stay put!"

Parker ignored her and checked Wright for a pulse.

Their eyes met, confirming what she already knew.

Kate brought a shaking hand up to her mouth as tears flowed. For the first time, she cast a blurry glance at the other motionless man. Jack's original assailant. Even in the dim light, she recognized him: FBI Deputy Director Stan Baker.

She felt too many things: the loss of a friend and lover, a torn sense of duty . . . and a desire for revenge.

Over the knot in her throat, she forced herself to study the placements of Jack's chest wounds: one to his right shoulder and two more over his heart, inches apart. Precision shots to destroy the organ beyond repair. He no longer had the muscle to generate a pulse.

Jack was dead. She couldn't save him, but she could get his murderer.

Kate broke into a sprint, ignoring the protection of the trees and soccer shelters, racing straight down the asphalt sidewalk in the direction of Jack's killer.

DEBRA FORD SLOWED TO a jog. Kenneth her driver waited dutifully beside the Town Car. Without a word, he gestured to the vehicle.

She needed no explanation.

He opened the passenger's door.

She handed the driver Baker's pistol. "Keep an eye out."

Tossing the laptop case on the backseat, she got in and closed the door. "Is my ex-husband dead?"

She slowed her breathing and uncapped a bottle of water.

The man in the front seat watched her via the rear-view mirror.

She noticed his bandaged nose immediately. Actually, it was hard to miss.

"Shot him myself, Princess," Gene Thornton said. "His body was incinerated. Unfortunately, your children won't be able to schedule a viewing. Hope that isn't an inconvenience."

Debra Ford took a swig of water. "Gene, you look like crap. Do I know the guy who mauled you?"

"Princess, you just did me a favor and shot him."

She slid her dark hair out of a ponytail and fluffed it out. "The men in my life better stop calling me Princess, or I'll wipe the earth clean of them."

Thornton laughed. "You have my package?"

She shoved the laptop case toward him. "Gene, none of this better come back to me."

He unzipped the bag to verify its contents. FBI evidence labels plastered a laptop.

"Debra, your resourcefulness never ceases to amaze me."

She unzipped her fanny pack and slid out a two-inch dagger, while keeping her gaze on Thornton's reflection in the mirror. "I hear someone beat you to Parker's lab. That's unfortunate. And very costly." She pursed her lips and blew him a kiss. "You're not bi, are you?"

Thornton faced her with a mischievous flicker. "I was about to ask you the same thing, Princess. I feel double-crossed."

"As do I." She leaned forward, mere inches behind the front seat. Her hand with the dagger rode up the back of the seat, ready to strike. "Parker's research equipment carries a market value of thirty million. I had a buyer in France offer double its value."

He sighed. "Well, Debra, that's capital we're both cheated out of."

She shook her head. "You think this Frontier is worth it?"

Thornton nodded. "I've stocked the institute with enough guinea pigs to make a real go of things. Their initiatives are promising. And for the two of us, the payoff will be to die for."

KATE CLEARED THE TREES at the western edge of Poe Field and spotted a man in a suit standing beside a black car. He held a gun and scanned his surroundings.

She leaned against a service van and took aim. "FBI! Drop your weapon!"

The man pointed his pistol in her direction.

Kate squeezed the trigger three times in rapid succession. A round blasted out the rear windshield of the car, another hit the truck, and the third blew a hole in the man's chest.

The man in the suit thumped to the pavement.

IN THE BACKSEAT OF the Town Car, Debra heard the muffled shout of a woman's voice. She had barely turned head when she felt the spray of glass hit her face and heard the sound of gunfire. Another round pounded the trunk.

"Damn, that woman is persistent!" she barked, dropping her dagger and reaching into her fanny pack for a compact 9mm pistol, a Ruger LC9. She kicked open the passenger's door and left the vehicle.

On the asphalt, Kenneth lay dead.

Debra Ford leveled her weapon and fired consecutive bursts. Her smaller pistol carried seven in the magazine and one chambered round, so she made shots count.

The woman ducked for refuge behind a white van.

Thornton nudged up beside her with a semi-automatic of his own.

"I'll keep her pinned down," Debra Ford said. "Load Kenneth in the backseat. We're not leaving without him."

Thornton feigned annoyance and manhandled the dead chauffeur into the car.

She fired two more shots. "Get in, Gene! I'm driving!"

Thornton rolled the dead man into the backseat, aimed his pistol through the fractured spider web of a hole in the rear window, and pulled the trigger.

Debra Ford slipped behind the wheel, fired up the engine, and slammed the gearshift into reverse. Wheels screeched against asphalt. Smoke churned up from the tires. The Town Car lurched backwards. More bullets contacted the trunk. Debra Ford wrenched the steering wheel hard and floored the gas pedal, and the car rocketed out of the parking lot.

In the distance, new sounds emerged: sirens.

29
THE AFTERMATH OF
BROKEN ASSOCIATIONS

**Poe and Pardee Fields, Ice Rink Parking Lot,
Princeton University, Princeton, New Jersey**

WITH RINGING EARS AND a tear-streaked face, Kate slid out
from behind a white maintenance van with her Glock seeking a
target. She watched in utter dejection as an executive-style sedan
sped away, despite a shattered rear window. A man in the back seat
fired at her, forcing Kate to duck for cover again.

Bullets peppered the side of the van that shielded her.

Taillights faded into the darkness.

She was on foot with no way to continue pursuit. Without a
target, she lowered her weapon.

Somewhere in the distance, the sound of sirens grew louder.

Adrenaline still surged through her veins. Her chest heaved,
catching up on needed oxygen. Kate blinked in disbelief, and for
the first time she felt the coolness of the night air paint her cheeks.

Jack was dead, gunned down by a female assassin.

The senator's laptop was gone.

Randy Wang's voice broke through her subconscious—*Thomas
Parker is the mission.*

In the chaos, she had abandoned him, and Jack.

Kate holstered her semi-automatic and broke into a run.

As she cleared trees, she noticed the emerging radiance from bedroom windows in the dormitories. More lights came on. Faces appeared. Outside, students came to the edge of the grass to check out the scene.

Not believing she could, she ran faster as cool air stung her face. The night sky was darker than remembered, its stars barely visible to her now. The open grass seemed like an endless void, until her feet found the evenness of an asphalt sidewalk.

Ahead, Parker knelt beside a body. Another form lay ten feet away from the first.

When she got to him, his face was a troubled mask. Nervously, he tucked something into his pocket.

"They're dead," Parker said, his hands wet from blood. "I tried… compressions."

Out of breath, Kate's lips trembled and she fought back more tears. "I know."

She turned and dried her eyes. Across the field, in the direction she had just come, flashing red and blue lights from police cars appeared, as did the roaming beams of handheld flashlights.

"Thomas," Kate said, sniffling, "if we stay, authorities will ask questions that I don't have the answers to. I can't believe I'm saying this, it's everything I don't stand for, but you and I must leave. Now."

"What do you mean?" Parker asked.

She reached down and hauled Parker to his feet. "Jack said this may be 'one of those cases where everyone is expendable.'" She pointed. "That man is the Deputy Director of the FBI. Our second-in-command came here to kill Jack. He wanted the laptop. Then that woman shows up. I don't know who she is or what's going on, but we can't stay to find out."

Kate pointed to a sidewalk that sloped out of view. "Get going, doc."

Parker shook his head in confusion, then turned and ran.

She glanced at Wright's lifeless body.

Kneeling, she placed her fingers against his lips. While he carried the wounds, she felt like her heart had been ripped from her chest. She let the tears flow. No sense holding back.

"I'll always love you, Jack."

Flashlight beams drew closer.

Kate rose and followed Parker into the darkness.

Princeton, New Jersey

SOUTHEAST OF THE UNIVERSITY, just before the bridge over Carnegie Lake, Debra Ford pulled off the road and turned off the Town Car's headlights. She spun the wheel and faced the vehicle toward the water. She lowered its windows three inches, left the engine running, and got out.

"Is it deep enough?" Debra Ford asked.

"Not really. It's a shallow reservoir." Thornton wrestled the dead driver out of the back seat and loaded him into the driver's seat. "Average depth of nine feet at thirty five feet out. Parallel to the bridge it's twenty feet deep. Aim there. At about six a.m., the water's full of rowers. Oh, I hear the Princeton men are favored for the Compton Cup against Harvard."

Their heads snapped sideways as a crackling band of color blazed through the night. A cop car with lights flashing raced along Harrison Street on its way to the university.

Debra Ford ducked into the backseat.

Thornton laughed. "Princess, you looking for this?"

He held up a dagger, its stainless steel blade glistening in the night air.

She reappeared with the laptop case and a day bag.

Her eyes narrowed. "Don't call me Princess."

"As you wish, darling."

Debra Ford shoved the laptop and her day bag into his chest, then twisted the dagger from his grip. His calculating eyes studied her, anticipating her move.

"Relax, Gene, I'm not going to carve your heart out. Not just yet." She flashed a flirtatious smile. Moving to the car, she leaned across the dead chauffeur, half in/half out of the car, and used the dagger to auger a hole in the floor mat. She looped a water-soluble wristband through the new hole and hooked the other end to the gas pedal. The car's engine screamed and she slapped the gearshift into drive. The vehicle lurched forward, speeding down a shallow embankment. Holding open the car door, she somersaulted onto a patch of grass just as the car plunged into the lake. Momentum carried it across the water's dark surface. The vehicle's engine roared even louder without resistance against its wheels. It drifted parallel to the bridge. About a third of the way out, its engine finally choked in the water. The car's nose dipped under the weight of its engine. The waterline swallowed the hood and lapped the edges of the car windows.

Debra Ford returned the dagger to her fanny pack and walked back to Thornton.

He watched her cautiously. "I guess this is where we say goodbye."

They locked eyes, untrusting. Two coldblooded killers, occasional lovers parting ways.

"Maybe I'll see you on a beach sometime." She snatched her day bag from him, then handed him a slip of paper with an address on it. "Gene, I need you to do me a favor."

Thornton laughed coldly. "Really?"

She fluffed out her hair. "The GPS dot on Sam's laptop located a house in Princeton. With Jack Wright dead, his partner will likely return there. And make no mistake, the NSA and FBI both pose a threat to us. Eliminate everyone. Do it tonight."

His gaze sharpened. "Darling, why exactly am I taking on this errand for you?"

"Our agreement was for you to deliver Thomas Parker's lab. Your failure cost me. A lot." She slung her day bag over her shoulder. "Don't forget, I delivered my ex, all wrapped in a pretty pink bow. Be a sweetheart, Gene, and pay your debts."

Thornton sighed. "Then we're even, Debra."

"Deal." In a sultry French accent, Debra Ford said, "Au revoir, mon amour. Jusqu'à ce que nos cœurs se rencontrent à nouveau." *Goodbye, my love. Until our hearts meet again.* She blew him a kiss and trotted off down Harrison Street, toward Route 1.

Debra Ford, the nighttime jogger, disappeared into the darkness.

30
TAKING STOCK

Princeton, New Jersey

KATE FELT AS IF part of her had died. And alcohol only dulled the shock.

Occupying a living room couch, she watched the front door, waiting for would-be intruders to storm the apartment. Her bureau-issued Glock with a full magazine rested in her lap. Wang's warning haunted her: *If the transfer goes south, do not come back to this safe house.* Parker offered his place, but whoever had turned it over could return. Since non-red-light, non-no-tell motels required credit cards, those destinations were eliminated as hide outs. Rebecca Ward's NSA-hosted apartment became the next logical choice.

No reason to suspect anyone to return.

Knowing the apartment had been under surveillance, her first order of business was to remove the cameras and store them in the freezer—go ahead, NSA, *watch the inside of a frozen box if you must.*

Parker insisted on picking up bottles of Apothic on the drive from the university. The blended red warmed her, but couldn't thaw the ice in her soul. The tears in her bloodshot eyes had dried, and fatigue pulled at the vulnerable thread binding her together. One firm yank, and she feared she'd come emotionally unraveled for good.

Thomas Parker is the mission.

The directive rang hollow, the line between duty and purpose blurred.

She'd failed on many fronts. Her incompetent handling of the situation got Jack murdered. His death was all on her.

And Ford's laptop was in the possession of an unknown killer, rather than back at the bureau where it belonged, where investigators could data mine its files.

Questions poked through her alcohol-fed stupor.

What was Baker's role in the madness? Who tipped him off? Why did the deputy director shoot Jack, who never stood a chance? Then there was the femme fatale who gunned both men down. How was she involved?

And even if Baker was corrupt, he still deserved to be brought to justice.

His death was on her, too.

Kate wrenched her eyes closed and tried to recall the woman's features and the man at the car with her. She had shot another, perhaps a driver. The sedan was clear enough. Black, the type used to usher executives around, with a Washington DC license plate mounted on its trunk. While the features of the assailants were indistinguishable, something about them seemed familiar.

Perhaps that was mere hopefulness and the alcohol doing the thinking.

Kate gulped the rest of her wine and stared at the bottom of an empty glass.

Nothing added up.

Slogging into Becky's kitchen, she refilled her glass and set her pistol on the counter.

Firing up her bureau-issued laptop, she scanned the files copied over from Ford's machine. Smart insurance, in hindsight, even if her version of the files wouldn't be admissible in court.

Email exchanges linked the White House National Security Advisor and Deputy Director Stan Baker. The White House's view of neurological singularity and all associated technologies, public and private, was that it posed a grave threat to the United States of

America. DARPA lobbied for competing technologies to be confiscated. Overnight, ANCRI became the sole research lab authorized to bring the sentinel achievement to fruition. The Frontier grew into the modern equivalent of putting an astronaut on the moon. Deputy Director Baker declared that the radical technology would usher in an evolution in fighting crime.

A shiver rippled through her, causing her skin to tingle.

Kate remembered what Parker said he'd been asked: "What would it take to read a human mind?"

That was it. The government wanted the technology to read minds—interrogate people.

The Supreme Court would strike that down as unconstitutional, an invasion of privacy. But neurological singularity would change law enforcement and intelligence gathering forever. Especially with enemy combatants, since they weren't U.S. citizens.

That made sense. The Frontier was a radical technology. One worth killing for.

Kate snatched up her semi-automatic and staggered to the back couch. Slumping against a pillow, the glow of a nearby table lamp faded in and out of view.

She had to learn everything she could about this magical Frontier, and bring the killers, whoever they might be, to justice.

And Thomas Parker was her way inside ANCRI—for vindication—for Jack.

In Becky's bedroom, stretched out across her bed, Parker stared at the textured ceiling. On the nightstand, his wine glass sat empty. The bullet hole in his side ached less, thanks to five milligrams of Vicodin followed by a wine chaser. Strangers had hijacked his world, and the peculiarity of his plight gnawed at him.

Becky's pillows still carried the scent of the lotion she wore.

He thought of the night spent with her.

How odd. He was lying in her bed, without her, thinking about her.

Assaulted, taken hostage, maybe experimented on? What was she going through?

She helped him transform nascent ideas into reality. Losing his teaching gig and research and getting shot felt trivial now.

From his pocket, he retrieved a blood-stained, handwritten note scrawled on an Alchemist & Barrister bar napkin. He'd found it beside the dead the FBI agent.

KATE, NO MATTER HOW MANY TIMES I SAID I WAS SORRY, IT WAS NOT ENOUGH. YOU DESERVED BET-TER. IF YOU'RE READING THIS, THINGS DIDN'T GO WELL TONIGHT. NOTHING IS YOUR FAULT. NOTHING. WANG'S RIGHT, THE FRONTIER IS WORTH KILLING FOR. USE PARKER. SAVE THE 28 IF YOU CAN. LOVE, ALWAYS. JACK

Her FBI counterpart penned the intimate note.

After the shootout, he wanted to give it to Kate, and wasn't sure why he withheld it from her. Perhaps because it named him like a dull tool—in case of emergency, break glass and use Thomas Parker, MD. Perhaps it was simple jealousy. They'd been involved, lovers. Wright had hurt Kate somehow. If the handoff failed, the schmuck didn't want Kate to harbor guilt over his death.

ANCRI's Frontier: an advanced technology worth killing to protect.

Incomprehensible for the modern era.

The U.S. government's track record on sponsored human ex-perimentation and its ethical limits had never been stellar: infect-ing people with cancer cells, giving black men syphilis, exposing prisoners to malaria and yellow fever, whooping cough aeration, transorbital lobotomies, radiation exposure, mustard gas poison-ing, Agent Orange, electric shock treatments, and LSD and ELF and mind control. The list of atrocities was long.

No government could be trusted with mind control.

It was crystal clear that authorities considered neurological singularity a secure-at-all-costs prize, where human sacrifice was an inconsequential expense.

And what did Wright mean by SAVE THE 28?

ANCRI had Becky. Was she one of the 28?

Hell if he knew.

He wondered if Kate knew.

One thing was certain. He was no tool for a secret lab, the government, or the FBI.

He was going to ANCRI not just to save Becky, but destroy their research.

Nothing the FBI nor NSA did could deter him from that purpose.

31
CLOSING OUT BUSINESS

Lewis-Sigler Institute for Integrative Genomics and Carl Icahn Lab Building, Princeton University, Princeton, New Jersey

INSIDE A DARKENED SECOND floor conference room overlooking Pardee Field, a kaleidoscope of illumination strobed through windows with pulsing colors as Randy Wang targeted an open door with his semi-automatic.

In the hallway outside, a figure appeared.

"That's far enough," Wang said. "Set your firearm on the floor."

Gene Thornton stepped forward, hands where they could be seen. The fractured radiance beaming in from the windows lit him up. He produced a Glock and set it on the floor. In his free hand, he carried a soft-sided briefcase.

"Kick the gun away."

Thornton surveyed the room, stopping at a camera aimed out the windows. In front of the glass, a telescopic, low light, high definition digital video camera synched to a parabolic microphone and targeted the fields below. The fatal dead drop had been recorded.

"I like what Jack Wright did to your face." Wang's gaze narrowed. "You alone?"

Thornton nodded. "This was a dangerous gambit, just to clear the name of a dead friend."

He cautiously appraised the hired contractor. "It was warranted."

A ruthless killer, Thornton was a man not to be trusted.

Wang waved his weapon at what the man held. "Place it on the table."

Thornton shook his head. "Not so fast. Thirty million was wired to the Bank of Canada in the Grand Caymans. Phillip Derman won't need those funds in his present condition."

Wang considered the statement. "You underestimate your leverage. Samuel Ford's laptop isn't worth fifty cents to me. I have what's on it. I suspect the FBI does as well. And the bottom line remains: you failed to deliver Thomas Parker's equipment as negotiated."

"How could I? You grabbed it first."

Wang chuckled. "Your facts are wrong. Debra Ford just murdered the man who did. Face it, she was never going to split Stan Baker's finder's fee with you. Baker was eliminated so she could claim the prize for herself."

Thornton stepped closer. "Is that so?"

Wang shrugged. "Phillip Derman promised Rebecca Ward a share of the thirty million, but he sold out to Debra Ford. Everyone involved got cheated. Baker thought Becky was his ace in the hole. She just wanted the easy money. Speaking of my operative, is she... dead?"

Thornton frowned. "You kill my men?"

Wang's eyes twinkled in the sparkling lights. "A couple that I recall. Self-defense."

Thornton seethed. "Your interference will cost you one field operative, or trade her for thirty million."

Wang nearly smiled. "For that price, keep her. Do what you will with her."

Paying a thirty million ransom was hardly a concern. The money was neither his nor the NSA's, having originated from a 770 straw man account under the FBI's Office of Partner Engagement.

He produced a credit card with an embedded USB flash drive and set it on the table. The card bore the logo of the Bank of Canada.

Thornton focused on the card. "What do you want?"

"Manea," Wang said, his eyes sharp, focused. It was INTER-POL's nickname for Debra Ford, a former U.S. State Department intelligence agent: Manea, Roman goddess of the dead. Her nickname came after she assassinated an Italian diplomat during an investigation over €500 million stolen Eurozone funds from a humanitarian aid account. She singlehandedly tracked the stolen funds to Sberbank in Moscow, and brutally tortured four Central Bank of Russia officials until the full funds were restored to the European Central Bank, minus a ten percent commission for herself. After four Russian bankers had died from excessive interrogations, Moscow labeled her the Silent Raven. Their 100 million-ruble bounty was still available for collection. "Where do I find Debra Ford?"

Thornton frowned. "Can't help you, Colonel."

"Not the answer I want to hear." Wang let his statement hang in the air. "Thornton, you're no more loyal to Debra Ford than I was to Jack Wright; than she was to Stan Baker; than I am to my operative. The exchange is simple. I want Manea. She'll lead me to Parker's lab equipment. Thirty million. Not negotiable."

Thornton did the math: a one for thirty million trade. His eyes remained on the plastic card. "All right. Here's what I know. Her driver was killed in the shootout. Their car was ditched in Carnegie Lake. Near the bridge. She's traveling light. Tonight she'll hustle some chump at a bar and steal his wheels. Debra loves Christmas in Barbados, but will likely visit the French Riviera."

Wang slid the card across the table. "Plug it in to any networked device."

Thornton set the laptop case on the table and unzipped it to reveal the evidence-marked computer.

Wang motioned to the door with his pistol. "Leave your hardware. You won't need it again tonight. And Thornton—this concludes our business. Do yourself a favor. Spend some of the money and get your nose fixed."

The man snatched up his newly acquired money card and backed tracked out the door.

Thornton darted down the nearest stairwell. He could have killed the NSA's CYBERCOM liaison. It would've been easy. The sacrificed pistol was a decoy, one he'd acquired from Debra Ford. Nestled in the small of his back was his own weapon, within quick reach if needed.

The trade went better than expected, especially since he held no leverage.

Almost too easily, in fact.

Best of all, he didn't have to split thirty million with anyone: not with Debra Ford, the Phoenix Consortium, Phillip Derman, or the inexperienced, in-over-her-head NSA operative Rebecca Ward.

Normally he wouldn't have shared information. Not his style. But thirty million dollars? No doubt, Debra would've done the same. They thrived in a killer's game where money ruled. Manea, the Silent Raven was smart, resourceful, and lethal. A twisted soulmate in the lonely business of espionage and murder for hire.

The NSA colonel took the bait. Debra was careful with her tradecraft. No one knew her next move, except her. While she adored the warmth of the Caribbean, fond of Paynes Bay in Barbados, she'd make her way to an international airport and take a non-stop across the Atlantic. Since her goodbye was in French, smart money meant Marseille or Lyon, where she'd avoid a broader exposure of Paris or the French Riviera.

The NSA colonel was as naïve as his field operative.

Authorities would waste days, months searching for Manea.

Outside, Thornton blended into the growing mass of onlookers. His eyes worked the chaotic crowd: cops, firemen, and students in all manners of dress.

Sirens raged in the distance, which would be true for the rest of the night.

Thirty million. An easy payday but it did not compensate him for the loss of his men.

That was a score still to be settled. A brief stop at a house in Princeton would make reparations and check off the favor he owed Debra Ford at the same time.

RANDY WANG LOWERED HIS weapon and grinned with satisfaction. He wanted his foe to feel that he'd gotten the better deal and cared less who ended up the beneficiary of the FBI slush funds. He reached below the conference table, dislodged a digital recorder, and clicked it off. He synced it to a satellite phone and downloaded the audio file to a preprogrammed email address.

He hit SEND.

Minutes before Thornton's arrival, Wang emailed partial video clips from the camera overlooking the dead drop to the same account.

The recipient was the White House National Security Advisor, Gordon Abbott.

Wang's grin broadened.

This will grab someone's attention.

THURSDAY, OCTOBER 8th

Neuroscientists are novices at deception.
Raymond Teller

32
PERILOUS CESSATIONS

NSA Safe House, Princeton, New Jersey

MIDNIGHT. THORNTON PARKED HIS car two blocks from the address Debra Ford provided. He appraised the two-story, century-old Victorian. A quick count of windows offered a probable layout: four upstairs bedrooms, a living room, kitchen and a bedroom or den on the first level. Likely had a basement. He grabbed a small tool bag and made his way to the rear of the house.

A detached garage stood away from the house in a corner of the backyard.

No lights were on inside.

Trees formed an unbroken canopy over a backyard. Ambient light was minimal. He slid on night vision goggles for a better view, and tugged on a pair of tombstone-like cellar doors. Locked from the inside. He turned and saw double-hung windows. Stripping away the caulk to remove a pane of glass would be easy, but the task would generate unwanted noise.

The back door was the logical point of entry.

From his tool bag, he retrieved a 13-piece lock pick set. He slid the L-shaped torsion wrench into the lock's bottom plug, and the rake pick above the wrench. Moving the rake in a methodical in-and-out manner, he excited the lock's pins, bouncing them up and down along the sheer line, until the contours of the pins came close to its mated key.

It was a routinely practiced drill.

Twenty seconds later, the lock turned and its bolt retracted.

He retrieved a semi-automatic and threaded a silencer on its end.

He moved into the dark house, his gun leading the way. Oak floors creaked under the burden of each step. He rebalanced his weight and walked more on his toes. Through the goggles, he scanned for alarm systems and motion detectors. The internal landscape had nothing to worry about. Manila folders covered a dining room table. He'd collect those on his way out. He swept through rooms and passed stairs. A razor and can of Barbasol lay on an unmade bed in the first floor's only bedroom.

Retreating to the stairs, he glanced up.

Thornton smiled with satisfaction. One floor to go.

Keeping his weight to the outside of the stair treads rather than the middle of the rungs, he made barely a noise as he ascended.

A LOW VOLTAGE TRIP-SWITCH in the cellar, wired to a back-door sensor, activated an electronic three-way gate valve on the main gas line. The valve dialed open, flooding the cellar with pressurized natural gas. Volatile vapors accumulated rapidly, waiting for an ignition source.

UPSTAIRS, THORNTON TRANSITIONED INTO a central hallway. A communal bathroom anchored the far end. Four bedroom doors were shut. Keeping his back to a wall, he turned the first door handle and listened to old hinges squeak as the door was opened. He slid into the room, his silenced gun ready to fire. Another empty room.

He frowned, cocked his head, and listened to a quiet house.

Three rooms to go. *This will go quick.*

IN THE CELLAR, UNRESTRAINED gas built up. The smell of sulfur intensified in the confined space. On the second floor, the house's only occupant approached the last bedroom just as the line-voltage solenoid to the basement's water heater arced across its contacts and ignited a blast equal to a hundred sticks of dynamite.

Like a funnel, the cellar channeled the nearly 200 million joule shockwave upward, the concussive force shredding the hundred-year-old home. Shards of wood and debris mushroomed in every direction. The eruption rocked the earth and shattered windows in nearby homes, triggering car alarms for blocks, and woke every neighbor in a ten-block radius.

The blast reduced the house to fragments, leaving its cellar nothing but a crater of splintered lumber and trash.

Two houses away, twisted and mangled, Gene Thornton's lifeless form dangled upside down in the top of a blue spruce, skewered through the chest by a tree limb.

The White House, Washington, D.C.

5:00 A.M. ACROSS THE hall from the Oval Office, portraits of two former U.S. Presidents adorned the walls of the Roosevelt Conference Room: Franklin, seated as usual, behind a desk with glasses and wheelchair nowhere in sight, and Triumphant Teddy, the famous Rough Rider, on horseback. Near the fireplace hung the Nobel Peace Prize awarded to Theodore Roosevelt. At the opposite end of the room, a muted television in a walnut hutch delivered news coverage of the tragic events in Princeton.

The President's National Security Advisor sat across from the Secretary of State at a walnut conference table. Rarely did the public know that the President's staff worked 24/7. Since the world never slept, National Security Advisor Gordon Abbott slept when he could.

Abbott wrung his hands together in distress.

Two anonymous emails had arrived in his White House inbox overnight, both with the subject line PERILOUS CESSATIONS. The emails had attachments. The first, a partial video clip, showed the murders of two members of the FBI: its deputy director and a special agent. The second file was an audio clip.

Both men had reviewed the electronic files.

"Neither the White House nor the State Department are mentioned," the Secretary of State pointed out. "It only implicates the FBI."

Abbott took a sharp breath. "The video is incomplete. What's on the rest of it? Samuel Ford's laptop is our worst nightmare. And I don't know how he got copies of our emails, but our correspondence cannot be made public or get to the media."

"Does the President know?"

Abbott shook his head. "No. But I have to brief the President at some point."

The Secretary of State nodded.

Abbott rubbed his brow. "Debra Ford assassinated two people. The press will link her to her ex-husband's disappearance, and by extension to the State Department. Stan Baker's involvement will prove fatal for both of us."

"She's been off our books since Moscow."

Abbott threw him a hard glare. "Involving the White House in this Frontier was your doing. This is a botched mess. Given the situation, we must cut our losses."

The Secretary of State pushed forward on his elbows. "Damn it, grow a spine. We need this tech for the War on Terror. Neurological singularity changes the world, and not just politically. ANCRI's Frontier is transcendent. We will win hearts and minds like never before, build peace where the world hasn't had goodwill in years. The West will win over jihad. Our world will embrace life, liberty and the pursuit of happiness. All because the U.S. developed the capability to reprogram our enemies' psyche. Our President will be known as the President of Peace on Earth."

Abbott gritted his teeth. "The press will follow the breadcrumbs from you to my office to the President."

"Debra Ford was a stellar operative," the Secretary of State said. "Emphasis on *was*. Clearly, she went rogue. Acted without directive or influence from our government. Her malicious actions are reprehensible, but they're hers and hers alone."

"Where is Manea?" Abbott asked, using Debra Ford's INTERPOL nickname.

"Unknown." The Secretary of State shifted in his chair. "Her Maryland home is under surveillance. Her phones are tapped. She's on the TSA's watch list, and we're staking out airports in the proximity of New Jersey. When she pops up, and she will, we'll take her down or get INTERPOL to assist on the other side of the pond. If she swims to Barbados for the holidays, well—tragically, Debra Ford will be floating dead in the crystal blue waters of the Caribbean."

Abbott pointed at the Secretary of State. "Terminate Manea, secure this technology, and get Ford's computer, or we'll both swing from the hangman's noose, world peace be damned." He took a breath. "You have four days to make this mess disappear. Come Monday morning, if matters are not resolved, we'll shutdown ANCRI and make everything disappear."

Harrisburg, Pennsylvania

6:10 A.M. DEBRA FORD ditched a stolen pickup in a parking lot on the Penn State Harrisburg campus and walked the final mile to the Harrisburg International Airport. She'd planned to leave the country from Newark, but nixed that in favor of an easy-in/easy-out regional airport with less TSA scrutiny and a non-stop to the upper Midwest.

No one would look for her in Chicago.

Operating undercover was nothing new, a skill acquired from her father.

Gone were her weapons and black outfits. She traveled light with a single carryon. She wore a gray casual two-piece suit and coordinated jacket. A light cinnamon-colored, shoulder-length wig concealed her dyed brunette locks. Black-rimmed glasses perched on her nose.

She'd purchased different round-trip tickets matching different passports online: Harrisburg to Chicago, Chicago to Paris. Both non-stops. Both first class.

Law enforcement flagged one-way tickets first. Round-trip bookings drew less scrutiny.

Once past TSA screening, Debra Ford caught the news on a television in the gate area.

Princeton was a downright disaster.

A fresh out of college reporter stood in front of the university's Blair Hall, using its rooked clock towers as a backdrop. Law enforcement personnel passed in and out of the camera frame.

A late-night shooting spree had left two people dead. The police were withholding their names, pending notification of their next of kin. Remarkably, no students had been injured. Classes had been cancelled while authorities conducted investigations. In related news, divers from search & rescue probed a lake for a car seen leaving campus around the time of the shootings, and police had obtained a warrant to search a professor's home in connection to the theft of university lab equipment.

Meanwhile, less than half-a-mile away, a catastrophic explosion had leveled a home. From aerial footage, the scattered debris looked like tiny broken toothpicks. A PSE&G source cited a possible gas leak as a potential cause of the explosion, which had left one occupant dead.

It was exhilarating to be back in the game.

She took out Baker's cell phone and typed a text message to a preset number: PREPARE SHIPMENT FOR SEA FREIGHT. DESTINATION IS LA ROCHELLE FRANCE.

She powered down the device and dropped it into a trashcan.

Loudspeakers announced the boarding of her flight.

Time to leave the chaos of the States behind and disappear for a while.

Beaming pleasantly, she handed the gate attendant her boarding pass.

Although it was only six in the morning, Pennsylvania time, it was noon at her final destination. Debra Ford hoped Chardonnay was available in first class.

A toast was in order. It had turned out to be a successful return to espionage.

33
THE MIRAGE OF HEAVEN

Advanced Neurological and Cybernetic Research Institute (ANCRI), New Jersey

8:00 A.M. PARKER STOOD on a wooden bridge, impressed with structure before him. The guard at the property gate called it the clinical neurophysiology annex. Beside him, a haggard-looking Kate stood in her alter ego, Cassondra Meir, a neurophysiologist who'd just escaped the South Pole. Over breakfast, they rehearsed a common backstory and an extended relationship after meeting at a neuroimmunology conference at the University of Colorado during his fellowship programs.

WHEN SHE ARRIVED IN town, naturally she looked him up. They were shocked to learn that ANCRI had in fact recruited both of them. *What a coincidence!*

"Dr. Meir," he said, turning to Kate, "if you're not too hungover, let's go find Becky and your missing senator, and see what the hell we signed up for."

"I didn't drink that much last night."

He arched an eyebrow. "Says the lush who drained an entire bottle of red."

She covered her face with her hands.

"Well, Ms. Pity-Me-Misery," Parker said rolling his eyes, "good thing we're just pretend friends, because I can honestly say you look like a train wreck this morning, and I'd hate to be seen with you in public. Now, come on."

A muscular, chiseled guard named Earl corralled them into the main building's sally port, where he processed Doctors Thomas Parker and Cassondra Meir. Bulletproof glass and hardened walls separated research spaces from the outside world. Behind the guard's desk, a bank of monitors showed glimpses to a protected world. Security cameras seemed to watch every move the staff made.

The no-nonsense guard pointed to a placard on the wall: AU-THORIZED PERSONNEL ONLY. NO CELL PHONES, CAMERAS, OR OTHER ELECTRONICS PERMITTED.

"Personal effects will be returned when you leave."

Parker shot the man a skeptical look. "Really?"

"I don't make the rules." Earl squared his shoulders and tapped the sidearm on his hip to emphasize his point. "Just enforce them."

They placed their belongings into plastic bins for storage.

Earl started to collect biometrics: fingerprints and retinal scans. An emphatic banging of a palm against glass interrupted the process.

"Any day now!" a man shouted from behind the bulletproof barrier.

Earl's face lit up with annoyance.

"Where in the hell are they going to go?" The man gestured with his arms. Script on his long white lab coat identified him as Noam Levine, M.D.

Earl released an impatient huff. "They're your responsibility, Dr. Levine."

"Yes, yes, of course," the man said. "If they turn out to be raging lunatics, you can hunt them down and kill them later."

Parker and Kate exchanged looks.

The man grinned. "I'm only messing with you."

Earl the guard issued them temporary visitor badges on lanyards, hit the button to open the sally port door, and watched them make their way into the annex.

"Hell, if I had left you in there much longer, wow—both of you would have ended up strip searched with your body cavities probed for contraband. Security takes their business around here way too seriously. They'll encroach on your personal boundaries if given a chance."

The man stopped in midstride.

"Where on earth are my manners?" he said with a broad smile. "Noam Levine. I'm the neurological lead at ANCRI. I manage the programs while Dr. Richards leads the charge. You'll meet the master shortly."

They exchanged handshakes.

"Welcome to the Advanced Neurological and Cybernetic Research Institute. I was told to wow you, but, honestly, that won't be hard."

The main hall was three stories tall and circled the core of the building. Above, clear windows drew in natural sunlight and complemented interior spaces. The tiled floors shone, sparkling in daylight. They passed doors labeled Neural Architectures, Synaptic Modeling, Advanced Cybernetics, Pharmacology.

Parker noticed Kate scanning for security measures. Each door had its own camera and access card reader.

"Our facility has no equal," Levine continued. "You're in the clinical neurophysiology annex. CNA for short. It's the heart of everything done here. ANCRI has the most advanced research capabilities in the world—quantum computing power that makes Google jealous, clinical labs, R&D spaces, MRI suites, and even a holographic neurophysiological projection lab. When someone says look inside my mind, you can do that here."

Parker nodded politely and wondered how much of Levine's propaganda matched substance.

"Our achievements." Levine pointed to a string of panels that ran the length of the main corridor. Each displayed a research theme: a microscopic snapshot of neurons firing, artificial cellular generation, organoids, DNA sequencing, bio-printing of human organs.

Parker shook his head. "Publish or perish."

"ANCRI is focused on human consciousness. We call it The Frontier. The last frontier."

"Ah, the grand quest," Parker said, "to read the human mind?"

Levine led them to a pair of sliding doors without replying. A placard read NEUROPHYSIOLOGY LAB, next to several warning signs.

AUTHORIZED PERSONNEL ONLY
BEYOND THIS POINT
BIOHAZARD RADIATION

Kate's eyebrows rose. "What doesn't kill you makes you... stronger?"

Levine chuckled and swiped his badge at a proximity sensor. A small LED screen flashed his name. Mechanical doors swished open, and he guided them into the anteroom. The doors shut behind them with a whoosh. "Welcome to our inner sanctum."

As the room pressurized, Parker looked toward a small window in the opposing door. Diagonal hatched safety glass showed a glimpse of a world beyond.

"Is this real?" Kate nudged closer, their shoulders touching.

A set of new doors parted open.

The neurophysiology lab was an enormous, two-story lab.

A sterile chemical smell filled Parker's nostrils.

The spectacle dazzled him, as if he'd died and gone to heaven. Heaven for medical nerds. It surpassed anything he'd ever imagined.

A small army of nurses and technicians in green and gray medical scrubs moved about capsules identified as Pod 1, Pod 2, and so on. Overlooking the ward, a monstrous electronic wall delivered a barrage of information: patient telemetry, vitals tagged to pod numbers, ECG wavelengths, 3D neurological modeling.

"We call it the Wall of Knowledge," Levine said, walking toward a group of technicians.

The bio-data on display left Parker speechless. Turning away from the Wall of Knowledge, he counted five rows, six egg-shaped participant pods deep. Thirty total. The patients were prone, outfitted in black, astronaut-like, amorphous suits. Masses of cables and tubes radiated out of each bio-suit. The headgear that encapsulated their skulls shrouded their faces as well. Bouquets of multi-colored fiber optic wires sprang out of the helmets, terminating at nodes inside each pod. Other than the numbers one through thirty, nothing distinguished one patient from the next.

Nothing about ANCRI was medical.

It was research, pure and simple, secretive work centered on thirty anonymous test subjects.

Kate's mouth fell open.

Parker whispered in her ear. "We'll never leave here alive."

He approached a pod to study it in closer detail. A local monitor showed a patient number, vitals, and electrocardiogram waves. The function of the patient's unflattering bio-suit was obvious: keep the subject alive. The gadgetry, wires and cables and tubing, made it impossible to distinguish whether the patient was male or female. Labeled tubes bonded to the bio-suit: cannula for oxygen, nasogastric tubes for liquid nutrients to the stomach, intravenous tubes for drug administration, catheters for urine and waste removal. Wires from EKG leads and blood pressure cuffs crossed the patient to the monitor. The patient wore a three-quarter faced helmet with only the lower jaw-line exposed. The helmet was structured in hexagonal quadrants like a soccer ball, with terminals that streamed bundled strands of neon fiber optic out of the helmet to posts in the egg-shaped pod. "Impressive."

"We call them participants," said a new voice. "Fragile human beings in semi-vegetative comatose states. They've been admitted to our unique medical program because of their similar neurological conditions."

Parker turned to see a man in a pressed white lab coat approach from a central row of consoles.

Stewart Richards. The master of ceremonies himself.

"Glad you decided to join us," Richards said with a crooked grin.

"Is that what I did?" Parker's eyes narrowed with the suspicion that the devil himself was in charge of running heaven.

"Dr. Parker, let's dispense with pretenses, shall we?" Richards said. "From the moment you walked in here, you knew ANCRI was the next chapter in your career. You're intrigued."

"I'm that transparent?"

Richards gestured to the lab. "The effect is the same on everyone."

"What's the status of their underlying medical conditions?" Kate asked.

"Easy now, Dr. Meir," Richards said. "We'll get to that."

She pressed. "Does the institute have patient consent and authorized custody for the medical treatments you're performing?"

Richards looked at her sternly. "Everything's in order." On the terminal attached to the pod, he swiped his badge across a scanner. A menu appeared. "Once you've been issued badges, you'll have limited access. Select the icon marked 'Patient Records' to access historical information. Pertinent consent forms will be at your fingertips. In order to protect participant confidentiality, the records do not include names or personal information. Each participant is issued an identifier, one through thirty."

"Human beings are not numbers," Kate countered.

Richards' jaw tightened.

Parker furrowed his brow. "Your process is a single-arm, blind, intervention model?" In response to misleading, ineffective approaches and sloppy research protocols, the National Institutes of Health and other groups had established parameters for conducting research trials, especially with human subjects. If ANCRI wanted its research to be considered valid, the institute would follow established practices. Single-arm was the simplest method, centered on a target group. "Blind" meant that trial investigators would not be able to discern the trial's strategy from precise details about individual subjects, so investigators could not be swayed and would not be pre-disposed toward participants who received a certain type of medical intervention.

Richards shrugged. "The approach was logical. Treat participants equally. Keep tasks universal and objective. Reducing unreasonable influence protects patient confidentiality."

"Has ANCRI ever experienced a serious adverse event during its research efforts?" Parker asked. "Serious adverse event" was one of the culture's nicer euphemisms: bluntly, a serious adverse event in a medical trial meant death.

Richards looked scornful. "No. Phase Two is our first foray into substantive medical trials."

Parker almost smiled, sensing he'd struck a nerve. He thought of the dead woman in the photograph: Amy Richards, with 64 EEG placements burned into her scalp. Richards? Father and daughter? An odd coincidence. Perhaps Amy Richards had been Phase One.

Studying the sea of pods, he wondered if Becky was among one through thirty.

"What's the gender mix of the intervention trial?" Parker asked. "Ages, ethnicity, socioeconomic backgrounds? The human conscious is an amalgamation of who we are in the world, influencing our perceptions, how we think, and even our synaptic associations."

"Fourteen men, sixteen women," Richards said without missing a beat. "Adults over the age of eighteen. One participant is older than thirty. Pertinent details can be released on a case-by-case basis, and as essential for treatment of their underlying medical conditions."

Parker leaned into one of the capsules, inspecting a patient's jaw line and the underside of the helmet. He could hear the soft rises and falls of breathing. The inner skin of the skullcap's neural sensors looked similar to his Princeton research. Spaghetti-thin multicolored cooling tubes and fiber optic bundles terminated in the headgear. "Amazing job your team has done, considering I was the first to engineer one of these."

He ran an open palm down the torso of the participant. The cables and tubes coming and going from the bulky bio-suits masked the natural contours of the human form. He had no way to visually determine the sex of the participant. If Becky lay within, he'd never know it. That seemed to be the objective.

Richards smiled thinly. "We've made some improvements."

"SQUIDS?" Parker asked, referring to the superconducting quantum interference devices mounted inside the headgear, which served as weak magnetic field recorders for detecting ion current transfers across synaptic junctions within the brain. Superconductors were tuned to specific ultralow working temperatures, which required liquid hydrogen, liquid helium, and liquid nitrogen. Researchers had first investigated SQUID-based neurosensors in the 1980s in a series of electrophysiological and magnetoencephalography experiments. No one had been able to translate the weak brainwaves into definitive neural firings until he'd pulled it off at Princeton.

Parker twisted his mouth, knowing the answer to the question before he asked. "How did you go about solving uncorrelated synaptic extractions and non-linear communicative propagation?"

Richards nodded. "We haven't." He stood like a man at ease, a man with the upper hand on the situation. "Doctors, the researchers I need are the ones who keep one eye on the details while the other eye roams the horizon. Medicine has no shortage of brilliant, highly skilled researchers, but few have what it takes to solve enigmatic puzzles, overcome the impossible." He turned to Kate. "Each of you possesses a unique talent. This facility, ANCRI, was built for you. Comprehension of the human consciousness is the greatest frontier ever to be explored. Here—"

An interruption stopped Richards in mid-sentence.

They turned to see Earl enter the lab, careful not to venture too far inside. He waved Richards over.

Richards showed concern. "Pardon the interruption. It appears my presence is required. Dr. Levine will continue your tour and introduce you to the rest of our team."

Lab doors swooshed closed behind the master of ceremonies.

Parker leaned to Kate. "I wonder what's going on."

34
LAY OF THE LAND

AT THE SURVEILLANCE STATION, Richards took in the news. None of it was good. His vision shifted to the bank of monitors, where Doctors Parker, Meir, and Levine progressed from the CNA neurophysiology sector to the research annex.

He faced the guard. "You sure about this?"

Earl nodded. "The sheriff's department confirmed that Thornton was killed in a house explosion. Natural gas buildup is suspected. Unrelated, two FBI agents died in a shootout and a dead man connected to their murders was fished out of a car in a lake. And Princeton police searched Thomas Parker's home—something about theft of university equipment."

Richards could not believe what he was hearing. Other interested parties sought Parker's research. Not entirely surprising. The involvement of the FBI might pose a problem. Yet the death of ANCRI's Board's external consultant came as an unexpected turn in events. An opportunity. With Thornton out of the picture, there was no one to stand in the way of his vision, his dream, The Frontier.

He returned to the monitors as first impressions gnawed at him, as did the antagonistic attitudes of his newest hires. Their bluntness undercut ANCRI's core premise. Passion and intrigue was expected, at least blind acceptance of the research, especially from Thomas Parker.

Cassondra Meir was a different story entirely.

Her South Pole interview via Skype raised no red flags. Now, red flags were abundant, anything from the slight difference in her physical appearance displayed via an across-the-world video session to the edginess of her tone.

He hoped their naïveté were not obstacles to the research.

Fooled once, Caroline Wang's enthusiasm inspired him to take risks, even to the extent of sacrificing his daughter, Amy. His trust in Caroline was repaid by her betrayal. Luckily, Noam Levine offered a competent replacement, while Caroline embraced his daughter's legacy—as participant 30.

Richards grit his teeth and watched Parker and Meir on screen. The pair revealed a slight closeness, almost a fondness for each other. That sensitivity signaled trouble if the two required separation. Meir was expendable. Parker was essential.

Perhaps a realignment of attitudes—classical conditioning—was compulsory.

AFTER AN IMPRESSIVE FIRST stop, Parker prepared himself for the low-rent district and the nickel tour. A wide swath of slate-colored flooring broke away from the CNA core and opened up into a two-story atrium. Paneled windows with coronal-plane sheltering grates overlooked a central courtyard outside.

The atrium looked like the one in the Lewis Sigler Institute, the building across from Parker's PNI complex back at Princeton, except shades of gray replaced natural woods and soothing tans. A handful of researchers milled about. The atrium's central feature was waterfall art, a fractured charcoal-like monolith with crystal clear water cascading down its rugged features into a shallow pool.

"What's ANCRI's turnover rate?" Parker asked as they walked. "Anyone leave lately?"

Levine shrugged. "Never thought about it. After Phase One concluded, we had some departures. Mostly low-hanging fruit, those kind of folks. But for Phase Two, we've ramped up nicely. Of course, having you two here raises everyone's game."

Parker looked at Kate, then back to Levine. "No pressure, eh?"

Levine's eyes narrowed. "Dr. Parker, you're here to change the world."

Kate tapped Levine on the shoulder. "Ever work with a gal named Caroline Wang?"

Levine stopped in his tracks. "Caroline was one of those who left during the transition." His eyes flashed cold. "Dr. Meir, how exactly did you know her?"

Kate fluffed out her hair. "Oh, we met during a recruiting visit to Ann Arbor. She was one of my hosts on a campus tour at Michigan. We just seemed to hit it off, you know, girls' stuff. I hoped to catch up with her, that's all."

"Well, Caroline and I weren't that close," Levine said. "I can't say where she went after her departure. I know she made substantial contributions to Phase One efforts. Gave her heart and mind to our cause as it were."

Levine hustled them toward a large pair of doors marked RE- SEARCH ANNEX. He waved his badge at a card reader. The doors powered open, revealing a broad expanse filled with modular labs where slate-colored floors changed to graphite-colored versions.

This new open structure populated with independent cubes drew Parker in.

Ahead of them lay sophisticated, autonomous labs with semi-frosted glass walls and rounded contours. Spacious corridors separated the discrete modules. Bands of colored neon accented and trimmed each modular unit.

"ANCRI has twenty-four research labs," Levine said. "Twelve are biological-chemical-neurological in nature, eight focus on cybernetic and neurocircuitry, and four are dedicated to artificial super intelligence, ASI, applications. Each of you is assigned to a homeroom."

They paused at the first series of windows, where glowing trim cast a soft violet splash across the glass. The lab was filled with flasks of liquid, test tubes parked in trays, and double-barreled stereo microscopes.

"This is our neurotransmitter applications lab."

Inside, technicians matched petri dish samples to specimens on glowing screens.

"Come, there's more to see." Levine led them further into the matrix.

At a peach-banded lab, Levine swiped his badge across the card reader. A door marked SYNAPTIC ANATOMICS opened.

This lab was a disaster, as if a tornado had devoured it and left a wasteland of litter and debris in its wake. Empty coffee cups, papers, charts, books, and lab samples covered counters. Monitors glowed green and displayed mangled, mutant spaghetti-looking images populated with knots and knobs: the microscopic world of neurons, dendrites, axons, and synaptic junctions at work. Pulsing red and blue bursts migrated between synapses.

"Riley Johnson," Levine said.

Parker studied the man. Johnson's dark eyes shone with an innate curiosity. His thick head of black hair was chopped and bound in thumb-sized dreadlocks. A chronic five o'clock shadow painted his lower face. Parker had never met anyone quite like Riley Johnson.

His disheveled look was surfer-meets-Hendrix—part reggae musician, part geek—as if the man spent the morning sleeping on the beach. His lab coat was something a disturbed five-year-old might wear, tie-dye gone wrong painted over an endless series of hand-scribbled mathematical expressions. Dryer-hardened blotches stained the coat: coffee, blood, indecipherable chemistry smears. The breast pocket of his coat had ripped off, revealing a virgin square, the only clean spot on the entire coat. Inside the sacred white patch was a commentary: LEFT ROCKET SCIENCE AND HIGH EXPLOSIVES TO BECOME FULL-TIME SOLVER OF P VS NP.

"If the NP-intermediate set is empty," Parker said, recognizing the nerdy P VS NP declaration was more about character transformation, a beam me up Scotty moment, than enlisting in an as-of-yet unsolvable mathematical crusade, "then P equals NP."

Kate frowned. "I don't get it."

Johnson shot up an eyebrow. "If computational complexity were complete, I would have no reason to join ANCRI."

Kate still looked blank.

Johnson noticed her expression and welcomed the opportunity to elaborate. "P versus NP. It's a quandary. A notoriously unsolvable puzzle in the realm of complex computational theory. P is a class in polynomial time. NP is the complexity class in nondeterministic polynomial time. Richard Ladner, the pioneer of accessibility technology, posted the NP-intermediate set, which contains problems that are neither in P nor NP-complete. Solve the P versus NP quandary and you win a Millennium Prize."

That much, Kate recognized; the Clay Mathematics Institute offered a standing prize of one million dollars for each of its Millennium Prizes. P versus NP, apparently was one of them.

"It's not the money, though," Johnson added. "A realized solution in complexity theory has profound effects on everything—global economics, energy, game theory, artificial intelligence, quantum mechanics—and, for our purposes, neurophysiology."

Parker showed his concern. "Some say solving P equals NP would destroy human society. Are you working on the end of the world?"

Johnson laughed at the obvious jab.

"Dr. Johnson," Levine said, "has modeled repeatable functions in synaptic architectures."

Johnson pointed to a screen. Using his thumbs and index fingers, he expanded the digital frame to highlight a specific neuron cluster and its synaptic knob.

The stunning clarity of the image was unlike anything Parker had ever seen, with the God-like cosmic ability to home in and see precise signal migration within a neuron and the synchronous wave of pulsating ion charges jumping across a neuron's synaptic cleft.

"Is this a computer simulation?" Kate asked.

"It's organic." Johnson beamed and pointed to a movement of red microbursts. "I discovered a method to tune synaptic couplings to the instantaneous firing rates of individual neurons. Down the line, we'll be able to alter the progression of neurotransmitters and action potentials, and train neurons how and when to fire. That will lead to the ability to reprogram neurons. Rebuild them. Talk to them. Make neurons speak any language we want."

Parker frowned. "You're out to rewire the brain?"

"Or repair it." Johnson turned to Levine. "Have they seen our organoids?"

Kate wrinkled her nose. "Organoids?"

Levine shook his head. "You're our first stop."

Johnson chuckled. "Damn honored."

"Our neurobiologists replicate nerve cells, nerve-electronic hybrids, biological-cybernetic interfaces, mini-brains," Levine added.

"Mini-brains?" Parker knew science was making radical breakthroughs in the fields of microbiology and cellular transformation in terms of three-dimensional nerve generation, including the growth of induced pluripotent stem cells, fibroblast skin cells, embryonic cells, and immune cells. Science was close to creating thinkable, miniature-sized human brains. It was just a matter of time until researchers wired either synthetic nerve inputs or biologically fostered inputs into cultured organisms. Mankind had evolved to become the Creator, or at least the Replicator, of life.

The benefits of emerging mini-brain organoids fueled the fields of neurology, pharmacology, and molecular biology. Mini-brains let scientists study disease-impacted nerve cells and what drug variations countered life-debilitating neurological disorders.

Johnson clasped his thumb and forefinger together. "Up to the size of a golf ball."

Levine jumped in. "Our researchers collaborate through an interactive platform called CrossTalk. A core principle here is dynamic engagement, the sharing of ideas. Neurobiologists grow the specimens. Johnson stimulates them."

"To test nerve stimulation propagation," Johnson glanced at Parker. "I've read about your research. It's impressive."

Parker frowned. "I haven't published anything."

Johnson glanced to Levine. "I—"

The door swished open, saving Johnson from a clumsy reply.

The new arrival was a dark-haired, mocha-skinned man with a beard and mustache.

Everyone turned to find Talib Makara, who Parker thought looked like the Disney character Jafar, from *Aladdin*.

"Hey there, Pigpen," Makara said, his voice deep and gravelly. He bumped Levine aside and waved to Johnson.

Johnson nodded, not appearing to be insulted.

Makara turned to Parker. "So you're the daft apeth who's here to save ANCRI? Well, doc, you don't look like much."

"Hold on," Levine interjected. "This is not the time—"

Makara ignored Levine and spun back to Kate, his eyes dialing in on her. "We've met before."

"No. Don't think so." Kate swallowed over a knot in her throat. "You're mistaken."

"Not possible." Makara ogled her up and down. "You look different, Dr. Meir. Less tree-hugger-like. More... hot."

"Dr. Makara!" Levine snapped.

Parker laughed. "That's funny. I told Kate she looked like a train wreck."

"Oh, please," she said.

Makara approached Kate. "Yes. I remember now. You gave a putrid presentation on transcendent approaches for revamping neurogenesis and cortical plasticity. It was so poorly received you fled to the South Pole, hiding out as an outcast with the National Science Foundation."

"You are out of line." Levine stepped between Makara and Kate.

Makara arched up his eyebrows up and down several times. "I'm so brilliant, everyone must tolerate me."

Levine steered Kate toward the door. "Let's continue the tour, shall we?"

Stepping forward, Parker came nose-to-nose with the biggest asshole he'd met. And med school had been full of arrogant know-it-alls like Talib Makara.

"Besides tearing people down," Parker said, "you do anything useful around here?"

All smiles, Makara patted Parker's chest.

"A lot, actually." Makara retreated and started picking his nose, jamming his long middle finger deep into a nostril. "Dr. Parker, I'm your new best friend. Gosh, I can hardly wait to work together. Ah, this moment… it gives me goose-bumps."

Reaching back, Levine snatched Parker by the shoulder.

"Be seeing you around," Makara said, behind a white smile and a wagging middle finger.

The lab door slid closed between them.

THE DAY KEPT GETTING better. In his second floor, executive office in the CNA sector, Richards watched more monitors relaying footage from the research annex. While security cameras blanketed the facility, audio was not available. But visual cues and outcome were obvious. Parker and Meir had an untimely encounter with the planet's largest ego, Talib Makara.

Makara was crude and excellent at pushing buttons, trashing people's sensitivities. Other than his sheer brilliance for neural quantum mechanics, neuroarchitectures, and computer programming, Makara possessed few admirable traits—the ultimate human resources nightmare disguised as a spectacular researcher.

The takeaways from their confrontation were enlightening. Meir looked shaken. On the other hand, Parker defended her and exposed a chip on his shoulder.

Richards leaned back in his chair and folded his arms across his chest.

A man with a chip on his shoulder and something to prove could change the world.

THE TOUR CONTINUED. KATE had a hard time staying engaged in the ever-changing conversations. She felt robotic. Shake this hand. Shake that hand. Smile here. Look interested in this cool application, gadget, or gizmo.

She should have been in awe, but her sense of investment waned.

Talib Makara had exposed her as a fraud. Thankfully, neither Levine nor Johnson seemed to notice. At least, she hoped they hadn't. Makara was a playground bully, an egotistical tyrant who preyed on the weak. She fought the urge to circle back and confront him, along with the fierce impulse to crush his larynx and shut him up—for all the tree-huggers in the world.

More amazing sophisticated spaces came and went, as did more introductions to talented researchers. Their faces and names blurred together.

Parker lingered closer to her side after Synaptic Anatomics. He too was quieter, asking fewer questions. His smile looked painted on. Makara's comments rattled him, too.

Levine pointed to a pair of enormous doors and talked about a first-ever, three-story, quantum-based supercomputer data center with ten times the computing power of its closest competitor—500 petaflops was the low-end processing speed. Fastest in the world.

Warning signs plastered the doors.

UNOCCUPIED DATA CENTER. NO FOOD OR DRINK IS PERMITTED BEYOND THIS POINT. INHALATION DANGER. WHEN ALARM SOUNDS, VACATE PREMISES IMMEDIATELY. FIRE SUPPRESSION CHEMICALS AND TOXIC SUBSTANCES PRESENT. PERSONNEL SHALL POSSESS SELF-CONTAINED BREATHING APPARATUS (SCBA) PER OSHA REGULATIONS.

Parker elbowed her. "You okay?"

She shook her head. "There's a lot to take in."

"Excuse us, Dr. Levine," Parker said. "I'm sure you have other duties requiring your attention. We're going to take a break and get some coffee."

AT A TABLE IN the dining hall, Parker noticed Kate still looked troubled and they sipped coffee in an awkward silence.

"What's wrong?" he finally asked.

She thumped her hand against the table. "You know what's wrong, Thomas."

Earl the guard interrupted them to finish recording biometrics. He captured fingerprint and retinal scans on his tablet, and had them sign a series of digital forms. After the process was completed, they each received photo IDs on lanyards.

"You can't access the data center," Earl said. "And basement levels are off-limits."

After the stiff-necked guard left, Kate asked, "You think I was made?"

Parker shrugged. "Makara never said you weren't Cassondra Meir, just that you looked different. A couple of years have passed. He used the word 'hotter.' That doesn't sound like a man who believes you're an impostor."

"Lovely." Kate rolled her eyes and leaned across the table. "How do we access the participants?"

"Right now, we don't need to." Parker resisted what he saw as a rash course of action. She wanted to get to the participants immediately, disconnect them from their artificial hosts, and see who came up looking like Samuel Ford, Becky, Caroline Wang, or twenty-eight missing college students—undeniable proof the institute engaged in human trials on innocent people. "Our job is to fit in. These pretend patients aren't going anywhere."

She huffed. "We have to help them."

"Yeah, I know. I suspect they're in chemically induced comas. Drugged into submission. But there will be ways around those obstacles."

"You think ANCRI will pull it off?"

"What?" Parker asked. "Pick apart the brain? Read a memory? Talking heads have proclaimed for years that organic life, our unique human condition, is nothing more than four and a half billion years of evolution and the consequence of applied chemistry. They say consciousness, our intellectual and cognitive functions and sensorium that makes us who we are, is merely repeatable patterns and the outcome of molecular physics, a chain reaction of ions and atoms coexisting in an organic host. It's a matter of time before someone solves this grand biological riddle and maps our intellectual universe. So why not this place?"

Kate shook her head. "Sounds like you're going to help them."

Parker's expression revealed nothing. "Do we help change the world forever, or sabotage ANCRI and delay the inevitable?" He hesitated. "I wasn't sure I was going to help you, and look where we both ended up."

She offered a thin smile. "Yeah, but the institute was already recruiting you."

"I'm not buying into the notion of fate. But Becky and Derman did screw me over, I got shot chasing Derman down, and you saved my life. Those twisted events led me here." He looked at his hands. "I'm sure I haven't properly thanked you for saving my life."

Kate reached out to grasp his hands. "Help find Samuel Ford and we can call it even."

Parker clasped her hands in his. "I know how to do that."

35
CATCHING UP TO CURRENT EVENTS

KATE FELT LOST AT times, and hated Parker for his overwhelming enthusiasm and boundless attention span. He enjoyed himself thoroughly. Midway through the tour, he'd scribbled out titles of journal articles for her to read: five papers on the causes, diagnostics, and treatments of comas and vegetative states, and four more on trends in clinical neurophysiology. It was supposed to mask any obvious weakness as a pretend expert in the field of neurophysiology.

Homework! She hadn't endured the brutality of monotone, wake-me-when-I'm-dead scholarly reading since med school.

Called away by pressing matters, Levine relinquished the tour duties to Riley Johnson.

More names, faces, cool-looking labs, and awe-inspiring research came and went.

The BIOMECHANICS LAB was the homeroom to the institute's green thumb. A Japanese woman in her fifties, Rikona Tanaka was decked out in a head-to-toe bunny suit, sterile booties covering pink sneakers and a white sterile cap wrapped over a dark head of hair. Her inquisitive brown eyes shone behind bifocals perched on a flat nose.

In her hand Tanaka gently swirled pink-tinted fluids in a six-pack, petri-dish set.

"Stand behind that line," she ordered, gesturing to the thick red-line taped to the floor, the delineation between sterile and non-sterile areas of the lab.

Tanaka looked over her audience. "Anyone interested in suiting up?"

Everyone shook their heads no.

"Very well," she said, "but I won't show you mine, if you can't protect me from yours."

Johnson was the only one who laughed at the joke.

Kate studied the wall-to-wall span of jars and tubes and specimen dishes, stainless steel contraptions, fume hoods, bioreactors, incubators, microscopes, and shelving packed with organoids suspended in fluids—anything from ears and noses to kidneys and livers to hearts and mini-lungs. The centerpieces of her work—mini-brains.

Parker gestured to the petri dish set in Tanaka's gloved hand. "How old?"

Tanaka strolled to the red line and showed off her current batch. Tiny white clumps smaller than sesame seeds drifted in transparent pink embryotic fluid.

"Two weeks. I'm moving them to a bioreactor. After that they'll go into an incubator for another couple of weeks."

Tanaka explained her process; taking an organic base of skin and embryotic cells, transforming them into adaptable stem cells through a process akin to genetic gymnastics, and cooking the cultivated bio-product in a sort of Easy Bake Oven until the cells reproduced and matured to have a mass equivalent to a non-simulated brain of a five-week old fetus.

Parker almost crossed the red line when Tanaka started to talk about positive outcomes with advanced cerebral organoids, replicating neurological biological structures that responded to sensory stimulation.

His eyes gleamed. "Johnson says he's developed repeatable synaptic-firing models based on your work."

Tanaka nodded. "We have several modeled scenarios."

Parker stroked his chin with his fingers. "What do you have for the behavioral characteristics of ganglia and astroglia cells?"

Tanaka's eyebrows almost touched her hair cap. "We've recorded sensory inputs for a broad variety of neurons. What is it you're specifically after?"

"Voltage gradients, harmonic interactions, and ion action potentials for neurons. I want to incorporate them into a new model."

Kate opened her mouth to chime in, but yawned instead. "Is this going some—?"

A rap on the outside glass grabbed everyone's attention.

Earl, the no-nonsense guard, glared at them through the windows.

Johnson opened the lab doors. "What do you need?"

Parker nudged Kate. "We boring you?"

She shook her head. "Now you ask?"

"Dr. Parker, Dr. Richards wants a word with you," Earl said. "Alone. Dr. Johnson, Dr. Makara is asking why you're late on some assessment. I understood nothing that man said. Quantum superposition states in combinatorial optimization learning algorithms?" He turned to Kate. "Dr. Meir, your presence is not required at this time."

Kate was caught between insult and a chuckle. "Well, I'll take a break."

Parker noticed Johnson clutched a tablet under his arm. He snatched it from the man's grasp and passed it to Kate. "You won't mind if she borrows this, will you? Dr. Meir mentioned needing to catch up on some light reading."

Johnson frowned, then turned to Kate. "I'll track down another one."

"Great," Parker said, all smiles.

"You've got to be kidding me," Kate said.

Parker leaned to her. "Head back to your dorm room. We'll connect up for dinner."

"Dr. Parker?" Earl the guard asked.

"Lead the way," Parker said, following the guard down the corridor.

Johnson came up beside Kate. "You alright?"

She sensed the man was just being polite, his attention clearly focused on pleasing Makara and solving his delinquent assignment.

Kate raised the tablet. "I'm fine."

36
DARK MOMENTS

IN THE DORMITORY WING, Kate found her assigned second floor, one-bedroom suite, but discovered its door ajar. An electronic lock linked the door to an ID badge. She pushed it open. It was dark inside. She flipped on a light switch. Standing in the doorway, she studied her modest sitting room. Her delivered luggage sat beside a pile of lab coats and light-blue scrubs—gifts from housekeeping.

She closed the door, set Johnson's tablet aside and let her hands tighten into fists. Methodically, she turned on lights and progressed through rooms. The bedroom, its walk-in closet, and bathroom were vacant.

Kate dropped to a knee to peer beneath the bed—no monsters there either.

Standing, she released a pent-up breath.

Housekeeping failed to close the door on their way out, that's all.

She rubbed her eyes and yawned.

She'd half-expected to encounter Makara, even fantasized about ripping his head from his shoulders and recalibrating his full-of-himself id.

That would cure her case of the yawns.

Facing Parker's laundry list of mandatory reading, Kate felt a hot shower was required to reinvigorate her. After turning on the shower above the bathtub, she stripped out of her clothes.

Somewhere in the distance came the sound of a mechanical snap.

The rooms in her suite plunged into darkness.

The spray of shower water rumbled into a dark tub.

Her head snapped around. *This a-hole is in for the surprise of his life!*

Kate brought up fists and took a balanced stance, a technique she'd learned at Quantico. The faint light breaking past window curtains didn't give her much light to see by as her pupils struggled to adjust to darkness.

Footsteps.

A shadowy figure came at her fast.

She took a breath and led with a front kick, the balls of her foot midsection high.

Her attacker stumbled, avoiding the strike.

In the fraction of a second, she recognized the outline of a man.

A loss of balance sent him low, diving at her legs.

Hooking her kicking leg with an outstretched arm, he launched at her like a wrestler who was content to strike and counterstrike in close-quarters. She was vulnerable. The man pushed forward and locked up her posting leg. Kate felt powerful arms around both of her bare legs.

Interlocking her fists, she slammed down against the small of his back.

Behind a tennis-like grunt, she struck again and again.

Her attacker finally buckled, the blows sending him to his knees.

Maintaining his grip, he jerked her down on top of him.

Straddling his back, Kate thrust an elbow into his kidney, which cleared recoil space to deliver another jab to his other kidney. She targeted his vulnerabilities again.

On his knees, the man let out an alarming groan and shot upward, his bull-like reflex ejecting her backwards.

Kate felt her bare feet leave the firmness of a tile floor as she sailed through the air. Hands reached for anything but found the uselessness of air. Her mind estimated her trajectory and destination—the bathtub.

The landing was brutal and the back of her head smacked the tub spout.

Water splashed everywhere as the shower continued to flow.

Stars filled her vision, leading a wave of lightheadedness.

Kate slumped into the tub as cascading water rained down upon her.

Beneath her, the drain plug in the bottom of the tub sealed.

Firm hands latched onto her throat. The tub basin afforded her no room to maneuver and put her at a severe disadvantage. A torrent of water flowed unrestrained into her face. Holding her breath, she tried to kick herself free, but her assailant straddled her and pinned down her legs. She slugged stiff arms. The grip against her throat tightened. Her fists reeled against elbow joints. The human force above her didn't budge.

Behind clenched teeth, Kate shut her eyes and grimaced.

Dizziness washed through her as water lapped at her ears. Her lungs burned, unable to take in oxygen, and her neck seared.

If she didn't die from the stranglehold, her assailant would drown her.

In a last ditch effort, Kate used both hands to claw at buttons and cloth and a breast pocket. Grabbing material, she yanked her attacker toward her. The man pitched forward. With two stiff fingers, she struck a single target hard—an exposed trachea.

It worked.

The man straddling her buckled. His grip on her throat retracted.

Hacking, she leaned away from the waterboarding splurge.

Fight!

She kneed him hard in the groin, and followed with a punch to the side of his face.

Water splashed everywhere as two bodies grappled in a confined space.

The man slid sideways.

Seizing the chance, Kate launched herself. As her feet cleared the tub, a hand seized a bare foot.

Kate croaked out a scream, hoping someone would hear.

Her hands found little traction on a wet bathroom floor.

The man's free hand snatched a fistful of wet hair.

Kate screamed again as her scalp burned. Her attacker was reeling her in. She latched onto the side of the tub. An arm wrapped around her throat. She tried to pry the stranglehold grip loose. Bent backwards, her feet slipped from beneath her and she collapsed onto her attacker.

The man hauled her into the water-filled tub, leaving her legs to dangle over the side. Growling in her ear, he asked, "Who are you spying for?"

The grip around her neck loosened just enough to allow a reply.

Kate coughed. "What?"

"I won't ask again. Are you a spy?"

"No," she said, hacking and trying to draw oxygen into her lungs. "Who are you?"

She tried to place the man's voice. Her assailant was masking his tone. She took frantic breaths trying to build enough stamina to launch a counterattack, knowing her situation was a dire one. Her attacker held every advantage: leverage, position, and darkness.

With his free hand, the man slammed a fist into her exposed midsection.

"Stop!" she gasped.

"Your name."

"Meir... I'm a... doctor..."

The stranglehold grip around her throat tightened for good.

Desperately, she pried at the suffocating grip. It was no use. In a last ditch effort, she kicked the side of her tub hoping to get traction and punched back at her attacker.

She landed a punch, but it came at a cost. Her energy was spent, and her will to fight started to evaporate.

"You should have stayed at McMurdo," the man snarled.

Kate succumbed to lack of oxygen and finally went limp.

37
THE POWER OF MESSAGES

PARKER WAS IRRITATED. THE nickel tour turned out to be worth the price of admission, and he'd enjoyed it more than he expected. He hated to admit it. ANCRI was nothing short of amazing. Now he had been summoned to an audience with the master of ceremonies.

Earl led him to a conference room in the neurophysiology sector.

Richards stood over an interactive screen that also functioned as a high-tech conference table. The table displayed a series of composite images: colored MRI brain scans, 3D topographic profiles of ECG scans, and recorded neural stimulations. The participant label read Pod 30.

"Take a seat," Richards said, offering a thin, plastic smile as he cleared the table with a swipe of his hand.

Parker appraised Richards, who had shed his pressed white lab coat in favor of a black suit and tie. A Rolex was strapped to a wrist. The man's gray eyes lacked warmth, and Parker thought Stewart Richards could pass as the devil's brother.

Like the devil, his brethren always wanted something.

His gaze panned across the conference room. A curio cabinet in the corner prominently displayed two brains bathing in formaldehyde. The jars were labeled ALPHA and BETA. On the back wall, black and white portraits hung side by side. He recognized them as the Three Fathers of Neuroscience. At the center of the high-tech table was an artist's rendition of the Palms of God holding His ultimate creation, the human brain.

Richards seated himself, folded his hands, and watched him. "Dr. Parker, every object in the universe can be defined in mathematical terms. The biological form known as the human species is no different. In crude way, we're merely a subset of elements governed by the laws of physics and chemistry. But then, what is the human mind?"

Parker shrugged. "'The energy of the mind is the essence of life.' Aristotle."

Richards' eyes sparkled. "If our ultimate goal is the discovery of consciousness, then the whole is indeed greater than the sum of its parts."

Parker took a seat opposite him, signaling he was listening.

Richards gestured to the portraits on the wall. "Each laid achievements before the Altar of Science."

Parker welcomed the test. "Santiago Ramón y Cajal, the father of modern neuroscience. Jean-Martin Charcot, the father of modern neurology. And, as a Yale grad, I would be remiss if I did not recognize Harvey Cushing, the father of neurosurgery. Of course, the Goldman Sachs clan would argue that Ernest should be present. But Yale reminded me more than once that Cushing was nominated 38 times for a Nobel Prize. Ernest Sachs not so much."

Richard's eyes narrowed. "Each faced unknowns, misperceptions, yet, they bore the inherent ability to see what others could not. As we do here. The Frontier is our *terra incognita*. This is our moment in neuroscience."

Parker liked the sound of this. Richards was playing to his vanity. Cognitive mapping and the extraction of consciousness were quests fraught with moral traps and ethical quandaries. One thing was certain—the starter's pistol had fired, and the sprint for the Frontier was underway. The winner would claim victory, the secrets of human consciousness and world-wide recognition, as had the Three Fathers, while the loser would fade into historical insignificance.

Richards pushed the Palms of God across the table. "Atheists believe that the Creator is a perpetuated fairytale—a concocted artifice promoted by manipulative and treacherous men to coerce the weak, and instill the fear of an Almighty incarnation in the form of childish superstitions. Thomas, this is your chance to see directly into the human mind—to pick up the phone and talk directly to God."

"If you talk to God, you're religious," Parker mocked. "If God talks to you, you're psychotic. Greg House, M.D. I can't see where using the human mind for a collect call to God gets me any closer to curing my deep-seeded psychosis."

Richards shook his head. "We're not as different as you pretend. We want the same thing. The Frontier won't wait for differences of opinions."

"Dr. Richards, you and I are very different." Parker slid the Palms of God aside, rested his elbows on the table and turned to the curio cabinet. "Who'd you kill to fill your jars?"

Richards' gray eyes probed him like a disappointed parent. "Compliance is required."

Parker shrugged. "Or what? You'll fire me like the university?"

Richards sighed deeply. "How long have you really known Cassondra Meir?"

"None of your concern."

"Everything in your life is a reflection of a choice you've made." Richards removed an unlabeled keycard and slid it across the table, got up, and walked to the door. "No different from your Ivy League faculty position, research, companionship. Tragically, life can be stripped away one precious element at a time. Be mindful of the choices that lie ahead."

Richards left the room.

Parker stared at the keycard on the table. *Kate.*

SPRINTING TO THE DORMITORY wing, Parker ascended the stairs to where medical researchers were housed. Room assignments were random.

He recalled her assigned room, four doors down and across the hall from his.

His side ached and heart pounded as he swiped the mystery card across the access reader to room 233. The door's lock disengaged with an electronic click. He wrenched the handle down and swung the door open.

The suite was dark. Faint daylight pierced window curtains.

"Kate?" he called, flipping on a light switch.

All dorm rooms held the same cookie-cutter layouts and generic furnishings. Her sitting room was vacant and he progressed into the bedroom, turning on lights along the way. Clothes were scattered about.

Parker spun toward the bathroom. Water glossed the floor.

A slender hand lay on the tile.

RICHARDS STROLLED THE PODS in the neurophysiology lab, pleased with himself.

He held no reservations about a harsh challenge to Thomas Parker.

His blatant contempt would not be tolerated or appeased.

Thomas Parker had been put on notice, genius or not. *Get with the program or face the consequences of poor choices.*

The Frontier was not for the faint of heart.

It required personal sacrifice, and full compliance.

PARKER FOUND KATE LYING naked and face down on a wet bathroom floor. He rolled her over and placed an ear to her chest.

Her heart thrummed steadily. Thank, God, she was alive.

He closed his eyes, content to listen to the steadiness of her heartbeat and the natural rises and falls of shallow breathing.

He raised his head and studied the situation. The tub was half-full of water. Water covered the floor. There had been a struggle. Someone had attacked her.

He turned his attention back to Kate.

Redness and bruising coated the soft tissues of her neck. He saw no other afflictions or wounds.

Someone left her alive for a reason.

The message was clear—*make the Frontier happen, or pay the consequences.*

Parker carried her into the bedroom, laid her on the bed, and pulled up bedding to cover her naked form.

He ran his fingers through her damp hair. "Kate, can you hear me?"

Peeling back the bedding, he rubbed his knuckles against her bare sternum to elicit a pain response.

Kate groaned and her eyes rolled back.

"Who attacked you?" he asked returning the bed sheets.

Her eyes fluttered open.

"Thomas?" Her voice was hoarse. "A man. It was dark."

He placed a palm against her cheek. "You're okay."

She grabbed hold of his hand. "I fought…"

"Too bad you didn't have your gun."

She tried to laugh, but coughed instead. "What did Richards want?"

He hesitated. "To send a message."

Kate told him what she remembered, which wasn't much, and mustered a tired smile. "I didn't get my reading assignment done, professor."

He waited to catch her gaze. "We'll find out who did this to you."

Kate leaned against him. "Trust no one. That's what I was told. Maybe we're even, doc."

Parker pulled her close. "Not even close, Kate. I'm burning Richards' little sanctuary to the ground, his Frontier be damned. That's more than a promise, it's a choice."

38
TRADES AND NEGOTIATIONS

University Medical Center, Plainsboro, New Jersey

MERCER COUNTY SHERIFF JOSEPH Kennard snapped at the desk clerk in the hospital's morgue. "How does a body go missing?"

The clerk spun her computer screen around to make it visible. "Our department logged in no one named Jack Wright."

The sheriff crossed his arms. "Your own ER pronounced the man DOA."

"Take that up with the Emergency Department then."

"This sounds like a predicament," a new voice added.

Kennard turned to find a Chinese man in a suit.

The man placed two objects on the clerk's counter: a laptop case and a camera. He produced an Armed Forces Identification Card with a photo and the name Randall Wang, U.S. Army, Active Duty, Pay Grade O-6, Colonel.

Wang spoke directly to the morgue attendant. "Bring me the personal effects of the John Doe killed in the Princeton house explosion."

Kennard stared down at the shorter man. "I don't think so. Anything that man in his possession is evidence. Now, colonel, if you get a court order, then the Army can have anything it wants."

"Sheriff," Wang said, "your department is trying to piece together a very troublesome set of crimes. I can help fill in details."

Kennard scrunched his brow. "You have my attention."

Wang directed the clerk to retrieve Thornton's personal effects as he laid out an abridged version of the previous night's chaos in Princeton, careful to leave out details of his or the NSA's involvement.

"How do you know this, colonel?"

"Because I recorded it." Wang slid the first of two gifts across the counter: an HD video camera. "FBI Special Agent Jack Wright was one of the good guys and my friend."

The clerk returned with a small bag of possessions carrying the identifier JD-AA104.

"Your John Doe was named Gene Thornton." Wang opened the bag, retrieved a wallet, and slid out a thick Bank of Canada credit card. He returned the wallet and tucked the bank card in his pocket. "He was a trained killer."

The sheriff looked skeptical. "What did you take?"

"A USB drive. It never belonged to Thornton."

"USB? As in a computer memory card, USB?"

"Yes."

Kennard flinched at the new information, as if he were drinking from a fire hose.

Wang slid the laptop bag across the counter. "Under no circumstances should your office return this to the Federal Bureau of Investigation without negotiating its release through the Department of Justice. Go ahead. Read its files. You'll learn more than you'll want to know."

Kennard unzipped the bag.

His eyes widened upon seeing FBI evidence stickers. "What the hell is this?"

"It belonged to an Oklahoma Senator. As your office is aware, Samuel Ford is a missing person. Computer files implicate the FBI, White House, and State Department."

Wang turned to leave.

Kennard held him up. "Colonel, I cannot let you leave with that USB thing."

Wang bobbed his head at the camera. "Yes, you will."

FRIDAY, OCTOBER 9th

It's a basic truth of the human condition that every-body lies. The only variable is about what.
Gregory House, M.D.

39
THE OATH OF SERVANTS

Advanced Neurological and Cybernetic Research Institute (ANCRI), New Jersey, 3:20 a.m.

THE SANCTUARY OF SLEEP for Parker proved a fleeting endeavor. Held captive to his mind, he wrestled with an endless series of incoherent thoughts. ANCRI was a place where the sanctity of life had become inconsequential, where sacrificial hosts were laid before the Altar of Science. Thirty unwitting victims were wired into a machine, and waited for their minds to be probed for changes in chemistry and ionic transfers of energy. It was science gone awry.

Prophetic questions plagued him. *What would it take to read an unmapped mind? Decipher a memory from scratch? Carry on a two-way conversation with a total stranger?*

Parker slid out of bed, leaving Kate to sleep. She needed the rest. He'd convinced her to move into his room after her attack. Sticking together, they could survive the madness. Moving forward, they'd do everything together.

Almost everything.

He turned on the shower and stepped into its streaming warmth, lathered and rinsed. He probed the bullet holes in his side with his fingers. The wounds were tender, but healing nicely.

Kate had done an outstanding job stitching him up.

Parker was invested in ANCRI because of her. Now Kate was at risk because of him.

He had become a willing conspirator in a distorted quest almost overnight. Part of him wanted to escape with Kate. Run away with her. Yet another part felt helpless to resist forces beyond his control, the esoteric laws of destiny and karma.

He also yearned to test the iniquitous premise: read an unmapped mind.

It wasn't as if he never thought about it or even attempted it. Many had and failed.

Parker dried off from the shower and dressed in the navy-colored scrubs the institute provided. After donning his lanyard, he set out for the neurophysiology annex and the pods.

He'd meet up with Kate later, but wanted to snoop around first without her. She was a federal agent on her own mission. His quest was a different one entirely.

Just as Levine had done, Parker swiped his badge across the card reader and stepped into the anteroom. The air pressurized before the inner doors opened. He marched into the neurophysiology lab as if he owned the place. The enormous room was quiet, the monstrous Wall of Knowledge inactive. His gaze raked the landscape, registering the thirty egg-shaped pods that glowed like idling alien spacecraft.

Faces attached to medical scrubs watched him invade their inner sanctum, as if he were a thief out to steal something—or worse, a madman who would start unhooking participants from the contraptions engulfing them. Behind a console, a woman dressed in light blue picked up a phone and made a call.

Since the patients were comatose, Parker deduced that the staff dress code wasn't for the psychological wellbeing of the patients, but more to establish a hierarchy—like stripes and bars and leaves on military uniforms. He guessed green meant nurses, gray signaled technicians, and light blue was reserved for floor-level physicians. Yesterday, he had caught a glimpse of navy beneath Levine's lab coat. His own scrubs were navy, which he found odd.

Green scrubs moved about the pods like bees pollinating flowers, while the gray ones worked a row of consoles. The woman in light blue rose and intercepted him.

"May I help you, Dr. Parker?" she asked.

She knew his name. Someone told her to be on the lookout for Thomas Parker.

He made a fast summation of the gatekeeper: mid-forties, attractive, rich brown skin, intense brown eyes, and black hair tied into a pony tail with gray emerging near her ears. She kept her chin up and shoulders broad, as if she was ready for a fight.

Parker cracked an inviting smile. "You can start by telling me your name."

She took a breath. "Alexis Hicks, one of the attendings."

"Pleased to meet you," he said, taking the crook of her elbow in his and steering her down a row of pods. "Now, Dr. Hicks, I'm a chronic insomniac. I know why I'm up before the crack of dawn. But you've got to tell me, how did you get stuck on the graveyard shift?"

Her features thawed a bit. "The institute has three ICU docs. Unfortunately, I drew the short straw for the first week."

His eyebrows arched. "You've been at ACNRI only a week?"

Hicks shrugged. "More like a couple of days, tied to the arrival of our participants."

Parker stopped at the pod numbered 16 and took in the cockpit of gadgetry surrounding its human host.

"You mean patients, don't you?"

"Of course I do," Hicks said, "but the institute is adamant about calling them participants. I'm told the terminology is tied to legal contracts."

Parker reached into pod 16 and took the gloved hand of its participant. "Okay, I get labels: patients versus participants." He eyed Hicks closely. "*I remember that I do not treat a fever, a cancerous growth, but a sick human being.*"

Behind pursed lips, she stiffened. "You're reciting the Hippocratic Oath."

"You know it," he said. "Historians tell us our oath was written between the fifth and third centuries BC. An earlier version contained the line: *nor shall any man's entreaty prevail upon me to administer poison to anyone.*"

Hicks' posture went rigid.

Parker turned to the pod.

Sixteen could be anyone, male or female. The exposed jaw line showed a tint of complexion, suggesting Hispanic or Asian ancestry. He studied the amorphous, indistinguishable form and thought of Becky. A mass of tubes and IV lines and wiring snaked away from the suited figure. The pod was like an incubator, keeping its host alive for trials and testing. It was impossible to discern the sex of the participant from a small patch of flesh or the unisex contours of the body suit.

He missed Becky, not for their unexpected rendezvous, but from what she'd brought to his research. She'd made him whole. No matter how she was involved in the theft of his research, Becky Ward would always be his partner.

Parker turned to Hicks. "Patient sixteen. Tell me about the patient's medical state."

She stole an anxious glance at the pod. "Do you have a specific question, doctor?"

"I have several," he said. "First, what's their underlying medical condition? Present to me their ailment or the calamity that produced their unconscious state. Each patient has a GCS, I presume," he said, referring to the Glasgow Coma Scale, a neurological measure of a person's conscious state. "Really, the question troubling me the most is, why the hell are these people in comas?"

"I'm not privy to those records. Our participants are here for medical assessment, and, as applicable, treatment. If you desire patient history, please consult Doctors Richards or Levine."

Parker stepped toward her. "Dr. Hicks, why are you here? What's your job?"

"I'm hired to manage the physiological stasis of the participants. Not cure them."

Across the room, the lab's doors opened.

Noam Levine entered, looking haggard, as if he had been rousted from a sound sleep.

Parker maneuvered past Hicks, then abruptly spun back to trap her between the pod and himself. "You mean, keep them alive for experimentation, don't you?"

"How dare you," she snapped. "Who are you to judge me?"

"I'm no judge. That duty rests with God." His eyes probed hers. Edging toward her, Parker forced Hicks to lean back over the pod to maintain her personal space. He gripped her hand to steady her balance. "You and me, are we here to cure 'em or dissect 'em?"

Hicks looked uneasy. "I'm not here to harm anyone."

He whispered in her ear. "Not sure everyone here feels the same way."

"Dr. Parker!" Levine called from across the room, "is there something I can help you with?"

Parker yanked Hicks upright. "Alexis, look me up sometime. I'll buy you a drink. Oh, I forgot—ANCRI prohibits alcohol in the facility. Now that's a damn crime. See you around, Dr. Hicks."

Parker faced Levine. "Dr. Levine, I have my first complaint. This dry workplace mandate is going to torture me. Short of alcohol, you offer no vices except dangerous narcotics. Who do I talk to about getting into the pharmacy?"

Levine frowned, looking from Hicks to Parker.

Parker spun Levine toward the door. "Last night, I could not get one iota of sleep. Incurable insomnia. Just like the night before my first day of med school." He appraised his new friend. "Sir, you don't look quite awake. You gettin' enough sleep? If not, as a physician, I can write a script for zolpidem, zopiclone, or ramelteon. How about we hit the cafeteria, slam espresso shots, and talk about the keys to the pharmacy."

Alexis Hicks caught herself holding her breath as she watched Parker escort Levine out of the neurophysiology lab. She glanced to coworkers moving about the pods, most having dismissed the interruptions and gone back to their duties.

She clenched her hands into fists to keep them from trembling. Like most doctors, she hated being challenged or lectured. She notified the charge nurse that she needed a break and left, but in the opposite direction of Parker and Levine.

Hicks headed straight to the women's locker room.

Popping open toilet stall doors, she ensured each was empty, and entered the last stall. Taking refuge on the toilet, she locked the door and tried to process what had just happened.

She opened a palm and exposed the crumpled note that lay inside.

Thomas Parker passed it to her when he caught her balance.

YOU DON'T KNOW ME. I NEED YOUR HELP. LOOKING FOR A FRIEND. SHE WAS TAKEN HOSTAGE. HER NAME IS REBECCA WARD. FRIENDS CALL HER BECKY. CAUCASION. 28. BRUNETTE. I NEED HER POD NUMBER.

Hicks took several breaths.

Her recruitment out of the Naval Medical Research Center in Silver Spring, Maryland, had doubled her salary and given her the opportunity to put her TS clearance to use in the private sector. She was used to the military system of need-to-know, classified operations, and staying focused on the tasks at hand.

Never had anyone questioned her ethics or challenged what she stood for.

Hostage? The implications were ominous.

Who the hell was Rebecca Ward?

She didn't want to know that answer.

She didn't need to know that answer.

Hicks dropped the note between her legs and flushed the toilet.

40
CLASSICAL CONDITIONING

THE MORNING CAME EARLY, and Kate awoke to find the other side of the bed vacant.

What a mess.

Her mistakes got Jack killed. The laptop was lost. She should have anticipated the attack and avoided putting herself in a vulnerable situation.

She resented being the victim.

Oddly, her life had been spared. That could not be a coincidence.

The lingering effects of a sedative Parker provided made her thoughts even fuzzier. She remembered the attack, waking to find Parker, and listening to his plans, which included moving her into his dorm room.

She lifted the bedsheets and peered down the length of her body to make sure clothes were still on. Nothing happened on that front.

Kate glanced to the empty space beside where she lay.

A smile stretched across her face. *Thomas Parker is the mission. I can't get any closer to him than sharing his bed.*

A romantic entanglement with him was not a horrendous thought.

Kate checked the bedside clock: 7:30 a.m. They agreed to meet at his lab then grab breakfast.

Parker's presence made her first undercover experience different than expected, much different from her work as a forensics investigator.

And she sort of liked it.

IN THE RESEARCH ANNEX among the individualized lab spaces, neon green bands of lighting encircled the outside walls of his assigned Lab 12.

Parker chuckled. A green lab was just another sign. Green for go.

Inside, he studied equipment specs to the participant pods on a digital whiteboard. He had to admit, ANCRI had all the high-tech toys a researcher could ever want. The interactive touchscreen gave him a large electronic workspace to break down the technology into digestible chunks. On the surface, ANCRI appeared to hide nothing. He had access to everything: files, specs, vendor submittals, links to concurrent research efforts. It wasn't until he drilled down into individual patient records that he encountered his first roadblock.

So he backed up and cross-referenced files on the participant pods.

Each unit was identical. The localized environments were unisex. Nothing distinguished one from another. The differences in bio-suits were based on the size of the human form, not the suit's functionality.

On the board, he used his fingers to jockey files around and detail out the bio-suits. The suits performed expected life-monitoring functions with embedded electrocardiogram, ECG, probes and O_2 sensors, but they also incorporated environmental regulation with integrated heat and cooling panels and had pressurized extremity cuffs and dual-channel electronic muscle stimulation. The suits had designated penetrations for feeding and respiration tubes, IV tubes, and urinary and anal waste.

The NASA-inspired amorphous suits were built to keep vegetative hosts alive for years.

He brought up a color schematic of the IV lines piped to the participants and traced upstream tubing to a series of reservoirs and pumps.

He found what he needed. A string of IV tubing connected to a dedicated drug infusion pump marked SLAVE, which interfaced with an upstream master controller.

The lab door swished opened.

"Am I disturbing you?" Kate asked, her gaze taking in the space.

He waved her over. "Not at all. Take a look at this."

She moved beside him, close. "Thanks for letting me sleep in."

He kissed her on the cheek. "You needed it."

She smiled in return.

They'd agreed to expand their charade and display a romantic closeness. To anyone watching on surveillance systems, they would appear inseparable, a team.

On the board, Parker flicked non-essential elements aside and expanded a schematic.

"MIT came up with the original auto-pilot concepts to manage barbiturate-induced comas. ANCRI uses a master controller to regulate levels of consciousness, metabolic rates, and oxygen demands through ECG signatures and biological suppression patterns. Their sedatives have code names, but they've got to be along the line of propofol, pentothal, or thiopental."

Kate pointed to the screen. "If we intercept the sedatives depressing their central nervous systems, we can wake everyone up and get them the hell out of here."

"I thought you wanted to find Samuel Ford."

She looked uneasy. "That was before I was assaulted and put into a choke hold until I passed out."

He took her hand. "ANCRI will never let us leave. Not us. Not the patients. Our buddy Earl will shoot us before we could get a single person disconnected."

She pulled her hand away and made fists. "What Richards is doing is unlawful. You and I both know these people are held against their wills. ANCRI is running an illegal human trials program. Regardless of whether or not we find incriminating evidence linking them to the abduction of Samuel Ford and the murder of his girlfriend, we have them on at least thirty counts of kidnapping, aggravated assault, and criminal endangerment. If we do nothing, we're no better than Richards."

"Well, you're not entirely wrong." Parker brought up a layout of the neurophysiology lab and pointed to the array of pods. "Who's Pavlov?"

Kate tossed him a confused look. "You mean, the guy with the dog?"

"Yeah. It's classical conditioning. Richards has to prove he's in control. The Frontier is his show. We're just paid performers. Hurting you was behavioral reinforcement—for both of us. Work hard, you get rewarded. Get out of line, you get punished."

"You mean choked to death." Kate shook her head. "This is insane."

Parker cringed. "I think the insanity has just begun."

In his office, Richards studied surveillance footage playing on desk monitors. Inconveniently, audio was unavailable.

On screen, Parker and Meir worked on a wall display in Lab 12.

Suddenly, he wished he could read lips or read minds.

Levine entered without knocking. "Parker's predictable, I'll give him that. Don't buy into his romance with Meir. Their relationship seems contrived. He's protecting her. Can't figure that part out, though. And Makara is right. Something about her is not genuine."

Richards glanced at his second in command. "It looks like she put up a fight."

Levine touched a small bruise on his cheek. "Meir wasn't that difficult to handle."

He almost smiled. "What did you get from your conversation with Hicks?"

"Nothing. Parker was fishing for patient information, just like we thought he would."

"Did she indicate which participant?"

"No one in particular."

Richards grunted. "He's searching for Rebecca Ward. He knows she's here."

"Thornton abducted her without anyone's knowledge. Besides, let him search. He won't find her."

Richards thought for a long moment. "On the contrary, that's exactly what we want him to do. He'll try and communicate with her."

"How? The participants are in comas."

Richards zoomed in on the surveillance screen and pointed. "The first thing Parker evaluated was the IV network to the pods. By now he's deduced we're using a combination of propofol and thiopental to keep the participants sedated."

Levine frowned. "How long you think before he tries to circumvent the drug induction system?"

Richards grunted. "That's our advantage. We control the sedation, to which he doesn't have access rights. And at some point, if we don't reduce sedation, successful cognitive interfaces will be unfruitful."

"I see your point," Levine said finally. "You think Parker knows we'll drop off sedation and then he'll make a move to contact her?"

Richards rubbed his chin. "Let's not make this too easy for him. Swap pods one and ten and make the appropriate program updates. That'll put Rebecca Ward in the middle of the population. And while we're at it, move Caroline Wang's pod from thirty to position twenty. It'll be interesting to see if Parker can keep up."

IN HIS GREEN LAB, Parker shuffled graphical objects and files around on the interactive display until he homed in on a set of parallel IV lines responsible for delivering chemicals to the participants.

Kate edged closer, studying the diagram. Using her fingers, she traced tubing to a central pump controller titled NMB-PSI. NMB-PSI electronically-controlled gate valves were in the closed position, meaning no chemicals currently flowed in that string of tubing.

"NMB-PSI," Parker said, "must stand for neuromuscular block and postsynaptic influence. It's the protocol that delivers paralytic drugs."

Kate scrunched her forehead. "So when the patients aren't drugged into unconsciousness, they're injected with neuromuscular blocks to keep them paralyzed?"

"Think about it. You can't read the mind of a drug-induced coma person—they're deep asleep. At some point you must limit sedation. But fully awake, they'll freak out. To counter that, the logical solution is to create paralysis. ANCRI has devised a method to transition patients from one protocol to the next."

Kate's face went pale. "You're saying the patients will be cognitively awake but unable to move, when we probe their minds?"

Parker's gaze fell distant. "Pretty much, that's what's going to happen."

41
HAPPIEST PLACE ON EARTH

RANDY WANG CLEARED ANCRI's perimeter guard station, using a fake identification in the name of Li Randall, a consultant specializing in data centers. At the clinical neurophysiology annex, a coffee-pounding guard named Earl processed his site-specific badge and escorted him to the office of Dr. Stewart Richards.

Earl introduced him and retreated to wait in the hallway.

Richards took a seat behind his desk.

"I'm here to implement software ecosystem enhancements," Randall said.

Richards eyed him closely. "Ecosystems?"

Randall nodded. "Think of it as high-performance software upgrades that increases holistic productivity. You'll be able to do more work in less time."

"It's essential that these upgrades are performed now?"

Randall handed Richards an authorization letter on Phoenix Consortium letterhead. "RMG Solutions assigned me as your executive systems analyst, which your own security protocols validated. Dr. Richards, I already have access to the institute's networks, I just need your authorization to physically enter the data center to complete ANCRI's service upgrades."

Richards frowned. "How long will it take to perform this work?"

Randall shrugged. "Two days. You won't even know I'm here. And best of all, your staff won't even see a blip in network performance."

Richards contemplated this. "See the guard outside. He'll take you to the data center."

AFTER A LUNCH, PARKER and Kate returned to his green-trimmed lab. Since they had spent the morning breaking down bio-suits and life-support/life-suppressing systems their afternoon migrated to neurological interfaces, headgear, and the pods.

Parker examined the systemic interfaces, while Kate scoped out the details of the pods. In the glow of screens, from her terminal to his interactive whiteboard, they shared files, drawings, schematics, and data sheets back and forth.

He was intrigued. "ANCRI's reverse engineered, and oddly improved on my concepts."

She nudged up beside him.

On the whiteboard, Parker separated the headgear into distinct units: multilayer superconductor sensors, cooling systems, and neural interfaces. A 3D model demonstrated how ANCRI's brain-machine interface (BMI) enveloped the skull to target specific anatomic regions within the brain. The high-tech BMI had the unique ability to communicate with individual neural neighborhoods, no matter the depth of their cognitive placement.

A device on the screen was labeled SQUID, its tiny fissures and valleys visibly bonded to nanowires and carbon nanotubes for heat rejection and cooling.

Kate pointed to the screen. "Squid?"

"Superconducting quantum interference device. SQUIDs detect extremely subtle magnetic fields, such as those in our brains. Brainwaves can be ten thousand times weaker than those in the heart. On a larger scale, similar tech is used in magnetoencephalography imaging. A Princeton team designed a kissing-cousin named spin exchange relaxation-free magnetometer, but it requires the use of lasers and encapsulation in potassium vapors. Try putting that contraption over your head."

From the pool of participants, he randomly selected a neurological scan belonging to the host in pod 1. The wrinkled lobe structures were pre-identified with automated tags, words like frontal, temporal, parietal, and occipital. The brain topography clearly belonged to a dormant brain, signified by the preponderance of shades of gray marked with faint splashes of pink and blue. A rainbow color-code was located in the lower corner of the screen, the vertical color scale ranging from light gray (inactive) to yellow (highly stimulated).

"Question," he asked. "Percentage wise, how much of our brain do we use?"

She punched him in the shoulder. "You're testing me."

Parker grinned, but said nothing.

"That fact was drilled into me in med school," Kate said. "The 'ten percent' brain use myth can be attributed to revisionist citations taken from an article by William James, a psychologist. James said, 'We are making use of only a small part of our possible mental and physical resources.' Even famous people like Einstein have misquoted the underlying sentiment. Our brain is wired with multiple neural pathways and redundancy. And since every region of our brain is active, we use a hundred percent of it, even though a hundred percent use may not be necessary at any given time."

Parker laughed. "Half my students get that answer wrong. On their own, neurons are not particularly bright. But cram 100 billion of them together in a compact space and let them start talking together, and we get brainstorms. Cerebral communications are inefficient and neurons cohabitate in a very noisy fishbowl. There's a lot of chatter to filter out."

Kate nodded to indicate she was keeping up.

Parker continued, "Most of the brain's energy is used on synaptic energy transfers, the shuffling around of sodium, potassium, and calcium ions. When ions cross a synaptic junction, energy is released, like a micro-micro-burst. The brain has an overall magnetic field of ten to the minus fifteenth Tesla—that's real, real small. Since superconductors have a current density of roughly zero, they can detect a weak magnetic flux and self-generate a corresponding pulse of energy. If enough sensors are available, in theory we can read 100 billion neurons."

She pointed to the BMI on the screen. "I don't see 100 billion of your super-sensors."

"A one-to-one ratio isn't required." He expanded the SQUID component view to reveal a layered sandwich of low-temperature and high-temperature semiconductor wafers. "As you pointed out, our brain is wired for redundancy. If our singular goal is to read a thought, we can ignore mechanisms such as motor sensory stimulation, respiratory management, and primitive physiological functions."

Kate fell silent, then said, "A thought is more than one neuron firing. Ion transfers across a single synaptic junction are not enough to create a twitch of an eyelid, let alone enough to generate energy transfer to create a conscious impression. Multiple neurons must fire together and cohesively stimulate other neurons, which, in turn, propagate signals to more neurons until the collective electro-chemical migration is enough to generate the slightest thought or feeling. If I recall correctly, millions of neurons are needed to produce the most trivial thought."

Parker saw her interest grow as she put the pieces together.

She turned to him, her mouth nearly agape. "You already know how to build a neurological template that filters out the extraneous noise."

He took her hand and led her from the lab. "Let's discuss it over dinner."

RANDY WANG, IN HIS alter ego of Li Randall, data center consultant extraordinaire, swiped into ANCRI's data center. Safety regulations required him to carry a self-contained breathing apparatus (SCBA), which he grabbed from a locker at the door and slung over his shoulder.

A perpetual, low-frequency mechanical hum churned through cool air and penetrated everything. Since the data center was an unmanned space, interior lights blinked on as he progressed deeper into the two-story structure and down a long grated metal platform.

Mystified, Wang stopped dead in his tracks. He had seen the layout from RMG's construction drawings, but data center was beyond impressive.

His vision took in the upper level with its rows of glowing blue, high-density neural network servers. Below, through the diamond-shaped gaps in grated flooring, he spotted translucent-green, like the color of antifreeze, emanating off super-frigid coolant ponds that bathed honeycomb groups of submerged 2,048 qubit quantum supercomputers.

Quantum computers required the most complex superconductor integrated circuits in the world. They operated on the laws of molecular physics and quantum mechanics, and exceeded the computational horsepower and speed of supercomputer contemporaries. The disadvantage was that quantum-based microcircuits required operational temperatures close to absolute zero, colder than interstellar space—thus the need for the coolant ponds and super-cooled encasement. Quantum computing benefited from a metaheuristic principle called quantum annealing and duality states for its qubits—quantum bits—that could superpose themselves and reside in classical states of zero, one, or both conditions simultaneously.

The RMG design incorporated a hybrid of quantum supercomputers, neural network supercomputers, and high-capacity, nano-engineered photonic data storage systems.

For computer nerds, ANCRI's data center was like visiting Disneyland, the Happiest Place on Earth. Wang's NSA colleagues at the Agency's Utah Data Farm and Fort Meade would be so damn jealous.

After his sense of awe passed, Wang set out for a small glass-walled control room in the heart of the two-tiered data center.

At an operator's terminal, he patched in a remote hard drive he'd smuggled in and went to work analyzing the data center's architecture. Using passcodes obtained from the RMG servers, it was relatively easy to establish himself as a network administrator.

Wang's official directives, code-named Synaptic Touch, were simple—construct a portgroup and anonymous network bridge to a mirrored DoD server in Maryland, and build in supervisory control of ANCRI.

His personal plan involved finding his daughter, Caroline.

BACK IN THE DORMS, Kate washed up for the night and sat on Parker's bed. The imaginary world that they had created came with his and her sides of the bed. All business, Parker sat upright and leaned against the wall, seemingly oblivious to her presence.

She studied him. His shirtless torso showed toned features and unsuspecting muscular definition, counter to what she'd expect from a geeky professor-type. She could see the stitched up bullet hole in his obliques. Absorbed in his tablet, he read a journal article on "Action Potential Initiation and Propagation: Upstream Influences on Neurotransmission."

If that couldn't cure insomnia, she didn't know what would.

Kate slid under the covers, grabbed her tablet, and opened her homework assignment. She stared at the screen, thinking that she landed in an alien world of his and her dueling tablets, and a place where their every move might be under surveillance.

She peered up at the ceiling. "You think we're being watched?"

It took Parker a moment to realize that she'd spoken. "Huh?"

"Thomas, do you think they're watching us?"

"What, right now?" He squinted at the ceiling. "Do you?"

"I don't know." She leaned over and kissed him on the cheek. "That's for just in case we are."

She fluffed her pillow and settled in as he returned to his reading.

Over dinner, Parker had laid out a grand plan for mapping and interfacing with the human consciousness. His scientific vigor was almost infectious. She imagined what it was like to spend time with him on a daily basis, and wondered if Becky once felt the same way. He obviously cared about her, enough to try and save her even after she'd betrayed him.

"Do coma patients dream?"

Parker wrinkled his nose. "Post-event studies show some patients do."

"You know, Thomas," she said, "they're prisoners here, not patients."

Without looking away from his screen, he said, "Kate, we discussed this. There's nothing we can do for them right now. Not without risking getting people killed."

"Colonel Wang left a password for Ford's computer: FRONTIER28. A catamaran with twenty-eight University of Miami students aboard sank in the Atlantic. All were lost at sea. It's no coincidence. Simple math. If you add Becky and Caroline Wang to the participant pool, they complete the group of thirty."

Parker hadn't moved, so Kate reached over and clicked off his device, which went dark in his hand.

She touched his arm. "Thomas, I know this is a once-in-a-lifetime opportunity. But we can't torture people."

Parker glanced at her. "What do you want, Kate?"

She pursed her lips. "Regardless of what our government is sanctioning, we're involved in it. We're on the front line. This entire program is unethical. Prisoners or not, the legality of reading a person's thoughts hasn't been considered, but I can assure you the very act violates a person's civil liberties. Thirty people are prisoners under our watch."

"I won't argue." He took a slow breath. "This may sound vain, but if I don't help Richards in this distorted quest, eventually someone else will. Then, who knows what happens to the technology? ANCRI can't, won't, let anybody live. None of us. We've seen too much. But together we can stop it and get everyone out of here."

Parker rolled to face her.

The intimacy of his gaze caused her to blush, and she averted her eyes from his.

"In case anyone is watching," he said, turning her face toward his.

He initiated a touching of their noses and a brush of their lips.

Kate's pulse accelerated as their lips joined, and she did not resist. His kiss was moist and deep. She felt unable to pull away as their lips clung together.

She closed her eyes.

His fingertips drifted up the outside of her thigh. She sighed and let the air in her lungs go shallow. The intimacy was unexpected, yet welcomed, and for her a bit overdue.

She felt his lips progress to her ear and kiss her lobe.

He whispered, "Trust me. I need you to do that. For all of us."

SATURDAY, OCTOBER 10th

In the kingdom of the blind the one-eyed man is king.
Desiderius Erasmus, Dutch Theologian, from Adagia (1500)

42
WATCHFUL EYES

1:10 A.M. EVEN FOR a pretend IT guru named Li Randall, it took twice as long as Randy Wang thought it would to complete his non-sanctioned defense department network upgrades to ANCRI's data center. After nearly twelve hours in the facility, he still had not the slightest idea of the whereabouts of his daughter Caroline.

Security logs showed no recent activity for her, with her last proximity badge location being the anatomical pathology lab in the basement.

Before setting out to hunt for her, Wang modified the surveillance system so he could move unseen. A hacker's traditional approach was to loop-feed fake security footage for a camera input, but since he didn't have a video replicator, he cloned non-essential cameras and dropped out all of the cameras to the basement areas.

43
A FATHER'S OFFER

3:30 A.M. RANDY WANG was no closer tracking down Caroline. After searching the institute's basement, including the incinerator room and anatomical pathology lab, he decided that Caroline was either dead or among the pool of participants.

Neither outcome was comprehensible.

A fatherly intuition that he could not substantiate told him Caroline was not dead. He just knew it. But the alternative was horrifying. Caroline was undergoing human experimentation.

Wang took a risk and made a beeline to the anteroom outside the neurophysiology lab. Inside the buffered space, through a hatched panel of glass, he studied a dimly lit lab populated with glowing oval capsules. He counted thirty. A large billboard-sized screen along the front wall was dormant. A handful of staff milled about.

Which capsule housed Caroline?

He'd managed to track Thornton's long reach to the boating tragedy that claimed twenty-eight University of Miami students—lives that his band of miscreants had hand-delivered to ANCRI. Who in their right mind would ever think to look for the missing 1,200 miles north? He suspected that Thornton had added Rebecca Ward in retribution for his own men's deaths.

Did Thornton discover Caroline was his informant?

He dreaded what they might be doing to his daughter.

Part of him wanted to storm the lab and scream, "Where's Caroline?"

But his orders were precise: infiltrate, construct a network bridge to a mirrored offsite DoD server, and get out. Avoid tertiary matters not affecting Pentagon directives, and under no circumstances get caught.

U.S. Army Colonel Randy Wang followed his orders, even at the sacrifice of being a father.

But that wouldn't stop him from ensuring that others succeeded in his absence.

On his back, Parker stared at the tiny green light of the smoke detector above his shared bed. He could feel Kate's warmth beside him, and had been unable to turn off thoughts of her since their kiss. It was spontaneous, and he hadn't expected the surge of feelings. For her part, she hadn't resisted, and seemed receptive to his affection.

Kate Morgan was smart, attractive. *What was there not to like?* He wanted to swing for the fences, but chickened out, stopping at a caress of a thigh and a prolonged kiss. *It could have been great. You should have run the bases.*

Parker shrugged off the thought and rolled out of bed, trying not to disturb her.

"What time is it?" Kate asked sleepily.

"After three," he whispered. "Sorry I woke you."

Kate buried her face into a pillow. "Thomas, don't you sleep?"

"The last time I slept a full night, I woke to find my lab gone."

She clicked on a bedside lamp and sat up. "What's the matter?"

He stared at Kate, unable to turn his gaze away. Her lips formed a wrinkled little pout and a sleep line creased the side her cheek. Her long brown hair was a mess. She was perfect, in a morning-after way. Too bad it wasn't really a morning after.

"Nothing." Parker picked up his tablet and waved it at her. "I want to get through more reading. Go back to sleep. I'll be in the other room."

She collapsed into her pillow. "Wake me in a few hours. Don't let me sleep in."

Parker clicked off her bedside lamp and kissed her on the cheek. "Sweet dreams."

In the small sitting area, he closed the bedroom door, plopped himself down on the couch, and put up his feet on a coffee table. On his tablet, he was halfway through a lengthy article entitled "Modeling Spike Timing-Dependent Plasticity (STDP) and Postsynaptic Membrane Potentials" when he heard a faint rap on the hallway door.

He cocked his head and listened.

The three-rap sequence repeated itself, this time louder.

Cautiously, he traipsed over and answered the door.

Wang pushed inside and motioned for Parker to shut the door.

"Colonel!" Parker snapped in hushed tones. "Where the hell have you been?"

Wang looked him up and down, then glanced around the room. "Where is she?"

"Who, Kate?" He bobbed his head toward the bedroom. "She snores like a gorilla. I found it hard to sleep."

Wang eyed him carefully. "You two are...?"

Parker shook his head. "It's not what it seems. Kate's cover story may be compromised. A researcher met the real Cassondra Meir at a conference several years back. Stewart Richards felt the need to exert his authority. He had Kate assaulted."

Wang's face fell solemn. "She okay?"

"You want me to wake her?"

"No. I need to speak to you. Alone. Off the record."

"Sure." Parker felt a chill, sensing the onslaught of bad news. "How'd you know Kate and I were...?"

"Card readers and proximity sensors log staff movements. Both of you showed up in room 212."

His eyebrows shot up. "We're being tracked?"

Wang nodded. "Every move you make is under video surveillance, except the large lab, a holographic room, dorm rooms, and toilets." He grimaced. "Right now, I do not represent the Pentagon or the NSA. So I have no official presence here, and this conversation never occurred."

Parker frowned. "You're not recruiting me to be an NSA spy, are you?"

"No," said Wang. "Look, I need your help. I'll do anything you want. Anything. Just name it."

Parker grinned. "Anything? Okay, you have my undivided attention."

Wang took a seat in a chair. "The man that assaulted you and kidnapped Rebecca Ward was killed a few days ago."

Parker furrowed his brow. "You mean the NSA murdered him."

Wang shrugged. "Read into it as you will. Gene Thornton died in a natural gas explosion, and his death afforded me a narrow window of opportunity."

Wang handed Parker a thick credit card with the imprinted name and logo of the Bank of Canada Caymans Islands. "I said if you helped us get inside, I would return the favor. This covers the replacement of your equipment. The card has routing, account, passcode numbers. In sequence, type them into the pop up menu that appears."

Parker studied the card, flipping its USB plug in and out. "What do you want?"

"Stewart Richards may be the face of ANCRI, but a company called the Phoenix Consortium manages the program. ANCRI receives funding through a black budget multiagency grant. It's a bookkeeping method that allows federal agencies to avoid line item expenditures and shelter assets from congressional scrutiny. Fiscally, ANCRI's sponsors are DARPA, CIA, FBI, and the State Department. Tell me, who in that group does not want in on neurological singularity? The Frontier will make current methods of intelligence gathering obsolete."

Parker rolled his eyes. "Oh, yes, the quest for mind control."

"More than that. The U.S. government wants the ability to pick apart consciousness, probe the mind's depths and extract its secrets, and even alter the foundational framework to judgement and reality. The Frontier will subliminally turn enemies of the state into sign-carrying allies. The Secretary of State calls it creating Peace on Earth."

"And goodwill toward men?" Parker asked. "I'd expect the NSA to be at the head of the line on this tech."

Wang forced a smile. "Who says we're not? Why do you think I planted Rebecca Ward with you at Princeton? I had a hunch. It paid off. Unfortunately, Richards found you because of Rebecca. However, the rest of this disturbing yarn is woven entirely by others. The NSA had no knowledge or involvement in Ford's kidnapping or the assassination of the FBI's Deputy Director. That baggage belongs to the State Department. My intelligence suggests the White House will wash its hands of this mess and order the Phoenix Consortium to shut down this entire program on Monday. Dr. Parker, that gives you two days."

Parker laughed. "You're kidding, right? It took me and your hired hand two years to get as far as reading preschool shapes from a deck of playing cards."

Wang's expression darkened. "Think about it. Maybe ANCRI lets the staff live, if they sign a nondisclosure agreement in exchange for silence. Then again, maybe not. But ANCRI sure as hell won't let thirty test subjects survive. There's an incinerator for a reason."

Parker fell silent, his mind churning through scenarios.

Wang pushed forward in his chair. "Have you located Caroline? Her last proximity log is over three days old. What can you tell me about my daughter?"

"Not a lot." Parker shrugged. "Dr. Levine wasn't forthcoming about Caroline. He said she departed after Phase One. But we suspect she's among the participants, along with Becky. Patient records are restricted. There's no way of validating their presence."

Wang's gaze turned serious. "You will when you read their minds."

Parker pointed to the door. "Get out, Colonel."

"I offer a simple trade. Any resources I can provide in exchange for my daughter's life. Just name your terms."

Parker felt a rush of dread pass through him. "Two brains are on display in a conference room: Alpha and Beta. Clearly, Richards is obsessed with power and control. People around this place are expendable, interchangeable. From the looks of it, anyone can end up in his trophy case. And I'm not anxious in joining that display."

"I'm asking as a father: save my daughter."

Parker squinted hard at the man. "Can't help you or Caroline."

Wang stood and put a firm hand on Parker's bare shoulder. "You're the only person who can."

44
TRIALS AND TORMENT

THE UNRELENTING BURDEN WEIGHED Parker down.

Sitting on the couch, he stared at his palms, imagining that a three-pound organ rested in his mighty hands. Hands turned up, as if to mock God and heaven that mankind could reverse-engineer the universe's greatest evolutionary creation. He thought of the artist's sculpture and the Palms of God in Richards' conference room—hands that could be his own.

Parker had a general idea of what he was doing.

Thirty lives rested in his ability to overcome the improbable, if not the impossible.

His chest felt hollow. Doubt. Hopelessness, knowing his talents and skill might not save everyone. No matter how hard doctors tried, sometimes death prevailed. At some point in their career, all physicians experienced fear, failure, and guilt. Unavoidable doubt.

Parker took a solid breath. *Two days to read an unmapped mind?*

Maybe… it could be done… at ANCRI… but not without enlisting others.

The thought hit him like a volcanic eruption.

Bolting into the bedroom, he switched on the light and ripped back the bed covers.

"Come on, Sleeping Beauty," he said. "Rise and shine."

"What the—?" Kate said, reaching for bedsheets that did not exist.

He kissed her cheek. "Get your lazy butt out of bed."

Dazed, she pushed him aside to squint at the alarm clock. 4:30 a.m.

He untied the waistband to his scrub bottoms, dropped them to the floor, and paraded into the bathroom, leaving the door open.

"Join me if you want, but you have to hurry," he called.

TWO HOURS LATER, KATE found herself submersed in a confined realm of possessed metal, enduring a demonic clamor.

Why would anyone volunteer for this torture?

She had taken Parker up on his invitation. In hindsight, she couldn't believe it. He'd left the door ajar for her. From the bedroom, she could hear the rapid spray of the shower in the tub. She edged the door open and swallowed hard. Wet and naked, he offered her an extended hand. With a reluctant breath, Kate slid out of her garments and joined him.

She felt her hand melt in his and an intake of steam quickened her pulse.

Their second kiss under the invigorating spray of water was sensual. She closed her eyes and went with it. He kissed her neck and could hear his hands rubbing a bar of soap to stir up lather. His lips returned to hers as his hands worked their way down from her shoulders to her hips, lathering her body with suds. She touched his chest with nervous fingertips. His hands found her breasts. Under the cascading warmth, they took turns exploring each other, and jostling their bodies in a rhythmic ritual of affection.

His lips found her neck and she sighed.

Kissing her ear lobe again, he said, "I need to give you an MRI."

"What?" she snapped, digging her fingernails into his chest.

Magnetic resonance imaging, MRI, was one of the most unnerving experiences ever created. The unearthly mechanical throbbing encapsulating her head was the result of a magnetic field passing electricity through gradient coils, which caused the coils to vibrate and groan.

For Kate, understanding the science behind the ordeal did not make it go more smoothly. The human body was nearly 60 percent water. A molecule of water was a bond of one oxygen atom and two hydrogen atoms. As the simplest element in the periodic table, hydrogen carried an even smaller particle at its core, a proton, which spun about an axis, and a single electron orbited its nucleus. In normal conditions, water molecules in the human body were randomly arranged. An MRI's primary magnet caused water molecules in the body, the protons in the hydrogen atoms, to align in one direction. Introducing a second, perpendicular magnetic field as rapid on-and-off pulses, caused each hydrogen proton to fluctuate between an artificial higher energy alignment and its lower, relaxed energy state. Manipulating hydrogen atoms released thermal energy that showed up in an MRI scanner as detectable contrasts in organic tissues.

Nothing was natural about having your hydrogen atoms jiggled.

Too much jiggling and you cooked to death from the inside out.

Right now, confined in the heart of the mechanical beast, Kate hated all men, Thomas Parker included.

Flat on her back, a plastic facemask and blocks restrained her head, kept it rigid. Flat color images flashed over her eyes. Her retinas converted the light impulses to electrical-chemical signals that radiated into her visual cortex. The functional-MRI process detected contrast propagation and blood flow movement in her gray matter. The resulting model was something like watching cosmic dust storms spark alive inside a large walnut.

The throbbing mechanical groan ebbed and flowed as Kate recognized images that appeared in her field of vision. On the first pass, she concentrated on an object and thought about its name without actually speaking it. On a second pass, the same object reappeared and she wouldn't think about its name, instead letting her brain process the object without extended concentration.

Throughout the ordeal, Parker issued instructions through speakers near her head, his voice devoid of intimacy.

As the hour progressed, she endured more cognitive exercises, each task more complex.

"Take a break," he finally said. "Close your eyes, Kate."

The screen above her went dark, as did the MRI room around her.

The groans of the magnets lurked with her in the dark.

Kate snapped. "Relax? Come on, I was hoping to graduate to Where's Waldo?"

THE MRI CONTROL ROOM had a semi-circular layout, a blended observation platform and an image reading room. Panoramic windows gave Parker a view of the dim MRI suite and a soft glow painted Kate's outline. Closest to him, a monitor presented her vitals. All were normal. Walls of screens hosted spatial maps and sliced-and-diced sections of her brain in action, with one screen showing her neo-structural connectivity and brainwaves. An adaptive software platform called ATLAS processed her cognitive responses and posted them on more monitors. Princeton's 3-Tesla unit that his PNI team operated was more academic. ANCRI's unit came with more sophistication and a lot of bells and whistles.

The room was covered in warning signs. Signs at the doors displayed an upside-down horseshoe with lightning bolts coming out of it. DANGER MAGNET IS ALWAYS ON. NO PACEMAKERS. NO LOOSE METAL. NO METAL IMPLANTS.

"You asked to see me." Talib Makara came into the control room, his face a long bearded mask carrying intense dark eyes.

Parker muted the microphone that relayed his voice to Kate inside the MRI.

"Yes," Parker said, spinning in his chair to greet him.

"What can I help you with, Dr. Parker?" Makara asked.

Parker gestured to the MRI. "I need your voice."

"I'm not sure I follow."

Parker slid the technician's microphone over to an empty chair.

"I needed to cure my insomnia, so I read your vita. You have PhDs from MIT in quantum mechanics and neuromolecular algorithms, and oversee a half-dozen computer chimps. You intimidate and harass people because you can. The way I see it, you're an asshole and everybody is beneath you in intellect and cognitive capacity. You consider your time here as time spent with kindergarteners." He paused to collect his thoughts. "Now I'll come right out with it. I have less than forty-eight hours to pull off the impossible. I will make the Frontier a reality. But in order for me to do that, I need that big brain of yours without pushback."

Makara made a fist and extended his index finger. "Dr. Parker, did you call me here for a reason, or are you intent on consuming oxygen pointlessly?"

Parker pointed to the microphone. "Meir doesn't know you're here. Talk to her. Tell her I stepped out for a cup of coffee."

Makara crossed his arms. "Playing practical jokes on colleagues is an ineffective use of my time and talents. That's not ego speaking. It's fact."

Parker shrugged. "I need a fight or flight response. That's something you can provide. I'll get to squandering your time and talents later. Besides, you might consider this fun."

"Fun?" Makara arched an eyebrow and took a seat. He cleared his throat and switched on the microphone. "Good morning, Dr. Meir," he said, his voice low and unmistakable. "I've been asked to talk to you."

"What?" Kate asked, concern lining her voice as it came across the loud speaker in the control room. "Who—?"

"Dr. Makara." He paused for effect. "Your associate stepped out... to get coffee."

On the screen, Kate's vitals ticked up as her heart rate and blood pressure rose.

"He what?"

"Coffee." Makara cracked his knuckles and got comfortable. He eyed Parker to see if he should continue. "Dr. Meir, Cassondra, I thought we should get reacquainted. Talk about neurogenesis and cortical plasticity."

"I have no interest in getting reacquainted," she said, her voice rising in pitch. "I want out of this damn machine!"

Makara sighed into the microphone. "Don't be so impulsive. We're just talking, you and I. As I recall, you co-authored an article in *Nature America* on the irreversible effects on the loss and degradation of neurons in the hippocampus—"

"I'm done here!" Kate's vitals leapt in value on the screen. In the adjoining room, her bare feet kicked up and down on the MRI table. "I'm getting out."

"HOW DARE YOU PUT me through that!" Kate barked at Parker, her breathing labored.

The machine from hell was silent, for a change. She heard sadistic chuckling from Makara as he beat feet from the control room. She'd threatened to kill him.

She ripped the EKG electrodes off her chest from beneath her surgical scrubs, and slung them to the floor.

When she tried to bolt from the room, Parker restrained her.

"I needed an unsolicited fight-or-flight response."

Her heart throbbed as her eyes flooded with wild-eyed vengeance. "Thomas, hands off me because this won't be much of a fight, I promise."

She forged fists and readied herself to drop him with one strike.

"Kate," Parker said, his hands up and defenseless, "stop being hysterical."

"Fight-or-flight?" she snapped. "I have every right to be ticked off. I was assaulted. Makara might have been the one who attacked me."

Parker shook his head. "You can hate him. I get that. But it wasn't Makara."

She looked dubious. "You weren't there. How do you know?"

He took her hands. "Listen, the guard told Johnson he was delinquent on a task involving quantum superposition states. I confirmed that Johnson met Makara, while I was meeting Richards." He tried to catch her gaze. "I took advantage of your distrust in him. Emotions run high. I knew you would draw on an experience of vulnerability, and those feelings blasted through your thalamus, amygdala, and neocortex. The MRI recorded the event."

"You bastard!" She shoved him away. "You tricked me into being a test subject."

Parker shook his head. "Thirty participants have similar emotions. Alone. In the dark. Trapped. Helpless. Scared to death. If we want to communicate with them, we need a baseline of that cognitive state. It's an experience you can relate to, one that had to be real and unrehearsed. We'll fold your MRI data into a template, like an overlay."

Kate turned away. "I hate your guts."

He came up behind her. "I took advantage of our chemistry. I won't apologize, because you're our prototype."

STOPPING AT THE ONLY other car in ANCRI's parking lot, Parker's Jeep Grand Cherokee, Wang—as Li Randall—popped open the back hatch, retrieved a hard-sided carrying case, and lugged it and a large gear bag into the neurophysiology annex.

Earl the guard was at his post, draining a large coffee mug dry, and as diligent as ever.

"What do you have there?" Earl asked, scrutinizing the case and bag.

Randall hoisted the gear bag onto the desk and unzipped it to reveal boxed computer components sealed in manufacturer's plastic wrapping.

"Computer hardware."

Earl leaned over to rifle through the bag.

Pivoting ever so slightly, Randall drew close to the guard's unprotected coffee mug. With a free hand, he uncapped a vial and poured its odorless, tasteless contents into the mug.

Earl gestured to the hard-sided case. "And that?"

"Beats me." Randall set the hard-sided case beside the bag. He snapped opened the lid to the case and exposed an odd-looking sphere of nodes and wires formed over a glossy white mannequin's head. "I was told to deliver this for systems integration."

"By whom?"

"The Phoenix Consortium." He produced an RMG delivery manifest.

"Very well," Earl said, badging him through the sally port.

With the case and bag in hand, Randall ducked into a clean storage across from the neurophysiology lab. He closed the door behind him. From the gear bag, he broke open a box and took out a portable, wireless CCTV monitor and synched it ANCRI's camera systems through a preset IP address. He clicked through camera frames until he came to the security desk.

During his first check-in, Wang noticed the guard was a java consumer. The concoction added to the man's mug was part concentrated diuretic and part imipramine hydrochloride, the last ingredient an antidepressant carrying a side effect of urinary incontinence. On his mini-screen, Wang watched the guard finish off his coffee. Now it was just a matter of time until Earl really had to pee.

While he waited, Wang unloaded the gear bag and stowed its contents on shelving and out of sight. He saved a top shelf for Parker's hard-sided case. Movement on the mini-screen matched the bottom of the hour, when Earl abandoned his post and anxiously hustled to the toilet like a blue ribbon porker in a pig race.

Wang knew he had minutes. Reentering the guard's station, he located a small bank of lockers and retrieved the cell phones belonging to Parker and Meir, devices they'd relinquished in order to enter the premises. The entire process took less time than it did for Earl to return from the men's room, momentarily feeling a whole lot better.

With cell phones in hand, Li Randall returned to the clean storage and added them to the leave-behind box before making his way to ANCRI's data center.

Levine and Richards huddled around the interactive display embedded in the table of the main conference room. Levine cycled through the morning's video surveillance of the MRI suite.

"I know what Parker is up to," Levine announced. "He uses the MRI to construct a neuro-map. Parker used this technique at Princeton. It's crude, but somehow his method pinpoints neuronal activity, allowing him to translate the data into foundational template."

Richards frowned. "Why perform the baseline activity on Dr. Meir? She's not a participant."

Levine smiled, surprised he grasped the answer before Richards. "Dr. Parker came here with a proven process, if not the actual technique on how to build a large-scale cognitive map."

Richards' jaw dropped. "Bring up his network activities. Let's apply his application to a participant. Start with Rebecca Ward in pod 10. Probe her mind and see what comes up."

In the data center, Wang proceeded down the metal platform. Lights blinked on, illuminating his path as he closed in on the control room. Inside, he sat at a terminal and entered the administrator's passcode to bring up the institute's security access platform. ANCRI's access card system was similar to a 26-bit Wiegand protocol, with predetermined attributes set to a two-digit scale, 00 through 99. Stewart Richards had been the only one to carry the highest rank of 99 until Wang recoded Parker's and Kate's privileges to carry the same value, granting them unrestricted access to locations inside ANCRI.

Before logging off the mainframe, Wang granted Parker full control of the institute's video surveillance platform as well.

He stared through the control room's windows. The state-of-the-art data center glowed blue amongst the rows of supercomputer nodes. Green light from the cooling ponds pierced through slatted platforms.

It was an amazing sight. He hoped it wouldn't be his last.

What the NSA could do with this data center would be incredible.

Wang had deviated from his Pentagon directives, yet accomplished every milestone in his covert mandate. The White House and State Department would take the fall for sponsoring out-of-control research, while the Pentagon would become the benefactor of ANCRI's secrets. Publically, the technological initiative, Richards' grand vision of a Frontier, would grow toxic. Samuel Ford became the poster child for the consequences of a government program gone awry.

In the Pentagon's control, Richards' Frontier would live on in a more infantile form.

Wang smiled. It was time for Li Randall, data scientist extraordinaire, to disappear.

And time for Thomas Parker to hold up his part of the bargain and save Caroline.

45
TREASURES FOR ARMAGEDDON

PARKER'S MACGYVER MOMENT PROVED a challenge. Unlike MacGyver or Bill Nye the Science Guy, who could both assemble incendiary devices from toothpaste, duct tape, paperclips, and a Swiss Army knife within a 60-minute TV show, he had no aptitude for alchemy or applied chemistry. While past classmates reinvented the Hindenburg disaster by using electricity to extract hydrogen from water, he preferred to dissect frogs and study their brains under a microscope.

Parker now wished he paid closer attention to creating hydrogen.

On top of that, Kate wasn't speaking to him.

He wasn't getting very far without her.

In the research annex, Parker strolled the long way back to his lab and stopped at a neon pink-banded space. A sign on the door read BIOCHEMISTRY. He peered through the semi-frosted windows and observed that the lab was unattended.

He swiped his access card across its reader to see what would happen.

Doors slid open.

Moving quickly, he improvised a shopping list as he went. Parker knew the desired result—an explosion—chemical reactions with rapid release of energy and a significant increase in volume. ANCRI had to be destroyed, not just taken out of commission. And that effort started with applied chemistry.

He recalled a professor once lecturing him about a candy bar having more energy than a stick of dynamite, meaning if you're counting calories, the tasty mass of sugar wins. But whoever heard of an exploding Snickers? If only there were sticks of dynamite lying around. He thought it odd that the guy with a peace prize named after him had invented nitroglycerin-based high-explosives. Explosives and peace, like identical twins, they always went together.

Parker's ragged mind struggled to recall the essentials for explosive reactions: fuel, oxygen, and an ignition source or heat.

As expected, the chemistry lab was populated with the usual objects: plastic containers and scientific glassware, such as beakers, flasks, and pipets. Refrigerators formed one wall. Fume hoods another.

A poster with the original spokesman for *Dos Equis* read: I DON'T ALWAYS WEAR SAFETY GLASSES. OH WAIT, YES I DO. STAY SAFE MY FRIENDS.

Now a Dos Equis sounded like a spectacular idea.

Parker panned his gaze until he spotted a door papered with ominous signs and skull and crossbones. That was a place to shop for combustibles.

Beyond the door, Parker found compounds and mixtures categorized and easy to find. He collected bottles from shelves, starting with oxidizers labeled potassium nitrate, ammonium nitrate, and sodium nitrate, then shifting to shelf with flammable solids and plastic containers of sulfur and magnesium and potassium thiosulfate. Everything went into a cardboard box he found on the floor. He spotted a brown bottle marked Nitrobenzene. That sounded nasty so he grabbed it too. Before leaving the lab, he thanked *The Most Interesting Man in the World* for the reminder of safety glasses and to enjoy a *Dos Equis* when it was all over.

IN THEIR DORM ROOM, Kate stretched across the bed and buried her face in a pillow. The MRI's claustrophobic hole and mechanical chatter was hard to push from her mind, and she felt foolish for breaking down the way she did. *Thomas Parker is the mission.* She had showered with the man. What was she thinking? She felt lost without Jack Wright. Undercover work was not her forte, and clearly she was way off script. Finding evidence to Samuel Ford was her true mission, not being beholden to the NSA or Thomas Parker.

It was time for her to do her job and find the senator.

A knock on a hallway door tore her away from her thoughts.

Kate approached the door with added caution. Through the crease beneath the door, she detected shadows belonging to a pair of feet. With a palm against the door, she took a calming breath and answered it, opening it just a sliver.

A woman in light blue scrubs peered at her.

"Oh," the woman said, her face a mask of confusion. "I was under the impression this was Dr. Parker's room."

Kate evaluated the woman. Attractive. African American. A hint of an east coast accent, perhaps from the Virginia area.

"Thomas isn't here," Kate replied, opening the door wider. "I'm just borrowing his room while mine is being fumigated."

The woman responded with an awkward nod and turned to leave.

"Can I help you, doctor? I'm guessing you're a doc. It's the whole blue scrub thing."

The woman shook her head. "No."

Kate shrugged. "Come on. Obviously you came here for a reason."

The woman hesitated behind tight lips.

Kate stepped closer. "You can trust me."

"Tell him, ten," the woman said. "And he better hurry."

AT HIS POST, EARL the guard watched Thomas Parker enter Lab 18 and disappear into a storeroom. A minute later, he reappeared carrying a box. Surveillance cameras watched essential spaces, but not storage rooms. And from fixed camera angles, there was no way to see what was in the box.

Earl made a mental note to have the lab's supplies inventoried.

On a different monitor, he detected Meir making haste in the direction of Parker's homeroom lab. The two appeared to be on a collision course.

IN HIS GREEN-BANDED LAB, Parker set his box of chemistry treasures on the counter. Kate slipped inside and behind him before the doors shut. She was out of breath. He noticed the intensity of her gaze carried an unspoken: "I have something to tell you."

"Thomas—" she said.

"Hold on, Kate." He held up a palm. "Before you say anything, I need a second."

Turning his back to her and the surveillance camera watching his lab, he retrieved 500 gram bottles of potassium nitrate and magnesium dust and tucked them out of sight in a drawer.

Kate put her hands on her hips. "We don't have seconds. I have—"

"How on earth can I shut you up?" Parker leaned to kiss her.

She dodged his advance. "Stop," she said, keeping him at arm's length. "There's no time for this."

He placed an index finger against her lips. "Not another word."

Frustration panned across her face. "I have something to tell you."

He mouthed, "Not here."

Slow to catch on, her mouth fell open with his finger still pressed to her lips.

He shook his head. *Not here.*

Kate took a confused breath as he snatched her hand and whisked her out of the lab.

RICHARDS WAS PLEASED. THIS was a Phase Two test run of sorts.

He directed his staff to transition the participant in pod 10 from a chemically-induced coma to chemically-induced paralysis. Beside him, Levine worked at a console. Above them, the Wall of Knowledge displayed participant vitals and functional-MRI scans from the processing phase of Rebecca Ward. During their preparation, each participant underwent a rigorous MRI protocol before being suited up and installed in a pod. The f-MRI initiation allowed for the construction of a crude foundational neurological map. Since Rebecca Ward had been the first Phase Two participant to arrive at ANCRI, thanks to Gene Thornton, she'd had more preliminary testing than her twenty-nine peers. Rebecca Ward was the first in her class.

Richards directed Levine to overlay Meir's f-MRI scans taken from Parker's work against those of pod 10's host. While it was too early to construct a comparative model, since the f-MRI protocols were different, they could make assertions about like-kind cognitive associations.

The objective of the exercise wasn't to beat Parker to a workable solution, it was to replicate his processes and enhance his techniques, and at the end swoop in to claim the reward.

Richards smiled. The Frontier was all that mattered.

Thomas Parker's presence was merely as a tour guide and a means to that end.

ON THE ARRAY OF screens in front of him, Earl watched Parker and Meir enter the neurophysiology annex. He was disappointed, hoping they would reveal what's in the box from the biochemistry lab. For a man who made a living conducting surveillance, he found their couple-like behavior odd, as if they were siblings rather than lovers.

His gaze crossed to other monitors. Most displayed techs and lab assistants and researchers going about their duties. Video surveillance of the neurophysiology lab and a few technically sensitive areas were prohibited, so there were no eyes on those locations. However, a tracking of staff badges notified him that Richards and Levine were in the large lab, along with eight support personnel.

A flash of movement on another screen caught his eye. Talib Makara badged into a clean utility store room. Nothing concerning there, since Makara had access privileges.

KATE FOLLOWED PARKER AS he badged through a door that read IMMERSIVE SIMULATION. The door slid closed behind them.

"What is this place?" she asked, taking in the large smoke-gray, warehouse-like venue with a tall, domed ceiling. Hundreds of tiny blue lenses stared downward to a floor imprinted with inlaid fluorescent circles.

"It's a hybrid reality environment." Parker led her into the room, inside the bands of phosphorescent circles. "It's an off-body holographic theater."

She scrunched her forehead. "A what?"

He took her hands, turned them upward, and caressed her palms.

With her hands in his, she watched him expectantly, sensing he had brought her here for a reason.

"ANCRI," he said, "has two major spaces not blanketed by surveillance."

"Let me guess," she said with a shrug. "Richards' infamous pod room and this theater?"

From a pedestal in the center of the room, Parker retrieved a pair of operator's gloves, and slid them over her hands. "We can talk now."

Kate withdrew her hands from his and noticed that the fingertips of her gloves were silver. "A woman came to your room. Obviously, she didn't expect to find me there. She passed on the number 'ten' and said you 'better hurry.' She didn't say anything else. What does ten mean?"

Parker ignored the question. "Pat your hands together twice. Think of it as a double mouse click."

Kate popped her palms together.

The room engulfed them with a holographic radiance, where they stood at its origin.

Kate surveyed the cosmic-like environment. It was a spherical world, tinted with blue and highlighted with green reference grids. In front of her, hovering in mid-air, dangled a semi-transparent menu panel. She looked above her and noticed that the hundreds of glass lenses were alive and actually miniature projection screens.

"It looks so real," she said, reaching out to the phantom holographic display of user options. Menu buttons lit up as her fingers glided across them.

"The room is a spatial virtual-to-real realm, an aural environment, where virtual reality sensors and projection systems are moved off our bodies. Stationary wall monitors are no longer required. Screens can be wherever we need them. Nothing touches you, except those gloves of course, which act as your gooey, a graphical unit interface, G-U-I. Lasers beam light directly into our eyes, positioning objects with respect to the user. This can be a single-user or multiple-user holographic realm, so what you spatially interpret can be different than what I do. Go ahead, select upload."

From the menu choices parked in front of her, Kate tapped UPLOAD.

A new menu appeared. She took his cues and selected the next option: NEW FILES.

Under a directory, she found a file with Meir's name on it. She tapped thin air again, over the projected location for her name, and their spatial world morphed into a huge brain.

Kate was all smiles. "Is this mine?"

"All yours."

Parker donned a pair of operator gloves. A new menu panel appeared, this one facing him rather than Kate. His screen came equipped with two user choices: ONE TWO.

Parker swiped at the ONE button and his competing screen disappeared. He settled in behind her, his elbows touching her sides and his silver finger-tipped hands lifted hers higher.

She felt his body form into hers and she told herself to go with it.

He guided her hands through virtual space and expanded her cosmic-like brain to encompass them.

Parker pressed his lips to her ear. "I took a road trip to visit the University of Illinois Chicago to investigate tech they were developing. EVL," he said of the university's electronic visualization laboratory, "builds virtual reality environments under a product line called CAVE. Eventually, EVL progressed to taking the interfaces off-station, off the human form. I wanted to integrate that technology into our work at Princeton. Seems like ANCRI beat me to it."

Kate could see throbbing clusters of neural activity and waved her hands through the cyclic patterns. Entire neural neighborhoods blossomed in activity. A sliding time scale let her transition through her time spent in the menacing MRI unit. She was standing inside her own brain, watching it in action. From their position, she figured they were standing in her midbrain, her thalamus directly above them, her cerebellum and occipital lobe directly behind.

"Thomas, what does ten mean?"

She felt him rest his head against the side of her neck. The warmth of his breath tingled her skin.

"I suspect you met Alexis Hicks," he said. "She's an attending in the neurophysiology lab, and oversees the health of the participants. I asked her which pod Becky was in."

"Ten?" Kate turned around, the two of them standing close, inside a neon version of her brain. She could see apprehension in his eyes.

Parker released a strained sigh. "Everything we do here will be used to make The Frontier a weapon." He cleared his throat. "Your colonel friend came to the dorm room."

"When?"

"This morning."

Disappointment painted her expression. "You didn't wake me?"

"He didn't want me too. He told me the NSA cannot be linked to ANCRI. And he's not returning. Come Monday, this place gets shut down. Orders from the White House." He searched for the right words. "Richards hasn't been informed yet. Not yet, anyway. The colonel implied a lot of things, including that it's an open question on whether the staff and participants stay alive. The way I see it, the Frontier gives us leverage. It will make our government back off. That gives us less than two days to read minds and get everyone out of here."

Kate's shoulders drooped as she took it all in.

"I made a deal with him," he said. "Wang wants us to save his daughter in exchange for free latitude to do anything with no interference from the NSA."

"Thomas," Kate interjected, "my job is to find out what happened to Samuel Ford."

Parker smiled thinly. "Help me with the riddle of the Frontier, and we will do just that."

46
IMPLIED COERCION

KATE LISTENED TO PARKER as they stood inside her time-captured, virtual reality (VR), holographic brain. The intimacy between them ebbed as they faced the blunt reality before them.

She was hardly keen on his plan.

Her obvious concern was risking the lives of the patients, although, if they did nothing, Richards and Levine would forge ahead with their human trials regardless. Still, Parker's plan exploited innocent people in an effort to save their lives.

The second concern was destruction of all of ANCRI's technological interfaces with the sole objective of setting the covert program back years. Such a delay would give lawyers time to challenge its legality in court. As an FBI agent, Kate's involvement likely meant termination from the bureau.

And lastly, his plan relied on others, something she was dead against.

She reminded him: *Trust no one.*

Yet they had found a way to trust each other. *Why not others?*

They had little choice. Thirty lives were at stake.

Parker moved outside her ring of circles in the immersive simulation theater and opened his own VR station with gloved, silver-tipped fingers. Through the institute's intranet CrossTalk platform, he reviewed Riley Johnson's documentation on synaptic migration and voltage gradients in organoid neurons. She continued in her own holographic realm and reviewed real-time neurological read-outs from the patient in pod 10.

"If this is Becky," she said, flipping through tiled ECG brain waves like a virtual deck of playing cards for all thirty participants, "she's undergoing a fundamental change in neurological activity compared to the twenty-nine others."

Parker nodded. "They're bringing her out of sedation, for testing."

"What kind of testing?" a new voice asked.

They turned to find Riley Johnson, in his psychedelic lab coat. Doors closed behind him.

"You pinged me on instant messenger?" Johnson said of the institute's peer-to-peer communication. "What's all the secrecy?"

"We need your assistance," Parker said.

Johnson's eyes blazed with intrigue. "For what?"

The door to the theater slid open again and Talib Makara entered, carrying a box from the clean storage room.

"Dr. Parker," Makara said, his voice low and agitated, "I find no reason to participate in your schemes, and don't appreciate being a delivery boy."

"You'll come to see things differently," Parker said. He took the box from Makara, set it on a table, and exposed its contents. Everyone gathered around. After unwrapping cellophane from boxes, he retrieved a handgun and passed it to Kate, then snatched up a gold badge.

Kate dropped the magazine out of the pistol to inspect it. Satisfied, she slapped it back into the grip of her semi-automatic.

Stunned, the two men stared at Kate, who shrugged—*Who would have guessed?*

Parker grinned. "Meet FBI Special Agent Katherine Morgan. She's undercover. If you fail to cooperate, she'll shoot you." He lifted his scrub top to reveal the healing bullet wound in his side. "I have first-hand experience that getting shot hurts like hell."

"We've done nothing wrong," Makara said.

"Keep telling yourself that," Kate said, "and if you survive being shot, you can spend the rest of your life in prison. We have reason to believe a U.S. Senator was brought to ANCRI. I'm here to investigate his disappearance, along with thirty counts of kidnapping and human rights violations. Less than a week ago, twenty-eight university students were presumed drowned at sea. Normally a tragedy like that would be unrelated. However, we believe those students are here as participants. People held against their will, along with Caroline Wang and a Princeton University graduate student."

Makara and Johnson looked confused.

"Cooperate," she said, "and I'll make a deal with the U.S. Attorney General on your behalf. Full immunity."

Makara's expression hardened. "Perhaps we should consult Dr. Richards and let him discuss these matters with you directly."

Johnson nodded. "I agree. That sounds prudent."

Kate held her service weapon as if she knew how to use it and stepped toward the two men. "We believe Dr. Richards is at the core of the ANCRI's illegal and unethical activities. If you tip him off in any manner, I'll make sure authorities treat you as an accessory on all counts." She furrowed her brow and blinked, as if she was doing the math. "I'm a forensics investigator, not a prosecutor. But I'd guess that any unwillingness to cooperate on your part amounts to complicity in all crimes committed. At a minimum, that's thirty counts of at least five years each. So you're looking at prison sentences of one hundred and fifty years. Minimum." She let that sink in.

Parked interrupted. "It's also doing what is right."

Makara frowned and Johnson looked like he was still playing catch up.

From the box, Parker pulled out a black and white photo of a bald, emaciated woman lying topless on a gurney. Scrawled into her bare chest was AMY RICHARDS RIP.

"Do either of you know this woman?" Kate asked.

Johnson nodded. "Amy Richards. Dr. Richards' daughter volunteered as the Genesis participant. Most staff came on board after Phase One concluded. I didn't even know she'd died."

"Caroline Wang did," Kate added.

Parker retrieved a cell phone from the box, clicked on its camera feature, and took a selfie. He passed it and the photo to Johnson.

"What do you want?" Makara asked, concern filling his long face.

"Your genius," Parker said. From the box, he collected two hard drives and passed them to Makara. "Richards' version of The Frontier is not for the benefit of humankind. It'll be used as a weapon. A weapon our government wants to exploit. Our world, society, is not yet ready for that kind of dictatorship."

Makara studied the hard drives. "What are these?"

Parker grinned. "Our way to The Frontier. That is, if you're game."

47
BLACKNESS AND DECEPTION

BECKY WARD FELT HOSTAGE to a dream state of fractured time. A bone-chilling numbness paralyzed her. Her world was dull and void of light, as if she were strapped to the bottom of a closed coffin that had yet to be buried. She told her mind to search for a place of reference, but her senses could not penetrate her containment.

At an unmeasurable distance, muted sounds encircled her.

In utter darkness, Becky could hear the sound of her own breathing.

She tried to move her limbs. Nothing cooperated.

Disjointed thoughts ebbed and flowed, and vague, out-of-order memories emerged from her muddled mind.

Becky recalled a tiled room, flat on her back, awake when people in scrubs stripped off her clothes. Callous faces lurked above her. No one she recognized. She tried to scream, but no sounds came out. The recognition of paralysis and helplessness settled into her psyche as someone prepped her for a medical procedure.

A man broke into her apartment. Thornton. Somehow he knew of her lies and betrayal. He found her NSA service weapon. The biting stings of a Taser dug into her chest and rendered her helpless.

It was Thornton who had delivered her to this world of unsympathetic doctors and nurses.

Nothing made sense.

In her dark, box-like world, all Becky possessed were her own fragile memories.

A face emerged from the blackness. Thomas. Thomas Parker. Her mentor. Her lover. Her NSA mission. Asleep, he lay beside her in his bed. She yearned to linger, to watch him breathe, to watch his chest rise and fall in a natural rhythm. But she couldn't stay, because she'd sold him out. Becky slid out of bed, trying not to wake him, her bare figure illuminated by street lighting snaking through a crack in window curtains.

Parker awoke and turned to her, his face a mask of disappointment. Becky mouthed "Goodbye."

Regret coursed through her veins, and Becky wished she could take it all back.

RICHARDS HOVERED NEAR POD 10 as staff moved about their normal duties. The Wall of Knowledge was alive with data and ECG brainwave graphs. At a central row of terminals, Levine pulled up mirrored screenshots on the billboard-sized screen to reveal Parker's and Meir's current network activities.

Richards rapped his knuckles against the side of the pod 10. "Rebecca, Thomas Parker is searching for you. He knows you're out of sedation." He leaned over the pod and ran a finger along the slim patch of exposed skin to her jaw. "Rebecca, I want you to talk to Thomas."

THE MEMORIES INSIDE BECKY'S mind contracted. Voices began to penetrate her void, transitioning from noise to clarity. She felt pressure against her entire body and the tightness of an object encompassing her skull. Something hard was inserted into her mouth like a bit. Through the blackness, Becky realized she was inside a machine, connected to it, wired to it.

A distinct noise, like a rap against a car door, snatched her attention.

A man beckoned above the noise, "Rebecca, Thomas Parker is searching for you. He knows you're out of sedation."

Sedation? Why am I here? Please let me out!

She felt tingling and a human touch streak across her chin.

Her heart skipped a beat. *Thomas is here?*

The man continued, "Rebecca, I want you to talk to Thomas."

Thomas! Help me! Please! Thomas, help me!

RILEY JOHNSON FELT MANIPULATED.

In his synaptic anatomics lab, he liked nothing about Parker's requests.

It was counter to other obligations. Matters that he could not ignore.

Foundational mandates were clear. *Make the Frontier a reality.* That was where his loyalties lay, not with the newcomer nor his FBI agent girlfriend. However, the threat of going to prison came across loud and clear.

If law enforcement possessed legitimate concerns over ANCRI's research, the institute would be under siege. And a badge and a gun did not make Cassondra Meir—or Katherine Morgan, or whatever her name was—an actual FBI agent.

Something did not add up. Their scheme of coercion amounted to blackmail.

And on the course implied, Parker was no more innocent than Richards. Both seemed eager to venture into human trials; only one did it behind the threat of imprisonment.

Yet Johnson sensed the importance of the tasks Parker had assigned.

Using neural training algorithms based on reverse-engineered synaptic self-learning communications, he took Parker's selfie and the photo of a dead Amy Richards from the phone, and uploaded the images to the institute's network.

After completing these tasks, he set out to consult with Noam Levine about how he should handle matters going forward.

THE OPPORTUNITY FASCINATED TALIB Makara. Finally a task worthy of his intellect. To date, he'd been squandering his time at ANCRI on conceptual busy work and trivial preparation. ANCRI had the most advanced quantum computers in the world, paired to an equally impressive, next-generation of deep-learning, self-healing neural networks. Nothing had ever put the large-scale architectures through their paces. Until now.

In his red-banded artificial intelligence lab, Makara cabled Parker's hard drives into ANCRI's network. Converting Parker's legacy applications to ANCRI's software structures was not as simple as plug and play. It was closer to the linguistic exercise of translating two different language trees, converting his father's Arabic tongue into his mother's native French.

Given the time constraints, his team of AI and software programmers would grind through the night generating wetware-based code and translating neurological algorithms. Along with leading the programming efforts, he would spend the night constructing comparative subdural neurological template maps for the participants.

Makara considered the discovery of "Dr. Cassondra Meir" as an impostor. Years ago, he had attended a presentation by the real Meir. He hadn't even noticed that the two women were in fact different people. Western women confused the hell out of him, with their free spirits and demands for equal rights.

He thought about telling Richards, but it seemed prudent to hold his tongue and let matters play out.

Makara had been at ANCRI longer than anyone but Noam Levine. He recognized that the arrival of Phase Two participants had been contrived, a transition overseen in secret by Levine and a chosen few. A separate rumor linked Caroline Wang to a vacancy among the test population, but no one could confirm it. The federal agent's information suggested it was true. As for Amy Richards, only a fool volunteered to be a test subject. She deserved whatever fate had befallen her. The loss of the unwitting college students didn't bother him either. He had experienced far worse in his native Iraq before the fall of Saddam Hussein.

Governments carried out all sorts of atrocities against its people in the name of progress. The mighty United States of America had proven itself no different. The best course was to stay neutral and declare an allegiance when a winner emerged.

Richards was not the yielding type. Once Parker made his breakthrough, Richards would execute him.

As a tyrant King, Richards would eliminate all threats to his precious Frontier.

Makara knew he had no time to waste.

AFTER GETTING NO RETURN call from the biochemistry staff about their missing chemistry supplies, Earl took matters into his own hands. He left his post, and headed straight to Parker's lab.

NOAM LEVINE ENTERED THE conference room, where Riley Johnson waited nervously.

"What is so damn important?" Levine snapped.

"Sir, Dr. Meir is not who she appears to be." Wringing his hands together, Johnson recounted everything said between the FBI agent and Parker, and their directives to him and Makara. "I thought I should bring this development forward."

Levine mulled over every word before placing a hand on the man's shoulder.

"Riley, thanks for letting me know," he said. "I had no idea this kind of thing might happen. But I can say with extreme clarity, their accusations are false. Our work is vital to national security.

Extremely vital. ANCRI has gone to great lengths to ensure that everything is in order, from medical consent to the ethical treatment of our participants. It's absurd to think we're somehow involved in the disappearance of a senator from Oklahoma, or manipulate the lives of our staff after they leave the institute."

Left unsaid was Levine's recognition that Parker and his FBI counterpart posed a threat.

The enemy was inside the temple walls.

He took a thoughtful breath. "You know, what concerns me most is that their nefarious actions are tantamount to industrial espionage. They're here to spy on us. Steal our research."

Johnson hesitated. "What should we do?"

"Leave these matters to me," Levine said. "But let me say again, you did the right thing bringing this to my attention. I assure you, Parker and Meir will be dealt with and brought to justice." He sighed. "I need you to do something for me."

Johnson looked at him eagerly. "Yes, sir. What is it?"

"Keep this conversation to yourself, as our secret."

Johnson nodded. "Absolutely."

Without a word, Earl the guard entered and set a cardboard box on the table.

Levine ushered Johnson to the hallway door. "Continue to support their conspiracy. Befriend them. Stay close to them. Report back on all research progress they make. Can you do that for me?"

"Yes, Dr. Levine."

He thanked Johnson again and sent the man on his way.

Earl flipped the lid from the box. "Parker acquired these supplies from the biochemistry lab, which I appropriated from his lab."

Levine studied a bottle: ammonium nitrate.

"Dr. Parker's been a busy man."

"What is he up to?"

Levine surveyed the contents in greater detail. "I would say he wants to build a bomb. We can't let that happen."

From a credenza in the corner, he grabbed a pad of sticky notes and scribbled common household words like water, salt, flour, baking powder, and baking soda. The labeled sticky notes went on the tops of bottles. He returned the lid to the box.

"Take these to the kitchen staff," Levine ordered. "I'll provide instructions on how to make look-a-like substitutions, and how to store the original chemical compounds. When they're done, return the box with its substituted contents to Parker's lab. He won't be the wiser."

Earl gave a firm nod. "Consider it done."

Levine pondered the host of problems on his plate. "Meir is a federal agent. She's armed and conspiring with Parker. They intend to bring down the institute. Both require elimination, but at the proper time. I realize ANCRI is shorthanded on security personnel, but your remaining detail is now on 24/7 shifts. No one sleeps until this trouble is behind us. Post additional guards at the entrance to the neurophysiology lab and the data center."

IN THE IMMERSION THEATER, Parker studied ANCRI's surveillance feeds on a free-floating holographic panel. One screen shot tracked Kate darting through the basement area.

The access to the institute's surveillance network was a gift from the NSA Colonel—part of their negotiated arrangement.

A useful tool, considering what lay ahead.

He tiled over to a new surveillance snapshot. Riley Johnson conversed with Noam Levine. Earl the guard entered the conference room carrying his box of chemistry supplies.

Parker smiled.

What do you know? The ruse had worked.

The guard had taken the bait, and now Parker knew who would rat him out to Richards.

Riley Johnson was not to be trusted.

48
MOVES AND COUNTERMOVES

As soon as Earl left his surveillance post, Kate darted to the institute's basement, with the goal of getting in and out in less than ten minutes. While medical scrubs had come a long way in terms of modern fashion, they still resembled work pajamas, offering no easy place to conceal a pistol. The waistband to her holster dug into her side beneath her top.

Meeting no one along the way, Kate negotiated the labyrinth of sterile white corridors and found ANCRI's incinerator room without issue.

After pushing through the hinged door, she scoured the utilitarian bricked room for evidence, even checking inside the incinerator itself. Spotting the security camera above the door, she crouched to frame the incinerator along the same camera angle used for Amy Richards' RIP photograph.

Bingo!

This was the place where ANCRI disposed of its participants.

Kate stroked the walls with her fingers. The room had a mildly grimy feel to it, not particularly clean or dirty. No sign of peripheral ash. She made a mental note to have the crime scene detail check for fingerprints and hair samples, but doubted anything would turn up.

On her return trip, Kate badged through a door labeled ANA-TOMICAL PATHOLOGY.

Inside, the tiled and stainless steel room was packed with exam tables, sinks, counters, and test benches. She logged onto a computer using access codes Wang had provided. In no time, she tracked down the autopsy records to alpha and beta participants. Names were omitted from the digital logs, but she surmised the female alpha was none other than Amy Richards and the more recent beta entry belonged to a sixty-year-old male, Samuel Ford. The cause of death in both cases: undetermined.

Nonsense.

The authorizing signatures on the autopsies read Caroline Wang, M.D.

If her speculation was on mark, it meant ANCRI killed Ford to protect its secrets.

Incineration would destroy any physical evidence linking the senator to the institute.

Kate recalled Parker mentioning brains were on display in a conference room. If the organs were fixed in formaldehyde, significant DNA damage could occur, but modern extraction methods made it possible to recover viable DNA from brains saturated in formalin for well past a half a century. Those trophies would be Richards' undoing.

In addition to DNA evidence, the bureau needed Caroline Wang alive to place Ford at ANCRI at the time of his death. She was now the keystone to a federal investigation.

Caroline Wang had become the Singularity Witness.

Kate checked her watch.

Twelve minutes had elapsed. It was time to haul ass and stake out a watering hole.

STANDING IN THE MIDDLE of the participant pods, Richards listened to Levine give an update.

An odd look crossed Levine's face. "The FBI knows about your daughter and Caroline Wang. They even know about Samuel Ford."

Richards glared at pod 20 and its occupant. "Caroline Wang is the bridge that brought this trouble to us. She's the FBI's mole. That leaves us no choice but to dispose of her, immediately."

This blatant interference could not be tolerated. His instinct was to haul the FBI agent, armed or not, into the lab and have her shot dead on the spot, regardless of her association with Thomas Parker.

Levine cleared his throat. "Dr. Richards, perhaps we should let this play out."

Richards' jaw went rigid. "That would be rather dangerous."

"Just hear me out." Levine brought up the network activities of Parker, Meir, Makara, and Johnson, displaying their joint work on the Wall of Knowledge. "If the FBI had probable cause, law enforcement would have us both in handcuffs. But that's not the case. Parker seems to be calling the shots, not the FBI. My assertion? He's buying time, and will use the government to cheat you out of The Frontier."

That angle surprised Richards. Alarm bells clanged in his head. He furrowed his brow. "Go on."

"Parker's invested in the conspiracy he's co-created. Why else would he instruct Makara and Johnson to develop rapid Phase Two neuro-modeling? I don't know about you, but that doesn't sound like a man who wants the government to drop in and seize everything."

Richards turned to Levine. The line of reasoning made sense. "It's either shrewd or downright foolish for Parker to reveal that his fellow conspirator is an FBI agent."

Levine shrugged. "It's sleight of hand. A distraction. To keep us focused on her, not his research."

Richards nodded. The problem with schemes was that they worked two ways.

"If you're correct," he said, "and Parker came here with a workable neuromapping template, Dr. Makara and his programmers will modify Parker's applications to interface with ANCRI's software architectures."

Richards turned his gaze to the Wall of Knowledge.

Neurological scans, cognitive mapping overlays, endless streams of program code all radiated out of the enormous display. Makara's computer programmers appeared to be tackling a viable tangent, one that now made complete sense.

Richards saw the deeper genius in Thomas Parker. His applications formed a framework for building a large-scale, brain-machine interface.

The Frontier offered worldwide recognition for achievements to science. Once he'd been a distant runner-up for a Nobel Prize in Medicine. Second place was no different than last place. Not this time. The Frontier was *his* path to Nobel recognition.

He shook his head. Neither Parker nor his accomplice would live see their charade to the end. That much was certain.

Richards stared down at pod 10 and its inhabitant, wondering if Rebecca Ward had any idea what was happening and that she was about to take up the torch of history, become the beacon of light that would illuminate a new world, The Frontier.

Only one person would claim The Frontier.

And it would never be Thomas Parker.

PARKER NEEDED HELP, AND he got it after returning to his lab.

Earl the guard had returned the box of bogus chemistry supplies, placing it exactly where he found it. For the moment, Parker ignored it.

On his digital whiteboard, he studied Johnson's work on sensory stimulation on grid cell organoids. Edward Tolman, an American psychologist, had written *Cognitive Maps in Rats and Men* in 1948. The article set the stage for behavioral decision making matched to physical regions of the brain and primitive cognitive maps, a precursor to grid cell dynamics.

Parker's research at Princeton had taught him that the ultimate goal of unlocking the black box between the ears and accessing consciousness was a larger undertaking than his hand-me-down university lab could support. A week earlier, he'd been in no hurry to solve the mysteries of the mind, and considered neurological singularity half-a-century or more away.

Now ANCRI stood on the threshold of making singularity a reality, with or without his contributions.

Their investment and the lives of thirty participants were a winner-takes-all gambit.

Constructing interactive neuro-maps required not only a precision matrix for targeting three-dimensional neural zip codes, but also the inclusion of additional biotic factors, such as action potentials and voltage gradients, neurotransmitter signal frequency propagation, firing patterns and signal frequency of neurons and their next-of-kin associative neighbors, and identifying the correct million combination set of neurons to replicate the simplest of memories.

As the mind evolves, the brain's neural neighborhoods get synchronized to the pulsing of chemical-electrical charges. A conceptual representation of memory had eluded scientists for years because many focused on defining discrete neurons at specified brain locations and saying "X marks the spot for memory recall." The gaping flaw in their location-based logic was how neurons tuned themselves to become receptive to inter-neural specific communications.

On a digital screen, Parker extracted the quantitative data from Johnson's organoids, his mini-brains, and forwarded performance values to the modeling Makara's programmers were building.

The knowledge that Becky was his first test subject troubled him—although he knew she'd give him a load of crap if he didn't pick her as his genesis participant anyway. He just hoped like hell he wasn't going to scramble Becky's brain in the process.

MAKARA FELT CLEAR, LIKE a bolt of electricity storming down a lightning rod. The promise of the lines of streaming code on nearby monitors amazed him. Parker's neuro-maps and algorithms weren't exactly elegant solutions, but did blend promising aspects of complex structure deconstruction, neural training, and wetware-like intelligence.

He imagined ANCRI's data center with its 2,084 qubit quantum supercomputers and high-density neural networks hitting overdrive. Parker's crude applications gave the institute its first peddle-to-the-metal drive on a metaphoric autobahn, exactly what the fastest computer in the world was built for.

Using an approach first developed at UC Berkeley, Makara launched ANCRI's quantum-based, self-programming software applications. The days of writing individual lines of code and mathematical relationships had vanished, extinct as the dinosaurs. Automated AI now performed the heavy lifting, saving tremendous time and tackling the trivial aspects of high-performance and multi-thread code, while leaving the prowess of the human intellect to focus on solving higher level functions and investigating more intimate coding schemes.

Makara checked his watch and grinned.

His AI team was ahead of schedule.

At this rate, ANCRI would have a working interface by sunrise.

It was odd, he thought. As a pragmatist, he'd never bought into Stewart Richards' obsession with neurological singularity. A day earlier, he would have considered Richards' plans for a grand Frontier delusional, unattainable in his lifetime.

Not now.

ANCRI stood on a doorstep of the greatest discovery mankind had ever faced, the human mind, and Thomas Parker was the one who delivered it.

49
ACTIVATION

BECKY WARD DRIFTED IN a world of confining blackness, blinded by the absence of light. Faint, prickling sensations broke through her void and tingled her consciousness.

She willed her mind to fight the shackles of an infused dullness.

The sounds of her own breathing grew clearer, as did the rhythmic pulse of her heartbeat.

The muffled voices outside her confines grew louder.

People out of reach discussed vital signs and sensory stimulation. Something was going on. She was part of it.

A voice resounded louder than the others. "Pod ten is ready for initiation protocols. Dr. Richards, shall we proceed?"

Becky felt a chill course through her body. She must be pod 10. *Thomas! Find me! Thomas, please get me out of here!*

"Proceed."

USING THE PASSCODES WANG had given him, Parker hacked into ANCRI's surveillance platform and swapped out camera inputs, altering feeds that overlooked a service corridor near the dining complex and a cybernetics workshop in the lab annex. Next he retrieved his hard-sided briefcase that Wang had left him in the clean storage diagonal from the neurophysiology lab. As he exited the storage, it was hard to miss the armed guard standing in the corridor outside the lab.

Richards was taking no chances on incurring an unauthorized breach into his sanctuary for human experimentation.

That was fine by him.

The guard looked straight at him, broadening his posture.

Parker threw the man an indifferent bob of his head, to say *I see you, too.*

They needed to get into the neurophysiology lab, which meant either finding a way around the guard or taking him out. Earl was at the monitoring desk at the sally port, of course, providing lethal backup in case of trouble.

He figured Kate would have a solution to that problem, and he wondered how she was progressing on her own assignments.

AT THE WATERING HOLE, Kate staked out the monolithic waterfall in the center of the expansive atrium and waited for her victim. Night had descended on New Jersey. The daylight radiating through the exterior windows had waned. Since it was well past their traditional dayshift, staff in lab coats and colored scrubs meandered around the dining hall.

Parker had made it clear how much they needed this assistance.

Anyone who headed into the clinical neurology annex from the residence wing and the dining facilities had to pass right by the charcoal monolith.

Doubt crept into her mind, as she worried that she had missed her contact entirely.

JUST AS KATE WAS ready to abandon her post, Alexis Hicks bid farewell to off-duty staff and walked toward her, carrying a lidded cup of coffee. Using the water feature as a screen, she slid behind

Hicks and slung her arm over the other woman's shoulder, buddy-like, and clamped down hard on Hicks' collarbone.

Hicks nearly dropped her coffee. "What the hell—?"

"Oh, shut up," Kate said in a low, exasperated tone, "and keep moving."

Kate nearly cross-checked the woman as she guided her to an alcove before they breached a pair of doors that defined the boundary between building structures.

"How dare you—" Hicks said.

Kate clawed the soft tissue of the woman's shoulder and squeezed like hell. "I said keep moving, Dr. Hicks, or I'll knock your teeth out with the gun I'm carrying."

Hicks resisted, then felt something jab into her side. She looked down and saw a handgun.

Kate gestured toward the alcove. Reluctantly, Hicks badged them into a service corridor leading to the outside world. Kate shoved Hicks deeper into the semi-vacant space and closed the door behind them.

"I'll make this easy on you and dispense with any pleasantries." She showed her badge. "Katherine Morgan, MD, FBI. Which pod is Caroline Wang in?"

Hicks looked stunned. "What are you talking about? Who are you again?" She hesitated. "This is crazy. I should never have helped Dr. Parker."

"Dr. Hicks," Kate said, rolling her eyes, "we can play good cop, bad cop. But right now, I'm missing the good cop, and, honestly, I'm on the clock. So here's what's going to happen. You're going to tell me what I need to know or more than thirty people are going to die. If you help, you'll be a superhero and save lives. "

Hicks chewed on her lip. "And if I say no?"

"I'll make sure you go to prison. No parole. You'll end up an old maid and spending the rest of your natural-born life occupying a block cell, compliments of the U.S. Department of Justice."

Hicks' gaze narrowed. "If I help you, will you both leave me alone?"

Kate offered a thin, confident smile. "I'll consider it. But come Tuesday, if Dr. Richards doesn't have you killed, you better update your LinkedIn profile, because I bet you're going to need a job." She passed Hicks a thumb drive. "I need two things. First, what pod does Catherine Wang occupy? From what you told us, it's not ten. That leaves twenty-nine other positions. Second, I need you to stick that into the intravenous fluid delivery controller to the participants."

Hicks eyed the device. "What is this?"

"None of your concern. The master pump controller has an interface port on it. The controller is in the supply room adjacent to the neurophysiology lab. You have access to the room. No one will ever know of your involvement. Plug that into the USB port and walk out."

"WHAT GIVES, PIGPEN?" TALIB Makara barked from across his AI lab space as he matched modified paradigms to neural-net code generated by genetic algorithms.

Riley Johnson thrust his hands deep into the pockets of his colorful lab coat.

"Talib," Johnson said awkwardly, "I may have made a mistake."

Makara looked up from his screen. "What are you moaning about?"

"I told Levine about Parker and Meir."

Makara cocked his head. "Why on earth would you do that?"

"I thought it was the right thing to do. Now I'm not sure."

"You bloody figure?"

Johnson cleared his throat. "Dr. Levine said the institute had no involvement with a senator from Oklahoma. No one, not even the FBI agent, ever mentioned Oklahoma. So how would Levine know?"

Makara's eyebrows shot up. "You're a low-intellect English bint, Johnson."

He waved the man over and brought up a series of algorithms in tiled formats, then a translucent image of a brain showing sporadic neural fires dancing across its varied folds and geographic landscapes. He pointed to microscopic sparkling explosions popping up in an undefined randomness inside the see-through brain.

"Who am I looking at?"

"Pod ten," Makara said. "AI correlation of neurological outputs was fruitless, until I applied Parker's algorithms. Then something intriguing happened."

"How so?"

Makara stroked his bearded chin and typed RUN/ACQUISITION into a pop-up dialogue box. Regions in the semitransparent brain sparkled with greater intensity as a contrast of red sparkles dominated a broader spectrum of pulsating yellow.

Johnson leaned closer to the screen. "Incredible."

"You've seen nothing yet." Makara typed THOMAS PARKER into the same dialogue box.

Tags tracked the pathway progressions of evolving thoughts as pulsing colors progressed inside the brain, areas labeled hippocampal region of the medial temporal lobe to the anterior cingulate cortex to frontal cortex regions.

Off to the side, a hazy picture of Thomas Parker's face formed.

Johnson laughed. "You uploaded Parker's selfie to pod ten?"

Makara leaned back in his chair. "The FBI agent inferred a student from Princeton was among the participants. All I did was input his name. The participant did the rest." He let that sink in. "I hate to admit Parker will deliver The Frontier, not Richards nor his manservant whore, Levine. Between the two of us, Pigpen, I hope that FBI agent shoots you for jilting her. You deserve it. If I were you, I'd watch my bloody back."

BECKY WRESTLED WITH THE fractured thoughts tickling her conscious, frustrated at the torturous helplessness to her state of existence. Her mind seemed free from the bonds anchoring her down earlier, yet blackness still enveloped her.

A bristling sensation washed through her, overtaking any other emotion. She couldn't explain the change, only that it seemed like a subliminal force deep inside her, like water pressing against the skin when you enter a pool, but pushing at her from the inside out.

She thought of Thomas.

And could see his face.

They were in their engineering lab at Princeton. Beyond a glass partition, he watched her stow away equipment after their test run with the high school student.

His face grew clearer.

Help me, she mouthed to him.

His expression hardened, and his gaze turned distant. It was if he could read her thoughts, and knew all of her horrible secrets.

I'm sorry, Thomas.

RICHARDS STIRRED IN HIS chair, glancing to an image that crystalized on the Wall of Knowledge. He stood and his eyes went wide.

"Sonofabitch," Levine said. "That's—"

"Thomas Parker," Richards added.

On the expansive screen, an image of Parker emerged in a panel dedicated to sensory outputs.

Pod 10's vitals ticked up.

"Is Parker doing this?"

Levine shook his head. "No. The network shows he's offline. So is Meir, or whatever her name is. This response came from the participant herself."

Richards strolled to pod 10 and leaned over the suited participant.

"Rebecca," Richards said, his baritone voice clear and resonating. "Thomas looks sad. Ask him to smile. Ask him to smile for you. Tell him… you love him."

Richards folded his arms across his chest and waited.

On the screen high above the floor, the image of Parker showed a nervous smile.

OCCUPYING A CONSOLE IN the row directly behind Levine, Alexis Hicks froze in disbelief, watching the image of Thomas Parker appear on the screen.

Richards spoke to the participant in pod 10, the one she knew as Rebecca Ward, Parker's former research assistant.

Under her breath, she said, "She knows him."

Hicks felt for the thumb drive in the pocket of her scrubs, got up from her position, and badged into the adjacent supply room.

Once inside, a nameplate made it easy to find the intravenous central pump controller marked NMB-PSI. As instructed, the device possessed a USB port.

She inserted the thumb drive.

A tiny green light on the controller blinked on and off, then stayed green.

Hicks took a deep breath, exited the supply room, and returned to her station.

PARKER SWIPED INTO A crimson-banded, neon-colored cybernetics lab carrying his hard-sided case, the one he'd collected from the banker's safe at his house. The high-tech workshop offered all the essential tools, allowing him to modify his tech to interface with the institute's infrastructure and backplane.

From the case, he removed the pearl white mannequin's head carrying his Princeton skullcap and its long tentacles of fiber optic dreadlocks. Everything went on a test bench.

The similarities in neurological skullcap designs, the ones employed in ANCRI's pods and his version at Princeton, were striking. It was logical to assume that Becky or Derman had sold his prototypes, giving Richards a head start on the quest for immortality and neurological singularity.

He wondered if Becky had been connected in any way to Derman's murder. It didn't matter, but he found it ironic that Becky had become a test subject for the very people she had sold him out to.

Each terminal connection on the skullcap's dreadlocks required swapping out.

All told, the alterations took an hour, with another thirty minutes consumed with bench testing the new interface on a series of oscilloscopes and calibration meters.

Now it was time to test his skullcap on someone not among the participants.

SUNDAY, OCTOBER 11th

Memory is the scribe of the soul.
Aristotle

50
CONVERSATIONS THAT MATTER

MIDNIGHT. PARKER RETURNED TO the immersive simulation theater with his hard-sided briefcase.

"You get what we needed?" he asked as the doors slid closed behind him.

"Hicks came through," Kate said, working off a holographic panel dangling in mid-air. "Caroline is in pod 20, and we now have control of the drug infusion system."

She explained her approach to the participants, lowering their sedation and transitioning them from deep comas to states of minimal consciousness, while adding neuromuscular blocks—targeting physiological existences above a Glasgow Coma Scale of 9.

"Richards posted a guard outside his lab. You'll need to find us a way around him."

"Why me?"

"You're the one with a gun."

Her shoulders slumped. "I'm not shooting anyone, Thomas."

Parker slid a stool to the middle of the room, inside the circles on the floor, and unpacked his case, retrieving his modified skullcap and its massive fiber optic dreadlocks.

Kate turned to him, trepidation on her face. She pursed her lips. "I'm now reconsidering how much I'm willing to help you."

Ignoring her, he unspooled the skullcap's band of cables and patched them into terminals along the wall. Hoisting up the skullcap, he secured it to a makeshift frame of square tubing behind the stool.

Parker slid on a pair of operator gloves.

A new holographic menu flashed up between them, creating his and her sides of the lab.

From a CURRENT PROJECTS folder, he uploaded Kate's cognitive template, which exploded above them like a cosmic bang, ebbing and flowing in a magical tapestry of stars.

Kate minimized her console and looked at her neurological constellation, absorbing the breathtaking sight.

He snatched her hand and led her to the stool.

"Why do I have the feeling I'm going to be electrocuted?"

Under the ambience of luminous and flickering neon, he drew her close.

"I thought every woman wanted to find the spark in her life."

Her eyebrows scrunched lower. "A spark? Fine. An experience that burns you alive, no, not so much."

He pushed her down on the stool. His hands lingered on her shoulders before moving to caress her cheeks. She smiled apprehensively. After tucking her dark hair behind her ears, he lowered the skullcap over her head and clasped its chin strap.

Kate took a hesitant breath. "This device of yours isn't going to make me say or do anything I'll regret, will it?"

Parker chuckled. "Any secrets you don't want to share, Special Agent Morgan?"

"Yeah, a lot."

He uploaded new sensory connections to her virtual brain and the luminescence around them grew more vibrant.

"As an organ," he said, "our brains share common genetic and anatomic structures. Yet the mind occupying each of our brains is unique to its host." He pinched his thumb and index finger just under a half-inch a part. "A cubic centimeter of your cortex has roughly as many synaptic connections as there are stars in the Milky Way."

"You romance all the girls like this? Give them a stool, a mind-reading helmet, and talk synapsis and neurons and galaxies?"

"Only the ones who share a shower with me."

"I'm going to regret that, aren't I?"

Parker gave her a grin. "Let's make you participant thirty-one, shall we?"

MAKARA MASSAGED HIS FOREHEAD and tried to keep his sleep-deprived mind on task. Beside him, at another console, sat Johnson. In a small breakout area, a band of coffee-pounding pro-grammers huddled around an interactive table and team-checked coding anomalies.

An IM from the network pinged Makara's workstation.

"Well, this is a new development," he said.

Johnson leaned over for a better look. "What's Parker up to now?"

Makara retrieved a new string of images and shuffled them to a larger interactive screen along the wall.

Among the images was a new neuro-map tagged as pod 31.

Everyone crowded around the interactive board, including the programmers.

Johnson frowned. "How does adding a new participant help?"

An odd look crossed Makara's face as he turned to his team of programmers. "What's the ETA on our platform update?"

The lead programmer gave him a look that asked *are you an idiot?* "We're still vetting code, and have modules infested with incomplete script."

Makara folded his arms. "How long?"

The man looked directly at his boss. "Eight hours. Then two more to compile. Another two for quality assurance."

Makara brought up a clock app on the board and pointed to it. 12:35 a.m.

He squinted at the cast of characters before him. "All program-ming will be complete and functional in six hours. Not a minute longer. So get back to work."

The programmers dispersed, unhappy.

Johnson rubbed the back of his head. "Dr. Richards will kill us when he finds out we're helping Parker add a participant to the population."

Makara ushered Johnson back to his terminal. "I'm still rooting for the FBI agent to shoot you. That way I can blame this entire mess on you."

Johnson took a seat. "What's going on, Makara?"

"We're about to shock the hell out of Dr. Richards," Makara said with a menacing grin.

KATE'S HOLOGRAPHIC BRAIN FILLED the room. On the stool under the skullcap, she meditated.

"Has anyone ever tried this before?" she asked.

Parker looked up from his holographic console. "What? Brain-to-brain communication? Technically, yeah. Researchers at the University of Washington performed rudimentary communications over the Internet using EEGs and magnetic stimulation."

Kate pouted. "Well, that's a letdown. I wanted to be the first."

He chuckled. "I'll call Guinness and ask for their world record to be stripped." He worked his holographic console and brought up varied two-dimensional images, one at a time. "I'm targeting neurons in your visual cortex. Tell me what you see."

She closed her eyes in concentration. "Yellow. A yellow square."

"Excellent."

"No, wait, now it's a pink oval."

"ANCRI's supercomputers in the data center are learning how you learn and building a cognitive basis for an interactive neuromap. Becky and I leveraged work done by others on the Human Connectome Project to build an intricate pattern-based approach at Princeton."

"A green… triangle. This is amazing. I can sense objects before they materialize."

"The formation of memory doesn't happen instantaneously. It's a process, not a single action or location. Complex cognitive elements are parceled across multiple hemispheres and microstructural architectures of the brain. We're tapping into a broad network of neurons."

"Blue. No wait. Sky blue. A sky blue crescent moon."

Parker felt hypnotized, watching Kate on the stool, hands folded in her lap, her mouth twitching ever so slightly as she mouthed the names of cognitive objects.

His gaze turned pensive. "Hold up for a minute."

Parker typed in additional commands on his console.

"What?" she asked, her eyes opening.

He stepped behind her, out of her field of vision. "Kate, rather than receive an image, I want you to deliver an image. In the same format as the objects you worked through, think of a stop sign. Simple. Red hexagon shape. White lettering. A stop sign."

She took a breath and closed her eyes.

Parker's jaw dropped when a red stop sign appeared on a holographic console.

Stewart Richards dared not sleep, fearful discovery would elude him.

In a back row of the neurophysiology lab, his gaze took in the expansive space while he enjoyed a Montecristo. Cigar smoke churned in the dim air. Before him, a night shift crew of technicians and nurses worked in the glow of their monitors.

Pod 10's neuro-interfaces had yielded no new results in hours, and no more images of Thomas Parker adorned the Wall of Knowledge.

ANCRI had come so far. From a government think tank's conceptual endorsement to federal funding for human experimentation, provided that ANCRI's first test subject, its genesis participant, was a volunteer.

His daughter, Amy, became the perfect sacrifice.

ANCRI had gained so much since her death.

Like many pilot programs, Phase One evolved out of primitive methods. ANCRI's two-way communicative 64-electrode EEG terminal skullcap design came with devastating side effects: destruction of sensory functions, pain-filled psychosis, and the charring of tissue. Even though Amy complained of the intolerable pain, research could not stop. The sensory terminals in the genesis skullcap generated destructive high-frequency signals, like the invisible energy inside a microwave oven. The collateral neurological damage was deemed acceptable. Rather than stopping to redesign a better brain-machine interface, Richards gave the order to forge ahead, regardless of his daughter's peril.

Amy's fate had been sealed the day she volunteered as their genesis participant.

He had no regrets. Not one.

The Frontier required sacrifices.

Her death, albeit tragic, offered a plethora of lessons learned. ANCRI progressed to Parker's approaches for Phase Two and Thornton delivered the next generation of participants.

Richards got up and strolled to pod 10. The tip of his cigar glowed in the ambient light. His gaze fell on the participant in the containment vesicle. The Phase Two amorphous-style spacesuit was a vast improvement over prior form-fitting versions, and hid its occupant's physiology. It was impossible to discern that the person occupying the suit was a woman. As Parker's former research assistant, Rebecca Ward seemed an apt replacement to carry on his daughter's legacy. Of course, twenty-nine others would do the same.

A technician approached with a tablet and presented him with the current sedation and muscular-block levels of the participants.

Richards looked incredulous. "Those levels are incorrect."

"Sir, I've rechecked the data myself."

Richards scowled. "Have you recalibrated the drug infusion master controller?"

The man nodded. "We attempted recalibration, but the platform is not responding. It appears we're locked out of the pump controller."

Adrenaline coursed through Richards' veins.

ANCRI was under siege from within.

And Thomas Parker was the threat.

Richards scanned the lab and stopped his gaze at pod 10. "Inform the staff that the participants are being transitioned out of sedation. And call security."

51
TRAITORS

RICHARDS FUMED, STYMIED ON a course of action. Traitors threatened ANCRI's very existence. Everything he worked to build was at risk. He directed the guards to shoot on sight and the small faction of armed men stormed the immersive simulation theater.

Richards trailed behind by several paces. No reason to get caught in the crossfire.

The theater was empty.

The guards dispersed to continue their search.

Richards took in the stunning panorama. Neurons and synapsis crackled as streams of neurotransmitters ebbed and flowed across the contours of a holographic brain. Neon hotspots pulsed with activity.

It was genius. Very wetware, a bio-cybernetic representation of the central nervous system.

A tag to the brain identified it as Participant 31, whoever the hell that was.

He strode deeper into the theater and spotted a stool occupying a ring of circles. A crude skullcap was suspended from a metal framework. Next to it, a holographic panel floated in midair and presented an image.

A wave of uneasiness flashed over him.

The image seemed to be a photograph, but with significant distortions, a pathetic replication with facsimile-like qualities.

He studied it closer. A memory?

Fronting ANCRI's incinerator was a gurney. His daughter lay dead. Etched into her bare chest was AMY RICHARDS RIP.

Only one person had been present at Amy's incineration—Caroline Wang—the occupant of pod 20.

How had Parker extracted a complex image from memory?

Richards tingled as he contemplated the neurological pageantry on display. The memory had not come from Caroline Wang, but from someone else—participant 31.

Parker was taunting him with a message.

The Frontier threatened to reveal all secrets. Even his secrets.

Secrets that could not be revealed. Ever.

KATE SPRINTED BEHIND PARKER as they dashed to his green-banded lab. The time it took for her to unbuckle from his contraption nearly got them caught, affording mere seconds to escape through the immersion theater's fire exit.

Time was not on their side. And a whole host of problems lay ahead.

His lab would be the first place the guards would check.

On an illuminated screen, she remotely lowered the infused sedation to all of the participants, bringing them into a twilight state of consciousness. Soon, each participant would have the cognitive ability to process verbal commands, critical if they were going to survive this madness and get out alive.

Beside her, Parker logged into ANCRI's master security platform and overrode the institute's surveillance system and blacked out security cameras.

"Don't forget to delete system access for Richards, Levine, and the guards," Kate added. "That will slow them down."

"Done," he said as he logged out.

From a drawer, he retrieved two semi-white, plastic, 500 gram bottles and thrust them into her hands: potassium nitrate and granular magnesium.

Her eyes widened. "Thomas, I can't help you sabotage the facility."

"Don't shake those a whole lot." He took her arm and led her out of the lab.

"Or what, they'll explode?"

"I didn't have time to read the SDSs," he said, referring to the OSHA-required safety data sheets for each compound. "But they're pretty damn reactive."

A guard in the corridor blocked the path out of the research annex. His stocky frame took up the entire doorway. He clutched a radio in one hand and raised a pistol in the other.

They were exposed, with no cover.

Kate dropped the bottles and lunged at Parker, driving them both into an offshoot of the corridor. Their bodies collided violently and tumbled across gray flooring. A bank of pink neon from a neighboring lab loomed above them.

She wrestled her Glock free of its holster. "Thomas, we need to get out of here."

"We're in a dead end," he said, nervously scanning for a way out.

She sprang to her feet, keeping her pistol pointed in the direction of the impending threat, and stole nervous glances to their boxed in location.

He was right. There was nowhere to run.

The rent-a-guard rounded the corner, his pistol seeking targets.

"FBI! Drop—!"

Kate fired as the barrel of a handgun zeroed in on her. A muzzle flash sparked, with an eruption of gunfire. The guard's advance stalled as his torso lurched back, his gaze exhibiting disbelief. His eyes blinked at the spread of crimson painting the left center of his shirt. He teetered for a long moment before pitching face first to the floor.

The guard's radio crackled. Earl's voice demanded an update.

Parker rose to his feet and stared at the motionless guard.

Kate retrieved the bottles and the radio from the floor, but let his pistol lay where it fell.

"Hold out your hands," she demanded, shoving the bottles at him. "I killed that man to protect your scheme. This better work, doc."

He gripped the plastic bottles tighter. "If Makara's team finishes their coding, it will."

Kate motioned to a stairwell door down the hall. "Come on, let's keep moving."

MAKARA SPUN AWAY FROM an interactive white board at the sound of gunfire. A single retort echoed from elsewhere in the research annex.

"What the hell?" Johnson asked from across the AI lab.

"Did you guys hear that?" whined a programmer, popping his head up from a cubicle like a gopher rising out of the dirt.

Makara pointed to his subordinate. "You, keep working. No distractions."

"That sounded like a gunshot," the rodent man said.

Makara turned to Johnson. "It's probably that pissed-off FBI agent looking for whoever sold her out. Pigpen, go see what's going on."

Johnson crossed his arms. "Why me?"

Makara gestured to the gopher's workstation. "Because Mighty Mouse there needs to finish compiling code before the platform interface can be commissioned. You, on the other hand, don't code like he does, and are therefore expendable."

RICHARDS FOUND THE GUARD and a handful of shocked night shift researchers huddled around his body. Someone had rolled him over. A single bullet wound pierced his uniform and blood pooled on the floor.

Everyone looked at him, horrified. Their stares intensified as they waited for answers.

Murder. Murder at the institute. How could that happen?

Levine elbowed his way closer. "Folks, we need you to return to your dorm rooms while security deals with this situation." He waved them off. "Now, people. Go on."

The small group dispersed, whispering in concern.

Richards retrieved the guard's pistol from the floor and handed it to Levine. "They're traitors. Their presence threatens everything." He decided not to elaborate on finding the memory of the incinerator and his daughter. "Kill the FBI agent, personally. I'll deal with Parker in a more pragmatic way."

Levine eyed the gun in his hand and swallowed hard.

Richards seethed. "This FBI agent won't be as easy to deal with as Caroline Wang. Make sure she ends up dead."

"I messed her up the first time." Levine felt the weight of the weapon in his hand. "This time I'll blow her brains out."

Richards' gaze darkened. "Do whatever it takes. But leave Parker to me. I'll have a special encounter for him to die for."

FROM HIS VANTAGE POINT, Riley Johnson eavesdropped on Richards and Levine. Ahead, blood pooled on the gray sheen of the floor. A guard lay dead at their feet. Neither man showed any emotion for a fallen colleague, as they discussed murders of their own.

The mention of Caroline Wang grabbed his attention. What the FBI agent had said about Caroline now seemed valid.

His stomach churned.

This Meir, or Morgan, or whatever her name was, would soon be a dead woman.

Levine brandished the guard's handgun as if he intended to use it.

Out of breath, Earl the guard jogged past him and announced, "There's a breach in security. Cameras are inoperable. Supervisory access is deactivated. Security management platforms are locked out." He took a heavy breath. "We have no way to track Parker or Meir."

Richards' face flushed with anger. "Give me your lanyards."

Each man relinquished an ID badge and Richards swiped them at the nearest card reader. Each time the plastic card passed over the control sensor, it blinked red.

Johnson leaned out from his hiding spot for a closer look.

Richards' gaze hardened. "Collect IDs from everyone with high level clearances and test their badges. We'll use their access privileges until we can reinstall the security system off of backup servers."

"Should I recall our guard from the property gate?" Earl asked, glancing at the man on the floor. "There's only three of us remaining, including myself."

Richards shook his head. "Not yet. Keep him there in case they attempt to leave the premises." He paused. "Repost a man outside the neurophysiology lab. Parker and his fellow conspirator cannot be allowed entry. Earl, work with Dr. Levine to hunt down this FBI agent. Make her pay for killing your man."

52
FIREWORKS AND SACRIFICE

3:30 A.M. PARKER LED Kate into the residential wing and badged into ANCRI's kitchen. A world of industrial-looking stainless steel greeted them: counters and tables, stoves, ovens, hoods and baker-sized mixers. He glanced behind to make sure no one had followed, and closed the door.

"Locate buffet supplies," he said, setting the plastic bottles he carried on a counter. "Matches, igniters, Sterno, those sorts of things."

She looked around the unoccupied kitchen. "Why are we here again?"

"Who's going to look for us here?"

She mashed her hands against her hips. "I don't know, gun-toting cooks?"

He ignored the sarcasm and disappeared into a dry goods storage. Moments later, he returned with a box labeled "Fingerling Potatoes."

Rifling through random drawers, she found her scavenger hunt obligations.

"Ah, woman creates fire," she said, clicking on a butane lighter to test its flame.

He chuckled. "The kitchen staff swapped out my chemistry supplies." He pointed to the surveillance camera across the room. "And they thought I wouldn't notice."

Parker unpacked sealed plastic bags of various crystalline powders from the potato box. Handwriting identified their contents.

Kate frowned as she examined a bag: potassium thiosulfate.

"It's used in pharmaceuticals, wastewater treatment, and fertilizers. Mostly."

"But that's not what you're using it for, is it?"

"We talked about this, Kate," he said, handing her a fistful of drinking straws.

"No, Thomas, *you* talked about this."

He shook his head. "I can't do this without you."

She sighed. "So how does a medical doctor from Princeton learn how to make improvised explosives?"

He opened the box of safety matches and started breaking off their heads.

"My parents were archeologists at the University of Colorado. They dragged me off to every historically significant dirt spot imaginable. Mom homeschooled me between digs. Cave excavations sometimes required boulders to be cleared." He flashed a grin. "Dad taught me rock climbing and how to play baseball. And while most kids' moms baked brownies, mine turned out to be a part-time alchemist."

She laughed. "My childhood was far more refined. Mom taught first grade, and dad was a card-carrying electrician. He had me rewiring toasters by the age of ten. A useful skill for a tomboy who went onto med school."

He crushed match heads gently, using a wooden rolling pin, then mixed their pyrotechnic compound with equal portions of sugar, magnesium, and potassium nitrate. He left her to stuff the mixture into a series of straws to form makeshift fuses.

"I hated what my parents did for a living, and wanted nothing to do with dirt or blowing up rocks. They died in a plane crash coming back from a dig in Oaxaca."

"Sorry about your parents, Thomas."

Parker sighed. "If Yale hadn't accepted me for the fall term, I would have been on that plane with them in southwestern Mexico.

I spent half my childhood living in tents, exiled from civilization. So please, never ask me to go camping, okay?"

"No tent camping for Thomas Parker. Got it."

He poured the remaining bags of dry compounds together in a large stainless steel bowl and stirred them with a wooden spoon.

Kate held up a brown glass bottle. Her eyes widened. "What's nitrobenzene?"

"A highly toxic and volatile acid used to manufacture a lot of things, ranging from pain relievers like acetaminophen to cheap perfumes for soaps. Whatever you do, don't inhale its vapors—it's a carcinogen and will mess up your central nervous system. I thought it could be a last resort."

She set the bottle gingerly back on the counter. "Ya think?"

He spooned jellied cooking alcohol from the Sterno cans and filled the bottom of four jars, then packed in the dry compounds to make six bombs.

With minimal direction, Kate punched holes through the lids, spun them on, and inserted their improvised fuses.

She eyed him closely. "How much time will I have after I light one of these?"

"Kate, all I can say is, run like hell."

"How much time, Thomas?"

Parker cleared his throat. "Seconds?"

"Seconds?" Kate looked scornful. "Oh, that's comforting."

Kate took a spare fuse, set it on the counter, and lit it with the butane lighter. Her lips moved while she counted down seconds. A brilliant white and orange flame consumed an end of the drinking straw and rapidly burned its way down the straw's length.

"Great," she said. "Six seconds? Is that all I get?"

He shrugged sheepishly. "A second to light the fuse and five more to beat feet."

"Thomas, you're going to get me killed."

—¦—

RICHARDS STORMED INTO THE neurophysiology lab, brooding the entire way. Behind him, the anteroom doors stood blocked open with an armed guard outside.

The Wall of Knowledge was dormant, the lab eerily serene. He ran his fingers along pods in passing as he walked to the center of the lab. The night shift staff's collective gaze tracked him, and he noticed their postures were rigid as statues.

They undoubtedly knew about the dead guard. That kind of word would spread fast.

Their eyes held unspoken questions.

It was time to demand answers.

Richards wondered who among them had helped Parker. Who among them was complicit in sabotaging his Frontier? He might never know, but it was time for people to prove their absolute allegiance.

A man in a white lab coat tracked him down. "Dr. Richards, security systems remain offline, but we're making progress on a full restoration of access control functions. Systems should be operational in two hours. On the research front, we have been unable to reboot the infusion pump."

Richards thought for a moment. "Assemble everyone along the front wall."

The man looked perplexed. "Sir?"

"Everyone, form a line," Richards ordered. "Now!"

The guard standing at the entrance peered into the room.

Richards waved the man in. "Relinquish your sidearm."

The guard reluctantly complied, and returned to his position outside the lab.

The migration to the base of the Wall of Knowledge was a slow one. Fear, even panic showed on everyone's faces.

Richards spoke clearly. "Which one of you assisted Thomas Parker in bypassing the drug infusion system?"

No one answered.

Leaning into pod 10, he tore IV lines from the suited arms of its participant and manually disconnected her from the drug's delivery lines. Blood spattered his immaculate white lab coat. Blood from a needle still embedded in the crook of the participant's suited elbow drained onto the floor. One thing was certain: Rebecca Ward no longer needed the influence of sedation or neuromuscular blocks.

He waved the gun at the staff. "Thomas Parker received assistance from someone."

Again, there was only nervous silence.

Richards pointed the gun and fired.

The gun's discharge was deafening. Staff screamed as the man in the lab coat who had delivered the bad news seconds earlier crumpled to the floor. His eyes bolted wide from the shock of the bullet penetrating his sternum.

Richards tried again. "I intend to go down the line until the traitor confesses. It's your choice, people, but one of you better speak up."

Anguished whimpers came from the staff, many of them turning away from the sight of a dead man on the floor.

"No?" He raised the gun again and steadied its aim. The next in line would go.

A woman stepped forward. "Dr. Richards, you need not hurt anyone else."

Her light-blue scrubs caught him off guard. He'd expected it to be someone in green or gray, a nurse or technician. "You're a doctor?"

"Alexis Hicks," she said defiantly. "Third shift attending."

He looked into her intense brown eyes. "I'd ask you why you did it, but that is not as relevant as disclosing what you did to the pump controller."

She crossed her arms. "I'll tell you if you let these people go."

Richards contemplated her demand, before moving to pod 20 and ripping IV tubing from its participant. Caroline Wang was now free of her administered drugs. As before, blood pooled beneath her pod, the result of a needle lingering in her arm.

He stared at the frightened lineup and saw panic in their eyes.

"The quest for The Frontier," he said, "cannot tolerate subversive interference. We stand at the threshold of neurological singularity. Sacrifices from each one of us are required in order to succeed at the greatest undertaking humankind has ever faced. Our work here will change the world forever."

His gaze fell to Alexis Hicks.

"What did you do? If I don't get a response, each person beside you dies." He pressed the barrel of the gun against the forehead of a woman dressed in green scrubs. He started counting. "Three, two…"

"I inserted a thumb drive," Hicks blurted out. "The pump controller has a USB port."

Richards pivoted with the gun and pulled the trigger.

Hicks tumbled backwards to the floor, the result of a point-blank gunshot to her frontal lobe.

More screams erupted from the staff as they scurried away from him.

"Your cooperation was appreciated, doctor." Richards slid the pistol into the pocket of his lab coat and studied each staff member.

Terror painted their expressions as some cried and others shook.

He took a solemn breath. "Treason cannot be tolerated. The consequences for those who betray us are severe. Moving forward, the only thing that matters is The Frontier."

BECKY WARD'S WORLD GREW more oppressive. Her senses and extremities slowly came under her control. In a world of absolute darkness, she had no way to fight her confines. Her prison obliterated the passage of time.

Voices outside her realm came and went with more frequency. She could not hear their words clearly, but managed to catch phrases.

"Did you hear…?" "Richards ordered…" "Parker murdered a guard."

She could no longer recall Thomas' face with the same vividness she'd possessed earlier. It was like losing grasp of a dream after waking.

She yearned to see him, and beg for his forgiveness.

A voice commanded, "Everyone, form a line. Now!"

She recognized the man's voice. He stood close. Real close. She heard more phrases: "Thomas Parker", "drug infusion." The man was demanding answers.

Something yanked against her arm, delivering a searing pain. She tried to scream, but the bit in her mouth prevented anything louder than a moan. The burning sensation in her elbow tapered off, replaced by an inexplicable wet, cool numbness spreading through her arm and trickling down to her fingertips.

An abrupt sound thundered outside her blackness.

People screamed. Feet shuffled.

They're killing people! Thomas, help me!

5:00 A.M. BEING DOWN a man put Makara into a foul mood.

Richards had the audacity to confiscate one of his programmers to reinitialize the security management system off of backup servers. His team was not obligated to provide technical assistance outside their areas of expertise.

What the hell was he running, a Help Desk?

Richards inferred that Parker's actions were paramount to treason. Hijacking security systems and murdering a guard in cold blood had proved that much.

Makara was not a brainwashed puppet like most at the institute. He saw Richards as a tyrant king, a *de facto* dictator who thrived on micromanaging research and positioning himself to reap the glory of others' accomplishments.

His native Iraq had taught him the hard lessons of life under tyrants.

Richards had blood-stained hands after sacrificing his daughter at his Altar of Science. It was clear that Caroline Wang and her companions would incur similar fates.

Power to the people.

Power to Parker and his FBI counterpart.

And death to the tyrant king.

On an array of monitors, he cycled through commissioning routines and tested code as his remaining programmers passed it along. Using Parker's model, he constructed a cognitive neuro-template, based on participant 31, the badass FBI agent.

Being one man short meant he had to skip some quality control assessments.

Makara checked his watch and frowned. Where was Johnson? That idiot needed to get back to his terminal and back to making himself useful.

Riley Johnson loitered at the waterfall at the junction of the residence wing and the research annex. Across the atrium, he watched a small window in the door to the institute's kitchen. Inside, lights blinked off.

Someone was in the kitchen and it wasn't the cooks. The institute's culinary executives, as they were called, did not run a night shift.

He moved closer, as quickly as he could.

The kitchen door inched open and a dark-haired figure stepped out, holding a gun.

"The staff believes you murdered that guard," Johnson said, standing behind the arc of the door.

Kate spun toward him with a gun aimed squarely at his chest.

He held up his hands, revealing he was unarmed.

Parker closed the kitchen door. He clutched a burlap bag labeled Yukon Gold. It was a good guess that the bag didn't contain potatoes.

"Johnson," Parker asked, "what the hell are you doing here?"

He gestured to the shadows of the dining hall. "We need to talk."

Kate kept her pistol leveled at him. "I don't see a reason we should trust you."

"Suit yourself, but I'm not the ones being hunted. And the longer we stand here, the easier it is for the guards to find you."

"You first," Kate said, waving the gun.

Johnson drew them into a spread of shadows and out of sight of the atrium.

"What do you want?" Parker asked.

"I know you hacked into the surveillance cameras. It's no secret. You probably saw me talking to Noam Levine. Your warning only mentioned not speaking to Stewart Richards. I thought I could trust Levine. He proved me wrong."

Parker shrugged. "We don't have anything else to talk about, Johnson."

"Richards reposted a guard outside the neurophysiology lab."

Kate lowered her weapon. "Tell us something we don't know."

"They're down to three, now that you murdered that man."

"I didn't murder him."

Johnson feigned indifference. "Richards told the staff you did."

"It was self-defense," Kate said. "He gave me no choice."

Johnson didn't care. "Richards wants you dead, and Levine is out to finish what he didn't the first time." He paused to let the words sink in. "Yeah, everyone knows about the attack in your dorm room. Secrets like those are hard to keep quiet."

He could tell the point had hit home.

Johnson turned to Parker. "Richards has something special planned for you."

Parker's eyebrows shot up. "Like what?"

"He didn't elaborate, but he's looking forward to it."

Parker sighed. "How close is Makara to finishing his programming?"

"Maybe an hour."

Parker's shoulders slumped. "That's an eternity."

Johnson stepped closer. "I don't know what you two are planning, but the security systems will be operational in an hour. After that, you'll have a tough time moving about."

A flashlight beam swung into the dining hall, breaching its shadows.

Everyone pressed flat against a wall. Kate raised her pistol.

Johnson shook his head and whispered, "Take out Richards and that bastard Levine."

Kate nodded.

"Who's there?" the voice behind the light called out.

Johnson bounced into the open.

"Damn vending machines," he growled, marching into the spotlight. He raised his arms. "You're not going to shoot a fella for wanting a snack, are you?"

"Dr. Johnson," Earl said, targeting him with a flashlight beam and a pistol. "Everyone was ordered to their dorm rooms."

"Not me," he countered. "Those directives apply to others. Dr. Levine gave me special orders. Go ahead and confirm them with him. Man, I'm going to die if I can't get something to eat. You know, the vending machines are out of order. My luck, eh?"

Earl clicked off his light and holstered his sidearm.

Johnson wandered past the service counters, drawing the guard's attention.

"Where is Dr. Levine? The last I heard, he was with you?"

"I'm not obligated to disclose his presence," Earl said, watching him closely.

Parker and Kate slipped out of the shadows and tiptoed toward the stairs.

The potato sack Parker carried caught the corner of a utensil tray and sent it crashing to the floor.

Earl drew his pistol and whirled in the direction of the noise.

A mirror opposite, Kate responded in the same manner.

Johnson snatched a chair and swung it wildly, trying to knock the guard off balance. Like a wrestler, Earl spun into his advance and locked a free arm around his neck, using him as a human shield.

Johnson felt the guard's shoulder square into his back while the man's arm constricted his windpipe. He struggled against the suffocating grip.

Earl fired first, narrowly missing the FBI agent as she dove for cover.

Parker dropped the potato bag and found a temporary refuge.

His ears rang from the deafening discharge of the guard's weapon.

With two hands on her pistol, Kate searched for a shot. She pivoted on her toes behind tables and chairs and hunted for a better angle.

Johnson wheezed for a breath, realizing he was in a front row in a Mexican standoff.

Earl, tracking Kate's movements, squeezed off repeated shots.

53
CONNECTIVITY

LEVINE'S MANHUNT TOOK AN unexpected detour through the institute's data center.

Standing inside the glassed-in control room, he could hear the churn of cooling fans and pumps and felt the penetrating vibrations from their motors.

He checked his watch. "How long is this going to take?"

"Not long," said the programmer from Makara's AI team as he typed at an operator's terminal. The man pointed to the screen. "This is a work of brilliance. Almost never found it."

Levine squinted at the convoluted network architecture schematic on the monitor.

"What?" Levine asked, realizing he knew little to nothing about large-scale network solutions. "What am I looking at?"

"A portgroup... a very slick network bridge to a destination outside ANCRI."

Levine's brow furrowed as he tried to keep up. "A bridge to where?"

The man shrugged. "It's numeric and anonymous. Could be anyone, anywhere."

Levine rolled his eyes. "Okay, what's this bridge used for?"

The man clicked on a pop-up to show real-time data packet transfers. "Well, it looks like someone's cloning massive amounts of data from the networks." He tossed a high-level control module onto another screen and opened it. "This is a typical nodal tree structure with an insert of God- or parent-level authority over lower level functions. Meaning, everything below their control function is subordinate. Whoever is parasiting data could take over ANCRI if they wanted."

Levine cursed, then asked, "Can you disable this bridge?"

The programmer yawned. "Man, this ain't my specialty. I know enough about network management to be dangerous. If I tried to clean things up, I might vaporize some vital operation and we'd all be screwed. I don't think you want me to do that."

Levine cleared his throat. "What are our options?"

"Crap, the easiest thing would be to go off-grid, disconnect from the outside world. Except for my iTunes and Netflix, ANCRI is already self-sufficient."

"How long will that take?"

The man cracked his knuckles. "Five minutes."

"Make it happen." Levine turned to go, then stopped himself. "Where are you at in terms of rebooting security systems?"

The programmer grinned. "Cameras and card access were online ten minutes ago."

Levine keyed his radio. "Earl, surveillance is restored. Any sightings of Parker or Meir?" Nothing. He keyed the radio again. "Earl, provide an update. Over."

PARKER KNEW THEIR OPTIONS were limited. He and Kate had separated in opposite directions of the dining room when the gunfire started. Now both of them were trapped.

She sought refuge in an alcove to flee a barrage of bullets. Behind her, soft drink dispensers and reach-in coolers exploded, sending glass and plastic shrapnel in every direction and showering the dining area in carbonated beverages.

Using Johnson as a shield, Earl held his ground and blocked their way out.

The guard dared Kate to return fire, and barely glanced Parker's way.

From across the seating area, Kate's look told Parker what he already knew. She was boxed in with nowhere to run. She maneuvered closer to the wall separating herself from Earl and kept her pistol ready.

"Run, Thomas," Kate mouthed

He could read her mind. She was going to bait the guard into focusing on her. She wanted him to run and save himself.

The radio crackled. It was Noam Levine.

"Earl, surveillance is restored. Any sightings of Parker or Meir?" Another crackle. "Earl, provide an update. Over."

Parker held out a palm and motioned for her to hold tight.

Unarmed, he had no way to get past the guard.

But Kate could, if he became the distraction.

He stole a glance at Earl.

The guard nudged his protective shield in Kate's direction. Johnson resisted, but the massive grip around his neck made it futile. Earl seemed determined to close the gap and set up for an easy target.

Parker returned his gaze to Kate, then pointed to the potato sack he was clutching.

She shook her head adamantly. *No.*

He stood and yelled, "Call Levine and tell him you found me!"

The radio crackled again. "Earl, radio in."

Parker flung the burlap potato sack across the gap between him and Kate.

The toss distracted Earl.

"I hear Richards wants to see me!" Parker yelled, stepping into the guard's line of sight. He kept his arms up and wide, offering a broad target.

"On your knees, Dr. Parker," the guard snapped. "Do it now."

Parker glanced to Kate, his eyes telling her it was time to move.

"Or what? You'll shoot me?" He offered a feeble laugh. "You do that and Richards' grand plan will evaporate. Isn't that right, Johnson?"

Johnson croaked out a whisper. "That's right. Richards has plans…"

Earl bobbed with his pistol, trying to secure a shot in Kate's direction.

"If you want her, you'll have to go through me."

Earl's face went red. "Move, doctor, or I'll—"

"Now, Kate!"

Parker gambled and charged the guard, betting Earl didn't have the guts to shoot him without Richards' permission.

Kate rounded the corner with burlap sack in hand, dogging tables and chairs and sprinting into the atrium.

Parker kept his gaze fixed onto Earl, tracking his eyes and parrying his movements to shelter her escape. Frustrated, the guard recoiled and drove the butt of his gun into Parker's shoulder blade. Pain exploded through him, leaving his left arm numb and useless. His heart pounded and he inhaled a panicked breath. Using his other hand, he latched onto Johnson and yanked backwards, trying to tip them all to the floor.

Earl sneered, released his grip on Johnson and let the fools crumble to the floor.

Steadying his balance, the guard fired shots in the direction of the closest stairwell.

Parker cringed at the pain in his shoulder and cocked his head in the direction of the stairwell. A bullet-riddled metal door shut. Kate was gone.

Earl screamed like a madman at the lost opportunity.

"Earl!" Levine shouted over the radio. "What's going on? Report in!"

Parker dropped his head to the floor and took a breath.

Johnson rolled off him and their eyes met. Parker cracked an exhausted smile at the corner of his mouth. The spontaneous, ill-conceived feat had worked. Kate escaped.

The guard's eyes lit up with rage. He glanced down and aimed his pistol at Parker.

Earl keyed his radio. "Parker is in custody. Meir escaped in the northeast stairwell. She's in possession of the chemicals that Parker stole from the biochemistry lab."

"What—?"

Earl bared his teeth at Parker and holstered his weapon.

The consequences of his actions became obvious as the guard clamped down on his ears. With an incredible, near skull-crushing force, the man lifted Parker by his head. Dangling, the tips of his toes cleared the floor. Having his skull squeezed like a piece of fruit was more painful than Parker could have imagined. He tried to retaliate. It was useless. In a Herculean move, the guard drove him headfirst into a building column.

Parker blacked out.

National Security Agency, Fort George G. Meade, Maryland

5:20 A.M. SOMETHING HAD gone wrong.

In the west building of the joint CYBERCOM, National Security Agency, and Central Security Service complex at Fort Meade, US Army Colonel Randall Wang sat in his ninth-floor office watching the vehicle lights streak north-south along the Patuxent Freeway.

He felt defeated.

ANCRI's network connectivity was lost.

The swath of data siphoned off the institute's servers had not been enough for the Department of Defense to establish a creditable neuro-intelligence initiative.

Minutes earlier, Wang had notified a four-star general that his mission, Synaptic Touch, had failed. It was a facts-only briefing, one that would never be documented or acknowledged. The general ordered Wang to stand down and let events unfold.

At this point, the objective was plausible deniability.

Wang thought of Caroline, whose life hung in the balance. He could interfere no further and wondered whether Parker or Morgan saved her, Rebecca Ward, or the 28 college students.

Not that the Pentagon cared.

Of course, if they perished, the White House and State Department would get the blame. The Pentagon would make sure others took the fall for botched oversight of the rogue research efforts.

It was an ugly business, war. The Department of Defense was in the business of measuring the value of human capital, assessing and categorizing tangible assets on a variety of balance sheets. Human capital was indispensable, but sometimes had to be expendable. George Patton had said it best: *Wars may be fought with weapons, but they are won by men.*

Caroline had found herself in a different kind of war: one of science, the science of tomorrow, with casualties that could be considerable.

As a father, he had taught his daughter to place her faith in science, what was known, rather than succumbing to the frailty of human superstitions.

He had failed her on so many fronts.

Outside his office windows, the first wisps of a sunrise emerged.

Wang shuddered. He had no way to help Caroline without violating his orders. He had already stretched his covert mission beyond acceptable limits.

A father's hope rested with Thomas Parker.

54
REPERCUSSIONS

Advanced Neurological and Cybernetic Research Institute (ANCRI), New Jersey

PARKER WOKE WITH A crippling headache. He could taste remnants of blood. It took several blinks to clear the cobwebs from his eyes.

The air reeked of cigar smoke, which seemed odd.

He took a labored breath and realized that zip ties bound him to a chair behind a row of consoles in the neurophysiology lab. He closed his eyes and concentrated. Earl the guard had smashed him against a wall or a column, causing him to black out.

But Kate had escaped.

His head throbbed as he looked for Riley Johnson, who was nowhere to be seen.

In front of him, technicians and nurses moved about pods. Fear seemed etched into their collective faces. He glanced to the Wall of Knowledge. Streams of antiquated neural images and obsolete cerebral grid schemes stood on display. Obviously, no one had consulted Talib Makara about updating modeling techniques.

He almost missed the two people lying at the foot of the huge screen. Both had been left where they died. Gunshot wounds were obvious. He didn't recognize the man, but knew the woman in light blue as Alexis Hicks.

His blood ran cold. He'd gotten her killed.

"You murdered them," Parker said, knowing the madman lurked somewhere nearby.

Wisps of gray smoke drifted closer, like clouds announcing an oncoming storm. Stewart Richards emerged from behind him, holding his cigar.

"Circumstances demanded extraordinary actions," Richards said. "The Frontier is grander than a few inconsequential casualties."

"Inconsequential? Tell that to their families."

Parker heaved against his restraints but the zip ties held firm.

He was going nowhere.

Richards moved to face him, and Parker found himself staring into the vile eyes of Satan himself. The splotches of blood dotting the man's lab coat filled him with dread.

Richards took a deep draw on his cigar, allowing a cherry to build, before extinguishing it on the backside of Parker's wrist.

He writhed as a thumb-size ember charred his skin.

Richards exhaled. "You, Dr. Parker, have become an obstacle that requires removal."

Parker looked away from the raw welt on the back of his hand.

Richards extracted a pistol from his lab coat. "ANCRI exists because of my vision. It's by invitation only. I offered you a chance to work together, yet you chose a different path. You conspired with the FBI to cheat me out of the Frontier."

Parker gasped at the sight of the gun. "What? Richards, you're insane. You yearn to be worshipped as the latest father of neuroscience, just like a portrait on your wall."

Richards' gaze darkened. "Do not lecture me."

"Really? I saw the photo of Amy. You sacrificed your daughter. Must've murdered Samuel Ford when he learned of your research." He tossed his head in the direction of the big screen. "Alexis Hicks never deserved to die. How many others have to die for your bloodthirsty ambition? Medicine is the science of healing, not this delusion you've concocted."

Richards scowled. "You don't understand the legitimacy of our cause."

"Enlighten me."

With his gun in hand, Richards spread his hands wide like a sidewalk evangelist preaching on a street corner. "The Frontier will deliver a treasure trove of advancements, anything from switching on and off individual neurons to improving cellular architectures. Replacement nerves cells can be grafted into dead neural pathways and spark a slumbering mind. The brain can be physically repaired, even recoded. Designer drugs will heal synaptic junctions. My Frontier will save countless lives, far more than the few lost on its road to fruition."

Parker's muscles tightened. The man was obsessed with fame and absolute power.

Richards flicked the butt of his cigar to the floor and raised his pistol. "It's time to show that your traitorous actions have repercussions."

MAKARA WAS ASTONISHED THAT compiling the neurological interface went off without a hitch. That rarely happened. As Parker had requested through a string of IMs, Makara inserted executive-level control commands and named the application APPLIED MIND.

He took an exhausted breath and activated Applied Mind on the network.

The live model synced with the thirty participants in the neurophysiology lab.

The door to his lab slid open. He craned his head around to spot Riley Johnson dressed in his usual colored lab coat. The door closed as quickly as it opened.

"Pigpen, where did you disappear to?" he snapped.

Johnson looked flustered. "Dr. Levine needed assistance with a matter of importance."

"Well, you twit, that's a waste of your time." Makara shook his head. "The baseline template developed for participant 31 allowed us to expand beyond discrete, singular-moment memory extraction and obtain multi-event cognitive recall. Now we have an authentic neural-interface that can extract dynamic cognitive associations."

Johnson pinched his brows together. "It's operational?"

Makara stroked his beard. "Let's just say our work is no longer academic supposition."

Johnson showed his pistol. "Dr. Makara, where are your programmers?"

Makara's eyes widened. "Why do you have a gun?"

"Where is your team?"

"Getting coffee." He frowned. "Explain yourself, Johnson."

"Who else knows you have a working neural interface?"

The directness of Johnson's tone surprised him. Behind tight lips, he let silence be his response.

Johnson's face became a mask.

Makara rose from his console and stood over the shorter man. There was no way he was going to be bullied by the likes of Riley Johnson, pistol be damned. And Johnson didn't have the nerve to hurt a fly.

The man looked flustered.

On a broad monitor, Makara taunted him by selecting the interface for participant 31. He typed RILEY JOHNSON into a dialogue box and hit EXECUTE.

Johnson twitched and he raised the gun.

Makara chuckled. "*The difference between stupidity and genius is that genius has its limits.* You, Johnson, seem to be afflicted with stupidity."

Riley Johnson appeared on the screen in his psychedelic lab coat. The image showed his introduction to Parker and Meir. The reflection was crude, like watching a VHS tape recording of a historical moment. In fact, it was history in the form of a memory.

Johnson looked startled. "What's this about?"

"Damage control."

Johnson cocked his head at the answer. Taking a steadying breath, he pulled the trigger.

Makara heard the eruption then felt the bullet pierce his stomach. Pain ripped through him, and his mouth opened in protest.

He gasped. "Why—?"

Johnson did not move. "I'm on clean-up duty. And your pompous ass is no longer of value to me or the team."

Makara's knees buckled and he crumpled to the floor.

He vaguely noticed Johnson's shoes turn and leave through the lab's sliding doors.

Lying on the tile floor, he was unable to move. Makara felt the ragged throbbing of his pulse pool blood around him. The sensation in his extremities had been lost, and his mind told him that Johnson's bullet severed his spinal cord.

In that instant, Talib Makara knew death was certain, inevitable.

RICHARDS WAS EXHILARATED. THE technology showed tremendous promise, and his place in history was assured, Thomas Parker be damned. He had won. The traitors had been discovered. Johnson closed out Makara's band of rogue programmers, leaving Levine to eliminate the FBI mole. With those obstacles eliminated, it was time to get to the business of the future—The Frontier.

A special surprise awaited Parker, one that surely would drive home the point that Stewart Richards was not a man to be cheated.

He pointed his pistol at Parker, still bound to a chair. "Who helped you hack the security systems?"

BECKY WARD WAS ON the verge of panic. Someone was experimenting on her—trying to read her mind. It was the only explanation that made sense.

The deep-seated fog she had endured dispersed, and her head felt clearer. Under restraints, her entire body ached. Discomfort was chronic. She chomped down against the airway bit in her mouth and tried to break it. No luck. And it kept her from communicating with the outside world. She yearned to scream, but realized that too was futile.

The burning pain in the crook of her arm receded, and she no longer felt like she was bleeding out.

Somewhere beyond her darkness, people were shooting.

Questions plagued her. Where was she? Why were people doing this to her? Who was shooting? Why was Thomas Parker part of this?

Answers remained out of her grasp.

She only had one power: the ability to listen.

A man's voice returned. Firm. Authoritative. She associated him with pieced-together conversations—Dr. Richards. He sounded like the man in charge.

"It's time," Richards said, "to show that your traitorous actions have repercussions." There was a pause and she sensed he stood closer. "Who helped you hack the security systems?"

Becky groaned through the bit in her mouth. "Traitorous... hack... what? Thomas, get me out of here."

PARKER SIFTED THROUGH POSSIBLE scenarios and prepared himself to be shot.

Bound to a chair, he sat dead in sights of the handgun.

He swallowed hard. "I'll give you everything, just let me go."

"This is not a negotiation," Richards said.

He saw the staff distance themselves from Richards like the parting of a sea.

Richards swung the gun to pod 10—Becky's pod.

"Wait!" he blurted out. "The government gave me the passcodes."

"Who, the FBI?"

He shook his head. "No. The FBI is only here because you kidnapped a U.S. senator." He paused as the surrounding staff absorbed this revelation. "Our government wants to use neurological singularity as a weapon. They could care less about advancements in medicine. Their sole interest is mind control. Your Frontier is in the crosshairs of those who brandish patriotism as a patch on a sleeve and fight enemies of the state in places most Americans don't know exist."

He could see Richards processing a reply.

Out of the corner of his eye, on the monitor facing him, Parker caught sight of a command icon that appeared on the network: AP-PLIED MIND.

About damn time, Makara.

He leaned forward in his chair. "Richards, for God's sake, I am not your enemy."

The man's eyes narrowed. "Your little coup has lost. At this very moment, your FBI associate is being hunted down."

Parker's heart thundered in his chest. Kate was in trouble.

That explained the absence of Earl and Levine. They were the hunters.

Richards stood beside pod 10, keeping his gun aimed at its inhabitant.

Parker tried to gather himself. "Killing a federal agent only exacerbates your problems. And hurting Becky offers no leverage. Be reasonable. Put down the gun. I'll cooperate."

Richards squeezed the trigger.

The shot rattled Parker, resonating in the large room.

"No!" he screamed.

Richards pulled the trigger again and again.

Parker wrenched against his restraints as tears flowed unrestrained.

Scared staff shuffled to the perimeters of the room. Only Stewart Richards stood in the center of his grand lab, alone.

Parker's heart stuttered as malice crushed his soul.

The grand display showed a flatlined electrocardiogram. Other vitals fell to zero.

Becky was dead.

55
PREDATORS AND PREY

KATE BOLTED FROM THE stairwell, grateful not to be dead. The shots Earl fired in the dining area had nearly took off her head. Out of breath, she scanned basement corridors and clutched Parker's potato sack of makeshift explosives a bit tighter. She hoped he was all right.

Ahead, placards provided directions.

She negotiated a series of metal doors leading to the data center.

Passing a janitor's closet, she doubled back and badged into it. Inside, she rifled through cleaning supplies, searching for flammable chemicals. No luck. Everything was environmentally safe, but she left with a door prize: a broomstick.

Carrying the broomstick like a samurai sword, she arrived at a dead end. Two side-by-side doors stood under surveillance. Attacking the CCTV camera like a piñata, she turned the device into shards of plastic and metal with a few solid whacks of the broom handle. She imagined the shock on Earl's face as he watched the monitors.

Multiple signs plastered doors labeled DATA CENTER and CENTRAL PLANT.

Ignoring warnings about inhalation danger, the possibility of electrocution, and excessive noise, she badged into the data center's lower level.

A frigid gust chilled her cheeks, the air driven off cooling ponds and submersion tanks. Lights blinked on in the distance and illuminated a world of machines, deafening pumps, and endless runs of piping.

The entrance was full of metal lockers marked SCBA.

Wrenching open lockers, she jerked out two self-contained breathing apparatus packs and hauled them into the corridor. The first tank became a doorstop, blocking open the data center's entrance. She badged into the central plant and performed the same routine with that door.

Anyone following would have to decide which path to take. Their indecision might buy her enough time to pull off Parker's absurd plan.

Hustling into the central plant's tunnel, Kate navigated a series of concrete corridors. Similar-looking intersections came and went. Nothing was marked or pointed to a central destination. She tried to recall the floor plans seen on the network, but her sense of direction was messed up. Underground there was no north or south, no reference to above-grade annexes. She went with her instincts and followed piping.

A musty smell permeated the air. Everything felt damp.

Lighting at fifty feet intervals led to the merger of enormous piping runs. Power cables snaked along spans of trays mounted to the walls.

She found a metal platform with a ladder that dropped another twelve feet down.

More piping ran in that direction. Just like following the Yellow Brick Road.

Take Your Kid to Work Day had paid dividends. As a tomboy, once a year she'd shadowed her father on his job as an electrician in downtown Chicago high-rises. The day's reward was investigative tours in the subterranean routes between buildings. During their father-daughter spelunking adventures, her father told ghost stories—a kind of metropolitan-era, Huck Finn-Tom Sawyer adventures.

No sooner had her feet touched down and sounds echoed in the concrete chasm, emanating from the upward direction she had just come.

Kate took a breath and broke into a sprint, darting deeper into the tunnel.

Shots rang out.

Bullets slammed into concrete and piping. Bursts of steam showered the tunnel with scalding vapors. She ducked and plowed ahead, the broomstick and a potato sack still in hand.

Scampering down the passageway, she began to club lights, busting their lamps and plunging everything into darkness.

She heard movement back near the ladder.

Keeping the whack-a-mole efforts going, she plunged the tunnel into darkness. It made her pursuer's trek more challenging, and the trailing footsteps slowed.

Ahead was the proverbial light at the end of the tunnel, at least ANCRI's version—its central plant—a world with more lighting than she could obliterate with a broomstick. The musty air was alive with a high-pitched churn that came from centrifugal chillers and compression pumps, the life force keeping ANCRI alive.

Kate broke into a world foreign to most people. Its mechanical shriek was deafening.

No wonder ear protection was required.

She didn't have time to get the lay of the land, but knew her primary targets—the chillers. Without the chillers and compressed gas cooling systems, ANCRI's data center would melt down.

Kate peered into her potato sack, which contained the six explosives and a bottle of nitrobenzene. The last item she had no idea what to do with.

The central plant's layout placed twelve chillers in a row.

There were more chillers than she had explosives, and she had no idea which unit fed which part of ANCRI. Parker's plan required taking out the ones serving the data center.

Seconds mattered, so she guessed.

Blow up the biggest units and see what happens. Those sat packed in the middle of the others.

With a propane lighter, she lit two explosives and heaved them.

Her six-second makeshift fuse clock started.

A man appeared at the tunnel's edge. Noam Levine. He carried a pistol.

Levine's gaze latched onto hers. He fired.

She had no time to sprint for safety, to distance herself from the blast or gunfire.

Kate dove to the floor as bullets pounded nearby pump housings. She cupped her ears with her hands and closed her eyes.

The concussive blast was deafening.

The entire below-grade structure shook. The air was filled with shrapnel and metallic piping. Lines burst and liquids sprayed everywhere.

Banks of vapors rolled her way.

Concrete panels broke loose from the ceiling and fell in thunderous chunks.

Her head throbbed and the ringing in her ears made it hard to think.

She raised her head and saw no trace of Levine.

Kate fought for a steadying breath and noticed there was not enough destruction. The bank of primary chillers looked to be intact and functioning. She reached into her sack, lit two more explosives, and chucked them at the bases of the biggest units.

On a six-second clock, she darted toward an opposing tunnel.

A gunshot rang out. A bullet struck a steam line just as she passed it. A scalding spray caused her to trip and skid across the concrete floor. A burning sensation rippled up her leg and across her back, and she crawled away from the threats on all fours.

Two simultaneous explosions again rocked the central plant.

A new wave of dust and vapors engulfed her.

-|-

ON THE EDGE OF his seat, Earl scanned the bank of monitors. CCTV coverage did not reach into the utility tunnels or the central plant, so he was flying blind with no way to direct Levine.

Faced with irreducible choices, Levine opted for the door to the central plant instead of the data center.

The subterranean passageways interfered with wireless communications. Earl lost contact with Levine as soon as he entered the tunnel. He watched the screens and waited for movement.

Alarms blared on the screen, green icons blinking to red as entire systems failed.

The central plant's cooling systems lost pressure, spiking temperatures.

Backup systems scrambled to cover the anomalies.

"What's going on down there?" Earl called into his microphone, knowing no one would respond. Panic rose in his throat. "Dr. Levine, do you read me? Over."

LEVINE STAGGERED TO HIS feet, his face painted with dust and grit. Everything throbbed. The world around him moved in slow motion. Ringing overwhelmed his hearing as his tired eyes scanned the twisted remnants of the institute's central plant. The remaining pumps clanked with a fierce intensity. A few chillers carried on undamaged. The air churned with vapors and sprays and began to generate a plume of fog. Chunks of concrete dropped from the ceiling.

Alarms blared and red lights flashed.

He staggered forward and aimed his pistol at a churn of gray.

A shadowy figure rose, more like a silhouette pressed against a tapestry of smoke.

It was the outline of a woman.

She heaved baseball-sized objects in the direction of the remaining chillers.

More bombs.

Behind clenched teeth, Levine pulled the trigger, hoping to get lucky before retreating for cover.

The second volley of concussive blasts knocked him to his knees.

He choked in dust for a long second and fought to stand. It was impossible to see through the dust-laden air.

Mechanical groans and the failing of mechanized steel thundered.

The woman was nowhere to be seen.

Levine fired random rounds into the whirling mass of gray, and screamed, "I'm going to enjoy killing you, FBI Agent Katherine Morgan!"

KATE COULD SEE NOTHING in the direction of the central plant. The clanging and banging of mechanical systems were relentless.

Using the broomstick as a crutch, she climbed to her feet and reached down for the potato sack. From a workbench, she snatched electrical wiring and duct tape and added those to her dwindling treasures.

Behind her, Levine bellowed over the blare of alarms. Kate couldn't make out what he yelled, and laughed from sheer nerves. She unholstered her Glock, and fired a round in his direction. *Follow at your own peril.*

Licking her lips, she noticed grit painted the inside of her mouth as if she had been eating dirt. She worked to build up enough saliva to spit and clear her palate, but it was nearly impossible not to inhale more dust.

She studied the central plant cast in gray then turned to the labyrinth of tunnels channeling out. The one routing the largest piping offered the most promise.

Her scalded leg turned running into fast limping.

The concrete chasm she entered was taller and wider than before. Again, lights spanned at even intervals. She put the broomstick to good use, taking out illumination along the way.

LEVINE PEERED INTO THE drifting churns of smoke and vapors. A fire sparked to life in one of mechanical units.

Clouds of rolling vapor hid the FBI agent.

She had targeted the large-framed chillers supporting the data center.

Her objective was to kill their research efforts.

Around him, alarms blared without reprieve and hazard lights flashed.

His congested head was just as fog-ridden as the central plant itself.

A gnawing pain caused him to look down and notice a short span of steel protruding from his abdomen. Adrenaline had masked it earlier. His grit-smattered lab coat showed blood. He clenched his jaw and yanked out the impalement.

Stripping off his coat, he pressed a palm against the one-inch gash in his gut to slow the bleeding.

Levine looked in the direction his prey had fled. He could pursue, but that would leave him a step behind.

There was another way. Backtrack.

Entering the data center through the other access tunnel would let him cut her off.

He could trap her before she wrought any more destruction. Levine smiled at a better plan, one she would never see coming.

56
ISOLATION

PARKER STARED IN DISBELIEF, stunned at the madman's heartless disregard for human life.

The consequences of his actions felt overwhelming.

Bound to his chair, he trembled in the glow of nearby monitors.

Helpless he watched timid staff disconnect Becky from pod 10 and a technician remove her headgear. Her pallid face and shaved head were troubling sights. The bulky suit she wore masked her wounds.

The night they shared sparked into his mind. He remembered the scent of her lotion, seeing her inquisitive brown eyes and chestnut-colored hair. He almost smiled and yearned to hold her and tell her it would be okay, but that kind of sentimentality only resided in a former lover's dream.

His gamble cost people their lives, He was as responsible for her death as the man who'd pulled the trigger.

Movement snagged his attention and jarred him from his thoughts.

An obedient nurse in green scrubs helped Richards don a crisp, new lab coat and discard his blood-spattered version. The change to a sterile cloak seemed to invigorate him, and the man's maniacal gaze flashed over to Parker.

"Rebecca Ward just created an opening," Richards said. "You will take her place."

Parker didn't flinch at the proclamation, yet noticed something odd.

Richards held nothing in his hands. The gun was not in sight. The last place he'd seen the weapon was in the pocket of the same coat the nurse had traded out.

His gaze followed the nurse as she deposited the bloodstained coat in a bin marked SOILED LINEN.

Stewart Richards was unarmed.

"I'm anxious to see what your mind has to offer," Richards said. "I assume the techniques used in the immersion lab were modeled on your Princeton research, which has influences from you as the primary test subject. My methodology will make you feel right at home."

Parker stole a glance at the monitor that resided three feet away. The APPLIED MIND icon still appeared on screen. If only he could activate the application.

Bound to a chair meant that three feet might as well be three miles.

Somehow he needed to get to the computer terminal. How?

Earl pushed past the guard at the lab's entrance. He looked panicked, and started a rapid conversation with Richards. They had a problem. The two men huddled away from the staff.

Parker inched forward in his chair, straining to hear their conversation. He picked up a few words: "systemic cooling system failure…" and "backup limitations…"

Parker let himself smile. Kate had taken down the central plant.

Someone in green scrubs bumped his chair, startling him.

He made eye contact with the female nurse who had discarded Richards' lab coat.

Ducking down, she sliced through one zip tie securing a wrist, then leisurely dropped a scalpel and a handgun in his lap. Without a word said, she moved onto an open workstation.

Seizing the moment, Parker used his free hand and the scalpel to sever his remaining bonds.

He peeked up. Richards and Earl remained in their tense conversation.

He lunged for the console, selected the `APPLIED MINDS` icon, and launched the command `makeCONTACT` in the application window.

A popup window emerged: `PATIENTS TO ACTIVATE:`

Just as Earl departed under directives from Richards, Parker typed: `31,20,1-30`.

For a fraction of a second, the Wall of Knowledge flickered, waking from its slumber.

Silence settled over the lab as everyone's gaze turned to the enormous screen.

The centermost frame erupted to reveal a neuro-map for patient 31 superimposed over patient 20, Caroline Wang. 3D neurological profiles appeared for other patients. The flanking screens showed live synaptic exchanges between the patients—their brains communicating.

A dedicated frame began to transmit images—memories.

Gasps spread across the room. A picture of Amy Richards lying on a gurney appeared.

With pistol in hand, Parker moved swiftly.

On the wall beside the lab's entrance was a red mushroom button protected by a clear plastic cover. The sign above the button read: `EMERGENCY ISOLATION`.

Richards' gaze was a mix of astonishment and fury. He tore his eyes away from the screens and spun around, searching for Parker.

Their gazes met just as he snapped open the protective cover and pounded the red button.

The pneumatic door to the anteroom hissed closed.

Amber emergency strobes sparked on.

The lab was quarantined. Locked down.

Parker forced a somber grin and aimed the pistol at Richards.

Behind him, Earl pounded on the anteroom door, his irate face appearing through the small webbing of paned glass in the sliding door. He had no way to enter the lab, no different from everyone inside being trapped and unable to leave. Trapped, at least, until someone found the override mechanisms.

Richards patted his pockets of his lab coat and realized he carried no weapon.

57
END OF THE ROAD

LEVINE CLEARED THE TUNNEL to the central plant and radioed Earl.

Earl didn't answer.

Levine's ache had worsened, and the hand pressed to his abdomen was bloody. He cursed and stepped through the steel door leading to the data center. Several signs adorned the SCBA lockers in the tunnels' entrance. He was grateful to see one of them.

He yanked open the locker and found a first aid kit. No time for antiseptic or alcohol wipes. He only needed to slow the bleeding until the matter at hand was resolved. Stacking gauze pads together, he cinched them down with a self-adhering strip tight around his waist.

He clicked his radio again. "Earl, do you have eyes on the data center? Over."

Silence.

"Damn it, where are you?"

Levine cursed again and let his pistol lead the way as he trudged down the tunnel and into the bowels of the data center.

KATE TROTTED WITH A severe limp down the concrete passage, clutching her potato sack in one hand and eliminating lights with the broomstick in the other. Behind her, the tunnel was nothing but a dark hole. She lost track of distance and direction, but knew from massive piping runs that she was due east of her destination.

Her scalded leg hurt like hell as blistered skin stuck to the inside of her scrub bottoms.

She rounded a corner and spotted a wide expanse.

Brisk, cool air greeted her. The churn of more pumps announced that she had arrived.

A placard caught her eye as it hung from a piping rack.

```
UNOCCUPIED DATA CENTER. INHALATION DAN-
GER. WHEN ALARM SOUNDS, VACATE PREMISES
IMMEDIATELY. FIRE SUPPRESSION CHEMICALS
AND TOXIC SUBSTANCES PRESENT. PERSONNEL
SHALL POSSESS SELF-CONTAINED BREATHING
APPARATUS (SCBA) PER OSHA REGULATIONS.
```

Her dilemma was clear. She had no supplemental breathing equipment.

Parker's plan required a high-temperature meltdown of the institute's quantum computers and data storage systems. The goal was to make sure ANCRI's research never saw the light of day. Of course, protective systems prevented such catastrophes. And disabling the fire suppression system with explosives meant releasing toxic gases into a confined space.

ANCRI's pressurized fire suppression tanks weren't hard to spot, two stories tall and painted fire engine red. Warning signs were posted everywhere. The tanks contained enough chemical agents to asphyxiate a small town.

She caught sight of a metal ladder and her vision darted upward into a cavernous space. High above, a maintenance hatch led to ground level—a means for maintenance crews to fill and service the tanks.

She ran through the problem. How to blow the tanks and not suffocate?

Hell if she knew. She hadn't been trained in sabotage.

Levine had no idea where the FBI agent might be, but understood the data center's layout enough to know she would enter somewhere on the lower levels near the cooling ponds, or perhaps near the fire suppression tanks.

Ignoring the pain in his gut, he picked up his pace.

The two-level data center was a vast expanse of massive computers and peripheral mechanical systems, the most sophisticated complex in the world.

He passed through the translucent green glow of super-cooled ponds and automated pumps. Above him, diamond-cut grating ran everywhere and his gaze raked the upper and lower levels.

A footpath separated rows of cooling ponds.

He came to a stop and raised his pistol. She had to be damn close.

In the distance, Levine spotted his target. She was climbing a ladder.

The access ladder ran parallel to the red tanks, and gave Kate little room to maneuver. With broomstick in one hand and the potato sack in the other, she climbed one rung at a time. Her breathing grew labored from the exertion. The steam burn on her leg caused a constant grimace. Under the exertion of climbing, she allowed Thomas Parker to slip into her thoughts. She felt something for him, and wondered if he felt the same way. Perhaps when this nightmare was over, they could spend time together and find out.

The FBI was bound to terminate her employment, which meant she'd be out of a job. She smiled, thinking Parker too was unemployed. That gave them time together.

She wondered if he had escaped and confronted Richards. With the central plant compromised, the supercomputers would exceed their thermal limits and either drop offline, or stay powered up and catch fire.

Parker had a narrow window in which to extract memories.

The halfway point and the main level platform hung above her.

The broomstick she carried banged against the metal ladder ever so slightly, and she was thankful the data center was unmanned. Clinging to the ladder left her as vulnerable as a string of metal ducks at a county fair's carny stand.

LEVINE ASCENDED THE STAIRS to the main platform and closed in on the fire suppression tanks.

He could no longer see the federal agent, but she was there.

Twenty feet away, a span of ladder stretched before him and fronted bright red tanks.

He could hear her. Something clanked as she climbed metal rungs.

Was it her gun? It didn't sound like a gun.

He crouched and trained the sights of his pistol on the ladder.

Levine grinned. As soon as he saw her deceitful eyes, he planned to put a bullet right between them.

EARL RACED BACK TO his surveillance station. His frantic gaze scanned monitors and took in the broad array of red warning indicators. The institute's mechanical systems shut down in an accelerating domino effect. ANCRI was melting down on multiple fronts.

To make matters worse, Levine had gone silent on his manhunt and Dr. Richards was barricaded in the neurophysiology lab with Parker.

With no one to provide directions, Earl made the command decision to recall the guard at the property gate and order him to search for a hydraulic jack in the maintenance shop. Quarantine measures prohibited traditional overrides. But perhaps a jack's brute force could dislodge the sliding door and allow him to gain entry.

Then there was the matter of Thomas Parker being armed.

How had that happened? He didn't have that answer, but hardly feared the doctor's sharpshooting prowess.

Earl snatched up his radio and clicked its button. "Dr. Levine, ANCRI has multiple cooling system failures. Central plant operations are failing at a rapid pace. Do you read? Over?"

LEVINE'S RADIO CRACKLED, KILLING his element of surprise.

"Dr. Levine," Earl's voice erupted across the radio, "ANCRI has multiple cooling system failures. Central plant operations are failing at a rapid pace. Do you read? Over?"

Levine frantically muted the radio's volume button.

JUST AS HER HEAD cleared the main platform, Kate heard a radio and spotted Levine reaching to silence Earl's voice. His pistol pointed her way.

She chucked the broomstick at him and reached for her Glock.

Levine ducked the stick and squeezed off a random shot.

Lead struck structural steel, narrowly missing pressurized fire suppression tanks.

Her fingers lost their grip and Kate dropped a rung, nearly plummeting thirty feet to her death. She grasped for handholds with sweaty palms.

"I should have drowned you," he taunted from a superior vantage point.

Her gaze identified movement through diamond grating. She let his words hang in the air, without a reply, and she fought against a raging heartbeat.

Approaching the platform edge, Levine angled for a shot.

She had nowhere to go—not up or down.

Then, out of the corner of her eye, she spotted a horizontal run of power cable trays four feet away. The gap between solid objects seemed huge.

Without thinking about it, Kate coiled her legs and leapt from the ladder. Sailing through the air, she hit the u-channeled tray hard, smacking her head against its sharp edges.

Levine stood directly above, searching for her. Only slatted metal separated them.

His eyes met hers. Surprise lit up his face as he swung his pistol toward his feet.

Kate did not hesitate, squeezing off three consecutive bursts.

Levine crumpled to the platform, dead. His eyes transfixed to hers, lifeless, his face resting against grating no more than a few feet above.

Blood from his wounds dripped through the platform's perforations and onto her.

"That's payback, asshole." She slumped into the tray of power cables and touched a painful laceration in her scalp. Closing her eyes, Kate caught her breath, and tried to ignore throbbing streaks of pain and the eyes of a dead man.

If Earl hadn't radioed, she'd be the corpse.

58
THE IMPORTANCE OF ECHOES

PARKER GLARED AT THE madman across the lab. His finger tightened against the pistol's trigger. In the weapon's sights, Richards stood emotionless and unapologetic.

Amber strobes continued to flash.

The Wall of Knowledge displayed pictures. Pulsing neurological models crackled neon with activity. A grainy movie image projected without sound. Amy Richards was loaded into the institute's incinerator.

An extracted echo, a memory from Caroline Wang in pod 20, reran history.

The APPLIED MIND program imprinted her memories onto the others, making them all witnesses—singularity witnesses.

The staff's collective gaze gradually turned from the transmission toward one person—Stewart Richards. Their eyes, which had been fearful, now showed disdain.

Parker gestured to the screen as Caroline Wang's hand pressed a red button.

Richards' features hardened in defiance.

"No one deserved to die," Parker said. "Not even Amy."

Richards faced him. "Her sacrifice led us to the promontory where we find ourselves." His face turned incredulous. "Who have you sacrificed, Dr. Parker? Rebecca Ward?"

Parker marched across the room, his pistol unwavering from its target. Behind gritted teeth, he struck Richards in the face with the butt of the gun, sending the pompous ass to the floor.

A mob of people dressed in green and gray scrubs crowded around.

Richards spit out blood. "Your moral superiority is tenuous at best. My Frontier is worthy of all sacrifices."

"Put Dr. Richards in pod 10. Make sure his restraints are tight. We'd hate for him to slither away."

Richards scoffed. "Influential forces are invested in ANCRI. You said it yourself. The government wants mind control. I intended to provide it. You thought me naïve. Hardly. The Phoenix Consortium and its investors were a means to an end, as was my daughter. I assure you, they will hunt you down Dr. Parker, along with those who assist you."

The anger-filled staff seized their boss. Richards tried to break free, but too many hands were latched onto him. A nurse muzzled him by shoving a plastic airway bit into his mouth. Others lifted him and loaded him head first into the vacant pod 10.

Parker's eyes narrowed as his gaze met Richards'. "Welcome to your Frontier."

On a computer terminal, he typed: SAMUEL FORD.

The headgear slid over Richards' head and covered his eyes. The man squirmed before accepting his fate.

The monstrous screen came alive with a new memory echo. Two men stood around the only occupied pod in the lab. Caroline Wang was there too, her memory serving as the historical record. In the pod, a male participant writhed in pain. The bio-suit and headgear worn were different, less sophisticated. Even without audio, the tension among those present was unmistakable.

Gene Thornton pulled out a pistol and targeted Richards, who indifferently lit a cigar. Richards taunted his counterpart before raising the pod to an inclined position. Caroline's hands removed goggles from the participant, revealing the anguished face of Oklahoma Senator Samuel Ford. His eye sockets were dark and sullen.

Vacant eyes stared into space before sputtering to life. His exhausted gaze settled on Thornton. Ford agonized before his lips mouthed, "Please" and then "Thank you." Thornton fired two shots. Monitors confirmed the obvious: Samuel Ford was dead.

The staff whispered among themselves, many pressing their hands to their faces.

BLACKNESS. RICHARDS COULD HEAR people outside his dark realm. People poked and prodded him as he was connected into the pod.

He knew what was coming.

Unexplained sensations trickled into Richards' consciousness. Slow at first, then as rapid fire. He'd often wondered what the experience felt like—not the aggressive and often traumatic approach he'd implemented to hyper-stimulate the minds of his daughter and Samuel Ford, but rather Parker's Phase Two neuro-mapping.

Teetering in the dark, jealousy surged through him.

Parker had delivered the Frontier and reduced him to a mere spectator.

That ate at his soul. He had been swindled out of his life's ambition.

Richards' mind prickled as new neural associations pulsed through him.

He was reliving Caroline Wang's memories, experiencing them from her perspective.

Everything to him felt so real. He was exposed, vulnerable.

Flat on his back, Richards' eyes sprang open. Treetops ablaze with autumn colors lurked above him. Indifferent faces moved about him and gloved hands touched his exposed flesh. His skin prickled in the cool air. Anxiety spurred breathing shuttered in his chest while he twisted against unrelenting bonds. Levine appeared holding a syringe. Fluid glistened at the tip of its needle. He knew the contents: a neuromuscular blocking agent. Smugly, Levine tugged on his neck and injected the fluid into his carotid artery. The stab of pain made him wince. The effects of the chemical tingled his bloodstream.

Richards wrenched his eyes closed and tried to drive Caroline's sensations from his mind. He wasn't interested in living out someone else's moment of weakness. The Frontier was meant to be a grander encounter.

UNDER THE GLOW STREAMING down from the Wall of Knowledge, Parker huddled the staff together.

He fought to clear his throat. "I'm sorry about Alexis Hicks. I never meant for her or anyone else to get hurt."

The woman in green scrubs who had freed him touched his shoulder. "She risked her life to save others. So did you."

His heart felt heavy. "I have no idea of what happens next. Richards may be right. The government funds the lab and there's no doubt that powerful people do whatever it takes to protect secrets." He struggled for a breath. "I know you have questions, but this is not the time or the place to answer them."

The others nodded.

"Let's get these people out of here. Remember, they're scared and have been bedridden for days, so be gentle."

The staff broke the huddle and started liberating patients from their living hells.

Parker turned to the enormous screen and took in its brilliance.

New synaptic associations formed in the minds of the patients. Richards wasn't wrong. The human mind was the greatest frontier yet to be explored. He'd never thought it was possible, at least in his lifetime.

The newest frontier in science now made a great many things possible.

Neurological singularity was a radical technology.

A dangerous technology with the potential to destroy the world.

A console beside him flashed red warnings. The data center's supercomputers exceeded thermal parameters, and were preparing to batch archive data in the high-density neural networks before systematic shutdown.

A clock appeared, counting down from three minutes.

It was time to destroy the brains of ANCRI.

He dropped into the chair behind the console and accessed the `APPLIED MIND` application. He typed the coding phrase / `GLOBAL/PRISYS` into the dialogue box and hit `ENTER`.

A new command screen appeared with a prompt.

He took a breath and typed from memory.

`PATIENTS TO ACTIVATE: RESET,10,10,10-10,NULL SWITCH=YES`

A quick glance to the Wall of Knowledge confirmed what he knew would occur.

He had just killed a man without technically killing him.

The massive screen showed the neuro-map for a single participant. Pod 10. Stewart Richards. The action was immediate, irreversible. Lethal. A second's worth of impulses vaporized a rice-grain portion of the man's claustrum, a tiny area deep buried inside the brain that functioned as an on and off switch to consciousness. The monitors showed his breathing decelerate. Physiologically, his body remained alive. His condition wasn't brain death, either. The madman simply lost the ability to interface with multiple regions of his brain. Cognitively, Richards was a timeless prisoner within himself.

Parker typed closeout commands.

```
[FINALRUN] /purgeMEM/ mainMEM, secMEM, auxMEM
killSYSTEM
   {
   closeMIND,
    justice(((i-j)=0)?(i-j, k):-(k)),
   closeANCRI
   } final_states=0;
```

He took a breath and hit `ENTER`. A confirmation screen appeared. `YES`, he typed, and hit `ENTER`.

The Wall of Knowledge fell dark, plunging the neurophysiology lab into twilight. The flash of warning lights grew more prominent.

Parker rose from his chair, feeling like a failure. He had come to ANCRI to rescue Becky, at least in part. She never deserved to die.

Becky had been a kindred spirit, and he loved her.

He noticed that the staff made headway as patients sat up in pods and took in their bizarre surroundings.

A single pod, pod 10, remained untouched.

Parker wanted to feel remorse, but couldn't.

As long as neurological singularity remained viable, Stewart Richards posed a threat.

"Doctor," the nurse in the green scrubs called, "someone wants to speak to you."

Parker turned and saw Caroline Wang sitting up in her bulky bio-suit. Her face was deathly pale and she wore a tired, grateful smile.

At least, he'd managed to keep his promise to her father.

59
BREAK OF DAY

The White House, Washington, D.C.

7:20 A.M. IN THE West Wing, the President's National Security Advisor, Gordon Abbott, finalized morning briefing notes for the President. The private cell phone clipped to his belt came alive. He peered at a number he did not recognize.

Reluctantly, he answered it.

"Alfred Heinz," Abbott said, using an alias from Nixon's National Security Advisor's middle and first names. No sense revealing his identity to unwanted callers. The media constantly trolled the private cell numbers of the White House staff.

"Mr. Abbott," a voice said over the phone, "several days ago you received two emails. 'Perilous cessations.' The communications contained attachments."

He cringed. "I have no recollection of such emails."

"Sure you do."

He gathered his thoughts. "I seem to be at a disadvantage. Who am I speaking to?"

"That's not relevant. You have a briefing with the President at oh-eight-hundred."

"Look—"

"Mr. Abbott, if you want to protect the President, get with the program. The media hit the lottery today. The White House supported a research facility. ANCRI. It's in New Jersey. Of course, you knew that. Senator Samuel Ford was murdered to protect its secrets. Your secrets. Firefighters will soon rescue a group of university students. Your job is to shelter the President from this fallout."

He swallowed and squirmed in his chair. "What do you want?"

"Debra Ford."

Abbott rubbed his forehead. "And if I assist you?"

The voice on the phone cleared his throat. "The President can deflect allegations and raise plausible deniability. The State Department and CIA will be the patsies in this incestuous affair. You know how the media circus works. Make it happen."

Advanced Neurological and Cybernetic Research Institute (ANCRI), New Jersey

JACK WRIGHT LURKED IN the shadows as the morning's first rays of sunlight crested over the forest surrounding the institute.

He clicked off his cell and winced at the pain he felt.

The call to the National Security Advisor was no different than chumming the water prior to throwing a line in. Gordon Abbott would act in a predicable manner, and he needed political favors to help track down Debra Ford. Wright wanted nothing more than to repay the witch for shooting him in the chest.

Wright leaned against a tree and struggled to breathe. Doctors had ordered strict bed rest.

But he needed to be here.

He was damn lucky Debra Ford hadn't shot him in the head— that would've been fatal. Instead, she stuck to her Queen of Hearts MO. The blunt force trauma broke four ribs and bruised a lung. Beneath his sweatshirt that night an armored skin protected him, similar to Hollywood stunt wear. The CIA designed the tech for faking staged informant assassinations. Thankfully, Randy Wang passed along the lifesaving materials in the nick of time.

The bullets had released a chemical cocktail to fake his death. Artificial blood spewed through pores in the armor to make it look like he was bleeding.

Except for a select few, the world believed Jack Wright had died at Princeton.

Kate deserved to know the truth.

There would never be the right time to tell her.

Someday she would learn of his miraculous resurrection… but not today.

KATE WRENCHED OPEN THE flush-mounted maintenance hatches to the data center and climbed out into brisk morning air. Dawn broke through the tree-lined outskirts of the property. The forest glowed in the sun's rays. She soaked up the radiance before propping open the steel doors with her broomstick. The tops of the giant red tanks below stared at her from the void, like two red alien eyeballs, their pupils a fixed set of relief values.

She reached into her potato sack and snatched the last of the makeshift explosives. Climbing down onto the tanks, she wedged the devices against the valves and mouthed, "Fire in the hole."

After lighting both fuses, she somersaulted out of the vertical chase onto to the coolness of a wet lawn, and covered her ears.

Concurrent explosions shook the earth. Pressurized gases rocketed past her.

The discharges slowed.

Looking up, she spotted the dual plume of a white ash mushroom.

Her chest heaved, taking in the outside air. Without cooling and fire suppression, ANCRI's data center would continue its catastrophic meltdown.

Kate struggled to her feet.

Unexpected movement snatched her attention.

Dazed and trying to clear his ears, a guard lugging a hydraulic jack lumbered around a building corner.

Kate's heart throbbed as a hand slid to her side. "FBI!"

Their eyes met. The man dropped the jack and reached for a weapon.

In a fluid movement, Kate drew her Glock and did not hesitate. Two shots fired.

The guard collapsed backwards as lead slugs struck him in the chest.

Kate lowered her weapon and let her shoulders slump.

The man lay motionless on the grass.

Exhausted, she trudged over and collected the man's pistol and access card. She studied his firearm, a Sig Sauer P226. After holstering her Glock, she nestled his weapon in the small of her back.

Ash started to settle on the grass like a thin frost of snow.

She thought of Christmas. But it was not Christmas.

Sirens sounded in the distance. She wondered who called the authorities.

There was no telling, and it could be reinforcements sent to secure the facility.

Kate kept moving. There were people to rescue.

60
END OF THE ROAD

RILEY JOHNSON RETURNED FROM the research annex, where Makara's programmers had been rounded up and shot dead. If Levine eliminated the FBI agent, the remaining threat was Thomas Parker.

Johnson's hybrid mission was different from that of others. He was the government spy. The mole inserted to monitor ANCRI's technical progress, with directives centered on containment—orders from the U.S. Secretary of State.

Earl intercepted him outside the neurophysiology lab. The former Army Delta Force soldier looked nervous, a rare expression for a trained killer. The guard recapped the trouble. Multiple system failures. Levine was MIA. Parker controlled the lab.

Frustrated, Earl shook his head. "We can't get inside."

Johnson soaked up the news and stepped into the anteroom to peer through the small pane of glass in its door. Nurses and technicians tended to the participants. He saw no sign of Richards. A fragile Caroline Wang embraced Thomas Parker.

From across the lab, Caroline's eyes found him like a compass needle striking magnetic north. She pointed and screamed.

Johnson retreated from the window. "No one lives. Not even Richards."

Earl held his breath and blinked before speaking. "We're killing everyone?"

Johnson's eyes narrowed. "Not a single person leaves here, alive. Except you and me. Is that understood, soldier?"

From her vantage point in the corridor, Kate overheard everything. The two men were plotting mass murder. Parker had said that Johnson could not be trusted. The man seemed adept at playing all sides.

She knew taking on two armed killers was a good way to die.

She carried her Glock in one hand, potato sack in the other, and a dead guard's Sig Sauer in the small of her back.

A plan formed loosely in her mind. Good thing she was an electrician's daughter.

She yanked open the sack. Inside were a spool of wire, duct tape, and nitrobenzene.

It was a ludicrous plan.

Johnson looked through the hatched window in the anteroom's interior door. There was no sign of Richards. Every pod was empty, except one.

Johnson's expression darkened. "Richards must be in that pod. The poor bastard." He turned back to Earl. "I count twenty-nine participants and ten staff members. Parker and Richards raise the count to forty-one people. We'll breach the door like you planned. Eliminate staff first. Those guinea pigs in there won't put up a fight, so they'll be easy pickings."

"Affirmative," Earl said. "Let's put down those rodents."

The anteroom's outer door to the corridor slid shut and locked. Johnson and Earl lunged at it.

Earl swiped his ID badge across its card reader. No use. The door's status indicator refused to blink from red to green.

They were trapped between the corridor and the lab.

Johnson pressed his face against the tiny frame of glass in the outer door.

"What do you see?"

Across the corridor stood a haggard FBI agent, her face bloodied and hair matted.

Rage swelled behind her bloodshot eyes.

Well, that explained Levine's disappearance.

The woman clutched a wad of wire, its ends stripped bare. Beside her was a power outlet in the wall. The wire in her hands snaked across the floor, to the door.

Earl pointed. "What the hell is that?"

Johnson spotted a brown bottle at his feet. Its top was sealed with duct tape. Wires slithered out of the bottle and disappeared through the jamb of the sliding door.

He understood her intentions and felt borderline panic. They had nowhere to run.

Survival instincts took over. Johnson did the only thing possible. Hurling himself, he tackled Earl and drove the man hard to his knees. Earl toppled over the bottle as Johnson rode his back.

The eruption of light was blinding. The blast deafening.

Time crawled in slow motion.

Johnson's head was groggy. His ears rang.

He found himself ejected across the anteroom. Contorted, his body slumped against the inner door. His left foot was mangled, but attached. His decorated lab coat was bloody from shrapnel wounds.

At least he'd survived the blast.

Locating the other body trapped in his confines was easy. Earl had not been so fortunate, his wounds extensive and deadly.

But Earl had proved an adequate shield.

Iron-colored fumes filled the small space and choked Johnson's lungs.

Ventilation fans hummed to life. The dense smoke slowly shifted upward.

A pistol rested two feet away. Even though he was injured, perhaps even severely, it remained possible to complete his mission. His orders were absolute.

Johnson clawed himself upright and secured the weapon.

Lungs burned as he gasped for clean air.

His mind told him to escape the fumes.

The effort proved futile and he slumped to the floor. Through the stench, he noticed both anteroom doors had buckled outward, dislodged from their tracks by the concussive blast. The neurophysiology lab was finally breached.

A silhouette approached.

The FBI agent pointed a pistol at him.

He fought to raise his gun as gravity seized him, sapping his remaining energy. The weapon slipped from his grip and clunked to the floor. He patted the floor for it and hacked out a bloody cough. Darkness settled over his vision and he felt colder.

Riley Johnson thumped face first to the floor.

61
HUMAN EFFECTS

The Oval Office, The White House, Washington, D.C.

AFTER THE BRIEFING, GORDON Abbott sat on a beige sofa and told the President what had happened. A reporter from the Washington Post rattled the White House Press Secretary, insisting on a "confirm or deny" response regarding undue influence on a research program called The Frontier.

"If Samuel Ford was murdered," Abbott said, "the media may infer that the White House sanctioned his killing."

"Preposterous," said the President.

Abbott wrung his hands. "May I speak freely?"

The President nodded.

Abbott took a long breath. "The news will get ugly and drag out well past the upcoming elections. However, we can deflect criticism. Most of it. The Secretary of State and CIA brass need to own their sins. They entangled your administration in unjustifiable, incomprehensible research. Of course, you had no idea they would harm people. There is no alternative. Any figurehead linked to these atrocities must be sacrificed."

The President rose from the chair and strolled to the bulletproof windows overlooking the southwest lawn.

Abbott stood. He knew the response before it came.

"Do what needs to be done," the President ordered. "Put as much separation of fact and fiction between those responsible and my administration. Congress will demand hearings. The DOJ will lead the investigation, not the FBI. Make damn sure we're meticulous in our alliances."

Abbott grinned. "Strategic relationships are already being cultivated."

The President sighed. "This neurological singularity endeavor was supposed to deliver Peace on Earth. Now it's done just the opposite."

Advanced Neurological and Cybernetic Research Institute (ANCRI), New Jersey

IN THE NEUROPHYSIOLOGY LAB, Parker targeted the anteroom's sliding door with the pistol.

Riley Johnson was the last known threat, except for the guards.

After she stopped screaming, Caroline Wang had told him that Riley Johnson was a spy. She had found network files linking him to the State Department. Johnson was the real reason Richards and Levine made her a participant.

The explosion had buckled the door. An iron-brown haze saturated the anteroom.

Parker surmised Kate found a use for the organic compound, nitrobenzene.

While he stood watch, staff stripped the scared and fragile patients out of their biosuits and dressed them in traditional open-back gowns. He could hear them discuss their vivid memories. Eerily similar, disturbing memories. Lab research. Murder. Mad scientists.

When the toxic haze dispersed, Kate shoved the sliding door open.

Two men lay motionless in the tiny space behind her.

He took a breath and lowered the gun.

Kate looked bloodied and battered, but happy to see him.

Parker gave her a sad smile. "Becky is dead. Richards killed her."

She swallowed hard. "I'm so sorry, Thomas." She glanced around. "Richards?"

He couldn't answer her, so he said nothing. How would she, as an Agent for the FBI, handle his admission that he gave an unarmed man an internal lobotomy? Vaporizing the bastard's brain tissues was a premeditated act of malice. Since the computer systems had been destroyed, no evidence could implicate him or prove wrongdoing. It was as if his and Makara's Applied Mind application never existed. What plight befell Stewart Richards? Impossible to know, unless he confessed.

Kate took the pistol from him.

"You going to tell me what happened in here?"

Parker scratched his head and pondered her question.

He had crossed too many lines. Morally. Ethically. Legally. As a doctor, he'd selectively discarded the vows he'd taken. He had become no different from a cheap mirror image of Richards himself.

Parker dropped his gaze, unable to look at her.

Kate raised his chin with her fingers. "Did it work?"

He nodded.

"Thomas, you saved a lot of people today."

She leaned into him and kissed him. Their lips clung together before separating.

"It'll be okay," she said.

He ran his fingers gently through her matted hair and felt a lump within a knot of blood.

"Ouch" she said recoiling. "I need a doctor to take a look at that. Have any referrals?"

He broke a half-smile. "A few."

They were about to kiss again when a band of firemen and paramedics stormed through the battered anteroom. The newcomers' expressions carried the same look—shock and awe.

"Who's in charge?" a fire chief called, loud enough for everyone to hear him.

ANCRI's remaining staff turned to one another, then to him.

Parker shook his head. *Not me.*

In a patient's gown, Caroline Wang staggered forward. Her weakened voice was raspy and horse. "No one is in charge. Not anymore."

The chief frowned. "So who in the hell is going to tell us what happened?"

Parker nudged Kate forward. "This is your cue."

She looked into his eyes. "My first act may be to place you under arrest. You're not going anywhere, Thomas."

One of the paramedics shouted. "Hey, what's this man doing in this machine?"

Kate drew him close, cupped his ear, and whispered, "Thomas, your secrets are safe with me. We'll get through this. Together."

He felt emboldened and stepped toward her, his wrists exposed and ready to be cuffed.

Kate reached beneath her scrubs top. She retrieved her badge and thrust it high in the air.

"We're going camping," she said with a defiant smile.

He rolled his eyes and wiggled his wrists at her. "Please. No. Just arrest me."

"Listen up!" she shouted. "Contact Princeton University Medical Center. These patients are to be segregated into a single wing for specialized care." All business, she tracked down the fire chief. "I need a radio or phone. Now. This facility is to be secured by the Department of Justice. They have an office in Newark. Get ahold of them. No one leaves this facility without my authorization or until my DOJ replacement arrives."

PARKER STROLLED THROUGH ANCRI's courtyard, alone. It was a beautiful terraced area with trees and earth-toned stonework. Caroline had told him this was the area where Levine and company staged the participants before bringing them into the facility for human experimentation.

A paramedic provided an update. The patients had been transported to Princeton's hospital in Plainsboro, as had all the bodies. Becky. Hicks. Makara. Johnson. Levine. The technician. The guards. The six programmers. Richards rested comfortably in intensive care. Perplexed, the doctors grappled with his unresponsive condition.

They could do nothing for the maniacal bastard. He was bound to a lifeless shell and an eternal state of unconsciousness, at least for the rest of his natural life.

It was hard for him to feel remorse.

Richards deserved far worse than he'd received.

Yet no one had appointed him judge and jury, the master of retribution.

Parker felt chilled and numb in the cool October air.

"I thought I would find you out here," a voice called.

He turned to find Kate, all cleaned up and wearing her own clothes.

"Officially, off duty and on administrative paid leave." She lifted her shirt to expose her waistline. "Look. No badge. No gun. Had to relinquish those until my review board hearing."

He smiled wryly. "I wouldn't say you're defenseless."

She drew close, and he swung his arms around her hips.

"You know, Thomas Parker," she said, "last time I heard, you don't have a job."

He shook his head. "Don't ask me to go camping."

She shrugged. "It's your loss. But I have thirty days of freedom until the bureau determines my fate. That means I have time to burn and nowhere to be."

He whispered into her ear. "Got any travel restrictions?"

Kate's eyebrows arched. "Not that anyone has told me."

Parker kissed her ear lobe. "Trade you? Sleeping on the ground under a swath of fabric for lounging on a sailboat and sunning on sandy beaches." He dug deep in his pocket and retrieved the USB credit card Randy Wang had given him. The device carried the logo for the Bank of Canada's Cayman Islands' branch. "I'm anxious to check out their financial institutions."

62
DESTINATIONS

70 Miles Northeast of ANCRI, Port Newark
Container Terminal, Port Newark, New Jersey

THE AFTERNOON WAS QUIET. East of Newark Liberty International Airport, a crane loaded wooden crates carrying diplomatic seals of the U.S. Department of State into a shipping container. An inspector initialed the manifest log and returned it to the special logistics liaison. Diplomatic property. General goods. Nothing to worry about. Materials leaving the United States were less of a concern than those entering the country.

The special logistics liaison took in a nostril full of heavy brine air that swept off Newark Bay. It was impossible to avoid the stench. The ambience of his job.

He collected the required signatures and made sure the forms were properly processed. Like a high-priced New York City escort, his job was to service clients in any matter required. In this case, that meant expediting the shipping container's contents through Port Authority bureaucracy. The container was logged and loaded without issue onto an MSC sea freight cargo ship bound for La Pallice, La Rochelle, France.

His job was to deliver, not ask questions.

Double the service fee, paid in advance, greased a lot of skids.

Although an interstate driver disclosed the origin as Princeton rather than the manifest's stated origin of Philadelphia, he was no idiot, just discreet. News broadcasts were in full swing: murders in Princeton, exploding homes, burglarized university labs, and now a terrifying story about human experimentation.

The freight could come from hell itself.

Origin. Destination. None of that mattered.

For the right price, he'd still put it all on a ship bound for France.

THE END

THIRTEEN ACROSS

A New Novel (Coming in 2019)
First Chapter

Dan Grant

Thirteen Across takes readers through a menacing scavenger
hunt for a dark truth that can only be revealed through an
evolving puzzle. More government secrets are disclosed
as dots on a map in Washington, D.C. are revealed.
Learn more by visiting www.DanGrantBooks.com.

MindScape Press, Inc.
www.MindScapePress.com

CHAPTER 1
MORNING COMMUTE—
FOUNDATIONS OF MURDER

East Falls Church WMATA Metro Station, Virginia

KATHERINE MORGAN HATED INQUISITIONS. The congressional hearing occupying her Monday calendar torpedoed the buzz of a tropical vacation. Two days earlier, the summons in the form of a stiff in a suit greeted her as she deplaned from a Grand Caymans flight at Dulles International Airport.

It seemed that the stars were aligned against her, while karma stood on the sidelines and watched as the world piled it on.

Now, standing on an outdoor platform, Kate wedged herself into the fluid mass of morning commuters. An eastbound Orange Line arrived. Doors opened. People crowded inside. Navigating the throng of bodies, she found a vacant vinyl seat and did her best not to stare. But it was impossible to ignore the gray-haired woman beside her. The woman's face was buried in the Bible. The page header noted the Book of Revelation. Gold bracelets clanked on her wrists when she turned a page and her lips moved in an animated fashion, as if she were a TV evangelist preaching to an unseen congregation and someone had muted her with the remote.

Kate rolled her eyes. *Reading about the end of the world? What a peaceful sentiment.*

Forcing her attention to *The Washington Post* in her hands, she skimmed a story on the bizarre murder of an Oklahoma senator. Secret research programs. Human experimentation. Tabloid news. And congress wanted to hear her version of it. She flipped to the entertainment section and the day's crossword puzzle. For her, the childhood addiction passed the time.

The train jolted into motion. Clicks and clacks of steel wheels on rails filled the air with white noise as the commute found a hypnotic routine. Minutes passed as the Washington Metropolitan Area Transit Authority (WMATA) train made stops.

"Foggy Bottom GWU," an automated voice said over the intercom.

Kate ignored the announcement. Not her stop.

Biting her lip, she studied the puzzle and dug the end of a pencil through her barrette-held hair to scratch her scalp. 12 DOWN. A twelve-letter word for ARCHAEOLOGIST'S TIME MEASURING-TECHNIQUE. The word started with C. D was the seventh letter. It ended with—

An explosion rocked the train.

Its shockwave reverberated like the blast of thunder that always accompanied a stunning flash of lightning. The train shuddered and dropped several inches, causing Kate's feet to lift from the floor. The unrestrained creaking and moaning of metal made her ears throb. More crackles of thunder raged as the train veered slightly.

Gasping for breath, she slung the paper aside and groped the bottom of her seat for a handhold.

Passenger screams competed with the sounds of tortured metal.

"We're going to die!" someone yelled.

Kate lifted her chin with a jolt and locked eyes onto the woman beside her.

The woman broke her muteness and chanted like a falsetto monk on speed, her words running together as indecipherable noise. "Holy Father…!"

Sparks streamed past windows. Cabin lights blinked off. Outside, cascading fireworks grew brilliant in the blackness of a railway tunnel.

Fears of her impending death seeded a thought of Thomas Parker. Their spontaneous tryst to the Caribbean came after surviving a deadly ordeal in Princeton. Kate yearned to retreat to the endless stretches of sugar white sand and sail under amber sunsets, and she prayed she'd see Thomas again.

Streaking lights stole her attention.

Running out of control on the concrete underlayment between tracks, the train's lead car skidded into a concrete side wall. The passenger cars in tow buckled under a sudden change in momentum and the train pitched forward. Plexiglas windows imploded, showering passengers with jagged bits of plastic.

Abruptly Kate lost her grip on the seat. A chorus of screams erupted as bodies tumbled through the air like rag dolls swirling around in a clothes dryer. The clamoring of metal was deafening. Within seconds, the menacing crescendo diminished as the train ground to a halt.

Wisps of haze clouded over dim lights.

She forced her haggard mind to catch up to current events, and noticed that her car, the second in a series, rested on its side. A ceiling faced her. A faint glow broke through smoky darkness as emergency lights replaced inoperative cabin lights. Unable to budge, she gagged on air saturated with metallic silt, and a caustic taste pasted the inside of her mouth.

Kate felt the pressure of people squeezing in on her and heard the drumming of her own heartbeat overtake the ringing in her ears. Peering around, she discovered she was buried among other passengers and atop a man who hung out a shattered window. His lifeless torso, crushed between the side of the passenger car and the tracks below, broke her fall and kept her from flying out when the train rolled onto its side.

"Oh, thank you, Father!" proclaimed the monk-chanting woman.

"I second what she said," Kate mumbled, assessing her condition. Nothing felt broken, just a few bumps and bruises—small prices to pay for survival.

Screams, lots of them, shattered her elation. Wrenching her head around, she couldn't make out what the panic was all about, until she heard a falsetto shriek. "Fire!"

"Get off!" Kate snapped, imagining the passengers above her swimming in a sea of molasses as they unpiled. Realizing she was a floor mat, she jammed her fists into the dead man and pushed. The muscles in her arms quivered and her heart raged defiantly as she wrestled free from the entangled mass of bodies. Nudging others clear, Kate gained enough room to stand.

Her eyes flashed wide at the sight of fire.

At the rear of her compartment, flames licked the edges of the twisted metal. Smoke carrying a blended odor of soot, grease, and melting plastic flooded the space, stinging her eyes, before breaking free and trickling out shattered windows.

The immediate threat wasn't death by suffocation, it was by incineration.

Around her, panic-stricken faces shared an orange glow of desperation—a "fend for yourself" hysteria.

For the first time, Kate saw the carnage in a coffin of wreckage. Debris and bodies littered the tipped over train. Moans from the injured competed for attention as panicked passengers climbed out and fled to safety above.

A wave of lightheadedness swept over her as she sucked in shallow breaths of soiled air. After several seconds, her head cleared and she discovered she was standing on the Bible. Her gaze absorbed the chaos. The monkish woman had vanished—as if she possessed a guardian angel who swooped down from heaven and whisked her away from tragedy.

An answered prayer. Who would have thought?

As the crackling of sparks and fire devoured more of the passenger car, she grew mesmerized by the splashes of heat touching her face.

Kate felt the presence of death—its fingers of fire claiming the fallen—it wanted her next.

ACKNOWLEDGEMENTS

OFTEN PEOPLE INFLUENCE THE choices you make and the paths you embark on. During my electrical engineering undergraduate program, Greg Larkin made technical writing and consulting for the CIA sound more glamorous that it was, which led me to exploring writing in different ways. Similarly, I was hooked on works by Clancy, Crichton, Cussler, and Grisham—their stories fed an alternative to engineering. Allen Woodman nurtured my courage to take flight and fostered the storyteller within; without his corruptive influence there is little doubt that I would've taken the leap of faith in any form.

The genesis of this story came from my master's thesis, and its current narrative form took years to cultivate. Although I write alone, I have a few people to thank for their editorial input and for helping *The Singularity Witness* become an actual book: Ellen Clair Lamb, Tiffany Yates Martin, and Trai Cartwright.

And finally, my wife Leslie has been beyond supportive and tolerant of my creative exploits. I'm grateful to her first reads, input, constant patience, and encouragement. She heard a radio spot for the Pike's Peak Writers Conference in Colorado. That event led me to resurrect nearly forgotten early drafts of *The Singularity Witness* from the imprisonment of a desk drawer.

ABOUT THE AUTHOR

DAN GRANT IS A licensed professional engineer with degrees from Northern Arizona University: a bachelor's in electrical engineering and masters' in college education and English with an emphasis in creative writing. His engineering endeavors have provided opportunities to work with a variety medical and technological applications, and get behind the scenes at military facilities. Besides engineering, he has taught college English and computer programming, and presented writing workshops. He lives in Colorado with his wife, two boys, and two dogs.

As a story backdrop and a place for characters to take root, Princeton University was selected because of its unique setting, historical connections, and its ongoing research efforts. For a year, Dan and his wife lived outside the town limits and just fell in love with the place.

Dan is working on his next novel *Thirteen Across*, a Kate Morgan thriller set in Washington, D.C. (the Chapter 1 insert was included in the previous section). And Thomas Parker will be back in *The Singularity Transfer*—Pandora's Box has been opened and threatens to change the world stage.

To get access to author's notes, go to www.DanGrantBooks.com/singularity-witness/ and use the code "Phoenix" to enter. Use the link there and sign-up to hear about the next in the Singularity Series. Connect with Dan at www.DanGrantBooks.com and on FaceBook.